"I HAVE NO ONE ANYWHERE," SHE SAID MATTER-OF-FACTLY, BUT DESOLATION ECHOED BENEATH THE WORDS.

He had a sense of everything coming together. After all the hell and blood that had gone before, fate had finally got it right. "Then I'll take you with me."

She was looking at him as if he had gone mad. Well, he felt a little mad at the moment.

"Come with me," he said. "It's clear you were sent to me as a gift and I never refuse a gift from the gods. How can you take care of your brother without help? He needs hot food and warm clothing. I can give you both."

She hesitated. "Why . . . would you do this?"

"Perhaps I wish to do my kind Christian duty and aid two orphans," he said mockingly.

Those clear blue eyes searched his expression. "But I think you're not a kind man."

"How clever of you to realize that fact, but you're not entirely correct. I do practice kindness . . . when it's convenient."

He turned and started back up the aisle. He had no intention of leaving her here even if it meant abducting her, but it would be simpler if she made the decision.

"Wait."

He stopped but didn't turn around.

She moved brusquely forward. "We'll go with you."

BOOKS BY IRIS JOHANSEN

The
BELOVED
SCOUNDREL

IRIS
JOHANSEN

BANTAM BOOKS • NEW YORK

The Beloved Scoundrel is a work of fiction. Names, characters, places, and incidents are the products of the author's imagination or are used fictitiously. Any resemblance to actual events, locales, or persons, living or dead, is entirely coincidental.

2012 Bantam Books Mass Market Edition

Copyright © 1994 by Iris Johansen
Interior art © 1994 by Steve Assel
Excerpt from *Stalemate* copyright © 2006 by Iris Johansen

Published in the United States by Bantam Books,
an imprint of The Random House Publishing Group,
a division of Random House, Inc., New York.

BANTAM BOOKS and the rooster colophon
are registered trademarks of Random House, Inc.

Originally published in mass market in
the United States by Bantam Books,
an imprint of The Random House Publishing Group,
a division of Random House, Inc., in 1994.

ISBN 978-0-553-59038-8
eBook ISBN 978-0-307-81572-9

Cover illustration: Wah

Printed in the United States of America

www.bantamdell.com

4 6 8 9 7 5

Bantam Books mass market edition: July 2012

This book is dedicated to Helen Johansen, who gave her love and warmth and very special grace to all of us.

The
BELOVED
SCOUNDREL

CHAPTER 1

February 16, 1809
Talenka, Montavia
The Balkans

The Window to Heaven was shattered.

Only moonlight and cold wind streamed through the huge circular cavity where splendor and beauty had once reigned.

Marianna dug her fingers into the door to keep herself upright as she stared at the devastation. The journey had taken too long. She had failed Mama. The pattern was smashed; the Jedalar was gone. Then she forgot everything else as the deep sense of loss over the act of sheer desecration hit home. She knew the Jedalar should be more important to her but, dear heaven, all that wonder and beauty gone forever.

Why was she so stunned? They had destroyed everything else in her life. Perhaps it was even fitting that this last beautiful remnant had died.

"Marianna." Alex tugged at her arm. "I think I hear them!"

She went rigid, listening. She heard nothing, just the wind whistling among the shelled and deserted houses of the town. She looked away from the shimmering splinters of glass scattered across the floor of the church, her gaze searching the ruins that had once been the town of Talenka. She still heard nothing, but Alex had always possessed sharper hearing than she. "Are you sure?"

"No, but I think . . ." He tilted his head. "Yes!"

She should never have come back. She should have taken the road to the south. Her mother would have forgiven her. They had not taken quite everything from her. She still had Alex, and by God, she *would* not let him die.

She slammed the heavy brass-studded door and dragged Alex behind her as she tore down the long aisle toward the altar, stumbling over a broken iron candelabra and several fat white candles scattered on the marble floor. The soldiers had wreaked their usual havoc here, she thought grimly. Everything of value had either been stolen or destroyed. The gold crucifix that had once adorned the wall beneath the Window to Heaven had vanished; the statue of Mary and the Child to the left of the altar had been toppled from the pedestal.

"Horses," Alex whispered.

She heard them now too. The sharp clip-clop of hooves on the cobblestoned street outside.

"They won't find us," she whispered back. "They didn't see us come in, and those pigs can have no traffic with either churches or prayers." She pulled the little boy behind a column beside the altar and crouched down beside him. "But we will stay here awhile and wait for them to go away."

Alex shivered and drew closer to her. "What if they do come?"

"They won't." She slid an arm around his shoulders. He was thinner than he had been last week, she realized in concern, and he had been coughing all day. The scraps of food she had managed to salvage from the deserted farmhouses outside the town had barely been enough to keep them alive.

"What if they do?" Alex repeated.

Heavens, he was persistent. "I said they—" She stopped. She didn't know the duke's soldiers wouldn't come, she thought wearily. She could not be sure of anything or anyone. She doubted if those monsters would come to worship, but they might come to loot and burn again. "If they come, we will hide here in the shadows and be very quiet until they leave. Can you do that?"

He nodded, his weight heavier against her. "I'm cold, Marianna."

"I know. As soon as we hear them leave, we'll look for shelter for the night."

"Can we light a fire?"

She shook her head. "But maybe we can find a blanket for you."

"And for you." He smiled at her—only a faint smile, but it was enough to light his face with the cherubic radiance that had led her mother to use him as a model in her last work. It was the first time she had seen him smile since the night they had—

Mama . . .

She quickly blocked the thought. She must not think of that night or anything that happened since. She had found it weakened her, and she must stay strong for Alex.

"A blanket for me too." She wanted to lean forward and kiss him, but Alex had reached the advanced age of four and regarded himself as too old for such a display of affection. "Just as soon as they leave the village."

But they weren't leaving. They were coming closer. She could hear the horses just outside the church and men's voices laughing and talking.

Her heart pounded as she drew Alex closer.

Let them go away, she prayed frantically. Mother of God, let them not come into the church.

Footsteps on the stone stairs.

The muscles of her stomach tightened painfully.

"Marianna?"

"Shhh." Her hand clamped over Alex's mouth.

The door creaked as it swung open. So much for prayers. Now she must do as her mother had taught her and rely only on herself.

Mama.

A tide of grief overwhelmed her. Tears stung her eyes until she could barely see the man standing in the doorway.

She blinked. She had not cried since it had happened, and she would not cry now. Tears were for the weak, and she must be strong.

She watched the man start down the aisle. He was tall, very tall, his stride long and purposeful, his dark cloak billowing behind him like the wings of a vulture. He was not in the duke's livery, but that didn't mean he wasn't the enemy. No one followed him, she noticed in relief. He had left those other pigs outside. She had a better chance of besting one man.

He stumbled in the darkness and muttered a curse.

She heard Alex's gasp beneath her hand. There had been many curses that night, curses and laughter and screams. She had held Alex to her breast so he would not see, but she had not been able to keep him from hearing. Her hand kneaded his thin shoulders in silent comfort.

The man stumbled again and then stopped, stooped, and picked up something from the floor. A few minutes later a tiny flame of light pierced the darkness as he lit the stub of a broken candle he had retrieved.

She shrank farther back into the shadows, her gaze raking the enemy to search out weakness.

Dark hair tied back in a queue, a long face, a glimmer of green eyes.

He lifted the candle high, his eyes searching the darkness until he found the gaping hole that had once been the Window to Heaven. His hand tightened on the candle; his face contorted in an expression of demonic fury. "Damnation!" His booted foot kicked out at the shards of glass on the marble floor. "Dammit to hell!"

He'd cursed in English. He must be English, like Papa, but she had never seen Papa in a fury like this.

Alex whimpered.

The man stiffened. "Who's there?"

He was turning toward them! She tried to think quickly through the sick terror tightening her chest. If he saw them, they would be helpless prey. Their only weapon was surprise.

"Stay here," she whispered. "Wait!" She pushed Alex still farther behind the column, darted forward, and charged the man.

"What the dev— Oof." Her head connected with the stomach and knocked the breath out of him. She grabbed the broken iron candelabra from the floor and brought it up between his legs. He gasped and doubled over in agony.

"Alex! Come!" she called.

Alex was behind her in seconds, and she grabbed his hand and ran up the aisle. But before they reached the door, she was knocked down and hit the floor, hard. He had tackled her! He flipped her over and leaped astride her. Helpless. She was as helpless as Mama had been.

"No!" She struggled wildly.

"Lie still, damn you."

Alex leaped on the man's back, his thin arms encircling his neck.

"Run, Alex," Marianna cried. "Run!"

She felt the man above her tense. "My God!" he muttered, and then added in disgust, "Children!" He leaped to his feet, throwing off Alex's hold. Marianna scrambled to her knees and reached for the candelabra she had dropped.

"Marianna!"

She looked up to see her brother struggling in the arms of the man. She lunged up at him, wielding the candelabra, but Alex was immediately lifted as a shield between them.

"Oh no, not again," he said grimly, this time in Montavian. "I will not permit a second assault on my person. I have other plans for my manhood."

As all men did. She wished she had a sword to cut his off. "Let him down," she said fiercely.

"Presently." He must be very strong; he was holding Alex as if he were weightless. "But only if you promise not to attack me."

"Put him down."

"Or?"

"I'll find a way to hurt you again."

"Ah, another threat. You're a little young to deal in threats."

She took a step closer.

He stiffened, his wary gaze on the iron weapon in her hands. "Keep your distance." As she stopped, he relaxed a little. "One of the first things you should learn is that the man who possesses the prize dictates the terms. Now, I seem to have captured an object you value." He backed away from her a few paces. "He's very small, isn't he? Small children are so easy to hurt."

Fear ripped through her. "I'll kill you if you—"

"I have no intention of harming him," he interrupted. "Not if you don't force me to defend myself."

She studied him. His thick dark hair had come loose from its queue and framed a long face that was all planes and hollows. His straight black brows slashed over startling green eyes, and his nose reminded her of the beak of an eagle. It was a hard face, a face as inflexible as stone, the face of a man who could be cruel.

"Answer my questions, and I'll set this young man down," he said. "I assure you I don't usually make war on children."

She did not trust him, but she had little choice. "What do you want to know?"

"What are you doing here?"

She searched wildly for an answer he would believe. "It was cold, and we needed shelter for the night."

"There's not much shelter here with that window broken." His gaze was on her face, reading her expression. He didn't believe her, she realized in despair. She had never been good at lying. He continued. "Perhaps you're a thief. Perhaps you came in here to see what you could steal. It wouldn't be—"

"Marianna wouldn't steal," Alex said belligerently. "She only wanted to see the window, but it was gone. She would never—"

"Hush, Alex," she said sharply. It wasn't Alex's fault. He was only defending her and didn't know the importance of the Jedalar.

"The window?" He glanced up over his shoulder. "Hell yes, it's gone." That terrible anger twisted his face again. "Bastards! I *wanted* that window."

He wanted the Window to Heaven. Then he must be one of them! "Who . . . who . . . are you?"

His gaze narrowed on her face. "Not Mephistopheles, as you seem to think. Who do you think I am?"

She moistened her lips. "I think you belong to the Duke of Nebrov."

"I belong to no one." His lips tightened. "Certainly not to that whoreson bastard. I don't— Ouch!"

Alex's teeth had sunk into his hand.

Marianna tensed, prepared to spring if he retaliated against the boy.

But he merely shook off the boy's teeth. "It seems the cub is also fierce."

"He's afraid. Let him down."

"I'll strike a bargain with you. I'll put him down if you promise not to run away."

He had seemed sincere in his dislike of the duke, but that didn't mean he was not the enemy. He wanted the Window. "You put him down and let him leave us, and I'll not run away."

"But then I'll not have my shield."

She smiled with fierce satisfaction. "No."

His lips quirked, but he did not smile in turn. "Done. I think I can protect myself from one small girl. Drop your weapon."

She hesitated and then dropped the candelabra.

"Good. Your promise?"

She had hoped he would not demand the words. "I promise," she said grudgingly, and then quickly added, "if I see no danger to Alex."

He set the little boy on his feet. "There's no danger here for the boy."

There was danger everywhere, and she must be prepared to face it. She turned to Alex. "Go to the garden and wait for me there."

"I don't want to go."

She didn't want Alex to go either. The night was cold and he was ill and she did not know how long this Englishman would keep her here. But there was no choice. Alex had to be sent out of harm's way. She took off her wool shawl and wrapped it around him. "But you must." She gave him a gentle push. "I'll be with you soon."

He started to protest, but when he met her gaze, he turned and ran toward the small door to the left of the altar.

She was alone with him. Mama. What if he hurt her the way they had hurt her mother? Fear closed around her heart, robbing her of breath, freezing her blood as she turned to face him.

You sent away my hostage," he said mockingly. He set one of the candelabras upright, found the candle he had dropped, and relit it. "It makes me feel excep-

tionally insecure. I don't know if I can tolerate—
Why the devil are you shaking like that?"

"I'm not." Her eyes shimmered with defiance.
"I'm not afraid."

He could see that she was more than afraid; she was
terrified. It was probably good that she feared him;
fear would produce answers, but for some inexplica-
ble reason he felt the need to save her pride. "I didn't
say you were. It must be the cold. You gave the boy
your shawl." He took off his cloak. "Come here and
let me put this around you."

She looked at the cloak as if it were a sword
pointed at her. She took a deep breath. "I will not
fight you, but you must make me a promise. You
must not kill me afterward. Alex needs me."

"After what?" he asked. His gaze narrowed on her
face, and he understood. "You think I intend to rape
you?"

"It's what men do to women."

"How old are you?"

"I've reached my sixteenth year."

"You look younger." In the loose, ragged blouse
and skirt she wore her body appeared to be as straight
and without womanly form as that of a child. She was
small-boned, delicate, almost painfully thin, with a
smudge darkening one cheek. Her fair hair was pulled
back in a long braid and added to the effect of extreme and vulnerable youth.

She stared at him scornfully. "What difference
does it make how old I am? I'm female, and men
don't care. They care for nothing."

She sounded so certain, he felt a surge of pity for
the waif. "Has this happened to you before?"

"Not to me." Her tone was suddenly reserved. He

could almost see her withdraw within herself, sidling away from the pain she would not discuss.

"And it won't happen now," he said grimly. "I'm not known to be above debauchery, but I don't rape children."

But she wasn't a child. The delicate beauty of her features should have reflected wonder instead of raw wariness; her clear blue eyes gazed at him with a worldliness far beyond her years, and her lips were set tight to prevent their trembling. He had seen the same look on the faces of the children in the towns and villages along Kazan's border, and it made him as angry now as it had then. "Where are your parents?"

She did not answer at once, and when she did, she spoke so softly, he had to strain to hear. "Dead."

"How?"

"Papa died two years ago."

"And your mother?"

She shook her head. "I . . . don't want to tell you."

"How did your mother die?" he repeated.

"The duke."

He remembered her earlier accusation. "The Duke of Nebrov?"

She nodded.

It was no surprise to him. The powerful Duke of Nebrov had launched an insurrection against his brother, King Josef, over a year ago. It had been a bitter struggle, and both armies had almost been destroyed before the duke had been forced to acknowledge a defeat. The king's forces had been too scattered and weak to pursue Nebrov to his own lands, where he was now licking his wounds and undoubtedly building a new army. As he retreated, he had made sure that Montavia suffered as much as possible and given his men free rein to rape and pillage as they pleased. On Jordan's journey to Talenka from Kazan he had traveled through town after town like this one that had been shelled and sacked, its inhabitants murdered and brutalized. "One of the duke's troops killed your mother?"

She shook her head. "The duke," she whispered. She stared straight ahead as if the scene was there before her. "He did it. He did it."

"The duke himself?" That was unusual. Zarek Nebrov was a brutal bastard, but his rage was usually cold and controlled, and he seldom indulged in spilling blood without reason. "Are you sure?"

"He came to our cottage, and he . . . I'm sure." She shuddered. "Mama told me who he was. . . . She had seen him before. He hurt . . . her, and then he killed her."

"Why?"

He received no reply.

"Did you hear me?"

"I hear you," she said haltingly. "If you do not wish to hurt me, may I go now?"

Christ, he felt as brutal a bastard as Nebrov. The girl was helpless and in pain. He should just call Gregor and have him send one of his men to find the girl's nearest relations and take her to them. But he knew he had to find out more. The coincidence was too blatant. She had come to see the Window and, by her few agonized words, it appeared the girl's mother had been tortured before she had been killed. Nebrov never did anything without reason. "No, you may not go." He held out his cloak to her again. "You will put on this cloak." He deliberately kept his tone hard, but he sat down in a pew so that he would appear less threatening. Standing, he felt like a giant looming over her fragile form. "Sit down."

"I won't talk about that anymore," she said unsteadily. "No matter what you do to me."

That painful memory was probably her biggest weakness, but he found he couldn't strike at it. "Stay," he said wearily. "I promise I'll never ask you to talk about that night again."

She hesitated, her gaze searching his face. Then she took his cloak and slipped it on but did not sit down. "Why do you want me to stay?"

"I'm not sure." He was probably wasting his time here. He had done all he could. Now that he knew the Window was destroyed, his only course was to meet with Janus so that he could carry the word to Kazan and then set out for Samda and try to find Pogani. Even if this waif knew something she wasn't telling, the Window was broken, dammit. Yet he couldn't let it rest until he was certain Nebrov hadn't discovered something he had not. His gaze returned to the cavity surrounded by jagged glass. "It seems strange that we were both brought together at this place and time. Do you believe in Fate?"

"No."

"I do. My mother had Tartar blood, and she must have instilled a belief in the Fates with mother's milk." His stare never left the empty window. "The town is sacked and deserted, you couldn't be sure the duke's forces wouldn't return, you and your brother are ragged and in want, and yet you picked this time to come to see the Window? Why?"

"Why did you?" she countered.

"I wished to acquire it. I heard it was magnificent, and I wished to take it back to my home."

"You wished to steal it."

"You don't understand."

"You wished to steal it," she repeated, her tone uncompromising.

"All right, have it your way. I wished to steal it." He met her gaze. "Now, why did you come?"

Those clear, fierce eyes slid away from his own. "I had to see if it was still there."

"Why?"

She didn't reply.

"It would be wise of you to answer me."

Her defiant gaze shifted back to him, and her tone was scornful as she echoed his own lie. "Why, I heard it was magnificent, and I wanted it for my home."

The girl had courage. She was still frightened, and yet she refused to yield. He was careful not to show the flicker of admiration he felt. "Shall I go to the garden and fetch your brother? I'm sure he would tell me why you're here."

"Leave him alone!"

"Then tell me the truth."

She burst out, "Because it was mine!"

Christ! He hid the excitement that jolted through him. "The pope would not agree. Everything in his churches belongs to God and so to him."

"It *is* mine," she said fiercely. "My grandmother gave it to me before she died last year."

He was careful to keep his expression impassive. "How kind of her. And what right did she have to bestow such a gift?"

"She created it. She said the church did not pay us for the work, so it was still ours."

"I fear she told you a falsehood. The Window was created by Anton Pogani, a great craftsman."

She shook her head. "He was my grandfather, but it wasn't he who was the craftsman, it was my grandmother."

His brows lifted. "A woman?" Surely no woman could have had the artistry and skill to create the Window's twenty-three panels portraying man's climb from the earthly plane to Paradise.

"That's why she had to let him lay claim to the work. They would not have accepted the work of a woman. It is always our women who do the work."

"Always?"

She nodded. "For over five hundred years the women in my family have worked with glass. We're trained from the time we leave the cradle. My mother said I have a special gift, and when I'm grown, I will be as great a craftsman as my grandmother."

A flare of hope shot through him. "And just how familiar are you with the Window to Heaven?"

He had deliberately kept his tone offhand, but she went rigid. Wariness when there should have been no such response. He retreated quickly and changed the subject. "What do the men of your family do while you're creating these glorious works?"

A little of her tension eased. "Whatever they wish. They are well taken care of."

"Then it's the women who work to provide the living and care for the men of the family?"

She looked at him, frowning. "Of course, it is our duty. We always— Why are you looking at me like that?"

"Forgive me if I find the idea extraordinary."

She shifted uneasily. "I must go. Alex is waiting."

"And where will you go? I assume your home is in ruins like the rest of Talenka."

"We didn't live here. Our cottage was just outside Samda."

Samda was over seventy miles to the west. "Then how did you get here?"

"We walked."

The journey from Samda through this war-ravaged land would have been a rough, dangerous trek even for a man on horseback, and yet the child had been driven to forge her way to the church on foot. "Do you have relatives in Samda?"

"I have no one anywhere," she said matter-of-factly, but desolation echoed beneath the words.

He had a sense of everything coming together. After all the hell and blood that had gone before, Fate had finally got it right! He hadn't even had to go to Pogani; the Jedalar had come to him. "Then I'll take you with me."

She stared at him, stunned.

"Come with me," he repeated. His eyes glinted with recklessness. "It's clear you were sent to me as a gift, and I never refuse a gift from the gods."

She started backing away from him, looking at him as if he had gone mad. Well, he felt a little mad at the moment. Despair and anger had changed to hope, and that could be a heady brew.

"How can you take care of your Alex without help? He needs hot food and warm clothing. I can give it to you."

She hesitated. "Why . . . would you do this?"

"Perhaps I wish to do my kindly Christian duty and aid two orphans," he said mockingly.

Those clear blue eyes searched his expression. "But I think you're not a kind man."

"How clever of you to realize that fact, but you're not entirely correct. I do practice kindness . . . when it's convenient. It is convenient now. Isn't that fortunate for you and your Alex?"

She shook her head, her gaze clinging to his.

He could see she wanted desperately to be convinced. All he had to do was say the words she wanted to hear. He tried to decide the best way to proceed. Persuading women to do as he wanted them to do had never been a problem for him. He had learned to charm and beguile before he left the nursery. Yet he was curiously reluctant to lie to this big-eyed waif. "You're quite right. I've never been known to follow the path of duty. I've always found it an abysmal bore." He continued crisply. "Very well, I do have a reason for wanting to help you, but I have no intention of divulging it at present. If you want to come with me, then you'll do so on my terms. You'll agree to obey me without question, and in return I'll promise that there will be food and shelter and protection for both of you as long as you're under my care. If you choose not to come, then you can stay here in these ruins and let your brother starve to death."

He turned and started back up the aisle. It was a gamble. He had no intention of leaving her here even if it meant abducting her, but it would be simpler if she made the decision.

"Wait."

He stopped but didn't turn around. "You're coming with me?"

"Yes." She moved brusquely forward ahead of him. "I'll go with you." She added quickly, "For now. But Alex stays in the garden until I'm sure it's safe. I'll take food and blankets to him."

"As you like. But you'd better make up your mind quickly. I intend to leave this town by sunrise."

"That's too soon," she said, panic-stricken.

"Sunrise," he repeated. "What did the boy call you? Marianna?"

"Marianna Sanders."

"Sanders." He opened the heavy door for her. "That's not a Montavian name."

"My father was English." She slanted him a glance. "Like you."

He recalled his outburst of profanity when he had seen the broken window. "And your mother?"

She looked away from him. "Montavian." She asked quickly, "Why is an Englishman in Montavia?"

"Because he wants to be," he said mockingly. "You've not asked me my name. I'm hurt you have so little interest when we're to be fast companions."

"Well, what is it?" she said impatiently.

He bowed. "Jordan Draken. At your service."

A sharp gust of wind struck them as they started down the steps, and she frowned. "It's getting colder. I need that blanket for Alex. I can't leave him out there without—"

"Ah, Jordan, you were in the church so long, I thought you were taking holy vows," a voice boomed.

Marianna stopped short on the steps as she saw the huge man coming toward them. She had thought Jordan Draken was tall, but this was a bear of man, towering almost seven feet.

The giant threw back his head, and his laugh again boomed out. "I should have known you would have found a woman to amuse you even in this deserted hovel." As he drew closer, the moonlight revealed a face as intimidating as his great bulk. He must be near his fortieth year, and his face reflected evidence that those years had been spent in violence. His nose had been broken, and his gray-streaked black hair was a wild, tousled tangle framing cheekbones that looked as if they had been chipped from a mountain. A jagged white scar curved from his left eye, across his cheek to the corner of his mouth.

"Easy," Draken said quietly. "It's only Gregor. He won't hurt you."

How did she know that? she wondered wildly. She looked beyond the giant to the men who sat astride their horses at the foot of the steps. There were at least fifteen of them, several bearing flaming torches, and they all looked as wild as this Gregor. They wore black fur hats and strange, quilted bulky tunics trimmed with fox fur and sheepskin, their wide trousers tucked into high leather boots that reached their knees. Rifles were holstered on their saddles, and each man wore a huge sword at his hip. Why had she consented to come with Draken? She knew the answer. Alex was ill. Alex must have warmth and shelter, and it had seemed worth any risk to see if this man could give it to him.

"Stay where you are, Gregor." Draken turned to her as the giant stopped on the fifth step. "No one will hurt you. I gave you my promise."

And he had not lied to persuade her to come with him, she remembered. He had given her a choice, and she had made it. She mustn't be a coward now.

She threw her shoulders back and demanded, "Tell him to give me a blanket for Alex."

An undefinable expression crossed his face. "Very well." He said to Gregor, "Go fetch a blanket for the lady."

He nodded his shaggy head and loped back down the steps to a giant of a horse. He opened a saddlebag and took out a sheepskin blanket. He turned, took the stairs three at a time, and stopped before Marianna. "Here." He thrust the blanket at her and smiled with surprising sweetness. "I'm Gregor Damek, and I know I'm an ugly monster of a fellow, but I don't eat children. I promise you."

In that terrifying visage, his hazel eyes were gentle, and she felt the tiniest ripple of warmth go through her as she took the blanket. "My . . . name is Marianna," she said haltingly.

"Take the blanket to your brother," Draken said to her. "We'll set up camp at the north edge of the town. There will be hot food and a warm fire for you both." He turned and started down the steps. "If you decide to trust me."

He had come for the Window. She couldn't trust anyone who wanted the Window to Heaven. Yet he was English, and why would an Englishman want the Window except for the reason he had given her? Perhaps she could trust him . . . a little.

"Wait." Her hand went to the fastening at her throat. "Your cloak."

"Return it to me later." He mounted his horse with loose-limbed grace and lifted his hand to his followers. He was not dressed as they were; his tight dark blue trousers, intricately tied cravat, and fine coat reminded her of the kind of clothes Papa had worn when he had visitors from England. Yet, curiously, he did not look out of place with these men. She had a sense he possessed that same wildness, but it was controlled, channeled, as theirs was not.

The hollow clatter of hooves echoed on the cobblestones as the horsemen turned north. He was leaving her, once again letting her make a choice. The knowledge brought a sudden lift of spirits as she clutched the sheepskin blanket to her breasts and hurried back up the steps.

What a frightened little dove." Gregor's expression was sad as he looked back over his shoulder at the doorway through which Marianna had disappeared. "There are so many wounded children in this land. It hurts my heart not to be able to help them."

"That 'little dove' nearly emasculated me," Jordan said grimly. "I assure you, she's far more falcon than dove."

Gregor's eyes twinkled. "Then you did try to mount her. For shame—and in a holy church too."

"I mounted her, but not in the way you mean. She tried to kill me with an iron candlestick."

"Because you frightened her. Her brother is inside the church?"

"In the garden."

Gregor frowned. "I will go and get them. They may be too frightened to approach us."

"No, let her come to me."

"But I think—"

"The Window to Heaven was shattered," Jordan interrupted. "It's completely useless."

Gregor gave a shocked exclamation. "Who?"

"Well, we know it wasn't Nebrov. I suspect it was broken accidentally when he tried to capture the town."

Gregor grimaced. "I would not like to have been the officer in charge of the troop who made that mistake. I wonder why he didn't secure Talenka before he marched on to the capital."

"Arrogance. He thought he would wrest the entire country from King Josef and then have all the time in the world to steal the Window to Heaven. It was only when he was defeated that the urgency of the matter hit home. He needed the Window to barter with Napoleon for power and support." He paused. "However, when they smashed the Window, it seems he tried to rectify the error. He took a troop and rode west to the cottage of Anton Pogani."

"The man who created the Window?"

"So everyone thought. Your 'dove' tells me the work was done by her grandmother." He briefly related the details he had learned from Marianna.

Gregor whistled. "Poor little girl. No wonder you're being so kind to her."

"For God's sake I'm not being kind. Haven't you heard anything I've said? She won't admit it, but she *knows* the Window to Heaven. She's been trained in glassmaking, and someday she may be as good a craftsman as her grandmother. It's a chance, but it's the only one we have."

"I heard you." He beamed. "You should not be ashamed of being kind. I know you like the world to think you wicked, but I promise I will tell no one."

"I'm not—" He stopped and shrugged. "The girl would disagree. She's already told me she knows I'm not kind."

Gregor glanced back over his shoulder. "I still think I should go back and get her. What if she flies away?"

Jordan reined in his horse as he turned a corner. "She's not going to fly away. Because you're going to go back to the church and stand in that alcove in the shop across the street. Send Niko to watch the back entrance to the garden. Neither of you are to let your presence be known, if she sets out in the direction of the camp."

"And if she doesn't?"

"Bring her to me."

Gregor's expression was troubled. "She thought herself free. You did not tell her the truth."

"I didn't tell her a lie. She is free as long as she makes the right decision. Sometimes it's necessary to hood a falcon to keep her from flying in the wrong direction." He added impatiently, "And stop looking at me as if I were going to harm your little bird. The only reason I didn't take her by force is that I know more will be accomplished by offering honey instead of lemon. I'm well aware I need to coax her into submission. I have no desire to have her claw at me again."

The assurance didn't please Gregor. He had seen Jordan offer honey to women before, share the sweetness, and then withdraw and walk away. "This is not a good thing. She's not like your usual women. She is wounded."

"You talk as if I was going to bed her," Jordan said dryly. "As you say, she's only a child."

"How old?"

"Sixteen. I don't seduce chits scarcely out of the schoolroom."

It was true Jordan preferred older, experienced women and avoided like the plague the young innocents who were thrown at him both in Kazan and London. Yet Gregor's instincts told him there had been something unusual in Jordan's attitude toward the girl a few minutes ago. "The schoolroom from which this particular chit emerged teaches more interesting lessons. You need the Jedalar. I think there is little you would not do to get it."

"Then you needn't worry about her for a time. She's incapable of giving it to me for at least a few years. Perhaps never." He nudged his horse into a trot. "I'll see you at camp." He glanced over his shoulder. "And, Gregor, my friend, while you're contemplating letting the little dove fly the cage, you might consider that the alternative to my guardianship is leaving her to starve or become a whore in this benighted country."

A convincing argument, Gregor thought gloomily, as he watched Jordan ride away. Jordan was a hard man and had grown even more ruthless since he had involved himself in Kazan's concerns, but, whatever fate he dealt the girl, it would be better than what she faced here. "Niko!" He wheeled his horse and gestured to the burly young man at the rear of the troop. "No rest for you yet. There's work to be done."

The campfire was burning brightly, a beacon in the darkness, luring her closer.

"Marianna?" Alex's hand tightened on hers. "Is it all right?"

She didn't know, she thought in sudden panic. She didn't know if they would be safe. She had stayed for hours in the church agonizing over this decision. Draken's followers appeared a wild band, and yet he was . . .

What?

Violent, hard, clever. He had demonstrated all of those traits in the short time they had been together. She had also discerned a relentless determination and a blunt honesty. Yet how could honesty live side by side with deception? Every instinct said he had not told her the truth about the Window.

Alex coughed and pressed closer to her. "I smell food. I'm hungry, Marianna."

Food and shelter and safety for Alex, Draken had promised her, and she had promised him nothing. After all, she could always escape later if she found the threat too great. In the meantime Alex would have a chance to heal and grow stronger.

"There will be food soon." She drew the sheepskin blanket closer about Alex's shoulders, drew a deep breath, and strode boldly toward the campfire.

CHAPTER 2

Huddled figures, wrapped in sheepskin blankets, lay slumbering a short distance from the campfire. Only Jordan Draken was awake, sitting staring into the flames.

He looked up as she entered the circle of the firelight. "You've been a long time," he said quietly. He turned to Alex. "And you look blue with cold, lad. Come closer to the fire."

Alex glanced up at her, and when she nodded, he edged closer to the flames. He dropped the blanket as the heat struck him and held out his hands to the flames. He gave a beatific sigh. "That feels good."

"Yes, it does. It's a raw night." Jordan gestured to the pot simmering over the flames. "Rabbit stew. Take a spoon and bowl and help yourself."

"I'll get it for him." Marianna stepped forward, then stopped as Draken shook his head. "He's not well," she said fiercely.

"If he can stand, he can use a ladle." He stood up and unrolled a sheepskin pallet a short distance from his own and sat down again. "You're the one weaving on your feet. Sit down."

Alex was already eagerly spooning hot stew into a wooden bowl, and she reluctantly sat down on the sheepskin pallet. The fire was blessedly warm, and she wanted to sigh with contentment as Alex had done. "I have to help Alex."

"After you eat yourself."

"I will help him." Gregor strode into the light of the campfire. He filled a bowl with stew and sat down across the fire from them. "Come, lad, and sit with me. We will eat together. I'm hungry as a wolf, aren't you?"

He looked like a wolf himself, fierce and scarred by battle. Marianna knew Alex would never go to him.

Alex solemnly stared at him and then said hesitantly, "You are dressed most strangely."

Gregor grinned as he saw Marianna's astonishment. "Ah, you thought he would be afraid of me? Children are much smarter than grown-ups. They rely on their instincts, not their eyes." He turned back to Alex. "And your instincts are right. It is my clothes that are different, not my soul. But even my clothes are different only in these tame lowlands. At home in Kazan you would be the different one."

"Kazan!" Her gaze flew to the north where high, gray-purple mountains separated Montavia from Kazan. Until now she had never met anyone who came from that wild, fabled country, and she was not alone. Not only was Kazan surrounded by mountains, but its inhabitants were rumored to be a fierce, warlike people who kept to themselves and did not encourage visitors to their land. Her grandmother had told her she had fled to Kazan from Russia, but she had been frustratingly vague when answering Marianna's questions regarding the country itself. Kazan had no commerce with Montavia, and if they engaged in trade with any country, it must be with Russia, their neighbor to the north. They had remained totally aloof during the recent war between Nebrov and King Josef. Yet here was Gregor, who claimed he had ridden across the mountains from that mysterious country. "What are you doing here?"

"At the moment I'm trying to beg this lad to keep me company while I eat." Gregor pulled a long face that made him look like a mournful gargoyle. "I hate to eat alone. It gives me a monstrous bellyache."

Alex chuckled and went around the fire and settled on Gregor's pallet.

Gregor nodded with satisfaction. "As for what else I'm doing in this boring country of yours . . ." He took a bite of stew and then nodded at Jordan. "I'm doing my duty and taking care that Jordan doesn't injure himself fighting with frail young girls. Did you really take a candlestick to his private parts? I'm sure that there's many a woman who would—"

"Eat." Jordan added with precision, "Fill your mouth with food instead of conversation, or you can go back on sentry duty."

"You'd send me back out in the cold? How cruel." Gregor sighed, but a sly smile remained on his lips as he applied himself to his stew.

"Where's Niko?" Draken asked.

"You told me not to talk." Gregor took another bite before he said, "Still on sentry duty. I sent him to look over the town. It appears deserted, but you can never tell." He drew a sheepskin blanket firmly around Alex's thin shoulders. "Gobble down that stew. How do you expect to grow as big as me if you have no nourishment?"

Alex shook his head doubtfully. "I don't think I could grow that big if I ate all the stew in the world." But he obediently dipped his spoon into the savory mixture.

Jordan filled a bowl and handed it to Marianna. "Satisfied?"

She wasn't at all satisfied. Her mind was full of questions and apprehensions, but she nodded and began to eat hungrily. The rabbit was tough, but the broth was hot and thick and flavored with herbs. She was vaguely aware of another man—Niko, Gregor called him—coming to the fire and filling his bowl before drifting away. She could hear Gregor's deep low voice across the fire as he talked to and teased Alex, but she could not make out the words. Draken was watching her, but she didn't care. The wind was howling, whipping sharply down from the mountains, but for the first time in days she felt warm and dry with real food instead of scraps to eat.

"More?" Draken asked when she had finished.

She shook her head and put down the bowl. She had eaten too much already. A full stomach made one feel deceptively content and safe. She looked across the fire and saw Alex curled up against Gregor, already asleep, and felt a little better. He should be in a bed, not a pallet on the hard ground, but at least he was warm and protected from the wind by Gregor's bulk. Gregor winked at her as he settled down, drawing the cover over both Alex and himself. In spite of the giant's kindness she must be the one to be there when Alex woke, she thought. It would be a chilling shock to come out of sleep to that scarred face.

"He'll be all right," Draken said, impatience roughing his voice. "Lie down and go to sleep. You're about to fall over."

"I am not." She sat up very straight, trying to keep her spine rigid. "We have to talk . . . I have to ask—"

"Questions I told you I wouldn't answer, no doubt."

"I have to ask about the Window." She met his gaze. "That's why you wish me to come with you, isn't it?"

He didn't answer for a moment. "Yes."

"You think I can give it back to you."

"I hope you can give it to me."

"Why?"

"What do you know of Napoleon Bonaparte?"

Napoleon. The emperor of the French was only a shadowy figure to her. She tried to remember what Papa had taught her about the man. He had admired the emperor's brilliance, but her mother had said he would not be satisfied until he devoured all of Europe. Two years ago when he had come near one of Montavia's borders, there had been whispers and days of tension until he had moved on and the threat was gone. Then Nebrov's attack had thrown all of Montavia into chaos, and Napoleon had been forgotten. "I know that he wants power as much as the rest of you."

"Even more than the rest of us. I have to stop him."

"So that you can grab everything for yourself?"

He ignored the question. "So far he's hesitated to attack this part of the world, but that won't last forever." He met her gaze. "When he starts his march, he must not have the Jedalar." He saw the ripple of shock that went through her. "Did you think Nebrov was the only one who knew why the Window had value?"

She had suspected the Englishman knew, but she had hoped desperately she was wrong. "The Window had value because it had splendor and beauty and—"

"Knowledge," he finished softly. "You're only a girl with a young brother to protect. Don't make yourself a pawn in a war you don't even understand. Give me what I want, and I'll see that you're both kept safe."

"So that you can use it as you choose. You're probably no better than this Napoleon. Why should I choose between you?"

"Because it's not safe for you not to make a choice."

"Then I choose not to believe any of you," she said fiercely. "I won't be used by you or this Napoleon or the Duke of Nebrov. I will go my own path and do what I please."

His eyes narrowed on her face. "And what would you do with the Jedalar?"

"Use it in any way I wish." She glared at him. "And answer to no one. You have no right to ask me what I will do with my own property."

He studied her expression and then said, "Suppose we come to an agreement? For now we'll forget about the Window to Heaven."

"You won't get it," she said desperately. "I'll never give it to you."

He smiled. "We'll discuss it later."

She stared at him in fascination and dread. She had not seen him smile before, and she suddenly realized he was quite splendid-looking. She had never seen a more beautifully shaped mouth, and that smile was nearly irresistible. It gave his irregular features a charm that softened and transformed the severity of the long planes of his face. It was as if he had changed before her eyes, taken on a powerful persuasiveness and magnetism at will.

Lucifer, she thought, the caster of spells, the shape-changer, the weaver of incantations. He would do very well for the figure of the Dark Prince when she created her own Window to Heaven.

It was foolish to be this frightened, she told herself. If you recognized Satan, then you could fight him.

His smile faded, and he looked back at the fire. "Did it ever occur to you the Duke of Nebrov could be searching for you?"

It had been part of the nightmare that had been her life since that night. "I . . . don't think he saw us. Mama made us hide in the woods." She said more firmly, "No, I'm sure he didn't know we were there."

"Nebrov wouldn't have given up after the death of your mother. He would have searched the house for any possible information, sent one of his men to ask questions of your neighbors."

"He had no time. Samda was being held by King Josef's forces, and there was a price on Nebrov's head. Mama thought we were safe from him, but our cottage was several miles outside of town." She shuddered. "I heard him raving and cursing as he rode away. He was terribly angry."

"If he took that kind of risk, then you know he'll come back or send one of his men to ask questions. Your neighbors will tell him about you . . . and

Alex." He paused. "I used your brother to get what I wanted from you. Do you think Nebrov is less ruthless?"

"No," she whispered. Waves of sickness washed over her. No one could be more cruel than that monster. "Oh, no."

"And I can assure you he will be as determined as he is vicious. Nebrov never gives up."

He spoke with such absolute assurance that she asked, "You've met him?"

"On many occasions." He saw her instinctive withdrawal and shook his head. "His lands border Kazan. Naturally he came to assess our military capability. He decided his brother's kingdom would be an easier target."

She stared with horror out into the darkness that hid the ruins of Talenka. Nebrov had almost destroyed Montavia and its people to feed his greed for power. "Evil . . ."

"Then you agree you need to get Alex far away from Montavia." Her gaze flew to his face, and he nodded. "England."

England. That alien, faraway country her father had sometimes told her about. He had hated England as much as he had loved Montavia. "You want to take us to England?"

"I doubt if even Nebrov would think to search for you halfway across the world. Alex would be safe."

He would not say she would be safe, she realized, because of that core of honesty she found so confusing. He would not promise her safety because of the threat that came from him.

"Sleep on it." He smiled again. "I'm sure you'll make the right decision once you're rested." He pushed her gently back on the sheepskin pallet and covered her with a blanket. "For Alex."

Sleep? She almost laughed aloud. How could she sleep when he had just told her that he wanted to take her to a land where she would be a stranger, dependent only on him, more helpless than ever in her life?

He lay down a short distance away and drew his cover over him.

The crackle of the burning wood was the only sound in the stillness.

"For God's sake stop shaking," Draken said harshly.

She hadn't known she was shaking. She contracted her muscles, but the trembling persisted. "I believe . . . I'm cold."

"I believe you're lying." He sat up on his pallet. "I tolerated it in the church, but I'm very weary of watching you pretend that you're as strong as Gregor." He was suddenly beside her, his arms enfolding her.

She stiffened in panic and tried to push him away.

"Lie still," he said roughly as he cradled her in his arms. "I'm not going to hurt you." In spite of the harshness of his tone, his hands smoothing her hair back from her face were wonderfully gentle. "Nothing is going to hurt you tonight. You don't have to be afraid."

"Yes, I do." As long as there were Alex and the Jedalar, fear was the only defense she had to keep them safe. The shaking become long, racking, shudders, and her teeth bit deep into her lower lip. "I'm sorry. I don't know why . . . I haven't . . . not since that night. . . ."

He gave a low exclamation, then lay down beside

her and pulled her into his arms. She started to struggle again, but he pinned her to the pallet and stared down into her eyes. "Look at me, dammit. Am I going to hurt you?"

Her gaze clung desperately to his. His pale green eyes blazed down at her, clear, mesmerizing, willing her to believe him. She *did* believe him. She slowly shook her head.

He tucked her face into the hollow of his shoulder and held her. He smelled of leather and musk and the pine-scented smoke of the fire. "Easy," he whispered. "You're exhausted and you're frightened and that's all right. Just let it go. Send it away."

Warmth. Safety. Strength. It was as if she were wrapped in a web of power where nothing bad could reach her. If she could just lie here for a moment and take from him. . . .

"That's right." His voice flowed over her like sunlight, warming her. She had always believed voices had color, and his was darkest burgundy. "Don't worry about anything. Let me take care of you. All you have to do is rest and let me hold you."

She should move, she thought hazily. Lying here was dangerous, not because he might hurt her as they had hurt her mother but because she had the strangest sensation she was melting into him.

You couldn't fight an enemy if you became part of him.

She didn't move. She would do battle tomorrow after she gathered strength. She was safe now. Strange to think of safety in connection with Jordan Draken, but no more odd than anything else that had happened tonight. . . .

No!

She suddenly rolled away from him and sat up, clutching the cover to her throat, her chest rising and falling.

He stiffened, and she thought he would pull her back down, but he did not. He only raised himself to lean his cheek on his hand. "You persist in making things difficult for yourself."

"I only recognize the difficulty that is there." She moistened her lips. "I'm very tired. May I lie down?"

He smiled and shifted slightly to one side. "It would be my pleasure. I never refuse a—" His smile faded as he met her gaze. "Don't look at me like that. I forgot, dammit. In certain circumstances words have a habit of flowing without thinking."

His smile had been purely sensual, and she knew the circumstances to which he referred. She didn't think he was a man who would speak without considering every import of his words. How many beds and how many women had made that response instinctive?

He said quietly, "You knew you were safe a moment ago. Nothing has changed." He moved to his own pallet and sat down. "Except that you're foolishly refusing something you need."

She lay down on her pallet and pulled the cover up around her. "I have no need of you."

"You need comfort, and I'm offering it." She kept her head turned away, but she could feel his gaze on her face. "You'll lie there, and fairly soon you'll start to think and worry, and then you'll begin to shake again."

"That was a temporary weakness. I told you I was a little tired. I'm fine now."

"The devil you are."

She didn't answer.

"Tell me about glassmaking." He saw her tense and continued impatiently, "Not about the Window to Heaven. We've agreed not to talk about that."

Not now. But the questions would come. When he thought she could give him what he wanted, there would come a time—

"Tell me about your work."

"Why should I? It's nothing to you."

"Do you like doing it?"

"Of course, don't be foolish."

"How does it make you feel?"

She had never thought about it, she realized. It had just always been there, a part of her. She was no more able to separate her work from her life than color from a pane of glass. "Good. Bad. I get angry sometimes."

"Why?"

"You wouldn't understand."

"That's quite true. Not if you don't explain."

Why not answer him? The subject was innocent enough. "There are times when you have the vision, and then your hands aren't clever enough or the color isn't right or it's too thick and you don't serve the sunlight."

"Serve the sunlight?"

"It's the light that streams through the windows that makes the glass come alive. Why else would we create, if not to serve the sunlight?"

"You make it sound as if you worship the sun god."

She frowned. "I'm not a pagan."

"I'm not so sure. What does it feel like when the work does go right?"

How could she describe it when there weren't any words? "It's like . . . something inside me flying apart."

"Really? How painful."

"It's not. While it's going on, it feels like a driving fever and yet . . . good, and then afterward there's a wonderful sense of peace." She helplessly shook her head. "I told you that you wouldn't understand."

"On the contrary you've described a state with which I'm very familiar." He paused and then chuckled in genuine amusement. "Yes, very familiar."

She frowned, puzzled. "You're an artist or craftsman?"

"I hope I can claim to raise my skill to artistry in some areas. What was your first work?"

"Flowers." She closed her eyes to better visualize it. "A small panel, very simple, with yellow daffodils. Grandmama liked flowers."

"Your grandmother taught you?"

"Grandmama and Mama." Pain suddenly rushed back. Mama.

"Tell me about the daffodils," he said quickly. "Did they serve the sunlight?"

Light streaming through brilliant yellow blossoms and making a pattern on the rush-strewn floor. Grandmama smiling proudly at her. "Oh, yes," she whispered. "They were beautiful. Everything was beautiful that day."

"Did the daffodils have leaves?"

"Of course, I was only four, but I wouldn't forget leaves. Pale green . . . The color wasn't as true as the yellow, but they weren't too bad. . . ." She yawned. "Grandmama liked them. She liked every kind of flower. I said that, didn't I?"

"I don't remember."

"The next year I did a panel with roses for her natal day. Pink roses . . . When the sun shone through it, the edges of the petals looked as if they were rimmed in gold. It was an accident with the stain, but Grandmama pretended I'd done it on purpose. The next year I gave her another one that I'd done correctly, but I think she liked the first one best."

Pink roses, rimmed with gold, daffodils and memories of kindness and love. They were all blending together like the colors of a stained-glass panel seen from a great distance.

"I'm sure she did."

She opened heavy lids to see him watching her, his expression enigmatic, his eyes the green of the daffodil leaves.

"Tell me again about the roses," he said.

She had already told him too much, she realized. She had pushed him away, and he had only circled and come back to claim a greater intimacy than when he had held her. He had won.

No, it was she who had won. He had given her back loving memories to replace the ones rooted in pain. It didn't matter what his motives were in giving her that gift; it could only heal and help her grow stronger.

"No." She turned on her side, facing away from him. "The roses are mine." She closed her eyes, deliberately shutting him out. She wanted to go back to that time when there was nothing but laughter and sunlight and Mama and Grandmama telling her that the gold around the petals was just right. . . .

• • •

Wake up, Marianna." Alex was shaking her. "We have to hurry. We're going to England! You know, the place where Papa was born!"

She opened her eyes to see his excited face above her.

"On a boat, a big boat. And Jordan says I'll see seagulls and dolphins and—"

"Shh." She groggily sat up and brushed the hair from her forehead. "Let me wake up before you—" She stopped as she saw Jordan standing a few feet behind Alex framed against the pink pearl of the dawn sky.

"Alex is right," His hand fell on the boy's shoulder. "It's nearly time to start." He nodded at the pond a short distance away. "Refresh yourself and then come back and get some bread and cheese. We'll not stop until evening." He turned and sauntered over to the fire, where Gregor sat pulling on his boots.

He was acting as if the decision was already made. He had even told Alex that they were going to England. She stood up and started down the hill toward the pond.

Alex scampered on her heels. "We have to go to the seaport at Domajo where the boat is waiting. Jordan says it will take a full day to get there."

Color bloomed in his cheeks, and he was more animated than she had seen him in days. He was full of the excitement of starting a new life, which only made her decision harder. What was best to do? Montavia was the only home she had ever known. The idea of leaving it was hard to contemplate.

She could stay. After all, it was not as if she didn't have a skill. Perhaps she could find work in the capital.

She would not find work. No guild would accept a woman in their ranks; Mama and Grandmama had both fought that battle. If there was no way to earn a living at her craft, how would she and Alex live? Montavia had been stripped and torn of its riches by the war launched by the duke. The people in the towns she had encountered on her journey from Samda had been struggling just to stay alive and rebuild their lives. Only the thieves and whores seemed to be prospering in the ruins.

She shivered as she remembered the painted women they had encountered in the towns on their way from Samda. She would not be able to bear such a life.

Of course she could bear it. For Alex.

But only as the last resort, after she had tried every other means available.

The Jedalar. All her life she had been taught that when the time came to act, her duty was to the Jedalar. Her mother had made sure Marianna had memorized the secret and the plan of action that must be followed.

But her mother had not known the Window to Heaven would be destroyed. She did not yet have the required skill to bring the Jedalar to life, and surely no one could blame her if she chose temporary safety for both Alex and herself.

England.

Jordan Draken wanted her skill and the Jedalar, not her body. She would not have to become a whore if she went with him to England, and Alex would be safe from the duke of Nebrov.

She glanced up the hill to where Jordan was still talking to Gregor. He was so confident, so sure that he could mold her to his will. Sudden anger flared through her. She would not allow it. She would take what she and Alex needed from him and then leave this England and go wherever they chose.

She whirled and began furiously splashing water into her face.

"Hurry, Marianna," Alex said. "Gregor says I can ride with him today. Did you see his horse? He said that he bought it in Kazan and that all horses are that large there. Do you suppose that's true?"

"No, I think Gregor was teasing you." She wiped her face and tidied her hair. "You must be careful not to believe everything these people tell you."

"Good advice." She lifted her head to see Jordan standing a few feet away. He continued blandly, "Gregor is given to embroidering stories. He says it makes life more interesting."

"But you always tell the truth," she said with irony.

"Whenever possible. I don't agree with Gregor. I think lies only complicate matters. I prefer simplicity." He turned to Alex. "Gregor is waiting for you."

Alex flew up the hill.

"You'll ride with me," Jordan said to her. "We have no extra horses. We were traveling fast and brought no pack animals."

"It wouldn't matter. Neither Alex nor I know how to ride anyway."

His brows lifted. "No? We'll have to attend to that as soon as we reach England."

"I didn't say we were going with you."

"But you are. You have courage, but courage isn't enough when the odds are so great. You're intelligent enough to know this is the best way out for you."

"I'll make sure it is." She added bluntly, "I intend to take everything you'll give me and give nothing in return."

"That attitude isn't new in my experience. I've lived with it all my life." His tone was laden with weary cynicism. "But I've not been cheated in a good many years. It's become a challenge to find ways of taking what I want too."

"You won't find a way this time."

"Are you going to abandon your work to keep from developing the skill you need? I think not. I understand you a little bit better after last night. You love what you do. You have to work. It's a passion." He smiled. "I understand passion."

"That doesn't mean I'll create a Window to Heaven even after I'm capable of doing it."

"True, but that's where the challenge occurs." He started up the hill. "I believe that, for reasons of your own, you want to do that window as much as I want you to do it. When we reach Cambaron, I'll supply you with all the tools of your craft, and we'll see if you can resist the temptation."

"Cambaron? Your home?"

He nodded. "Go and get something to eat while I saddle my horse."

Cambaron. Her hands clenched at her sides as she watched him walk away. She knew nothing about him or this place to which he was taking them, while she had revealed entirely too much to him last night. It made her feel frightened and uncertain.

She had to find a way to shift the scales.

He looked over his shoulder. "Coming?"

By the time she reached the group at the top of the hill, Alex was already mounted, sitting before Gregor on the giant bay horse, cradled in his arms.

"Good morning," Gregor said. He held out a small leather-wrapped packet to her. "Bread and cheese. I saved it for you. You must rise early to snatch food from these fellows."

"I'm not hungry."

"Eat it anyway. You ate practically nothing last night." Jordan swung onto his horse. "We'll wait."

She already felt more helpless than she could bear, and she would not let him command her in a matter this small. "I'm *not* hungry," she repeated with precision.

To her disappointment he didn't argue. "As you like." He walked his horse forward. "But don't complain if you grow famished before evening."

"I won't complain."

"No, you'll suffer in silence." He leaned down and lifted her onto his horse and settled her across the saddle in front of him. "As all proper martyrs should."

His arms encircled her; the heat of his body on her back came as a shock. "For God's sake, stop stiffening," he said in her ear. "You'll be a bag of bruises by the time we reach Domajo."

"I told you I wasn't accustomed to riding." She was also not accustomed to being this close to a lean, masculine form. It was not like last night, when she had been conscious only of the comfort he offered. Today she was aware of every muscle, every texture and scent, of him. It . . . disturbed her. "I'm not comfortable."

"Neither am I," he murmured.

"Perhaps . . . I should change places with Alex." She continued quickly, "Gregor's horse is larger."

"So is Gregor. You'll have to be content with me." He laughed grimly. "And I guarantee we'll be more than accustomed to each other by the time we reach Domajo." He pulled her back against him. "Close your eyes."

"Why?"

"You can pretend you're in a fine carriage. I'm sure you'd think that better than being held by my humble self."

She closed her eyes but immediately realized it was not better; it was much worse. She again had the uneasy feeling she was flowing into him.

Her lids flicked open. "I prefer reality to pretense."

"Pity," he murmured. "When pretense offers so many attractive faces. I suppose you'll just have to live with mine instead."

A breeze, wet, salty, striking her face.

Voices, loud, strident, but not threatening.

"Take her, Gregor. She's probably too stiff to stand."

She slowly opened her lids. Green eyes looking into her own, those beautifully shaped lips. She wished he would smile. . . .

The hands that lifted her from the horse were enormous. Gregor's hands, Gregor smiling down at her when Jordan would not. She shouldn't have worried about Alex waking to that scarred face, she realized sleepily. You noticed only the warmth of his smile. "We're there?" she whispered.

He nodded. "It was a hard trip. You stood it well."

Gray-white sails shimmering in the darkness. . . . Gregor was striding toward a ship.

"Alex?"

"He stood it even better. The scamp is running all over the dock."

"He'll fall in the water!" She was immediately awake and struggling in Gregor's arms. "Let me down."

"When we get to your cabin. Jordan is right, you need time to ease the stiffness." He strode up the gangplank. "Don't worry about the boy. Niko is watching him."

She felt like a helpless child herself, being carried like this. "I'm perfectly able to walk." She glanced over her shoulder and saw Alex climbing on a huge box with Niko standing beside him.

"Niko has children of his own. He won't let anything happen to him."

As if to prove Gregor's words, Niko laughed, plucked Alex from the box, and set him safely onto the dock. "I still want you to let me down, Gregor."

Gregor studied her face and then set her down, but steadied her with a hand around her waist. "It makes you uneasy to feel helpless. Why did you not tell me? Most women like to feel cosseted."

"I'm not accustomed to it." She felt better on her feet but was glad of Gregor's support. Her legs were numb, and her back felt as if she had been on the rack. "Where is Mr. Draken?"

"Jordan?" He nodded at a small building down the dock. "He had business with Janus. He will be here soon. He wants to sail on the midnight tide."

"Janus?"

"Janus Wiczkows, Jordan's cousin." He turned as he saw a man approaching and hailed him. "Captain Braithwaite, what a pleasure to see your smiling face. Did you think we weren't coming?"

The small man who stopped before them was not smiling; his long, deeply furrowed face seemed incapable of the act. He gave Gregor a dour look. "It took you long enough. I've been sitting in this port so long, I have barnacles on my own bott—"

"Permit me to introduce you to your passenger," Gregor interrupted quickly. "Captain John Braithwaite, may I present Miss Marianna Sanders."

The captain's sour gaze raked over her, taking in the ragged garments with disapproval. "I told His Grace I would take none of his harlots on board my ship."

Gregor's smile faded. "It is Jordan's ship, and I think he would be most upset if he heard you insult his . . . his . . ." He hesitated and then finished with a beaming smile. "His ward."

"His ward?" Braithwaite echoed suspiciously.

Gregor nodded. "She is the daughter of Justin Sanders, Jordan's close friend, who was killed in this terrible land a few weeks ago. Poor child. What trials and tribulations she has endured to escape death and dishonor. When we heard of Justin's death, we searched ceaselessly until we found her and her small brother."

Marianna stared at him in astonishment.

Gregor's eyes were misting. "Do you know where we found them? In a church, praying for rescue. I cannot tell you how . . . touched and full of pain Jordan was when he found this poor girl."

Touched. Pain. She remembered Jordan doubled

over when she had struck him between the legs with the candelabra. Gregor slanted her a look from beneath his lashes, but his mournful expression didn't change. "What could he do?" he continued. "The only thing any Christian soul would do. Take her back to England where she can be educated and given the chance to marry a man who will make her forget these tragic woes."

"I believe not a tenth of this balderdash," the captain said bluntly. "I've heard your tales before, Gregor." He turned to Marianna. "What is your name, girl?"

"Marianna Sanders." She met his gaze. "And my father *is* dead, and I am *not* a harlot."

He studied her and then nodded slowly. "I believe you." He turned and walked toward the gangplank. "In future let the girl tell the tale. She knows the value of brevity."

Gregor looked after him, outraged. "It was a very good story. One of my best. Just enough truth to make it sound true." He took her arm and propelled her along the deck. "And on the spur of the moment too."

"Did you have to lie to him?"

He shrugged. "I couldn't let him insult you. He has a mind as narrow as his body, but he's a good seaman. England rules the Mediterranean, but when we reach the Atlantic, we'll need a good captain to avoid Napoleon's navy. I thought it was better than crushing his head."

She found herself smiling. "Much better."

"But I should know more about you the next time. What was your father's given name?"

"Certainly not Justin. His name was Lawrence."

"We'll make that his middle name. Justin Lawrence Sanders. It goes well together. What was his occupation?"

"He was a poet."

"Jordan does not run with the literary set." He frowned. "We will say they knew each other as boys at Oxford."

She shook her head in bewilderment. "Why is all this necessary?"

"Things in England are not as they are here. There are many people who are like the captain. It would not be . . . pleasant for you." He smiled. "So we will make sure that there is nothing at which they can raise their brows or sneer."

She felt a surge of warmth toward him even as she shook her head. "I'm not concerned with these English or what they think. I intend to work. Nothing else matters to me."

"Then we will make sure you work in comfort and not be disturbed when the world brushes by you," he said soberly. "But it will brush Alex more than you. You would not want him to be distressed by name-calling. It is clear you want only what is best for him."

"He's an innocent child," she protested. "What names could they possibly call him?"

"If they cover you with their tar, then he will also be smeared. You do not wish this."

"No." She was beginning to dislike the thought of this England more each passing minute. She made an impatient gesture. "Very well, tell whatever story you wish."

He smiled. "I promise you I will make it most interesting. There are many possibilities. Would you like to be the daughter of a princess?"

"I just want to be left alone."

"Unfortunately, Jordan's position makes that unlikely. There are always people at Cambaron."

Jordan's position. She suddenly remembered how the captain had referred to him. His Grace. She asked warily, "And what is his position?"

"Did he not tell you?" he asked, surprised. "Jordan is the Duke of Cambaron."

"No, he didn't tell me."

Power. Jordan Draken might hold as much power in his country as the Duke of Nebrov did in Montavia. The thought sent fear through her and made this journey to England appear even more threatening. "None of the men addressed him as Your Grace."

"That's because no one in Kazan recognizes any title but the ones granted by our own ravin."

"Ravin?"

"Our leader. Our ravin is like your king Josef."

She wasn't interested in the intricacies of the Kazan monarchy. "What was an English duke doing in Kazan?"

For the first time he hesitated. "I cannot tell you."

"It has something to do with the Window to Heaven."

"Not entirely," he said evasively. "Jordan has visited us many times."

"Why does Kazan want—"

His big paw of a hand gently covered her lips. "Do not ask me. I know you feel uneasy and afraid and think knowledge will help you. I cannot tell you about Kazan. It is not my right."

His expression was sympathetic, but she could see he would not be moved. She moved her head to escape his hand. "Then tell me about Cambaron."

"Ah, it is a fine place. One of the richest estates in all England." He again began to stroll down the deck. "You will like it."

"Rich?" Bad fortune if Draken was not only titled but wealthy as well. His arsenal of weapons was growing by leaps and bounds.

"Very rich." He beamed. "His father died when Jordan was only a lad of twelve, and he inherited vast mining and shipping interests."

"How pleasant for him," she said faintly.

"Pleasant but not good. Too much money tends to lead to debauchery, and Jordan was ever one to do things with more intensity than others. We became most concerned about him."

"You knew him as a child?"

"Not exactly." He paused before a polished oak door. "This is your cabin. Alex will be next door. Are you hungry?"

She was starved, she realized ruefully, just as Jordan had predicted. "Yes."

"I will go to the galley and see if I can find something for you and Alex." His gaze went over her. "You are very thin. . . ."

She smiled. "You intend to fatten me up?"

He chuckled. "No, after I bring you food, I intend to go ashore and purchase you clothing to cover that skinny body. Jordan said you and Alex must have something to wear on the journey besides those rags."

"I wouldn't want to offend His Grace," she said ironically.

"You would not." He opened the door for her. "I've seen him more ragged than you on occasion. He only wants your comfort."

"That's not all he wants."

His smile faded. "No, that is true. He wants the Window. Can you give it to him?"

"I will *never* give it to him," she said passionately.

"Can and will are different words. You're saying it is possible." He shook his head. "I was hoping you would say no."

"I don't lie."

"It would be safer for you if you did. Jordan will not stop until he gets it, you know." He moved his big shoulders as if shrugging off a burden. "But we need not think about that now. We will enjoy what we have and worry tomorrow."

"I do not intend to worry about it at all." She suddenly smiled and said gently, "But I thank you for your concern, Gregor."

"So much for warnings." He sighed and turned away. "I will have Niko bring Alex to you."

"Are Niko and the other men going with us to England?"

"No, they return with Janus to Kazan." He smiled. "So you will have only Jordan and me with whom to contend. Does not that make you happy?"

He didn't wait for an answer but sauntered away immediately.

She lit the candle on the small table by the door and surveyed the tiny cabin. Its furnishings consisted only of a chest, a small bunk, and a washstand, but it was pristine. She was the only dirty object in the room, she thought wearily. She smelled of horse and was so grimy she doubted if she would be able to do more than remove the surface layer at that washstand.

Well, she would do what she could and ask about the possibility of a tub for a bath later. Cleansing herself would at least give her something else to think about besides the disturbing information Gregor had imparted.

Jordan watched Gregor as he strode down the dock toward him. The man could barely see over the stack of boxes and cloth wrapped bundles in his arms.

"Did you buy out all of Domajo?" Jordan asked dryly.

"How could I? Most of the shops were closed. I even had to persuade a few of the merchants to open their doors for me."

Jordan had seen Gregor's arts of persuasion. He started with a smile, but it usually ended with him knocking the door down. "I told you I wanted only enough for the journey. Domajo is hardly a center of fashion."

"Marianna will not know that, and perhaps a pretty gown will raise her spirits. I wish I could have found more for her." He balanced carefully as he strode up the gangplank. "What did Janus say?"

"What you would expect him to say. He wasn't pleased."

"The ravin will be even less so."

"Unfortunate. I'm doing all that I can."

"They know that," Gregor said quietly. "It will just be a disappointment. They worry about Napoleon. They're afraid he will make his move too soon."

"The whole world worries about Napoleon."

"Do not bite at me when you want to bite at him." He grinned. "Or I will knock you off this gangplank into the water as I would have done when you were a boy."

Jordan smiled reluctantly. "No, you won't. You

wouldn't wish to drop all those gauds you bought for your dove."

"True. I would wait." He shifted the packages. "There is the captain on the bridge. You should know I told him Marianna and Alex are your wards. You went to school with their father, who was killed in the war. His name was Justin Lawrence Sanders, and he was a poet."

"Wards?" Jordan said, stunned.

"I could think of nothing else on the spur of the moment." He frowned. "Though I admit casting you in the staid role of guardian is not very plausible."

"Nor in the least realistic."

"It will have to do." Gregor's jaw set stubbornly. "You may have to rob them of the Jedalar, but you must cause them no further hurt."

Jordan's lips thinned. "I have no intention of hurting them."

"You could hurt them just by being who you are."

"The Devil incarnate?" Jordan asked caustically.

"No, nothing so omnipotent. Merely the Duke of Diamonds." Gregor grimaced. "But it is still enough to ruin any innocent who is seen with you."

The Duke of Diamonds. The ridiculous title left a sour taste in his month. Christ, he could remember when the sobriquet had amused him, when he had even encouraged its use. But that had been at a time when he had embraced every pleasure and sexual excess with a recklessness that had made him a legend even at a court notorious for its debauchery. "I have no intention of being seen in company with this particular innocent."

"You intend to shut her in a dungeon and let her out only when she can give you what you want?"

"I didn't say that," he said testily.

"Or you could leave her here. We could tell Niko to find her a place of safety. You said yourself that it is a gamble. She may never be capable of giving you the Jedalar."

"It's a gamble I intend to take."

"Then we must do what is necessary for her well-being."

"I'll have to think about it."

"I have already thought about it. She is your ward, and when we arrive at Cambaron, we will get her a maid to accompany her and . . ." He paused. "What do they call them . . . an abigail?"

"Good God, a chaperon?"

"Of course, and then we can all live in peace and tranquillity." He shot him a sly look. "And your sudden virtue will redeem you in the eyes of the dowagers at Bath."

"I would have to become a monk to accomplish that feat."

"It is true they consider you lost to sin, but anything is possible." The captain was coming down the steps from the bridge, and Gregor said quickly, "It is only a small thing. It will do you no harm to protect the girl."

"What if she doesn't want to be protected?"

"She will accede to anything for the sake of the boy."

That was true enough. The girl had demonstrated she would walk through fire to safeguard Alex. "I still don't like it."

"I know," Gregor said. "And I think it is not because it will make you a favorite among the dowagers. You do not want her protected. Why?"

"She's a hostage of war." He smiled cynically. "It's going to be difficult enough winning what I want from her. Why should I let you strengthen her position when I prefer her vulnerable?"

Gregor's gaze searched his face, and then he slowly shook his head. "I do not think that is the complete reason. You may want her weak and vulnerable, but—"

"I didn't say weak," Jordan said sharply.

"No, that would be a blasphemy in one so strong and bold," Gregor murmured. "Ah, and you admire strength. It attracts you like a glowing fire. Perhaps you want to—"

"I want you to stop making surmises that have no basis in fact." Jordan turned and walked toward the captain.

"I will see you tomorrow morning at breakfast," Gregor called after him, and then added even more loudly, "I must take these packages to your poor wards."

He had made sure the captain heard his words, Jordan thought with annoyance. Whether he liked it or not, Gregor was trying to make sure his dove was settled safely in the niche he had placed her.

CHAPTER 3

The sun shone on the water, turning it a silvery blue so brilliant, it hurt Marianna's eyes to view it.

"Good morning. I hope you slept well."

Marianna turned to see Jordan Draken walking toward her. He was dressed in severe black and white, a stark contrast against the blue of the sea. "Well enough." She paused before adding deliberately, "Your Grace."

He smiled. "There's little enough grace in the way you say that. I think you must call me Jordan instead."

"I wouldn't think of it, Your Grace."

He studied her. "You're more annoyed with me than usual. I didn't think it possible." He leaned one elbow on the rail. "Why?"

"I have no liking for dukes."

"A natural enough reason. In your place I would feel the same. But I assure you I am no Duke of Nebrov."

"You are not in my place. You cannot know how I

feel." She added fiercely, "And how do I know you're not the same? You want what he wants."

"What is that?"

"Power. Do you deny it?"

"Yes, I already have more than enough power to suit me." He saw the flicker of expression on her face. "That's what you fear, isn't it? You think I'll use my power to make you give me the Jedalar."

"I'm not afraid." She met his skeptical gaze and said, "And of course you will use any weapon you have. Mama told me there would come a time when everyone would do whatever they had to do to claim it. She said that unless I—"

"What?" he asked after she broke off.

"Never mind. It's of no consequence."

His gaze narrowed on her face. "I believe it may be of the utmost consequence."

She tried to distract him from that slip of the tongue. "She was right, wasn't she? There's nothing you wouldn't do to get it."

He nodded wearily. "Yes, she was right." He changed the subject. "Where's Alex?"

"Gregor took him to meet the captain."

"Have you both had your breakfast?"

"Yes."

He smiled mockingly. "You see how concerned I'm being? The perfect guardian of innocent children."

"I told Gregor it was a ridiculous idea. You have none of the qualities of a guardian."

"I agree, but Gregor is adamant. So it seems we must all comply."

"Why?" she asked with sudden curiosity. "What is Gregor to you?"

"My friend."

"He says he takes care of you."

"He did at one time. But then, Gregor takes care of everyone. It's his nature." He looked out to sea and asked suddenly, "Do you play chess?"

She looked at him in bewilderment. "Yes, I used to play with my father."

"And are you adequate at the game?"

"No, I'm not adequate. I'm very good."

He laughed, his face alight with amusement. "My apologies. I meant no insult. It's my curse that I cannot bear to play with novices."

"I'm not a novice. After the first year of play I bested Papa all the time."

"Let us hope I'm better than Papa."

"You wish me to play chess with you?"

"It will while away the time. It will take us weeks to get to England, and sea voyages can be stultifying."

"Then play with Gregor."

"Gregor refuses to learn the game. He gets too restless."

"I'd think you would suffer the same malady."

"On the contrary, I can be very patient—if the prize is worth the game." He said softly, "And I think you would be an excellent opponent. You have a single-mindedness that bodes well for the match."

"I have no time for games. I have to take care of Alex."

"Ah, yes, your duty to the men of your family. I believe Gregor would be willing to watch over the child." He shifted his gaze to her face. "Doesn't the idea appeal to you? Think of it. You have a chance of humiliating me over the board and seeking out every weakness."

In her present state of dependency that prospect was very tempting. "And give you an opportunity to do the same to me."

"True, but I don't think you'd be afraid to meet that challenge." He smiled. "And it will keep you from going mad with boredom. I judge you're not one who can stand being without a task to do. Will you join me in the master cabin in an hour?"

He was right. She was accustomed to working from dawn to dusk, and this journey would become excruciatingly tedious if she had nothing to do but look out at that blue sea.

"Continuing to be so wary of me will be both exhausting and uncomfortable for you," Jordan said, sensing her wavering. "Propinquity brings a certain . . . acceptance."

"Tolerance," she substituted.

"If you wish to be blunt."

"I wish to be blunt." She frowned. "If I come, I won't answer any of your questions."

"Then how can we become acquainted?"

"I'll ask *you* questions."

"A very one-sided arrangement."

"Or we will not talk at all."

"But I'm a shallow fellow who cannot bear long silences."

She snorted. He was as shallow as this sea around them.

"That was very unladylike. I don't believe I've ever heard one of the females of my acquaintance make such a monstrous sound."

She stared at him uncertainly. His eyes were glinting with mischief. "You're . . . teasing me."

"How clever of you to recognize, if not respond.

Don't you ever smile?" He held up his hand. "Never mind, I'll regard it as another challenge."

"I've had little to smile about of late, Your Grace."

An undefinable expression flickered on his face. "I realize that, but perhaps it's time to start again. Now, you seem determined to address me with the respect due me. Is it that you think I'm your superior because of my birth?"

"You're not my superior. Respect should be earned, not given. What have you done to deserve my respect? Have you created a beautiful panel of glass? Have you painted a wonderful picture?"

"Not lately," he said mildly. "Since I'm so low on your scale of worthiness, don't you think it's absurd to address me by any but my given name?"

It was a small concession that would put them on a more equal footing, a status she desperately needed. "Jordan," she said tentatively.

"Much better. By the way, you're quite charming in that gown, Marianna."

Charming? Was he teasing again? She looked down at the high-waisted white gown she wore. Probably. The garment was a little large and, even if it had fit better, she still wouldn't have been able to fill out the bodice. "You're going to see a good deal of it. It's the only ready-made gown Gregor was able to find in Domajo."

"I won't get tired of it. I've always been fond of white."

"My father liked white too," she said absently.

"Did he? Then my taste is undoubtedly validated." He turned and sauntered away from her. "Though I take umbrage at being compared in any way to your father. Being a guardian is bad enough."

She gazed after him thoughtfully. A steely edge shimmered beneath the lightness of his tone, and she realized he disliked the position Gregor's lie had put them in as much as she did. She would have to remember that tiny break in his armor. It was a weapon she couldn't ignore, when she had so few.

The design on the panel of glass was very simple, the daffodils painstakingly executed. Yet it clearly lacked the skillful touch of a mature artisan.

"You found this in the cottage?" Zarek Nebrov held the small panel up to the light and then tossed it on the table. "It's nothing. This crudeness has nothing to do with the Window to Heaven. You've brought me *nothing*."

Marcus Costain protested, "I've brought you the information about the girl and her brother."

"They could be dead now." Nebrov strode over to the window and looked down into the courtyard. "You should have found out sooner about the children. We could have used them to make the woman talk."

"You were in a great hurry that night," Costain said impassively.

And in a fury of frustration about that stupid shattering of the Window at Talenka. He had almost lost everything, and the stupid woman had refused to reveal what he needed to know. If he hadn't been so angry, he would have brought the woman with him and wrested the information at his leisure. He would never have permitted the bitch to taunt his sergeant into killing her before he had what he wanted. Blunder after blunder. That fool had paid, but it had not given Nebrov the Jedalar.

"The farmer who lives next door to their cottage said this design was done years ago by a child of four. She brought it to them to show the farmer's daughter. The girl could be much more skilled now."

"Could she be hiding with this farmer?"

Costain shook his head. "She's not with them. He's too frightened to lie."

"Then she could be anywhere in Montavia. Do we know what she looks like?"

Costain nodded.

"Then find her."

"It will not be easy."

"Will she desert the boy?"

"The farmer says no."

"Try the stews first. It's the easiest way for a girl to keep from starving. A whore caring for a young brother should be fairly easy to find."

"I can no longer move freely about Montavia. King Josef is beginning to reassert his power in the west."

While Nebrov was forced to stay on his lands for fear Josef would send his army after him. The anger began to rise again, and he forced it down. It was lack of control and overconfidence that had caused him to be here licking his wounds when he should be on the throne of Montavia. He must never make that mistake again.

"Then go slowly, but find her. Even if the girl doesn't have the skill for the work, if she knows the secret of the Jedalar, it may be enough. I'll find another craftsman to give me what I need."

Costain hesitated. "It seems a great effort for—"

"Do it," Nebrov said softly. He gestured to the panel of daffodils on the table. "And don't bring me any more of this rubbish. I want the girl herself."

Costain shrugged. "As you wish, Your Grace." He turned and left the room.

As he wished? Nothing was going as he wished.

Very well, then that circumstance must be corrected. First, he must rebuild his army to make sure he was safe from that fool, Josef, and then he must set out in another direction. Josef would never be caught by surprise again, so he must discard Montavia from his plans.

Kazan? No, it was even stronger than Montavia.

He must have help if he was to gain dominance over either country.

Napoleon. He had been considering an alliance for some time, but he knew the emperor would never give Nebrov either Kazan or Montavia unless he was given something of equal value in return.

The Jedalar.

She moved her knight. "Why were you in Kazan?"

Jordan looked up and smiled. "Because I wanted to be there."

"You said that about Montavia."

"Forgive me for being repetitive. Truth has a habit of lacking originality. Gregor would tell you lies require much more creativity."

"What is it like?"

"Kazan?"

"That's what we were talking about," she said impatiently.

"As I recall, we weren't talking. You were asking

questions." He moved his queen. "Why are you suddenly so interested in Kazan?"

"Everyone in Montavia is curious about Kazan." She studied the board. She might be in trouble. "Because no one knows anything about it."

"Which suits the denizens of Kazan extremely well. They prefer to shut the world out and live in isolation."

"I can't believe that's true. Not if they resemble Gregor."

"But no one resembles Gregor. He's unique."

And so was the man facing her across the board, she thought. For the past two weeks she had studied him and found him to be as complicated as the pattern in the Window to Heaven. One moment he was guarded and faintly menacing and the next completely charming and witty, ignoring her distrust as airily as if it didn't exist. The quicksilver changes in his nature were as fascinating as they were unsettling. She had lived a secluded life in Samda and her acquaintance was not large, but she did not believe another Jordan Draken could be found on the face of the earth.

"You're truly fond of Gregor, aren't you?"

"Of course. I love him," he said simply. "You should know by now that he won't tolerate anything less. God knows, I tried to keep him at a distance, but he wouldn't accept it."

"Why would you want to keep him at a distance?"

"Because you and I are a great deal alike." He looked up and met her gaze. "Neither of us wants to give too much for fear it will be taken away from us."

"I'm not like you." At least she had not been like that before she had lost everything she loved, she thought with sudden pain. She had been as open and free as Alex before that horrible night.

"Are you going to make a move, or do you intend to sit there until we get to Southwick?"

His expression was impassive, but she had the uncanny feeling he had somehow sensed that agonizing memory and was guiding her away from it. "Don't rush me." Her glance returned to the board. Yes, she was definitely in trouble. "Where is Southwick? I thought we were going to London."

"I said England. It does comprise more than one city, you know. Southwick is the port nearest Cambaron, only a half day's ride."

"Ride?" she asked cautiously. She had no desire for another experience as intimate as the ride to Domajo.

From the look in his eyes, she knew he had again interpreted her qualms with exasperating accuracy. If the purpose of these hours together was to enable them to better read each other, then they had benefited Jordan more than her. At times she felt as if he could sense her every thought.

He said, "We'll get two very gentle horses for you and Alex and take the journey slowly."

"Very slowly," she said with emphasis.

"You should know by now I can be patient." His eyes twinkled. "For instance, I've been sitting here waiting for you to wriggle out of the box I've put you in for the past ten minutes."

"I'm not necessarily in a box." She looked down at the board. "And if I am, there's usually a way out."

"Then find it."

That's what she was trying to do, but she feared it

was futile. "Gregor says Kazan's monarch is called a ravin."

"That's true." He leaned back in his chair. "Why are you more interested in Kazan than your future home? You haven't asked one question in the last two weeks about Cambaron."

"I'll find out about it soon enough."

"And Kazan is far, far away, while Cambaron is on the horizon and a bit intimidating."

It was true, but she didn't know she had been so transparent. She tried to shrug carelessly. "I'm sure I will become accustomed to it."

"I'm sure you will too," he said quietly. "I told you when you came with me that I would protect you and Alex. Do you think I'm going to throw you into the dungeon?"

"Does it have a dungeon?"

His lips quirked. "A very small one and hardly ever used."

"A dungeon . . . That means it's a castle, doesn't it?"

"That appears to be what it means."

"I've never been in a castle. There was one on the outskirts of Samda, but I've . . ." She said haltingly, "I've never known anything but our cottage."

"A castle is merely a cottage with more rooms."

"That's ridiculous. You don't have to comfort me with falsehoods." She moved her queen. "Just because I'm not familiar with your grand castle is no reason to think that—"

"Checkmate."

She had made a mistake, and he had pounced. She frowned. "You distracted me."

He chuckled. "You knew you were going to lose two moves ago."

Her jaw squared. "I had a chance."

"Only if you changed the rules of the game."

"That's not true. I could have—" She could think of nothing and finally smiled reluctantly. "I *hate* to lose."

"That's come to my attention on a number of occasions."

"Not that many. We're equally matched, and I've won as— Why are you looking at me like that?"

"You're smiling at me. It's the first time I've seen you smile at anyone besides Gregor or Alex." He watched her smile instantly vanish and shook his head regretfully. "Ah, it's gone. Too bad."

She pushed back her chair and stood up. "I have to go find Alex."

"By all means run away." He stood up and bowed courteously. "There are signs of softening. If you stayed, you might even smile at me again."

"It's not likely." She moved toward the door. "It was obviously caused by the shock of losing, and I have no intention of doing that again."

She could never bear to let him have the last word, Jordan thought.

A smile lingered on his lips as he picked up the pieces and returned them to the leather box. That final verbal thrust was part and parcel of her dislike of losing. Lately he had found himself watching and anticipating it, rather like a fencing instructor waiting for a favorite pupil's lunge.

"Marianna tells me you won today," Gregor said as

he strolled into the cabin. "That should put you in good humor. Victory hasn't come that often to you of late."

"How kind of you to remind me." Jordan leaned back in his chair. "Have you had a pleasant afternoon?"

"Oh yes, our dour captain is teaching Alex how to sail the ship." He grinned. "Braithwaite is soft as mush in the boy's hands. It is most rewarding to see, when he's so difficult with everyone else." He went to the sideboard, poured a glass of whiskey, and drained it in one swallow. "Ah, that was good."

"I'm glad you enjoyed it. You do realize you've seriously depleted my stock on this trip?" Gregor took infinite enjoyment in all physical pleasures including liquor, but Jordan had never seen him drunk. He seemed to store the alcohol in some mysterious section of that huge body until the effects dissipated.

"It's the dampness." He refilled his glass. "I don't mind cold, but I hate damp and cold together." He refilled his glass.

"Since we've reached the Mediterranean, it's no longer cold," Jordan pointed out.

"Well, I don't like damp and heat together either." Gregor sat down and stretched his legs out before him. "Alex is very excited about going to Cambaron. He's been plaguing me with questions."

"His sister doesn't share his eagerness."

"She is afraid?"

"No," he said quickly.

"You denied that as swiftly as she would have done." Gregor smiled slyly. "You're beginning to sound like a proud father."

"What a sickening thought. And completely in error. You're the one with whom she's at ease."

"Does that bother you? You told me you wanted her to feel uncertain and vulnerable. You cannot have it all ways."

"It does *not* bother me."

Gregor took a deep drink. "Besides, if you wish to make her fear you, then you should not let her win so often."

"You know very well I don't let her win. She's a fine player."

"Oh, I thought it was some clever ploy to make her feel safe with you before you turned and rended her." He beamed. "It is just as well. The effect is the same. How can the girl be frightened by a man who not only loses to her with regularity but is actually proud of it?"

"I'm not proud of losing. I dislike it intensely."

"But you're proud of her," Gregor said softly. "I've watched the two of you, and I find it very curious. It's almost as if she were your own."

"Balderdash," Jordan enunciated precisely. "I told you, I don't feel in the least fatherly toward the girl."

"Then there is an alternative to consider."

"There is no alternative either."

"Unless you've considered it, how can you be so positive?"

"I assume you're intimating I have a passion for her?" He opened the drawer of the table, shoved the chess box into it, and slammed it with a little more force than necessary. "I told you I don't bed children, Gregor."

"But in Kazan a female of sixteen is a woman."

"This particular female has far to go before she reaches that state."

"I agree. She is somewhere in between. At times she still has flashes of childhood."

Jordan had a vision of Marianna sitting across from him, her gaze on the chessboard as she asked him about Cambaron. She hadn't wanted him to see her uncertainty and fear of the unknown but had been unable to keep herself from questioning him. She was so strong that when she did exhibit moments of weakness, it was all the more poignant and surprising.

"She is looking very well, don't you think?" Gregor took another long drink. "There's a fine color in her cheeks, and she's putting on weight. She's going to be a beautiful woman one day."

"Yes." It had been warm in the cabin, and she had rolled up the sleeves of the white gown to reveal arms that were sweetly rounded. Of late, her figure had taken on a certain fragile maturity, and her fair hair, though bound in the severe long braid, had shone with vitality.

"She's beginning to look like a woman, not the waif you found in Talenka," Gregor said.

Yet the fire that had illuminated that waif's every movement was still present. Jordan became aware of Gregor's intent study of his face and instantly made his expression impassive.

"What the devil is this about?" Jordan looked him directly in the eyes. "It sounds remarkably like you want me to bed her."

"On the contrary, my friend, it is what I am most trying to avoid. It would be the worst possible thing for both of you."

"Then why are you extolling her attributes as if she were a slave on an auction block?"

"Because you've already noticed them but refuse to think of them. That is dangerous." Gregor smiled gently. "You are drawn to her, and if you do not admit it and put up barriers, a moment will come when you will reach out and take. You drift closer to it every day."

"Nonsense."

"Have you not been restless when you go to your bed each night?"

"My dear Gregor, I've been without a woman since we left Kazan, and you know that's not usual for me."

"When your dreams come, who is the woman beneath you?"

"I don't know. She has no face. It's not her face that has my interest. For Lord's sake, Gregor, simply because I'm full of lust doesn't mean I'm going to leap on the first available female."

"It would be a mistake to do so. You would regret it." Gregor's expression was serious. "I have seen you kill men without a qualm, but to hurt her would eat at your soul."

"Not if she wanted it." The quick words had tumbled out of nowhere, and he instantly wished he had bitten his tongue when he saw how quickly Gregor leaped on them.

"Ah, you see?" Gregor nodded sadly. "You may not have realized it, but the desire is there. I know you can make women want you, but you must not make the attempt this time. These hours spent in your cabin are no longer wise."

"I disagree." He stood up and moved toward the

sideboard and poured himself a whiskey. "She's growing more at ease with me every day. She's gaining confidence."

"Which she will lose if you—"

"I will *not* bed her," Jordan said through his teeth.

"And you do not wish to give up these hours with her. Have you considered that portends something even more dangerous for you?"

"Good God, another alternative?"

"Affection," Gregor said softly. "You admire her, and where there is admiration, liking soon follows."

"I admire Napoleon's intelligence and military capability, but that doesn't stop me from wanting to cut out his heart."

"It is not the same."

"I assure you, Gregor." He turned and lifted his glass with a reckless smile. "Of the two alternatives, I would make sure I chose the first."

"Choose neither, and you will be better off." He rose to his feet and lumbered toward the door. "I will see you at dinner. Think on what I've said."

"If I don't, I'm sure you'll repeat it," he said dryly.

"I'm sure also." Gregor grinned over his shoulder. "But I don't believe it will be necessary. You are a hard man, but you do not intentionally hurt the helpless. It was only needful that I point out in what direction you were wandering."

As the door closed behind him, Jordan drained the glass and set it on the table. It was all nonsense. He would continue on the same course he had started with Marianna.

He did not lust after the chit.

He did not hold her in affection.

He was most certainly not going to let her sway him in his purpose.

To hell with Gregor's alternatives.

He poised, ready to plunge deep.

In just a moment he would be inside, closed in her warm tightness, and this agony of need would be over.

Her blue eyes looked up at him, bold, shining, eager.

Strange, the other times he hadn't noticed her eyes. . . .

My God.

He woke, hard and heavy and aching, and lay there in the dark, his chest moving in and out with his labored breathing.

He rose and moved naked toward the window and threw it open, letting the night wind rush in and cool him. Lord knows, he needed cooling.

Marianna.

Marianna glanced up from the board. "Why are you looking at me like that?"

"How was I looking at you?"

She frowned. "Peculiarly. Are you irritated because I'm beating you today?"

"I don't like to lose," he said noncommittally.

She lifted her hand to her cheek. "Do I have a smudge?"

He had been searching for a smudge, an imperfection, and had found many. Her features were fine but not classic; her eyes were too bold; her lips were well shaped but seldom smiled at him.

And she was scarcely more than a child, dammit.

He didn't want to have this passion for a young girl who had no experience and thought life should be seen through a stained-glass window. He didn't want to set out to bed a girl who had beaten him at chess and made him smile at his defeat.

"We all have smudges." He looked down at the hand toying with her queen. "What is that on your palm?"

"What? Oh, a scar. You must have seen it before."

"Not that one." He took her hand and turned it over. Her palm was nicked with a number of scars. He touched the long white one running across the center of her palm. "This must have cut deep."

"I work in glass. Sometimes I pay the price. I was clumsy and let a sheet slide off the table. I had to catch it before it hit the floor and broke."

Sudden anger surged through him. This was an old scar, so the accident must have happened when she'd been a very young child. Why hadn't they watched her, taken care of her? "It could have cut your hand in two."

"I work in glass," she said again. "I was never that clumsy again."

Her pulse was leaping beneath his finger as he gently rubbed back and forth on the scar.

She swallowed. "I wish you would not do that. It feels . . . most strange."

"Pain?"

"Not precisely."

It felt like pain to him, and the discomfort was growing by the second. A child would not have answered him as she had done. She was a woman and fair game in the sport he knew so well.

Christ, he was looking for excuses to seduce her.

He dropped her hand and stood up. "It's warm in here. We'll finish the game tomorrow."

She looked at him, startled. "I'm not warm."

"I'm not only warm, I'm hot. I need a stroll on deck." He strode toward the door. "I'll see you at supper."

If he distanced himself from her, then his need would go away. He had always been a self-indulgent bastard, and he was instinctively searching out qualities in Marianna that would give him an excuse to bed her.

"You look a trifle discomposed," Gregor said as he fell into step with him on deck. "How is Marianna?"

"Not lying naked and weeping on my bunk."

"Then it is good we had our talk." Gregor's brows lifted. "You must be behaving very well. It always puts you in vicious temper."

"Did you think that bringing all of this to the surface would solve the problem?"

"No, I knew you would be pulled back and forth once you recognized what you felt for her. There was a danger, but the threat was greater the other way."

He smiled crookedly. "Because you know my instincts are naturally to destroy?"

"No, your instincts are sound, but your habit was always to take. It's hard to break such habits." He clapped him on the shoulder. "But you grow better all the time."

"Thank you," he said with irony. "But this time don't be surprised if habit wins out."

"I will be surprised," Gregor said soberly. "And disappointed."

Jordan gazed at him with a wide mixture of emotions, foremost of which were exasperation, frustration, and affection. Gregor knew that last word from him would move Jordan when nothing else would. From the time he was a lad, when he wasn't fighting the reins Gregor tried to put on him, he had been fighting for his approval. He loved the son of a bitch. He smiled. "You bastard."

"Ah, you're in better temper." Gregor grinned. "Let us go and watch the dolphins. No one could be bad-tempered while the dolphins are jumping."

He was watching her.

All through dinner Jordan had teased Alex, chatted idly with Gregor, but had watched her. It was most unsettling.

It was not as if Marianna was not accustomed to him looking at her. During these past two weeks over the chessboard she was sure he had memorized every feature, every nuance of expression, as she had his.

But tonight there was something . . . different.

At the end of the meal Jordan pushed back his chair and rose to his feet. "There's a full moon tonight, and the sky is bright. Gregor, why don't you take Alex to the bridge and tell him about the stars?" He turned to Alex. "Gregor has a tale for every constellation in the sky. When I was a boy, he used to take me into the woods and weave his stories, but the sea is a much better tapestry."

"Oh, could we, Gregor?" Alex asked eagerly.

Gregor stared at Jordan an instant before he nod-

ded. "For a little while." He turned to Marianna.
"Would you like to come with us?"

"I'm sure Marianna is tired. I'll take her to her
cabin," Jordan said. "There are things we have to discuss."

Marianna stared at him in bewilderment. He had
left her only a few hours before. If there was anything
important to discuss, why had he not done it then?

Jordan turned to Marianna. "Will you come with
me?"

He had said almost those same words in the church
in Talenka.

He must have read her mind, because he smiled
and said softly, "It hasn't turned out too badly so far,
has it?"

The persuasiveness with which he was smiling at
her was irresistible. He was compelling her, willing
her to agree with him.

"Has it?" he asked again.

She slowly shook her head.

"You can talk later," Gregor said. "It would
not—" He broke off as he saw Marianna's expression.
He shrugged and rose to his feet. "You have her. One
of the things I will tell Alex is that what is written in
the stars will be."

"But you do everything in your power to change
it," Jordan muttered.

"As do you. Put on your cloak, Alex."

"I don't need it," Alex said mutinously.

Gregor put Alex's cloak around him with almost
maternal care. "The night wind is cool. You don't
want to get that cough again."

Marianna shook her head as Gregor led Alex from

the cabin. "He can do anything with Alex. It's magical."

"He can do anything with anyone." Jordan added sourly, "except keep his mouth shut." He grabbed Marianna's cloak and put it over her shoulders. "Come along."

"What did you want to talk about?" she asked as he propelled her from the cabin and along the deck. The breeze from the south was gentle on her face, but there was nothing gentle about Jordan. Now that he had gotten what he wanted, he was suddenly different. That mesmerizing charm had vanished, and there was an aura of suppressed violence about him. She tensed as a thought occurred to her. "I told you I wouldn't talk about the Window."

"For God's sake I'm not fool enough to waste my time in that fashion."

"Then I don't know why you—"

"What did you do when you were a child?"

"What?" she asked in confusion.

"What did you do? You must have done more than work at your precious glass."

"Of course I did."

"Then tell me about it."

"Why?"

"Because I want to *see* you as a child, dammit."

The answer made no more sense than his interest in the first place. "I don't understand what you want from me."

"All children play. What did you play at?"

"Working in the glass was play for me."

"You don't ride. Did you go for walks?"

"Sometimes we would go on picnics and take long walks in the hills."

"Ah, at last a sign of childhood. I thought you'd sprung full grown from a stained-glass window."

He was clearly in a temper for some reason, and she was growing tired of bearing the brunt of it. "Don't be foolish.

"You've barely mentioned your father, only that he died a few years ago. Tell me about him."

"Papa? He was very handsome. He had beautiful golden hair and fine features and he laughed a lot." She was silent a moment, remembering. "He was always laughing."

"Then he's different from the poets I know. They seem to thrive on tears and woe."

She shook her head. "Papa loved to laugh. He said life was meant for laughter."

"And not for work?" he asked caustically.

"He worked," she protested. "He wrote beautiful poems. He would sit under the tree in the garden and write for hours."

"While your mother labored to put bread on the table."

"She didn't mind. It suited them both very well."

"And I'm sure you can't wait to find your own handsome poet to lavish care and sustenance on."

"I wouldn't mind, if he was like Papa," she said defiantly.

That answer didn't seem to please him either. "What else did Papa do besides sit under the trees and write poems?"

"He gave me lessons. He taught me French and English and mathematics. He even tried to teach me to write poems like him, but I was never good at it. I didn't have the gift."

"But that didn't matter because you had a gift for the glass and could support him in his old age."

"You refuse to understand," she said. "I don't want to talk about Papa anymore."

"Neither do I. It's not succeeding anyway."

"Succeeding in what?" she asked in exasperation.

He ignored the question and was silent a moment before he said abruptly, "I believe we'll dispense with our chess games from now on."

"Why?"

"I'm growing bored with them." He smiled cynically. "Gregor will tell you that I grow bored with exceptional ease."

She felt a queer pang she refused to admit was hurt. He had been a little strange, but she was sure he hadn't been bored this afternoon. Yet how did she know? She couldn't read him nearly as well as he did her. Perhaps he had been bored during their entire time together. She lifted her chin. "I certainly don't wish to continue. I was growing bored with them also. I'll be glad to spend more time with Alex."

They had reached her cabin, and he opened the door and flung it open. He stood there looking into the darkness, his stance tense. It was almost as if he saw something waiting for him in the shadows.

"Jordan?"

He turned to look at her. She inhaled sharply as she saw his expression.

She moistened her lips. "Is . . . something wrong?"

"It could be." His pale green eyes were glittering recklessly, his lips sensual. "But wrong is always the most wicked of delights, isn't it?"

"I don't understand what you mean."

"I could teach you. It would be my—" He broke off as he saw her take an instinctive step back. He took a deep breath and whirled on his heel. "Good night."

She watched him stride away. His dark hair gleamed in the moonlight, and his long stride was faintly animallike in its grace. She had thought she had begun to know him, but tonight he had been everything that was strange and bewildering and hurtful. She should be angry but instead felt bruised and a little afraid.

She was more fearful of Cambaron than she would admit to herself. She knew nothing of castles and dukes and this England her father had hated. Her world had been small and tight and loving, and now it seemed to be growing, yawning like a beast ready to swallow her.

Yet she would rather face a hundred Cambarons than the man who had turned on her tonight. She had thought she had armored herself against him. How had she let him come close enough to hurt her?

CHAPTER 4

The four towers of Cambaron could be seen in the distance, the pennants flying over a massive gray stone castle that was far grander than the one Marianna had seen in Montavia. The place looked strong and cold and alien. The sun was shining brightly, but Marianna involuntarily drew her cloak closer about her.

"Do you see it?" Alex, who had been riding ahead with Gregor, came trotting back and reined in before her. "A castle, Marianna!"

She quickly hid her first reaction and said dryly, "It would be hard for me not to see it. Castles have a habit of being rather prominent."

"Is it all right if I ride on ahead? Gregor is going to show me the stable."

She nodded. "But be careful and keep that pony to a walk."

"If that pony moved any slower, we'd have to bring Cambaron to her," Jordan said. "We'll have to get Alex something with a little more spirit once he's had a few lessons."

"I like this one." Alex patted the pony's neck. "What do you think I should name her?"

"It's a great decision to make. Why don't you think about it?"

"I will." He turned the pony and trotted back to Gregor. "Hurry, Marianna!"

She didn't look at Jordan as she said, "Go on ahead with them. I'm as awkward a rider as Alex. It's foolish for you to let me keep you back."

"I wouldn't think of it. I'm not as eager to reach my ancestral home as your brother. I've never had any special fondness for it." He smiled. "And besides, such an abandonment wouldn't be in keeping with my duties as your guardian."

"We both know that's all nonsense."

"Perhaps I'm clinging to that nonsense to keep me from indulging even greater foolishness."

She didn't even attempt to decipher the cryptic statement. She only wanted to rid herself of him. She was nervous enough about that castle in the distance, and since they had left the ship at Southwick this morning he had been a silent, provocative presence by her side. "Go on ahead," she repeated. "You've made it quite clear my company bores you." After that night of several days ago she had scarcely seen him except at meals. He had been courteous but totally withdrawn and spent his time with Gregor and the captain. Even Alex had received his share of attention.

"Did I? Actually, I don't believe I ever said your company bored me. I only said I found the game boring." He nudged his horse abreast of hers on the trail. "And this particular game is growing less boring and more uncomfortable with every passing day."

He was obviously mocking her, and she was finding it surprisingly painful. Her gaze returned to the castle. "Why don't you have a fondness for it? It's your home."

He shrugged. "A home is just a place like any other."

It had not been so for her. She had passionately loved the cottage where she had been born and raised until that night of horror. "Did you not enjoy your childhood here?"

He lifted his brows. "Are you trying to search out my secrets?"

"You shouldn't object to questions. You ask me and Alex enough of your own."

"True." He was silent a moment before answering lightly, "I regret to say I have no gloomy secrets to impart. My mother departed this life when I was only two, and I was indulged by all and sundry. Every servant in the castle vied in an attempt to thoroughly spoil me."

"What of your father?"

"Oh, he indulged me too. When he had time. However, it was difficult to find a few minutes to spare when he was determined to become the greatest drunkard and libertine in all of England." He smiled crookedly. "He might have succeeded, but he broke his neck in a fall from a horse when I was only twelve. What a pity."

"You didn't love him?"

"I probably loved him at one time. Why not? He was quite an engaging fellow and a fine example. After his death I threw myself into a similar quest for the ultimate in debauchery. I would have succeeded where he failed if I hadn't been distracted along the way."

"By what?"

"Not what, who. Gregor burst into my life." He reined in before a stream and dismounted. "You see how open I'm being? I'm lowering all my shields."

His defenses were still very much intact, glittering like beautiful faceted glass, but she was surprised he had been this frank with her. "Why?"

"To show you how harmless I am." He paused. "And to encourage you to lower a few defenses of your own."

"I have no intention of doing so."

"It's necessary," he said soberly. "If we are to live here together with any civility."

Together. The word sounded startlingly intimate.

"I know I angered you on board the *Seastorm*." He patted his horse's neck while the animal drank. "My behavior was abominable."

"Abominable. But I'm sure that is quite natural for you."

"Quite natural." He smiled coaxingly. "Forgive me, and I'll promise to reward you very generously."

It was the first time he had smiled at her since that night in his cabin. "I don't want any reward."

"Of course you do. Everyone wants something." The offhand statement was made with absolute assurance.

"Has that been your experience? That everyone wants something from you?"

He smiled cynically. "I've been as rich as a nabob from the day I was born. Before I left the nursery, I learned what's expected of me in the way of favors."

She felt a pang of sympathy for that little boy who had never known love without price but immediately dismissed the momentary softness. That child might have deserved pity, but not the man who stood before her. "And I'm supposed to seek out these favors?"

"Why not? It's to your advantage to bargain with me. You're in a very vulnerable position. I can make things very pleasant for you."

"What would you give me?" she asked curiously.

An undefinable expression crossed his face. It was foolish of her to think it might be disappointment. "Whatever you like. Diamonds? Women usually like a bit of flash."

Whatever she liked . . .

Her glance shifted back to those forbidding towers.

"Tell me," he said. "Ladies usually aren't this shy about making their demands known."

She was sure there had been many women who had been in a position to meet his demands with demands of their own. The thought sent a flare of unreasonable anger through her. "That's because men seldom allow us to reach out and grasp what we want ourselves. It's considered both unwomanly and un-natural."

His gaze narrowed on her face. "Is that what you prefer? I have no objection to yielding to such aggressiveness. I'll be happy to accommodate you."

"You mean you'd accommodate me by giving me what should be mine by right?"

He shrugged. "I regret that I cannot change the way of the world."

"Not *my* world." She looked back at the towers. "I . . . I . . . don't want to go there."

He went still, his gaze on her face. "Where do you want to go? London?"

"London?" She looked at him in bewilderment. "Why would I want to go there?"

"Shops, theater, masked balls . . . and, of course, all the lovely little trifles a woman wants and needs."

"I wouldn't know what to do with them."

He was silent a moment and then slowly shook his head. "No, you probably wouldn't. I'm afraid I'm guilty of trying to place you in the role I want you to play."

She scarcely heard him, as she nervously plucked at her horse's mane. "I'd like a cottage of my own. Just a small place for me and Alex."

He shook his head. "I can't let you reside outside the castle."

"You said I could have anything I want."

"I lied. It should be no surprise to you, considering your opinion of my character."

"You offered me diamonds," she said desperately. "A cottage would surely cost less than diamonds."

"You'd be too vulnerable outside the castle walls. I hope Nebrov won't discover you're here, but there's always a possibility."

She smiled bitterly. "And you can't risk him taking me away from you."

"Any more than you can risk him taking Alex."

"It isn't the same. I love Alex, and you care nothing for either of us."

"Don't I? Then you must put up with my arrogance and surliness and teach me. It's not an entirely impossible task. Gregor did it."

"I have no desire to teach you what comes naturally to others." Her hands clenched the reins. "Very well, I will live in that . . . that place, but I must have a workroom and tools and freedom to work with no interference." She gazed defiantly at him. "I'm sure you will make no objection to that. It's why I'm here."

"No objection at all," he said quietly. "But you still haven't told me what you wish as reparation."

She gestured impatiently. "Work is a gift. I *need* to work."

"Do you?" He studied her flushed cheeks and the tense line of her mouth. "I believe you do. Then of course you shall have it."

"At once?"

"Why not?" He kicked his horse into a trot. "I think it's an excellent way to make you realize that you have only to ask, and I'll supply your every need."

Alex came running toward her across the courtyard as soon as she and Jordan rode through the gates. "The horses are beautiful, Marianna. All of them! Gregor says Jordan invites half of England here for races every spring."

"London," Gregor corrected. "I fear even Cambaron could not accommodate half of England."

"We're going to be here for the races," Alex said. "You should see the stallion Jordan purchased from the Berber sheikh." He frowned. "What's a sheikh?"

"I'm sure Gregor will be glad to explain," Marianna said. She was certain Papa had mentioned these sheikhs, but she could not remember. For all she knew there were Berber sheikhs running all over this dratted England.

Alex's eyes were blazing with excitement. "You've got to see all of the horses. Come on, I'll show you!"

"Not now," Gregor said as he lifted Marianna

from the saddle. "I'm sure your sister has had enough
of the smell of horses for one day. Let her go to her
chamber and rest."

"Rest?" Alex stared at him in bewilderment.
"Now? Why would she want to do that?"

"Perhaps you could take Alex to see the racecourse
we've laid out in the south pasture, Gregor." Jordan
took Marianna's elbow. "While I introduce Marianna
to the servants and show her to her chamber."

He stood there, perfectly at ease. He belonged in
this great castle, wielding power, dispensing favors or
vengeance as it suited him, as his ancestors had done
for centuries before him.

Power.

The flesh of her arm tingled beneath his hand. She
felt suddenly suffocated, overwhelmed. She had to escape. "I'm sure Gregor can do that later. I want to see
the stable." She shook off Jordan's grip and grabbed
Alex's hand. "Come show me, Alex."

Jordan's hands slowly clenched as he stared at Marianna and Alex running across the courtyard. "What
are you waiting for?" he said roughly to Gregor. "Go
after them."

"Presently. It will take Alex a while to show her
through that first stable." Gregor watched the two
disappear through the stable doors. "She is afraid."

"Yes." Jordan gave him a sardonic glance. "But not
of me, I assure you."

"A little of you. It's a new world, and you are king
of it. You must make it easier for her."

"I tried." He glared at him. "What the devil do
you want from me? First, you insist I distance myself

from your dove, and now you want me to come closer."

"Not too close. You must walk a fine line."

"I'm not good at balancing on tightropes. Do it yourself."

"I will do my part." He smiled. "You were very good on the *Seastorm*. I thought perhaps I had lost you that night."

"I'm glad I earned your approval. It's my heartfelt goal in life."

"Why are you so angry with me? You would not have done as I advised if you had not known I was right. You would have kept drifting until it was too late."

And Marianna would have occupied his bed on the *Seastorm* and here at Cambaron, Jordan thought. The drifting Gregor spoke about would have culminated in an inevitable coming together. He would have found a way to seduce her, lure her. He would have taught her to please him, to open her thighs and welcome him into that tightness that he had been thinking about since Gregor had told him he couldn't have it. Dammit, he was hardening now at the thought as he did every time he saw her. "Did it ever occur to you that's what I wanted to do?"

"Yes," Gregor said. "A part of you, the part that was the decadent boy you were when I first came to Cambaron."

"That boy is still very much a part of me."

"But he is controlled by the man you are."

"Is he?" He looked back at the stable. Control had little to do with what he wanted to do to and with Marianna. The more he held back, the more intense the lust, the more erotic the imagining. "Don't count on it, Gregor."

"I do count on it," Gregor said serenely.

"Suppose I decide that it would be easier to make Marianna do what I want in regard to the Window if she's trained to please me in other ways?"

"It would not be a fair decision, and you are a fair man." Gregor started across the courtyard. "But I think it would be best if you visit Madam Carruthers as soon as possible. You have been without a woman too long."

God knows, that was true. He had fully intended to slake that lust as soon as he reached Cambaron. He would go visit— Dammit, he did not want to visit Laura Carruthers with her lush body and the insatiable appetites he usually found amusing. The thought was not at all appealing.

And neither was the task he must perform now, he thought grimly. He must talk to the servants and pave the way for Marianna with Gregor's lie, put her in a position where seduction was impossible.

No, not impossible, just more difficult. If he chose to circumvent the barriers, he could do it.

If he chose . . .

This is Mrs. Jenson." Gregor smiled at the plump gray-haired woman. "She is most kind and will be glad to serve you in any way you wish. How are you, Jenny?"

"Very well, Mr. Damek." She smiled. "Welcome to Cambaron, miss. We are all saddened to hear about your loss in that heathen country."

The woman was *curtsying* to her.

Heat flooded Marianna's cheeks. "Thank you," she said weakly.

"And where is the poor bereaved lad?"

She must mean Alex. "In . . . in the stable."

"We couldn't get him to leave the horses. William will care for him and bring him a little later," Gregor said.

"Yes, William Stoneham's a good man." She curtsied again to Marianna. "His Grace has instructed me to take you straight to your chamber. Will you come with me?" She did not wait for an answer but moved brusquely across the hall toward the wide stone staircase that appeared to stretch to heaven.

The housekeeper's words echoed hollowly off the high arched ceiling of the hall. Marianna carefully avoided looking around her as she followed the housekeeper up the steps. She had already had too much to absorb in the two hours she had been here. Cambaron was more a kingdom than an estate with its magnificent stables and carriage barns and now this dark cavern of a castle. There were more men and women here to serve one man than there had been in the entire village of Samda.

Mrs. Jenson said, "I've assigned Mary as your maid. She's young but very willing."

Maid? She cast Gregor a wild glance, and he smiled reassuringly. "Perhaps we will let Miss Sanders serve herself for a time. She is shy of strangers."

"But she must have—" Mrs. Jenson's glance encountered Marianna's, and she smiled gently. "Of course, it will take time to overcome the memories of such a terrible ordeal." She proceeded up the stairs. "In the meantime you must only give a tug to the bellpull, and someone will come."

She would rather jump from the top of this gigantic staircase than pull that bell, Marianna thought fervently. She wanted only to hide in her chamber and close everyone out until she could become used to the *vastness* of this huge place.

They were now going down a long, dim hall lined on either side with portraits of all sizes and descriptions. "These pictures are of His Grace's family," Mrs. Jenson said as she noticed Marianna's interest. She pointed to one large painting of a bearded man in hip boots and a jerkin that was puffed at his hips. "That was Randolph Percival Draken, the fifth Duke of Cambaron. He was a great favorite of Queen Elizabeth. She stayed here several times, you know."

"No, I didn't know." But she wasn't surprised. Elizabeth and her entire court would probably have scarcely been noticed in a castle of this size.

"And that is his lady." She pointed to a small, daintily formed woman in a gold-encrusted gown and a wide pleated ruff encircling her neck. "The duchess was considered one of the most beautiful woman of her day."

The woman she had indicated was pleasant-looking, with a pouty mouth, wide blue eyes, and tightly curled golden hair. "She's very— Who is that?"

The housekeeper's gaze followed Marianna's to the portrait a few feet down the hall. "Oh, that's His Grace's mother. It was painted a year after she came to Cambaron."

Marianna stepped closer to the portrait, searching for a likeness to Jordan. Even in the dim light, the full-bodied woman in the picture seemed to glow with life. Her shining black hair was darker and curlier than her son's and pulled back from her face by two emerald clips. Her eyes were the same green and tilted slightly at the corners. Tartar blood, Marianna remembered, Jordan had said his mother had Tartar blood. She wore a full-skirted green velvet gown that flattered her tall, strong figure, but the garment somehow seemed wrong. The woman should have been wearing something else. . . .

"She was a foreign lady, a very foreign lady," Mrs. Jenson said reservedly, then looked at Gregor apologetically. "I beg pardon, sir, I know she was one of your people, but she was not like you. She was more like His Grace when he was a bit younger."

"She was only seventeen herself when this was painted." A faint smile curved Gregor's lips as he stood looking at the portrait. "And you are right, she was just as wild as Jordan and just as compelling of affection."

"Some found her so." It was clear the housekeeper had not.

"She was from Kazan?" Marianna asked.

Mrs. Jenson nodded. "None of us had ever heard of the place. She was attending a school in Paris, and His Grace's father brought her back to England with him when he came home from his grand tour. There was a good deal of talk about the duke marrying beneath him."

"Everyone in Kazan thought the same thing," Gregor said. "She was a noblewoman of Kazan and therefore higher in estate than any Englishman. I assure you, that if she hadn't eloped, she would never have been permitted to marry Draken."

Mrs. Jenson looked faintly shocked. "Not permitted to wed His Grace? I can't believe that, sir."

"You were here when she came?" Marianna asked. "You remember her?"

"Oh yes, she's not a woman one forgets," Mrs. Jenson said without inflection. "In the three years she was here before her death things were most unsettled."

"She means Ana liked her own way and would move heaven or earth to get it," Gregor said with a grin. "She probably turned the castle upside down."

"Most unsettled," Mrs. Jenson murmured as she moved down the hall. "But His Grace's father was heartbroken when she died." She threw open a door at the far end of the corridor. "This is the Blue Room. The little lad's room is just down the hall. I hope this will be suitable?"

The large room was as dark and overpowering as the rest of the castle. All the furniture, from the enormous four-poster bed, draped in dark blue velvet, to the armoire against the wall, were crafted of gleaming ebony mahogany. A large desk with massive curving legs occupied the space directly in front of a long, narrow window that permitted only a weak strip of light.

Marianna felt a burst of homesickness as she remembered her small room at home. It had been filled with light that had streamed radiantly through the stained-glass rainbow panel Grandmama had created for her tenth birthday. Everyone should have a rainbow, Grandmama had said, so they would remember the storms of life do not last. Every morning Marianna would wake on her narrow cot and open her eyes to color and light and beauty.

Suitable? She could feel her chest tighten until she

could scarcely breathe. She would *smother* in this room.

"Marianna?" Gregor prompted gently.

She swallowed. "Quite suitable." She tried to think of something appealing about the room. Clean. The chamber was as spotless as her cabin on the *Seastorm*. "I wonder, could I possibly have a bath, Mrs. Jenson?"

"Certainly." Mrs. Jenson beamed. "I'll have a tub brought up at once. Are you sure that you don't want Mary to come and—"

"Jenny, why don't you go downstairs and wait for William to bring the boy?" Gregor asked quickly.

Mrs. Jenson nodded, curtsied again, and left the room.

"Is she always going to do that?" Marianna asked as she unfastened her cloak.

"Curtsy? Probably. Jenny was trained from childhood to show respect and obedience to all and sundry."

"I don't like it."

"She would be unhappy if you asked her to stop. You'll become accustomed to it." Gregor added gently, "You'll become accustomed to everything, Marianna."

"I know. . . . It's just that it . . ." She ran her fingers through her hair. "It's very warm in here, isn't it?"

"Your cheeks are certainly flushed." He entered the chamber and stepped aside for her to enter. "I think you'll find this room comfortable. If you need anything else, you have only to ask Jordan. His wish is for you to be happy here." He nodded at the oak armoire across the room. "Perhaps you'll find a few gowns in there that will serve you until a dressmaker comes down from London."

"Dressmaker?" She turned to look at him. "Can't we find someone in the village to furnish me with a few gowns?"

"I told you, Jordan wishes you to be happy. In his experience ladies require a certain standard of elegance to be happy."

"Because if I'm happy, I'll work harder?" She strode over to the armoire and threw it open. It was filled to overflowing with a colorful array of gowns of practically every fabric and description. "Who do these belong to?"

Gregor shrugged. "I doubt if Jordan remembers. The ladies in Jordan's set are not overly careful of their belongings. There's always something left behind after a house party."

His words evoked a mental picture of fashionable ladies drifting about these halls and over the carefully tended lawns, their soft bodies scented, their hair shiny and intricately curled, their only desire to please and charm.

To please and charm Jordan Draken, the Duke of Cambaron.

"If you'll forgive me, I'll leave you now," Gregor said as he turned away. "I must go and talk to Jordan. I'll send a servant with a tub and hot water."

She experienced an instant of panic as the door closed behind him. She did not want to be alone in this cell of a room.

She was being foolish. This was not a dungeon, and Gregor had said she would grow accustomed to it. She took off her cloak and hung it in the armoire. She wrinkled her nose as the sweet scent of perfume wafted to her from the gowns. She would be glad to rid herself of the rumpled, stained gown she wore, but she had a sudden repugnance at the thought of smelling like one of those women whom Gregor said Jordan had forgotten. She rifled through the garments, grabbed a plain blue silk gown, and took it over to the casement window. She threw open the window and laid the gown on the window seat for airing.

A little scent should not matter. She didn't usually let inessentials bother her.

It *did* bother her.

Why was she so unsettled? She was becoming as vaporish as the woman who had worn this gown. She must put an end to it and set things back in their proper place.

Work.

She would be fine once she immersed herself in the world she knew and loved. She could close herself away from all this disquiet. Yes, work was the answer.

After her bath she dressed in the blue gown and went in search of Jordan. After getting lost once and having to ask directions of two liveried servants, she finally found him in the library talking to Gregor. They broke off their conversation when she came into the room.

"Enchanting," Jordan murmured as his gaze ran over her. "I've never seen you in anything but white. Blue is quite delightful on you."

She snorted. "That was not my intention. It was the only gown I could find that didn't have a hundred bows. I have no desire to be enchanting, only busy."

"Do I detect a hint of displeasure?" Jordan asked.

"My workroom," she said brusquely. "I need to see my workroom."

"How remiss of me." Jordan snapped his fingers. "You've been in my home for at least half an afternoon, and I haven't given you what you value most." He moved toward the door. "Permit me to rectify the error at once." He said over his shoulder to Gregor, "I'll see you at supper, Gregor."

Gregor hesitated. "I could come along."

Jordan slanted him a glance. "It's quite safe. Her workroom lacks the piece of furniture necessary to the subject we were discussing."

"I can remember many times in villages on the steppes that you didn't find furniture necessary."

Marianna impatiently looked from Gregor to Jordan. "I don't care about this . . . this . . . furniture. I'll tell you what I need later. I want to see my workroom."

"How can I resist such eagerness?" Jordan strode out of the study. "Make sure Alex is settled, Gregor. I'll take care of Marianna."

"It is my earnest hope you will," Gregor called after them.

Jordan had moved so quickly, Marianna found herself having to hurry after him across the foyer and up the wide stone staircase. "Where are we going?"

"I thought perhaps one of the tower rooms would be best. It's isolated, and you receive light from all directions." He had reached the second landing, opened a door, and led her up another twisting staircase. "I trust that will be satisfactory?"

"I'll have to see it. I'll need tools."

"My agent tells me there are four craftsmen who

are completing the windows at the cathedral at Medoran. I've sent a servant to purchase whatever instruments you might need from them. It's only an hour's ride from here, so he should be back by night-fall."

Her eyes widened. "You've done that already?"

"You said you needed it."

"I'll also need a kiln to bake in the colors and a blowpipe and kettle for making the glass."

"You make the glass yourself?"

"Of course, every true craftsman has her own for-mula for the making of the glass. Different thicknesses and compositions take the color differently."

"Forgive my ignorance. It will take a little longer to produce those particular items of your trade. Will tomorrow do?"

She nodded. "I can use other glass as long as the work has little importance."

"I'm greatly relieved. I feared I'd have to post to Medoran in the dead of night myself." He threw open the door and stepped aside. "I hope this will be adequate."

Light!

The small circular chamber was without furniture, but that didn't matter. Brilliant sunlight poured into the room from six long windows. Dear God, the light . . .

Marianna slowly moved to the center of the room, closing her eyes and lifting her face so that the glori-ous warmth struck her face. The cold knot that had begun to tighten within her since she had arrived at Cambaron began to dissolve. She was dazzled, en-tranced. "Oh yes," she murmured, imagining the hues, the effulgence that would flood the room. "It's splendid."

"Splendid."

His voice sounded so strange, she turned to see him staring at her.

"You look as if I've just given you a rope of diamonds," he said thickly.

She shook her head. "Sunlight," she said softly. "There's nothing more beautiful on earth, and it cannot be given."

"But I just gave it to you, didn't I?" He didn't wait for a reply as he walked toward her. "The sun shone all the way on our ride from Southwick, and you weren't like this. Why is this different?"

"The windows. I can make this come alive."

His eyes narrowed intently on her face. "As it's made you come alive."

She *was* alive. She could feel the blood coursing through her veins, and she felt more alive than ever before in her life. He was only a few feet away, and the strong sunlight surrounded him, stark, unforgiving. She could see the lines around his eyes, the tiny indentation in his chin, the curve of lip and jaw. His eyes were shimmering pale green, and there was something behind them. . . . She stared up at him, caught, fascinated. She had a vague memory of planning on using him as a model for Lucifer in her Window to Heaven. Why had she thought he was the dark one? He wasn't afraid of the light. He belonged to it. She had the sudden impulse to reach out and warm her hands against him as she had lifted her face to the sun.

He was going to touch her.

She held her breath. She couldn't seem to move.

She couldn't tear her gaze away from his face. She felt a tingling in her palms, in the soles of her feet, in the tips of her breasts.

He stepped back. "What else will you need?" he asked hoarsely.

He had let her go. She swallowed, and it was a moment before she could speak. "Candles. Many, many candles, a long, sturdy table, and an inkwell and several large sheets of paper."

"I'll have them brought up tomorrow morning."

She shook her head. "Today. You said the tools would be here later this afternoon. I could start work this evening."

He studied her face, and then a smile lit his face. "Today." He moved toward the door. "I hope you won't object to delaying your labors until after supper?"

She didn't want to sit with him at a table, she thought desperately. She didn't feel as if she could bear to be in the same room with him. "I'm not hungry."

"But I'm sure Alex will be, and he'll be more comfortable if you're at the table. After all, this is his first night at Cambaron. You mustn't disappoint Alex."

She realized with relief that whatever she had seen in the fierce clarity of the sunlight had vanished, replaced by his usual mockery. She could deal better with this Jordan Draken who tried to manipulate the world to suit himself. "I'll consider it."

The chamber seemed darker after he had gone, as if the sun had hidden behind a cloud.

Imagination. It was still as bright as ever.

She was aware of a sweet, sickening fragrance in

the room. It was the gown she wore. She could have sworn there was no lingering odor when she left her chamber, but it was suddenly back.

Imagination again, because for a moment she had felt as that woman had probably felt when she had been close to Jordan. Weak and womanly and . . . wanting.

She closed her eyes as a shiver ran through her.

Not wanting. That could not be true.

Imagination.

CHAPTER 5

An army of servants moved about the oak-paneled dining room, deftly serving a meal that would have fed Marianna's family for a year.

Jordan sat at the head of the long, gleaming table, dressed in pale gray and white, an elegant figure against the muted richness of the ancient tapestry on the wall behind him.

He casually spoke to Gregor.

He patiently listened to Alex's excited chattering.

He was fastidiously courteous to Marianna.

And every time he glanced at her, she could think of nothing but that moment in the tower room.

She couldn't wait to mutter her excuses and escape. She put Alex to bed, kissed him good night, and then fled up to the tower room as if she were being pursued.

She slammed the heavy door behind her.

Safe.

And cold. The wind whistled around the tower, rushing into the room through the open windows.

It didn't matter. The cool air felt good against her

hot cheeks. Perhaps she had a fever. Nonsense. She was never ill.

She looked around the now-furnished room. She lit the candles in the three tall black iron candelabras on the long table and drew out a large piece of paper from the stack also on the table.

She sat down on the stool and quickly began to sketch.

This panel must be nothing elaborate. Nothing that she would be unhappy to leave behind . . .

There was a light in the tower room.

She was there.

The leap of excitement Jordan felt was like a jolt of lightning. Christ, he hadn't felt like this since his first time with a woman.

"You didn't visit Madam Carruthers," Gregor observed from behind him.

"No, I didn't." As he turned away from the study window, he added deliberately, "Nor do I intend to do so." He waited for a reply.

There was none.

"No argument?"

"I have done all I can. You want Marianna? Take her. She is only a woman . . . well, not quite a woman. But what is that to you?"

Jordan turned back and looked again at the tower. "My mother gave birth to me when she was only a year older than Marianna."

"Oh, you wish to get her with child?"

"No, I don't wish to get her with child," he said through his teeth. "I was just—"

"Defending your position. Why? When you will

do what you wish anyway. At the dinner table you were sending out waves like a stallion after a mare in season. Only the mare is not in season."

"The hell she's not." He whirled on him, his eyes glittering in the candlelight. "You're wrong, Gregor. She's ready for it."

"Because she's feeling the first stirrings of womanhood? Is that any reason to ruin her?"

"I would not—" He muttered a curse, turned on his heel, and stalked out of the study. It was ridiculous of Gregor to say that he would ruin the girl if he took her to his bed. She had no money or connections. What better life could she expect than the one he offered her? He could give her anything she needed. After she was persuaded to give him the Jedalar, he would set her up as his mistress. He would buy her a house of her own and lavish presents and attention on her. She would be well cared for in every way. She might be young, but he was experienced enough to know when a woman wanted him.

She had wanted him this afternoon in the tower room.

The knock on the door of the tower room was perfunctory. Jordan immediately opened the door. "May I come in?"

Marianna tensed. "No, I want to be alone, Your Grace."

"Jordan." He closed the door with a resounding click. "Don't be ridiculous. You can't turn back the clock because you wish it so." He strolled toward her, his gaze on the large sheet of paper on which she'd been drawing. "What are you doing?"

"You wouldn't understand." She paused before adding deliberately, "Your Grace."

"You said that once before."

She remembered that first night when he had given her back the gift of her childhood when she had needed it most. She quickly banished the memory. She could expect no such gift tonight.

"I have a reasonable intelligence." His smile lit his features with that curiously elusive charm. "If you explain slowly and clearly, I might possibly be able to comprehend, Marianna."

Her name always sounded strange on his lips, dark and smooth and rippling as sun-warmed glass. She put her pen back in the holder. "I have to have a design before I can execute it in glass."

"I can see that. You must be planning a very small panel."

"It's only the first sketch. My grandmother always said the first sketch was to let the heart run free. The second is done on an exact scale and dimension, and then thin pieces of card are pressed into each aperture on the sketch and then cut to shape. Then the cutline is added."

"Cutline?"

"The tracing of the lead lines that forms the pattern from which the glass will be cut. I can see the design in the abstract and get a feel for the rhythm of the piece."

"I agree rhythm is very important," he said solemnly. "It's one of my—"

"You said I'd be free to work," she interrupted. "I can't have you underfoot asking questions."

"I'm not under your feet, I'm merely here." He

turned and walked to the window nearest him. "It's cold as Hades in here. I'll close the shutters."

"No."

He glanced inquiringly over his shoulder.

"I like the cold, it keeps me alert."

"You mean awake." He noted the circles under her eyes. "You've had a long day, and you've been up here for hours. Why don't you go to bed?"

"I'm not tired," she said. "Will you please go?"

He glanced around the room. "There are no comforts here. I'll have a big chair and cushions brought up tomorrow."

"I don't need them. I come here to work. I had less than this in my workroom in Samda. I wouldn't use your 'comforts.' "

"But I will." He prowled around the room, stopping now and then to glance out one of the eight windows. His tone became self-mocking. "I'm not accustomed to such Spartan surroundings. You can't expect me to suffer both cold and discomfort. I couldn't endure it. I've told you how spoiled and indulged I am."

She had a sudden vision of him above her, holding her captive on the floor of the church, strong, primitive, completely different from the beautifully civilized man in this room. Then she felt the muscles of her stomach clench as she realized he was speaking as if this was not to be an isolated visit. "I expect nothing from you. Except that you leave me alone."

He glanced at her over his shoulder. "But I can't do that," he said softly. "I suddenly find myself utterly fascinated by the craft of making stained glass. Since you won't explain the process, then I must watch and learn for myself."

She drew a deep breath and turned back to the table. "There's no point in arguing with you when you're too arrogant to pay attention to anyone's needs but your own. I'd appreciate it if you would either leave or be silent."

She could feel his gaze on her as she picked up her pen. Please God, let him leave.

He didn't leave. She heard him move across the room but not in the direction of the door.

She ignored him, staring fixedly on the paper.

"Your hair is shining in the candlelight."

She started a rosette in the upper corner of the design.

"But not as much as it did this afternoon. I'm not sure you were telling me the truth when you said you weren't a pagan. When you stood in that pool of sunlight, you looked like an Egyptian priestess worshiping the sun god. You were almost in a trance. I remembered what you said about color serving the sunlight." He paused. "You serve the sunlight, Marianna."

His voice came from the darkness across the room, rich, disembodied, like a warm breath reaching out to her.

"I wanted to touch you. Do you know why I didn't?"

Her hand was shaking. She steadied it and completed the rosette.

"Because I didn't want you in a trance." He laughed harshly. "No, that's a lie. I don't give a damn if you're in a trance as long as I'm the one who cast the spell. I want to *be* that sun. I want to heat you and make you open to me."

Heat was moving through her now, she realized helplessly.

"One should never neglect an opportunity because it's not exactly what one wants. I should have taken what you offered and gathered up the rest later. I regretted it as soon as I left you. I regret it now."

Her head lifted swiftly. "I made no offer."

"No?" He was sitting on the floor beneath one of the windows, his legs crossed, as perfectly at ease as he had been in the forest and at the table tonight. His face was in the shadows beyond the pool of light cast by the candles, and she could see only a shimmer of green as he looked at her. "Think back on it."

She didn't want to remember that scene in this room this afternoon. She had been trying to forget that moment of bewildering weakness. She *would* forget it. "You're disturbing me."

"That's my intention."

She tried again. "I don't want you to come here anymore. And I want a lock on the door."

"I shall come here every day." He paused. "And there will be no locks between us. Not ever."

"Then I'll ignore you," she said desperately. "You'll become very bored sitting there talking to yourself."

"I won't be bored. I enjoy looking at you. I promise I won't bother you. I'll sit here meekly absorbed in my own thoughts." He smiled. "I'm sure you won't mind if I share one with you on occasion?"

"I do mind," she said fiercely.

"How unfortunate. But I really think you must tolerate my small demands when I'm showing such restraint and consideration in the larger ones. I never wanted this, but it's here, and we must both admit it."

"I will not admit to something I do not feel."

"You will . . . in time."

She turned back to the table and began to trace in the border. Ignore him. He is not here. The work is the only thing of importance. He is not here.

He was there. Silent. Tense. Compelling.

She could not bear it.

The border was blurring before her eyes.

"For God's sake stop weeping," he said harshly. "I won't have it!"

Tears were running down her cheeks. "It's the smoke from the candles." She wiped her eyes on the back of her hands. "And you have nothing to say about it." She dipped her pen in the inkwell again. "If you don't like it, go away."

"I don't like it." He was suddenly kneeling before her on the floor. He took the pen from her hand and jammed it into the inkwell. "And I won't go away, and I won't have you—" He pulled her from the chair, to kneel in front of him. He shook her. "Stop it!"

The tears wouldn't stop; they were only coming faster. "Do you think I wish to—" She broke off as a sob choked her. "I hate this place! It's huge and it's dark and there are too many people."

"Oh, for God's sake." He jerked her into his arms, his hand cupping the back of her head as he held her face against his shoulder.

"Let me go."

"Be quiet."

"I want to leave here. They . . . they *curtsy* to me."

"A terrible sin. I shall have it stopped at once."

"You're laughing at me."

His voice was hoarse. "Believe me, I see nothing at all funny about this."

She discovered she was clinging to him as Alex did to her when he woke from a bad dream. She tried to push him away, but his arms tightened around her. "Stop fighting me. I'm not going to hurt you."

"Yes, you will. You want to hurt me like those men hurt Mama."

"It would be nothing like that. You'd like it. I promise you'd like it." He stroked her hair for a moment before adding resignedly, "Or rather, you would have liked it."

"I wouldn't have liked it. You make me feel . . . strange and hot . . . and . . ."

"Shh, it's better if we don't discuss how I make you feel at the moment." He took a lace-trimmed handkerchief from his sleeve and dabbed at her cheeks. "And absolutely imperative that we don't discuss how I feel."

She drew a deep, shaky breath and pushed away from him. "I will not do . . . what you . . . that."

"No, you won't." He handed her the handkerchief. "Blow your nose."

She looked at the fine linen square and shook her head.

"Do it," he ordered. "By God, I'll at least have my way in this."

She blew her nose and immediately felt much better.

He rose to his feet and lifted her back onto her chair. "Work for another hour and no more." He turned toward the door. "And sleep late tomorrow."

He was leaving, she realized in astonishment. "I never sleep late."

"You will tomorrow." He glanced back to her. "Or I'll carry you back to your bed."

"I wouldn't let you do—" She stopped as she met his gaze.

"Don't," he said softly. "Gregor says it's necessary I walk a fine line, but I'm not sure it's possible if you're not equally cautious. It will take time and restraint." He opened the door, and the draft caused the candles to flicker. "We have the former, but Gregor will tell you how lacking I am in the latter."

Nothing could look less restrained than Jordan at the moment. His muscles were tensed, and his eyes glittered recklessly in the candlelight. "Where . . . where are you going?"

"I'm going to pay a visit to a lady of my acquaintance. Would you like me to tell you what we're going to do?"

She knew what he was going to do. She could almost visualize him lying in bed, his hair loosened from his queue, his eyes intent as he— "No!"

"I wouldn't have done so anyway. It would have been a shocking breach in conduct for a guardian." He swung the door shut. "Good night, Marianna."

Gregor was leaning against the stone wall beside the stable doors when Jordan rode out into the courtyard.

"I don't want to hear a word from you," Jordan said shortly.

Gregor ignored the injunction. "She wasn't ready."

"No." He looked straight ahead. "She *wept*, goddammit."

"Ah, you've never made a woman weep before."

"It made me feel— I hated it." He glowered at him. "If I didn't know better, I'd swear you'd taught her to say exactly the right words to bring about the result you wished."

"I did not have to do that. She had only to be herself. Where are you going?"

"Do you need to ask?"

He kicked the stallion and galloped out the gates.

Gregor gave a sigh of relief as he looked up at the tower. "It was very close, little dove," he murmured. In all the years he had been with Jordan, he had never seen him in such a passion for a woman. Jordan had learned to control his unruly nature in many areas, but he was still Ana's son, and the forbidden had always glowed like a beacon for both of them.

Well, Jordan himself had made the decision to avoid this particular forbidden fruit, so it might be possible that Marianna was safe from him.

He could only wait and see.

Ah, you're down early," Gregor said as Marianna came down the stairs. "That is good."

"It is?" Nothing could have kept her from disobeying Jordan's command to sleep late today. Only minutes after he had left the tower room, she had been overcome by shame and anger at the disgusting weakness she had shown. "Not that early. I'm usually up before first light."

"What a terrible habit. I myself prefer to sleep late when I get the chance."

"Then why are you up?" she asked with assumed casualness, "and where is Jordan?"

"He is not here." He paused as if debating whether

to elaborate. "He went to visit Madam Carruthers. She is an old friend."

He had spent the night in that woman's bed and was still with her. Something hot and hurtful twisted inside Marianna. It was not anger, she told herself. There was no reason for her to be angry.

Gregor took her hand and led her toward the dining room. "I'm sure he will return shortly."

Perhaps it *was* anger, but only for the sake of that poor woman whom Jordan was using to vent his lust.

She would think no more about him. "Why are you up?" she repeated.

"I wished to make sure you were comfortable."

Warmth flooded her at his kindness. "As comfortable as I could be in this place."

"I was uncomfortable here, too, when I first came." Gregor seated her at the long table and then sat down beside her. "There is nothing this grand in Kazan. We live very simply there." He sighed. "How I miss it."

"Why did you come here?"

"To take care of Jordan."

"He hired you to act as guard?"

"No, I was not hired. I just came." He saw her curious expression and shook his head. "I told you I could not tell you about Kazan. All I can say is that Jordan is part of all of us in Kazan. We do not like to see a part of us rot and become less than it could be. That is why I came to care for him."

She looked down at her plate. "He seems quite able to care for himself."

He laughed. "Ah, he did then too. He was only a boy of nineteen but as cynical as a man of thirty. It wasn't surprising when everyone treated him as if the world and everything in it had been created for his enjoyment. I've never seen a lad so spoiled." He grimaced. "Or so hot-tempered. We had many a match before we came to terms."

"His terms or your terms?"

"Why, my terms," he said, surprised. "It could be no other way. He had to be taught discipline, or he would have remained impossible."

He was still impossible. "It must have been very unpleasant for you. I wonder that you stayed."

"It was not all bad. Jordan can coax the birds to fly to him when he wishes."

"And it made up for the bad times?"

He nodded. "When he was himself and not what they made him, he was a boy to warm the heart." He nodded at the cup in front of her. "I don't wish you to eat breakfast this morning, but you must have nourishment. Drink. It is chocolate."

"Chocolate?" She reached for the cup. "I've never had it. Papa said it's wonderful."

"It's a beverage made in paradise."

She sipped it tentatively and then more deeply. "I like it."

"As do I." He drained his cup and gestured to the servant to refill it. "I have a taste for anything dark and uncommon."

"Then it's no wonder you have a fondness for Jordan," she said dryly. "For he is both."

"You're still angry with him? Actually, for Jordan, he is behaving toward you with singular virtue." He lifted the chocolate to his lips. "But you must help him."

"I have no intention of helping him in any way. I'm here to work and care for Alex."

"That will help. The less he sees of you, the better." He paused. "And, when he does see you, offer no challenge. Be as eager and childlike as Alex."

"I cannot pretend to be something I'm not."

"It would be easier for you if you could." He sighed resignedly as he saw her expression. "Oh, very well, do what you will. I will try to stand between you."

"Thank you." She reached out and patted his big hand. "I need no one to protect me, but it is a kind and generous thought."

"I like you," he said simply. "And even if I did not, I would still do it. It is my duty. Such a thing would not be good for Jordan either." He looked down into the depths of his cup. "I was sent not only to protect his body but his soul."

"I believe you should concentrate on protecting his body," she said tartly. "I've seen no sign of this elusive soul."

"I have," he said quietly. "I've seen him weep at the death of a child, and I've been with him when he carried a wounded man on his back for twenty miles across the steppes. I've seen him writhing with an inner hurt so terrible, he did not say a word for days. He does not show his soul, but it is there." He smiled. "And we must make sure he does not harm it by actions he cannot forgive himself. Finish your chocolate."

She obediently drained her cup and set it down.

He reached over and gently wiped her mouth with his napkin. "Paradise leaves an occasional mark upon those who taste its pleasures." He stood up. "Now we go to the stables."

She shook her head. "I'm going to my work-room."

"Not today. Today you and Alex have riding lessons. That's why I didn't want you to have a full stomach."

She frowned. "I'll do that another day."

"Today. And tomorrow you have dancing lessons, and the day after you and Alex will have schooling with the vicar."

"I will *not*."

"Yes, you will. It will keep you out of sight and away from Jordan."

She glowered at him. "I will not hide from Jordan even to save his precious soul. If you want me out of his sight, let me work."

"I would never think of depriving you of your work. I have it all planned. After today you will work from dawn until noon. The light should be better in the morning." He beamed. "That leaves all the after-noon free."

"I don't need dancing lessons, and Papa said that the education he gave me was better than most gen-tlemen received at—"

"Then you will surprise and delight the vicar." Gregor pushed her toward the door. "But you cannot deny you need to learn to ride."

"No, but I—" She stopped as she met his gaze. She suddenly realized how he had managed to over-come the wild, decadent hellion who had been young Jordan Draken. Gregor's expression was kindly but absolutely relentless. She said faintly, "I do need to work."

"After your lesson." He added, "And your hot bath. You're likely to be quite sore at first. Now, we must get you proper riding clothes. Perhaps there is something you can use in the armoire. . . ."

His Grace would like to see you, miss." Mrs. Jenson shivered in the doorway as a blast of wind poured into the tower room. "He requests your presence in the courtyard."

Marianna felt her muscles tense, and she looked back at her sketch. "Tell His Grace I'm busy at present."

Mrs. Jenson was scandalized. "He said at once, miss. He wishes to bid you good-bye before he leaves."

Her head lifted swiftly. "He's leaving? Where is he going?"

"To London, I understand." She shivered again and drew her shawl closer about her. "You should close those shutters. You'll catch your death in this cold."

"I like it," she said abstractedly. He was leaving. She had been scrupulously avoiding Jordan for the last week, and now it would no longer be necessary. She should feel relief, not this strange flatness. "Is Gregor going with him?"

"I'm sure I don't know." Mrs. Jenson added reprovingly, "You're keeping His Grace waiting."

And that must never happen, Marianna thought. Mrs. Jenson was completely under Jordan's spell and thought everything must be exactly as he decreed. She was not alone. Marianna had found that everyone at Cambaron held him in an affection that amounted almost to adulation. It was hard to comprehend considering Gregor's comments on the duke's character as a youth.

She put her pen back in the inkwell and stood up. "By all means, we must not cause him to tarry even a minute longer than necessary."

Mrs. Jenson smiled and started to curtsy. She stopped in midmotion and frowned in distress. "I do beg pardon, miss. You must think me a stupid old woman."

Jordan had evidently spoken to her after that first night in the tower, for the housekeeper had been attempting to stop the habit ingrained by a lifetime. She failed as often as not, and Marianna was fervently sorry she had blurted out those words to Jordan. She sighed. "It truly doesn't matter, Mrs. Jenson. Do as you wish."

"It does matter. His Grace will be very displeased with me."

"I will speak to him." She stood up and moved to the door. "It was only that I was unused to such a response. I've grown accustomed to it now."

It was a lie. She was still nearly as awkward in these surroundings as when she had come. She was not like Alex, who had adapted wonderfully and was happier than she had ever seen him. Why should he not be happy? He had lost everything and then was brought to Cambaron with a bevy of servants eager to cosset and amuse him and a playground a prince might envy. She would have to take care he was not thoroughly spoiled while he was here. When it was time for them to leave, she would not be able to give him anything more splendid than the gamekeeper's cottage.

Jordan stood waiting beside a light phaeton harnessed to two magnificent bays. "You took your time." He motioned to the stable boy to hold the horses and took her arm. "Walk with me."

She immediately tensed, and he smiled sardonically. "Don't be afraid. I don't intend to attempt you here in the courtyard in full view of the servants." He drew her away from the phaeton and walked toward the fountain in the center of the courtyard.

"I'm not afraid. I just don't like to be touched."

"A laudable attitude for a young virgin," he said. "If I wasn't your guardian, I might argue with you. I've noticed signs you could like it very much." His grip tightened as she tried to pull away. "But since I've decided that's my present lot in life, I'll make no such remark."

She snorted.

He smiled. "Do you know I'll actually miss that less than elegant sound? The ladies in London would swoon rather than—"

"I don't care what the ladies in London do. According to Gregor, they do nothing but paint teacups and worry about what gown to wear."

"Oh, they can be persuaded to venture into slightly less shallow waters on occasion."

"Like Madam Carruthers?" She had not meant to blurt that out.

His smile faded. "Gregor has been less than discreet."

"He only mentioned . . ." She tried to shrug carelessly. "You spent two days there."

"Laura is a lonely woman. She was widowed after only three years of marriage and likes company."

"You don't have to make explanations to me. Papa

told me it's the custom for gentlemen in England to take mistresses."

His lips thinned. "Then Papa is as indiscreet as Gregor."

"Papa believed both speech and spirit should be free, and one should not be concerned with what others think."

"Good God, if you hadn't already told me he was a poet, I'd have guessed it by that singular bit of philosophy. And do you believe the spirit should be free?"

"Of course, don't you?"

"What I believe is not necessarily safe for you. Laura is not my mistress. We merely amuse each other." He paused. "I will explain the status of mistress to you at a later time."

The air was suddenly heavy and hard to breathe. "I'm not interested in your mistresses or this—"

"Good, for I refuse to discuss them further with you." He leaned against the rim of the fountain. "It's indelicate for a young virgin to—"

"Will you stop calling me that!"

"I have to keep reminding myself. Gregor will tell you that I have a poor memory when it suits my convenience." He looked down at the water. "Actually, it does little good in this case. I don't care a whit whether you're a virgin or not. In fact, it makes the prospect of teaching you pleasure all the more appealing."

Heat flooded her face. "Mrs. Jenson said you wished to bid me good-bye. Good-bye, Your Grace."

"I had a few other things to discuss." He lifted his gaze from the water. "I want you."

Shock tore through her. She had not expected that

stark, raw sentence. "You want only a woman to sate your lust. Go back to Mrs. Carruthers."

"I assure you I shall, and many other women besides. I have no desire to have this passion for a stubborn chit who may someday prove to be my enemy. I have the greatest hopes this may be a temporary madness." He looked into her eyes. "I'm trying to be honest with you in this so you will trust what I say now." He paused. "I also . . . like . . . and admire you. I believe, in time, it's possible we may be friends."

She stared at him in astonishment.

"For God's sake, why do you think you weren't in my bed on the *Seastorm*?" he burst out. "You bound me, and you did the same in the tower."

"I did nothing to you."

"You bound me," he repeated through his teeth. "And I have no liking for it." He drew a deep breath, and then his expression changed and became mocking. "But I've accepted it and now must try to wrest something from the situation."

"What?"

"We will become friends."

She shook her head doubtfully.

"I repeat, we will become friends."

His tone was so grim, she found herself smiling. "Or you'll cut off my head?"

"That's not the alternative I had in mind." He turned and strode back toward the phaeton. "That's all I had to say. I thought you should have time to become used to the idea before I return from London."

She trailed behind him, staring in bemusement at the straight line of his back. "When will that be?"

"Within two weeks."

She said with irony, "How kind of you to give me such a long time. Your patience is truly astonishing."

"I never claimed to be patient. I prefer things done yesterday." He stepped into the phaeton and took up the reins. "I'm sure you have enough to keep you occupied while I'm gone, and I'm leaving Gregor here to amuse you."

She was careful not to reveal her relief. "Amuse me or guard me?"

"I'm not worried about you running away. You have too much to lose at present. You have no money, and you wouldn't cast Alex back into the same situation you faced in Montavia. I assure you, England can be just as cruel to the poor."

He was echoing every fear she had held since she had decided to come to this country. "I will stay here only as long as I wish."

"Then we must make sure you wish to stay here until both our purposes are accomplished."

The Jedalar.

He met her gaze and nodded. "You could agree to give it to me," he said softly. "We could work together. It would be a good deal easier for you."

"No, it wouldn't. That would be true only if our goals were the same." She started up the steps. "Good journey."

"Your chaperon will arrive this afternoon," he called after her.

She turned to look at him. "Chaperon?"

"Gregor suggested we hire a maid to act as your abigail, but I decided we need a more intimidating barrier between us." He grimaced. "As I find no one more intimidating than Cousin Dorothy, I sent for her."

"I will not have a chaperon. Merciful heavens, aren't there enough people at Cambaron?"

"You will think there are when Cousin Dorothy arrives." He snapped the reins, and the horses sprang forward. "Good luck."

"Cousin Dorothy?" Gregor was coming down the steps toward her. "What is this about Cousin Dorothy?"

She watched Jordan drive through the gates. "She is coming here to be my chaperon. He sent for her. Who is Cousin Dorothy?"

"Lady Dorothy Kinmar of Dorchester. Jordan's second cousin." A sudden smile lit his face. "This is good. Jordan has always found her a very difficult woman."

"It is not good. I don't need a chaperon. Why won't anyone listen to me? All I want to do is work."

"No one needs a chaperon as much as you, and Cousin Dorothy will do splendidly." He patted her shoulder. "Do not worry. I think you will like her. She has a tongue like an asp but a kind heart. She also has great learning for a woman. They call her a . . ." He frowned, searching for the word. "Bluestocking."

"I don't care what they call her. When she gets here, send her home."

He shook his head. "If you want it done, do it yourself." He grinned. "But be sure I'm here to see it. It should be very interesting."

CHAPTER 6

Where is she?" The words, boomed out by a voice that was a feminine counterpart of Gregor's, bounced off the arched ceiling of the hall. "I want to take a look at her."

"Cousin Dorothy," Gregor murmured. He gestured for Marianna to precede him out of the study. "Let us hasten and send her on her way."

The strapping woman standing in the hall must be near her thirtieth year, towered over six feet and exuded a tremendously forceful air. She was dressed in a fashionable purple silk gown that flattered her pale complexion and rich brown-red hair. A small hat decorated with purple flowers perched over her broad forehead and accented rather than concealed the mass of hair caught back in a sleek bun. She was not a comely woman, but her brown eyes sparkled with vitality, and her spine was rod straight, her carriage magnificent. She wheeled to face Gregor and Marianna as they came into the hall. "Good day, Gregor." Her gaze shifted to Marianna. "This is the girl?"

"I am Marianna Sanders, my lady."

"Gadzooks, no wonder Jordan risked sending for me." Her glance ran over Marianna from head to toe. "Exquisite. How old is she?"

"Sixteen," Gregor said.

"And how long has she been under his roof?"

"A week at Cambaron."

"And before that?"

"We brought her from Montavia."

Dorothy Kinmar groaned. "And he expects me to set this aright? There is bound to be gossip."

"He has supreme confidence in you."

Marianna was tired of them talking over her head. "I do not need a chaperon. It is kind of you to come, but I think you must go back to—"

"Be quiet, girl." Dorothy nibbled at her lower lip. "It is possible, but it will take all my considerable intellect."

"I will not be quiet," Marianna said. She had enough of this. She drew up herself to her full height, but she was still pitifully little in comparison with this giantess. "And I think you rude to suggest it. I do not need you, I will not have you, and there's the end of it." She turned on her heel and quickly climbed the staircase. She heard Gregor's chuckle and was aware of the woman's startled gaze on the middle of her back until she passed from view.

A few moments later she slammed the door of the tower room and hurried over to the table. A feeling of peace immediately surged through her, quieting the anger. This was her world. She was safe here, and she would not let them take her away from it. First, Gregor with his dratted lessons, and now this female dragon who looked at her as if she was a clump of dirt left by the chimney sweep.

"You do need me, you know."

She stiffened, her gaze flying to the doorway. Dorothy Kinmar came into the room and closed the door. She glanced around the barren tower. "This is quite nice."

Marianna stared at her in disbelief.

"Well, don't you think it is?"

"Yes," she said. "But everyone else thinks it's a desolate place."

"You do not wish comfort when you're bidding the muse to come to you. I have a room that is similar to this in my house in Dorchester where I do my writing." She smiled. "Though I confess I do pamper myself with a fire."

Her smile was surprisingly sweet, illuminating her bold features with warmth. Marianna's lips reluctantly curved in response. "I do dress warmly. You write?"

"I've written several books dealing with the shameful lack of freedom given women in our society." She added proudly, "And Mary Wollstonecraft herself did me the honor of writing me a letter of praise on one of my earlier volumes."

She was obviously supposed to know the identity of this Mary Wollstonecraft. "How pleasant."

She looked around the workroom. "You've not done much since you've been here."

"I've had interruptions. Which I'm now trying to avoid."

The woman ignored the broad hint. "Are you good at this making of glass?"

"I'm very good. I shall be much better."

This time the smile was wider, revealing large, even teeth. "At least you don't lower your eyes and stammer modestly. A woman should be confident. If she has something to say, she should say it. Did Gregor say your father was also a writer?"

"My father was a poet."

"Oh, that's right. I seldom read poetry." She came over to the table. "I've never heard of him."

"He had only one poem published five years ago. 'Ode to an Autumn Day.' It was lovely."

She looked at her searchingly. "Was it truly?"

To her astonishment Marianna found herself telling the truth. "No, he wasn't a good poet, but he was a very good man."

"So you lied to him and praised him and made him happy." Dorothy's lips curled. "And put your neck beneath the chariot of the oppressor."

"He was not in the least oppressive, and I see nothing wrong in making someone you care about happy." She was growing weary of defending poor sweet Papa. "It's time you left, my lady."

"Dorothy." She gestured impatiently. "I've offended you. You'll find it's a habit of mine. I'm not one to mince words." She looked around the workroom. "I believe we'll get on better than I thought. You're no milk-and-water namby-pamby. I was afraid at the first put-down I'd have to catch you as you swooned." She grimaced. "I have little patience for such nonsense."

"You will not have to display patience . . . in Dorchester." She paused. "I have no need of you here."

"Gregor thinks you do, and Jordan would certainly never have invited me here, if he hadn't had reason." Her eyes narrowed on Marianna's face. "Tell me, did he attempt you?"

Heat burned Marianna's cheeks at the bluntness of the question.

"You don't need to answer. Most unusual. Jordan has always determinedly avoided youngsters." Dorothy smiled cynically. "What is more unusual is that he's chosen to protect you from himself." She walked over to the window and looked out at the hills in the distance. "I might make the *ton* accept you, but I will—"

"I don't want anyone to accept me. I want to be left in peace."

"And what of your brother? Children can be savages and follow their parents' example. Do you want the village children to throw rocks and filthy words at him because his sister is a whore?"

"No!"

"Then you must not be a whore in anyone's eyes."

It was the argument Gregor had used, and the one she couldn't refute. "And I suppose you can prevent this by your mere presence?"

"No, it will take a good deal more than that. Though I have a certain presence that tends to cow the easily frightened."

And the not so easily frightened, Marianna thought.

"And, due to my father, who was a shameless gossip, I have a store of scandalous secrets on almost every family at Prinny's court."

"What good would that do?"

Dorothy's brows lifted in surprise. "That's the first hint of naïveté I've seen in you. One tends to forget how young you are. It is a weapon, my dear." She drew herself up to her majestic height. "Now, we must come to terms. I have no intention of fighting the *ton and* you. Will you give me your cooperation?"

What else could she do if she was to protect Alex? she thought resignedly. Life at Cambaron was becoming increasingly complicated. "Within reason." She added quickly, "And as long as it doesn't disturb my work."

"Done. We will work around it." She frowned. "We must have a plan."

"You mean a lie. You sound like Gregor."

"Actually, Gregor did quite well, but we must do better. You are fifteen, not sixteen. It's only one year, but considering everyone knows of Jordan's dislike of young girls, perhaps it will help a little. We will say you are a bookish young miss interested only in her lessons and her hobby."

"Working with glass is not my hobby."

"It is now. Craftsmen are not acceptable to the *ton.*"

"Then all the more reason why I should not try to enter their ranks."

"Your brother," Dorothy reminded her.

Marianna's hand clenched on the pen. "I will not spend one more minute than necessary on this nonsense."

"Don't worry, I could not trust you for long periods. You would ruin everything." She frowned. "Now, when Jordan is here, there must always be guests. On no account must you be alone with him."

"We are hardly alone with hundreds of servants and Gregor and—"

"It is not the same," she said impatiently. "And I shall tell him in public he must be indulgent, perhaps even a little bored in his attitude toward you." She shook her head in disgust. "I must be mad. What am I trying to do? They might believe it of some men, but not the Duke of Diamonds."

"Duke of Diamonds?"

"One of the titles that's not recorded as Jordan's birthright. He earned it himself." She saw Marianna's interest and continued, "He left the university at sixteen and became the darling of the court, just as he was the darling of Cambaron. He didn't come into his father's money until he was twenty-one, but he had inherited a fortune from another branch of the family that he could use at once. He became a notorious womanizer and gambler, into every wickedness imaginable."

It was essentially what Jordan had told her about himself. "What do diamonds—"

"One of the properties Jordan inherited was a diamond mine in Africa. He used to keep pouches of diamonds about for all those ghastly women with whom he cavorted."

"Diamonds? Women usually like a bit of flash," Jordan had said.

She had known he had spoken from experience, but this revelation was curiously hurtful. "He gave them gifts of diamonds?"

For the first time puzzlement crossed Dorothy's face. "I . . . don't think so. There was a good deal of laughter when the diamonds were mentioned." She dismissed the subject. "At any rate, there was no doubt he was a thorough scoundrel for a number of years."

"Until Gregor came?"

"Oh, and for a few years afterward. Jordan was not easy to tame. It was only when Napoleon did something to displease him that he settled down." She held up her hand. "And I do not know what he did. I'm not concerned with the doings of that little Corsican. There are too many injustices committed at the fireside to go looking for trouble across the channel. However, we can be grateful Jordan is so preoccupied these days that he's seldom at Cambaron, can't we?"

"Very glad."

"Then, smile, girl. You're far too serious. One should be solemn only about the important things in life. Heaven knows, there are enough of those to weigh us down." She started toward the door. "Now, I shall unpack and send my driver back to Dorchester. Which is your room?"

"The Blue Room."

"Gracious, that won't do at all. It's fine for Jordan's ladybirds, who never know whether it's day or night anyway, but you wouldn't be able to breathe in there. No wonder you're clinging to this tower. I'll see to the change. Something brighter and more open?" She saw Marianna's bewildered expression and said, "If you didn't like the room, why didn't you move?"

"I thought all the chambers were like that. Alex's is little better."

"Does he mind it?"

"He doesn't even notice. It's only a place to sleep and play on rainy days. He spends most of his time at the stables."

"But I think you notice everything about this place." Dorothy studied her expression and then said quietly, "Listen, Marianna, this is a new world for you, and that's frightening. Gregor tells me you have courage, but that's not enough. I think, if you look at Cambaron as one of your glass windows that you can change and rearrange to suit yourself, you'll be happier."

"Change?" Marianna repeated, startled.

"Did you think Cambaron has stayed the same for the past six hundred years? As long as you do not tear down the walls, I doubt if Jordan will object. Perhaps he would be grateful if you did. He has no fondness for the place." She smiled impishly. "Besides, he will not be here when you're doing most of the alteration and will have only the agent's report."

A heady lightness swept through Marianna. She suddenly realized her unhappiness at Cambaron had not been caused by the place itself but her lack of control to change and mold it. It had been a prison, and now Dorothy was throwing open the gates. "It doesn't seem possible. You're sure he will permit it?"

"Jordan sent word I was to keep you contented. If this will do it, he won't object."

Why, Cambaron could be a giant panel of glass that she could shape to serve the sunlight. The joy that had been tentative was growing stronger by the second.

"And we will have an enjoyable time spending Jordan's pounds. Better us than one of those doxies." Dorothy opened the door.

"Wait! Why did you come when he sent for you?" Marianna asked curiously. "It's obvious you don't approve of him."

"I like the rascal. Liking has nothing to do with approval. We are the same age and saw each other frequently as children. In spite of our quarrels, I find I miss him." She grimaced. "Besides, Dorchester is monstrous dull, and life is never boring around Jordan."

"And that is all?"

She hesitated and then shrugged. "No, I owe him a debt. He did me a great service at one time." She changed the subject. "You may work here for another four hours, and then you must come with me to inspect and choose a bedchamber while there is still light." She pulled the door shut behind her with quiet firmness.

For the first time since she had come to Cambaron, Marianna felt a burst of hope. Since that moment in the church at Talenka she had been walking on quicksand, not certain where to step, confronted by dangers and feelings she had never known before.

But now the ground was growing firm, and she could begin to see a path in the distance.

He was coming!

Marianna could see the high-spirited bays racing down the road toward her, Jordan guiding the reins with skill. Good heavens, she had not thought he would be coming at this breakneck pace. If she didn't stop him, he would be careening past her and leave her with nothing but a face full of dust.

She drew a deep breath and then stepped out of the underbrush and into the middle of the road.

The bays reared high!

The phaeton leaned perilously to one side as Jordan stood up and fought to get the horses under control.

Marianna stared in astonishment.

Jordan was cursing beneath his breath as he finally subdued the bays. "Good God, what are you about? Did you wish to kill us all?"

She stiffened defensively. "How was I to know they would behave so foolishly? My horse is not so skittish."

"These horses are bred for spirit and speed, not docility." He glared at her. "You don't jump out in front of a team like this and expect them to behave like plow horses."

"Perhaps if you'd train them to be better—" She stopped and scowled at him. "Very well, I'm in the wrong. I should not have done it."

"Yes, you are." He stared speculatively at her. "But you don't usually admit it so readily. What mischief have you been practicing?"

"No mischief. You speak as if I were as young as Alex."

"It's how I've been endeavoring to picture you for the last few days. However, I doubt if even Alex would have the lack of maturity to step out before a team of horses."

She gestured impatiently. "I wished to talk to you. I have a request to make."

"You couldn't wait until I reached Cambaron?"

"Dorothy is there, and she would . . . She is very determined to have her own way and has very strong opinions. She says you would not mind, but I have to be certain."

"This request is becoming lengthy, and it's not good to keep the horses standing." He held out his hand. "Get in the phaeton."

She cast a wary look at the horses as she sidled past them. As he pulled her up and onto the seat next to him, her stomach rolled queasily. She felt perilously high and vulnerable in the open carriage. "I think I'd rather get down and walk beside you."

"Nonsense." He flicked the reins, and the team leaped forward with a bound. "The request?"

She said in a rush, "Dorothy says you wouldn't mind if I made stained-glass panels for the windows at the castle." She added, "And perhaps decorations for some of the walls."

"Why should I mind? If your work is creditable, it can only improve the place." His gaze suddenly narrowed on her face. "Is that all?"

"Well, not exactly." She moistened her lips. "I wonder if you'd let me cut a hole in the roof."

He blinked. "I beg your pardon? Wouldn't that be a trifle drafty?"

"Not the entire roof. Just in the south wing where the ballroom is located."

"I see," he said solemnly. "I'm relieved we're to have a little shelter from the elements. I knew you had a dislike for Cambaron, but don't you think such destruction is a little extreme?"

He was not taking her seriously. "It will only be for a little while. We needn't start cutting for a long while, and even after the hole is there, we can cover it until I'm ready."

"Until you're ready for what?"

"A dome." She rushed on eagerly. "I've always dreamed of doing one. A beautiful stained-glass dome with flowers and vines and perhaps birds. Wouldn't that be splendid?"

His stared musingly at her. "It sounds utterly magnificent . . . and complicated. Are you sure you'd be capable of fashioning this dome?"

She nodded. "The panels themselves will not be too difficult. The precision and balance of setting the panels into the dome will make up the greatest challenge. I'm very good now, and the more complicated tasks I undertake, the better I'll get." With a touch of defiance she added, "And you do want me to improve. Isn't that why I'm here?"

He didn't answer the challenge. "And how long would such a project take?"

"I don't know. A long time. There's a great deal of work involved in such a project."

"I can see there would be." He added dryly, "And in the meantime I exist with a monstrous hole in my roof."

Her face fell with disappointment. "Yes." She bit her lip. "You're right, it's too much to ask."

He was silent a moment. "How big a hole?"

Hope leaped within her. "Not the entire ballroom. The dome would be in the center."

"How comforting."

She held her breath.

"Oh, the devil with it." He smiled recklessly. "What do I care if you chop up the place? Make your blasted dome."

"Truly?"

"Truly." He shook his head as he saw her luminous expression. "It takes very little to make you happy."

"This isn't little." She was so excited, she was having trouble sitting still. "It's very seldom a craftsman gets to work on such a project. My grandmama did only two domes in her entire life."

"Well, if you don't stop wriggling, you won't be alive to do this one," he said. "You're making the horses restless."

She didn't care. She was so full of joyful exuberance, even the dratted horses didn't intimidate her. "You seem to be able to control them."

"Would you like to try?"

She looked at him, startled. "Me?"

"A new experience." He put his left arm around her and transferred the reins to her hands, which he then covered with his own. "Hold tight, but don't pull."

Power. Excitement soared through her as she felt the pull on the reins. All that strength and spirit, and she was holding it in check, guiding it!

He chuckled. "You like it."

"Yes," she said breathlessly. "It's . . . wonderful. Take your hands away. Let me do it alone."

"Not this time." He moved his arm from around her and took back the reins. "Next time I come to Cambaron, I'll give you a lesson in handling the ribbons."

"Do you promise?"

"I promise." He smiled indulgently. "If I keep you sufficiently occupied, perhaps you'll delay poking a hole in my roof until the winter snows are done."

Perhaps this wasn't the time to tell him that the snows would come and go again before she would be through with the flower dome. "You're going away again?"

"Tomorrow morning."

"Why?"

"I have business to conduct abroad."

"When will you be back?"

He shrugged. "I have no idea. Perhaps in the spring."

Spring. He wouldn't be back until spring. She would be able to work with no interference and with no inner torment. The realization must not have set in yet, otherwise she wouldn't feel this curious flatness.

The gates of Cambaron were just ahead, and she was surprised at the sharp twinge of disappointment she experienced. Their short time together on the phaeton had been amazingly companionable. She had not been aware of even a hint of sensuality in Jordan's manner. He had been as casually indulgent as if she had been a younger sister.

She darted a glance at him from the corner of her eye. His expression was bland, controlled, faintly amused. Yet it was too . . . too smooth, as if he were wearing a mask.

He did wear a mask, she realized suddenly. She never really knew what he was thinking unless he told her.

"What are you plotting now?" he asked with mock alarm. "The ballroom is one thing, but I absolutely refuse to allow a hole in the roof of my stable. My horses are much more sensitive than any of the two-legged specimens of my acquaintance."

What did she care what was beneath the mask? He had said yes. He had given her the opportunity to create her dome! "I wouldn't think of it." She smiled happily. "You're not the only one who likes horses better than people. Alex would never permit it."

William says next year I'll be ready for a bigger horse," Alex said as Marianna tucked the covers around him. "But Gregor says not as big as his."

"I should hope not." Marianna smiled down at him. "You would need to stand on the top rim of the fountain to mount him." She brushed his hair back from his face. "But you mustn't be disappointed if you have to keep your pony. Horses cost a good deal of money, and we have no right to ask anything of these people."

"We don't have to ask; they just give to us." Alex yawned. "And Jordan won't mind. He told me he got his first horse when he was five, but he still rode his pony until he was too heavy for it."

"Why did he do that?"

"He said you don't desert your old friends when new ones come." Alex smiled sleepily. "So I won't have to give up Keely. I'll just make a new friend."

"You're making a good many friends here, aren't you?"

Alex nodded. "They like us." He frowned. "But I worry a little. Mama always said not to take unless you could give. I've been taking, Marianna."

She had been taking, too, she realized suddenly. Jordan had promised her protection for Alex, but he had also given kindness. He had brought them here to safety and treated Alex like an indulged younger brother.

But he had done it only because of the Jedalar.

No, he could have merely supplied her with a place to work. He had sensed she would not be able to resist the opportunity to create, to perfect her craft. He didn't have to be either kind or generous to them.

Perhaps he had been kind because he wanted her in *that* way.

But there had been nothing calculated in his lust; it had been as swift rising as a summer storm. When he had realized the storm would hurt her, he had sent it away.

"Marianna, what can I give him?" Alex asked. "He has so much. . . ."

"Take your time. He won't return until spring. You'll think of something," she said gently. She bent and kissed him quickly on the cheek. "Surprises are always best. Good night, Alex."

She blew out the candle and moved toward the door.

Alex was far wiser than she, she thought resignedly. She had told Jordan she would accept everything and give nothing in return, but she should have known she wouldn't be able to do it. It would have destroyed something within her. Gifts, no matter for what reason they were given, must be returned. It would have been so much easier if Jordan had remained the enemy who was trying to steal the Window to Heaven. Instead, he had begun to weave himself into their lives until he was now part of the fabric.

If she was to start anew here, she must learn to deal with that truth. He had said they could be friends. It could be that by offering her friendship, he only thought to persuade her to give him the Jedalar. It was far more difficult to refuse a friend than an enemy.

But wouldn't that also be true of Jordan? Wasn't he far less likely to use coercion toward her if their relationship were more harmonious?

Harmonious? The word was ludicrous used in connection with Jordan Draken. From the moment she had met him, her life had been fraught with conflict and uncertainty.

Yet on board the *Seastorm* there had been moments

of harmony and humor, and this afternoon he had been as kind as an older brother.

It might be possible.

April 15, 1809
Pekbar, Montavia

Well, what news? Have you found her?" Nebrov asked.

"Not precisely." Costain hesitated. "But I think I may know where she is."

"Then why isn't she here?"

"It may be difficult—"

"I don't want to hear about difficulties. I want to hear about how you conquered them."

"I had to come to ask if I should broach this particular difficulty." He paused. "I believe the children may be under the protection of the duke of Cambaron."

"Draken?" He frowned. He cursed viciously. "Why not? It should come as no surprise, what with the bad fortune that's plagued me. Are you certain?"

Costain shook his head. "But the duke sailed from Domajo only a few months ago. I made inquiries on the dock, and I was told he had come directly from Talenka."

"The Window to Heaven." Nebrov's lips curled. "Well, at least he didn't get it either."

"But he may have gotten the children, if they fled to Talenka after we killed the mother. Draken's man, Gregor Damek, scoured the shops before he left to buy clothing for a little boy and a young girl. He was in a great hurry because they were sailing at midnight for England."

"Then he does have them," Nebrov muttered.

"But does he know what he has?"

"Of course, he knows. He has a connection with Kazan. I'd wager he was sent to Talenka to get the Window to Heaven before I did." He smiled unpleasantly. "I would have liked to have seen his face when he saw it lying in pieces on the floor."

"But, if the girl knows the pattern, there's a possibility she could create another one."

"No!" Nebrov's hand clenched on the table. England. Why did Draken have to take the bitch to England, where he could not touch her?

But who said he could not touch her? he thought suddenly. Every stronghold could be breached if one was clever enough, patient enough. Draken was a formidable man, but Nebrov had detected a certain weakness in his character. He would have no compunction about killing an enemy, but he would hesitate in torturing the girl to get information about the Jedalar. He would not force the pace if patience would carry the day, and that weakness might give Nebrov the opportunity he needed.

Nebrov could be patient, too, if the stakes were high enough. Why not let Draken invest the time and effort and then take the prize away from him when the time was ripe?

"I think you must pay a visit to England, Marcus," he told Costain. "I believe we must learn what's happening at Cambaron."

CHAPTER 7

June 30, 1809
Cambaron, England

I t's just like you to give us so little notice, Jordan. A house party of seventy-five? Do you expect miracles?" Dorothy asked as she stood on the castle steps and watched Jordan get out of the phaeton. "Didn't it occur to you that not everyone in the world is waiting to rush to do your bidding?"

"No, I've found if you expect miracles, they have a tendency to occur." He smiled. "Particularly if you're here to provide them, Dorothy. I was at a masked ball last night, and I suddenly decided it was time to come home. Since you forbid me to come without a bevy of chaperons, I invited the entire party."

"Your sudden wish to come home is a bit surprising considering you were supposed to be home in the spring, and it's summer already."

"Did you miss me?" he teased.

"When have I had time to miss you? I'm far too busy with my own concerns to bother with thoughts of you." She searched his face. "You look tired."

"Dissipation."

"Do you think I don't know the difference? Have you been ill?"

"Of course not. Perhaps I'm a little tired. I just got back from France yesterday afternoon."

"That Corsican again." She waved a hand. "I don't want to hear about him. When are we to expect these guests?"

"They should be arriving today and tomorrow. The first are probably a few hours behind me." He started up the steps toward her. "And how have you been, dear cousin?"

"You mean how have I survived that obstinate young miss you set me to watch over? We're comfortable with each other now."

"I thought you'd approve of her. She has many of the same ideas you expound in your books."

"I've noticed that she has exceptional good sense." She added, "And a truly remarkable talent at her craft."

"Has she?" He felt a leap of excitement that dispelled the lethargy and discouragement he felt after two futile months of trying to undermine Napoleon's power in his homeland. The bastard had a stranglehold on half of Europe and was already looking to the East. "I've never seen her work."

"She's more artist than craftsman. She's done a tiger about to pounce from a tree for the window at the landing. It's magnificent." She shivered. "And chilling."

"I look forward to seeing it."

"It's still in her workroom. I believe she's been working on something else lately."

The Jedalar? No, it was too early to hope. "And where is this magnificent artist?"

"She's at the stable with Alex. The lad taught his pony a trick he wanted to show her." She looked beyond his shoulder. "No, here she comes."

He deliberately kept his manner casual and unhurried as he turned around. "I'm sure she will be as eager as you to bid me— Good God, what have you done to her?"

Dorothy stared approvingly at Marianna, who had just left the stable and was talking over her shoulder to someone inside. "What you sent for me to do." She smiled with satisfaction. "She looks very young, doesn't she? The dressmaker did very well indeed."

Marianna was wearing a loose high-necked white gown with a blue sash beneath the bodice that hid any hint of curves. Tiny embroidered white slippers peeped from beneath the hem of her skirt with every step. Her hair, divided into two loose braids tied with matching blue ribbons, shone in the sunlight. Even her skin appeared to glow with the shimmer that only children possessed.

"Christ, she looks as if she belongs in the nursery."

"Don't blaspheme. She looks exactly as she should look. She'll make a few appearances so that the guests can get a glimpse of her and appease their curiosity and then disappear. It would be better if she were less comely, but there's nothing we can do about that."

"No, there's nothing we can do." He hadn't allowed himself to recognize the intensity of his desire to see Marianna again. Now, he felt outraged, as if he had been robbed, as if she had been stolen from him. She was no longer half woman, half child. To touch this . . . this . . . infant would be unthinkable. Yet he knew with maddening certainty that the woman was still there, hidden, taunting him. He tore his gaze from her. "Where's Gregor?"

"I haven't seen him all morning." She raised her voice. "Marianna!"

Marianna's head turned, and she tensed as she saw Jordan. "Coming." She flew across the courtyard, looking more like a child than ever. She skidded to a halt before him and dropped a curtsy. "Your Grace."

He glared at her in astonishment. "What is this about?"

She looked up and smiled innocently. "Dorothy says it's improper to address you informally and that a curtsy is an entirely appropriate gesture for a young girl to show respect to a man of your years and august estate. Don't you approve?"

She knew very well he did not approve. She herself hated to be curtsied to. The little chit was teasing him, and in his present mood, he was definitely not amused. "I do not. Stop it."

"As you like." She stood staring at him. "You look terrible."

Dorothy's chuckle held a hint of malice.

"That appears to be the consensus of opinion. It must be my years and august estate. Why don't you run along and play with your toys?" He started up the steps. "I'm going to find Gregor."

To his surprise Marianna followed him. "I'll go with you."

Dorothy instantly shook her head. "You should not do—"

Marianna said impatiently, "Mercy, Dorothy, there's no danger of gossip. There's no one here yet." She hurried after Jordan into the hall. "All of this is nonsense anyway."

"I'm pleased you're so desirous of my company."

She ignored the mockery. "If you're looking for Gregor, he's in your bedchamber."

"How do you know?"

"He's doing something for me."

"Snakes in my bed?"

"No." She looked straight ahead. "Something else. A surprise."

"I'm intrigued. The last time Gregor arranged a surprise in my bedchamber, it was exceptionally interesting."

"This is *my* surprise." She frowned. "And I wish you would not say things that make me feel uncomfortable. You've been very kind to me, and I'm trying to think well of you."

"A great strain, I'm sure."

"Not while you're far away in London."

He burst out laughing. Dammit, he wished he could have stayed annoyed with her. "I accept the qualification." His smile lingered. "What kind things have I been doing for you?"

"You know." Her manner was suddenly awkward. "Alex. The windows. You allowed the workmen to make the new windows and cut the roof of the ballroom for the glass dome. It's all going to cost you a great deal of money."

"I have a great deal of money."

She lifted her chin. "That's true, and Dorothy says we can put it to better use than your doxies."

"That sounds like Dorothy. Have you forgiven me for unleashing her on you?"

"Of course, I like her very much."

"When she's not trying to tell you what to do."

"Sometimes even that's comforting. I know she

only means everything for the good." Her tone was wistful. "It seems a long time since anyone truly cared what was best for me."

She looked like a woeful little girl. He wanted to reach out and tug her braid, then tweak her cheek to make her smile. Good God, at this rate he would soon be patting her on the head and telling her bedtime stories. No, he would stay far away from anything to do with beds. "I'm glad you find her companionable."

She darted him a glance. "But you do not?"

"Dorothy has always wanted to change the world, and she thinks I'm the best place to start. She's tried to reform me since we were children."

"She likes you."

"I'm an eminently likable fellow." Then he added, "When it suits me. You'd be surprised at the number of people who hold me in affection."

She lowered her eyes. "I'm sure I would," she murmured.

"Wretch. You're not supposed to agree with me. A polite protest was in order." He stopped before the door of his bedchamber. "Do I call out before I go in? I don't want to ruin your surprise."

"Don't be ridiculous. Gregor was just supervising two of the servants. He may not even still be here. Besides, the room belongs to you." She shivered. "Though how you can stand it . . . It's even bigger and darker than mine was before I moved to another room."

"I'm accustomed to it." He opened the door. "It's the master's bedchamber, and I do obey some traditions. Dorothy will tell you that it's not a frequent habit, but I— My God." He stood in the doorway, his astonished gaze on the window directly across the room.

The five-foot panel of intricately cut stained glass shone like a radiant candle in the dark room. It portrayed a dark-haired woman riding a black stallion. She wore a rich purple gown, a silver breast armor, and carried a pennant. Mist-shrouded gray-purple mountains formed the background, but they were barely noticeable. The woman commanded all attention, with her hair whipping behind her and her green eyes shimmering with life.

"My mother," he murmured.

"I hope you don't mind," she said quickly. "I used the portrait in the hall to try to get the likeness. In glass, portraiture is terribly difficult. Most of the time you can give only a suggestion of a resemblance, but her features were so distinctive that I think I did a decent piece of work. Do you think it looks like her?"

"Yes, it looks like her."

"The ball gown was wrong," Marianna said. "She looked . . . it was wrong."

"And armor is right?"

"Yes." She moistened her lips. "As I studied the painting, I kept thinking of Galahad and Arthur and—"

"Joan of Arc?"

She shook her head. "Not Joan of Arc."

He turned to look at her. "Why did you do this?"

"I told you. You've been kind to Alex. You gave me Dorothy and Gregor." She shrugged. "I thought I could take and not give back, but I found I couldn't."

He nodded at the window. "And why did you choose her?"

"I thought . . . You never really knew your mother, and that's a terrible thing. It was a—" She stopped and then whispered, "I miss my mother. I would want more than a dark, cold painting to remember her by. I hope the sun will make her come alive for you."

He turned back to the window. "I don't think there's any question of that."

She was silent a moment and then burst out, "Well, why don't you say something? Do you hate it? Did I insult her? If you don't like it, I'll ask Gregor to take it out of here, but I won't have it destroyed. It's too good. I couldn't let—"

"I would kill the man who destroyed that window."

"You do like it?" she asked eagerly.

His voice was uneven as he tried to say lightly, "I'm so moved, I can think of nothing appropriately inane and trivial to cover the emotion. It's most disconcerting." He turned to look at her. "I thank you."

She didn't speak for a moment, her eyes meeting his, and then nodded brusquely. "I'm glad you like it." She turned and walked quickly out of the room.

He stood there for a full ten minutes, bathed in the radiant hues, contemplating the woman in the window. Then he turned and left the room.

It was another quarter of an hour before Gregor stirred from his chair in the deepest shadows at the corner of the room. He strode forward to stand before the window.

"She's a wise child, isn't she, Ana?" He chuckled. "Definitely not Saint Joan."

• • •

The lady's hair was a shining pale acorn brown and her eyes the color of violets. She was one of the most beautiful women Marianna had ever seen.

Jordan lifted the woman from the carriage and said something to her in a low tone that caused the woman to giggle and glance flirtatiously at him from beneath her lashes.

"Who is she?" Marianna whispered to Dorothy.

"Diana Marchmount, the countess of Ralbon."

"She's very beautiful."

"She's very ambitious," Dorothy said dryly. "She's seeking a permanent connection with Jordan."

A permanent connection. Dorothy must be speaking of marriage. Marianna felt an odd sense of shock. Somehow she had never connected the marital state with Jordan. Of course, it was foolish of her not to have done so. He must be considered a superb catch, and a man in his position must wish to carry on his line. "She wishes to marry him?"

"Heavens, no." Dorothy grimaced. "Well, perhaps, if she was not already wed. But then Jordan would have had nothing to do with her. He's always had an aversion to marriage."

"Why?"

She shrugged. "I suppose because his cynicism is too great and his need too small. Why marry, when ladies such as the countess are willing to pander to him?"

"Doesn't her husband object?"

"Her husband is only too willing to share her. He has little money, and Jordan is known to be very generous to his light of loves," Dorothy said. "I notice the earl isn't with her this time. He usually accompanies her when she comes to Cambaron. It lends her liaison an air of respectability."

Marianna shook her head. She did not understand these people and their dual codes. According to Dorothy, Marianna would be condemned and crucified at a hint of impropriety, and yet a woman could go to another man's bed with full consent of her husband as long as it was done discreetly.

Dorothy added in a low voice, "Keep your door locked this weekend. There are always improper goings-on in the hallways and bedchambers when this lot is here. Someone might stumble into your room by mistake."

"If she's already his mistress, what else does she wish from him?" Marianna asked, her eyes on the countess.

"He has no mistress. He amuses himself with her when it suits him." She watched Jordan's head bend attentively toward the beauty. "But it appears she's to be the choice for his stay this time." She took Marianna's elbow and gave a little nudge to start her down the steps. "Run along and have Jordan introduce you to her. He has her so dazzled, she'll scarcely notice you, and that's what we want."

Marianna didn't move. She didn't want to be here, she thought with sudden desperation. She didn't like the sensual curve of Jordan's mouth as he stared at the woman. She certainly didn't want to watch him dazzle her. The two were entering into a mysterious game with rules of which Marianna had no knowledge. She wanted to return to this morning, she wanted the Jordan back who had told her he would kill the man who destroyed her window.

"Marianna," Dorothy prompted.

She drew a deep breath and then started down the steps. She should not be upset. She and Jordan had started to forge an entirely different relationship. None of this had anything to do with her. He had told her he would go to these women. She had resolved to become at ease at Cambaron, and Jordan Draken *was* Cambaron. This careless lust was a part of the texture of his life, and she must become accustomed to it.

She would *never* become accustomed to it.

She reached the carriage. They didn't even know she was there. The knowledge filled her with unreasoning anger. To the devil with harmony. She searched wildly for a way to annoy him without endangering the elaborate lie Dorothy had concocted.

She reached out and tugged at the sleeve of his coat like an impatient child. When he looked at her in surprise, she smiled with openmouthed girlish delight and dropped him a low, low curtsy. "Oh, Your Grace, may I please be presented to the pretty lady?"

Marianna's door flew open, snatching her from sleep.

"Come along." Jordan strode into her bedchamber. "Hurry!"

She had never seen him like this. He was without a coat, his eyes blazed recklessly, his hair was tousled.

Marianna sat up in bed, her eyes wide with apprehension. "What is—"

He tore the covers off her and jerked her out of bed. "Hush! Do you wish to wake the household?" He grabbed her robe from the chair and shoved it at her. He pulled her across the room toward the door. "It's the middle of the night, for God's sake."

"I know it's the middle of the night. What— Let me go." She tried to free her wrist from his grasp. "Are you mad?"

"I don't think so." He considered the question and then shot her a gleaming glance. "No, only very, very drunk."

The smell of brandy and perfume that drifted to her confirmed his words and did not make her any more kindly disposed to him. "Then go to your room and go to sleep."

He didn't answer. He started down the stairs.

"Or go to the countess of Ralbon. No doubt she will be pleased to tolerate this—"

"Bored . . . All the same. Bored . . ."

"You weren't bored with her this afternoon," she said tartly. "Or tonight at supper."

"Knew it annoyed you."

It had annoyed her exceedingly, and she had done her best to annoy him in return. She had never expected her action to garner this violent a response. "Let me go back to my room."

"Can't do it. Journey. Have to go on a journey."

"Journey?" She stumbled as he started down the second flight of stairs. "The only journey we'll be going on is to the graveyard. You're going to kill us both."

"Nonsense. I'm very surefooted when I'm foxed." His words were slightly slurred. "Ask Gregor."

"Yes, let's do ask Gregor. I'm sure—"

He was shaking his head. "Gregor interferes." He threw open the front door. "So I locked him in his room. Not that it will keep him for long."

"Then let's go talk to Dorothy."

"I've already talked to Dorothy. She wasn't pleased, but she knows where we're going. Had to tell her. Not fitting for a guardian— You're confined to your room by a fever." He jerked her down the front steps toward a waiting carriage. "And I need no excuse. Everyone knows I have no sense of what is proper in a host."

"If I'm going on a journey, I need to get dressed," she said. Perhaps if he permitted her to go back to her chamber, she could lock herself in the room. "Let me go back to my room. It will only take—"

He shook his head. "No time." He put his finger to his lips. "Have to leave in the dead of night so no one knows. Not fitting . . ." He threw open the door of the carriage and half lifted, half pushed her onto the seat and then followed and settled himself opposite her. "Go, George," he shouted.

The carriage started with a lurch, and the next moment they were careening down the road at a breakneck pace. "Tell him to slow down."

He shook his head. "Promised Dorothy I'd have you back in two days. Have to hurry."

"Two days!"

"George can do it." Jordan settled himself in the corner of the seat and leaned his head against the wall of the carriage. "Fine hand with horses . . ."

"Take me back to the castle. I don't want to—"

He was asleep. She couldn't believe it. The drunken idiot was asleep!

She reached over and shook him.

No response.

"Jordan!" she shouted at the top of her lungs.

He sighed gently.

She stuck her head out the window. By what name had he called the coachman? "George, take me back to the castle."

The man didn't answer. It shouldn't have surprised her, she thought angrily. She was a stranger here at Cambaron, and he was no doubt accustomed to Jordan abducting women. It was probably a weekly occurrence.

There was nothing to do but wait until Jordan woke up and sobriety made him see reason. She leaned back on the squabs of the seat. How could he sleep when they were being jounced so hard, her teeth were rattling?

She shivered as a gust of wind blew in the window, piercing the fabric of her thin cotton nightgown. She quickly put on her blue wool robe. Good heavens, she was barefoot, she realized with exasperation. The fool hadn't even let her grab her shoes. Somehow this small inconvenience was the last straw.

She could not wait until he woke.

Jordan did not stir until midafternoon the next day, and by that time she was ready to throttle him.

He took one look at her expression and closed his eyes again. "Oh my God."

"Take me back to Cambaron," she said, enunciating every word through her teeth. "At once."

"Soon," he murmured.

"Soon!" she repeated. "You take me from my bed in the middle of the night. You drag me barefoot and unclothed into this monstrously uncomfortable carriage and then fall into a drunken stupor. I don't have an unbruised portion on my body because you gave orders to the coachman that he must—"

"Be still." His eyes had opened again, and he was glaring at her. "My head aches abominably, and your voice is pecking at it like a vulture."

"Good." She smiled viciously. "And I will continue to peck and rend you until you tell the coachman to turn around and go back."

He shook his head.

"You can't do this. I won't be subject to your drunken whims."

He closed his eyes and leaned his head back against the cushions.

He was paying no attention to her, she realized. She wanted to push him out of the carriage. "Where are you taking me?"

He didn't answer directly. "Soon."

"Why?"

"It seemed a good idea at the time." He opened one eye and regarded her balefully. "Christ, that nightgown is even worse than that other hideous garment Dorothy draped you in."

"Then you should have let me dress."

"I was in a hurry." The eye closed again. "I think."

"*Don't* close your eyes again."

"You will not tell me what to do." His lids opened, and suddenly there was no hint of drunkenness about him. "I have a raging headache, my mouth feels as if I'd slept with my boot in it, and I'm in extreme bad temper. We have a destination, and we aren't turning back until we reach it." His eyes closed. "Now I'm going to go to sleep again. I suggest you do the same."

She stared at him, fuming.

In an incredibly short time she realized he was asleep again.

They stopped twice at posting houses to change horses and refresh themselves but were back on the road in less than an hour each time.

Day became evening.

Evening became night.

Marianna dozed but could not sleep deeply due to the bouncing of the fast-moving carriage along the rutted road.

Jordan appeared to have no such problem. He slept as easily and deeply as a babe in a cradle. She would kill him, she decided. Or at least find a way to punish him horribly at the earliest opportunity.

It was near dawn when she became aware that the carriage was now traveling over cobblestones. She glanced out the window and saw the shadowy form of houses. As the light grew stronger, she could see this was a goodly sized town. "Where are we? London?"

Jordan roused and glanced out the window. "No, but we're right on time." He stretched. "Good man, George."

"Where are we?"

"Soon."

If he said that one more time, she would not wait until they returned to Cambaron to murder him.

The carriage stopped, and George jumped down and opened the door.

Jordan got out and lifted Marianna to the street. The stones felt damp and cool beneath her bare feet.

"Now will you—" Her gaze traveled up the cathedral spire. There could be no mistake. She knew where she was.

"The Minster," she whispered. "Sweet Mary, we're in York."

He nodded. "The Lady Chapel of York Minster, to be exact." He looked at the now fully risen sun. "Come along. It's time."

She took an eager step forward and then looked down at her robe and bare feet. "I'm not dressed. They won't let me in."

"They'll let you in." His lips set grimly. "I'll see to it."

Dazedly, she let him lead her into the dim chapel. She knew what she was going to see. Papa had seen it once, and her mother and grandmother had often talked of making a pilgrimage to view it.

Glory.

She stopped before the Great East Window.

Bold blues and reds and greens.

Sunlight wedded to brilliant color and superb artistry.

The arched window towered seventy-six feet high by thirty-two feet wide. Below the tracery panels of angels, patriarchs, prophets, and saints were twenty-seven panels, each three feet square, of Old Testament scenes, beginning with the first day of Creation and ending with the death of Absalom. Nine rows of panels followed, illustrating eighty-one scenes of dire prophecy from the Apocalypse. In the two bottom rows was the kneeling donor, Bishop Skirlaw of Durham, flanked by English kings, saints, and archbishops.

"It took Robert Coventry three years to create this

window over four hundred years ago." Jordan said. "He was paid the princely sum of fifty-six pounds. Do you think it's worth it?" When she didn't answer, he glanced at her expression and nodded slowly. "I can see you do. So do I."

"It's magnificent," she whispered. "It's everything. . . ."

"I thought you might like it." He smiled. "I can give you until noon to worship at Coventry's altar if I'm to keep my promise to Dorothy."

"Noon?" She shook her head. "I need longer. This is only one window. The Minster has one hundred and thirty."

"I promised Dorothy that—" He stopped as he saw her desperate expression. "Oh, what the devil. Sunset."

She nodded eagerly. "Then I can see the Great West Window properly." She turned back to the East Window and said dreamily, "Do you see how he combined color and grisaille? Isn't that wonderful?"

"Wonderful," he said, smiling indulgently. "I'll speak to the archbishop and see that you're not disturbed."

"I won't be disturbed."

"No, I doubt if anything could disturb you at the moment. I'll go to the nearest inn and see if I can find you shoes and a gown to wear on the journey back to Cambaron."

Coventry had added touches of humor to a few of the panels. Papa had not told her. . . . What had Jordan said? "That would be pleasant."

"Or perhaps you'd prefer to wear sackcloth and ashes?"

The blues were magnificent but, dear heaven, those reds. . . . "Whatever you like."

She was vaguely aware of him shaking his head and then the sound of his receding footsteps.

How had Coventry attained that astonishing shade of red?

Jordan came to the West Window to fetch her when the last light had faded from the sky. He took one look at her feverishly bright eyes and dazed face and led her quietly from the Minster to a nearby inn. She was scarcely aware of him thrusting a bundle of clothes at her.

Blues and reds.

Opaque and clear.

Light.

Above all. Light.

He lifted her into the carriage a short time later and settled himself onto the seat next to her. "I take it you had a successful day?"

"They'll last forever, you know," she said softly.

"They've lasted a long time already."

"You can burn a great painting. You can topple a statue, but those windows were meant to last forever."

"If fools like Nebrov don't meddle with them." He frowned. "Your cheeks are flushed. How do you feel?"

"The light . . ."

"I had George bring a basket of fruit. Can you eat?"

She felt as if she would never eat again. She was full, brimming with hues. "I feel like a pane of glass,

as if you can see through me, and yet I have tex-
tures. . . ." She shook her head. "I feel . . . most
peculiar. Is there something wrong with me?"

He chuckled. "I believe you're drunk."

She shook her head. "I couldn't be. I've had no
wine."

"There are more dangerous forms of drunkenness
than those derived from the grape." He pulled her
against his shoulder. "Rest. I'll be kinder to you in
your infirmity than you were to me in mine."

She stiffened against him. She vaguely remembered
that there was a reason she must resist this intimacy,
but it was hard to recall. She relaxed against him.

He had given her the Minster. He had given her
that wonder.

"Try to go to sleep. I doubt if you did more than
doze on the way here."

"I was very angry with you."

"I know."

"Why did you do this?"

"There's no accounting for the whims of fools or
drunkards."

"It was not a whim."

"If you don't wish to believe it, I certainly won't
insist. I need all available credit for good works to
balance the other side of the scales."

"It . . . was very kind of you."

"You must tell that to Gregor. It might save me
from severe physical punishment."

He would not be serious. Had he done it because
of the window she had crafted of his mother? She had
known he had been moved by it.

Oh, she did not know why he had done such a

wonderful thing for her. It did not matter. He had given her the Minster.

"Did you see the blues?"

"Yes." He stroked her hair. "Though I admit I saw the entire picture and failed to take each facet apart."

"It's hard to do in a work of that detail."

"Was it better than your grandmother's Window to Heaven?"

"No. Grandmother's work is better, but she was never permitted to work on so grand a scale. Seventy-six feet . . ."

"I think you'd better stop thinking about the Minster, or you'll never get to sleep. What happens after the cutline?"

"What?"

"You once told me how you prepared the final sketch for cutting. What comes next?"

She had not thought he had paid any heed to her words that night in the tower. All she could remember was shimmering sensuality and his soft voice in the darkness. There was darkness now also, and his voice was just as soft, but now there was comfort, not danger.

"I cut the pieces of glass with either a grozing iron or a wheel cutter. After that I grind the top colored layer from the glass with powdered stone."

"And then?"

"You don't wish to hear this," she said impatiently. "It can be of no possible interest to you."

"Since I'm to live indefinitely with a hole in my roof, I think I'm entitled to test your knowledge."

He would not know whether she was correct or not. She indulged him anyway. He had given her the Minster. "I attach the pieces of glass to an easel with melted beeswax and paint the lead lines. Then I check for light and flow through the glass." She yawned and realized she was growing drowsy. The excitement of Coventry's work was gradually being dampened by the details of the process itself. "I paint the glass and then apply silver stain to the white glass. I fire the glass in a kiln to set the color and then link the pieces and hold them in place with lead strips and cement."

"And that's what Coventry did?"

"It's what we all do."

"And much more besides." She realized he had guessed she had simplified and left out the more complicated problems and processes. "Will you let me watch you someday?"

A ripple of unease went through her. "No."

"Why not?"

"Because it's mine."

"That's why I want to watch you."

She shook her head and then burrowed against his shoulder. "I wish to go to sleep now."

"You wish to run away now," he corrected. He hesitated and then said ruefully, "Go to sleep. My halo's shining so brightly, I choose not to tarnish it at the moment."

Gregor was waiting with a closed carriage four miles from Cambaron.

He stepped into the road, stopped George with a wave of his huge arms, and opened the carriage door. His gaze raked Marianna's face. "Are you well?"

She nodded, smiling luminously. "I've been to the Minster."

His expression softened. "Dorothy told me. She

was most upset, but at least Jordan had the courtesy to inform someone."

"Did you break down the door?" Jordan asked.

"Of course." He grinned. "As quietly as possible." He lifted Marianna down to the ground. "And that is how we must get Marianna back into the castle. I'll take her ahead and slip her in through the scullery and up the backstairs to her room. You wait here for an hour and then show yourself."

"You've concocted a story for me, no doubt?"

"Southwick. It was unbearably hot, you were drunk, and you decided you wanted to go for a sail on the *Seastorm*. When you woke up, you found yourself halfway up the coast." He shrugged. "Considering your comparative tameness in latter years, it's not entirely believable. But the people who remember you as the Duke of Diamonds will not doubt it."

The Duke of Diamonds. Dorothy had told Marianna something regarding that title. . . . She had no time to think about it; Gregor was propelling her toward the closed carriage.

"You will make sure George keeps silent in the servant hall," he called over his shoulder to Jordan.

"He'll be silent."

"Wait." Marianna stopped and turned to face Jordan. "I thank you."

He shrugged. "There's nothing for which to thank me. I told you it was only a drunken whim." He climbed back into the carriage. "Get her to her room, Gregor. It's going to be very boring waiting here."

She didn't speak for a few minutes after Gregor's carriage had whisked them away. "It wasn't a whim, Gregor."

"Probably not."

"He was very kind to me."

"Yes, he can be kind."

She made a helpless motion with one hand. "I don't understand him."

He didn't answer; he merely reached across and gently patted her hand.

He thought she needed comfort. Well, perhaps she did. She had come closer to Jordan during this journey than she had deemed possible. She had seen him drunk and angry, indulgent and protective.

And he had given her the Minster.

How could she fight him when he did things of that nature?

Yet she must fight him.

She must perfect her craft and make plans on how to accomplish the task her mother had given her. Every day that she gave to Cambaron, she must give an hour to the Jedalar.

It would be the only way that she could keep her feet planted firmly on the ground in this bewildering world ruled by Jordan Draken.

> September 6, 1811
> Lost Coin Inn
> Southwick, England

Nebrov would be pleased.

Marcus Costain tossed the note he had received from Cambaron into the flames of the fireplace and watched as the paper curled and blackened. Of course, the information regarding the girl's growing skill could be faulty. His spy at Cambaron was no judge of such things. Still, she might now be good enough to suit His Grace's purpose, and that was all that was important. Nebrov's correspondence had grown increasingly caustic and impatient of late. Napoleon was looking eastward, and he wanted a bargaining tool.

What did the man expect of him? he thought sourly. These years of waiting had not been pleasant for him either. Nebrov had not wanted him to take any chance of Draken knowing Costain was watching the girl, and he had been forced to rely on reports from a paid informant while sitting in this boring hovel of a seaport. These English had no liking for foreigners and had made his stay as difficult as possible. He would make someone pay for all the indignities he had suffered here.

Thank God, this exile might finally be coming to a close.

He sat down at the table, picked up his pen, and began to write what might be his final report to Nebrov.

CHAPTER 8

January 12, 1812
Cambaron

"Don't put it there!" Marianna rushed across the hall and took the narrow panel away from Gregor, who was striding toward the dining room. "I want it for a wall decoration to complement the flower dome in the ballroom."

"You did not tell me," Gregor said mildly. "You have these panels all over Cambaron." He looked at the panel. "It is very pretty, but I thought you were tired of doing flowers."

She shrugged. "Flowers are fine for a ballroom. They don't mean anything but beauty, and people like to look at them."

"Not like the tiger you did for the window in the hall." Gregor grinned. "I caught a glimpse of it with the sunset behind it the other evening, and I would swear it was going to pounce on me."

"Excellent." Marianna smiled. "Then the work is good. Let's hope the guests tonight will think my dome of flowers is equally realistic." Her smile faded and became wistful. "I almost wish I could be there to see it."

"You see it every day. You've been working on the dome for almost three years."

"It's not the same. I've been imagining how it would be with all the dancers . . . they'd look like flowers themselves swaying beneath it." She knew the dream was impossible. Young girls still in the schoolroom did not attend balls, and she had become resigned to the idea that she remain the eternal child, if Alex was to remain safe from the hurtful gibes. She had been kept away from society as much as possible during these last three years, but she had found Dorothy's and Gregor's assessment of the shallow cruelty of the *ton* more than accurate. Only Dorothy's position and bold intervention had kept the poison from touching them. She tried to smile. "Oh well, you can tell me about it tomorrow." She held up the panel to the light and shook her head. "This won't do. It's not good enough."

"It's very pretty," he protested.

"It's common. I'll use the one I did last month." She raised her voice. "Robert!"

When the young footman came running, she handed him the panel. "Put it in the storeroom in the stable and fetch me the jasmine panel from the tower."

"Jasmine?" he asked in bewilderment.

"The white flowers."

He nodded and set off on the errand at a fast trot.

"You have enough discarded panels in that storeroom to grace every window at Prinny's palace at Brighton," Gregor commented.

She shrugged. "I may use them someday. Are the torches ready?"

"Of course."

"What if it rains?" she asked in sudden panic. "Or snows? It snowed yesterday. Why couldn't it be an afternoon party? The dome would be much lovelier in sunlight."

"Because Jordan invited everyone for a ball tonight," Gregor said patiently.

"And then doesn't even bother to come until the last minute."

"He's been in Sweden for the past two months. He returned to London only two days ago."

Marianna knew that but she did not feel like being reasonable. "I'm surprised he didn't bring the crown prince with him if he found him so entertaining. Or perhaps it was that crown princess Desiree. Dorothy says she's very charming."

"It was the crown prince." His eyes twinkled. "And I don't believe even Aphrodite would keep Jordan in that cold country if he didn't think it necessary."

"If he doesn't like the cold, why tell Dorothy he wants a ball in the middle of winter?"

"Why do you think?"

"How do I know what he is thinking? He comes, he goes. He does exactly what he pleases. He has no—"

"I told him your dome was finished. He wished to honor your work."

She felt the heat in her cheeks as her gaze flew to Gregor's face. "Truly?"

He nodded. "He has great pride in your work."

"He never told me," she whispered.

"Haven't you noticed he has difficulty talking about anything he feels deeply about? Does he not let you have your way in all things to do with Cambaron?"

"Yes." She cleared her throat of the sudden tightness. He was proud of her. She had pleased him. The thought meant too much, and she had to make light of it. "But he came close to missing this fine ball he's giving to honor my work."

"I know you regard it as only a small matter, but he was trying to convince Sweden to repudiate Napoleon and join in the Alliance."

Then it would probably come to pass, she thought. During the past three years she had caught brief glimpses of a Jordan Draken who was entirely different from the man she had met in Montavia and the man who came so rarely to Cambaron. The brilliant, complex man who hopscotched over Europe and manipulated events to suit himself was an enigma to her. Gregor had told her it had been Jordan who had convinced Napoleon's trusted General Barvoir to betray the emperor and come over to the Alliance. He had also hinted that the failure of the banks of Lyons that had almost caused France's economic collapse last year could also be laid at the duke's door. She suppressed a shiver as she thought of the single-minded obsessiveness that would engineer such destruction.

"Why does he hate Napoleon so much?"

Gregor shrugged. "Many people in England hate Napoleon."

He was evading her. "Why does he hate him?" she repeated.

Gregor hesitated and then said, "You are right. Jordan's hatred is entirely personal. He is threatening Jordan's possessions, and that is not permitted."

She frowned, puzzled. "Possessions in Kazan?"

"And here at Cambaron."

"He cares nothing for Cambaron."

"Because he denies any affection? I thought you saw more clearly than to believe him."

Who could see deeply into Jordan when he was always armored? "You are saying he lies."

"I am saying he hates above all things the idea of being chained by affection and so will not admit it even to himself. To Jordan such an admission has always been linked to possession, and he has always regarded that as a danger."

"Why?"

"What he has is his forever. It becomes a passion, an obsession. Jordan knows he must protect Kazan and Cambaron to the death because his nature will let him do nothing less. Napoleon is a threat that *will* be removed." He turned away. "I must ask Dorothy if she needs my help. She is crazed by all these preparations."

She did not want him to leave when she was receiving answers to questions that had tantalized her for years. "Gregor, how is—"

He had already left the room. He always walked away either physically or mentally if he did not wish to answer questions. In truth, perhaps he had told her more this time than she wanted to hear.

The picture he had drawn of Jordan's relentless obsession for protecting his own was chilling. A man who would attempt to topple an empire to bring down one man would not cavil over doing anything to gain his ends.

Gregor had not really told her why Jordan had chosen dead winter for this ball, she remembered with a sense of foreboding, and there had been that odd instant of hesitation in him when she had asked. Gregor may have spoken truth regarding Jordan's pride in her work, but this ball could also mean something else entirely. She had been growing increasingly uneasy this past year. Events were moving too quickly; everyone knew Napoleon was preparing to attack Russia. The clock may have run out for her, and this ball was the final chiming of their period of tranquillity.

Well, she had known this time would come. She had even prepared for it. She should begin to think of leaving Cambaron.

No, not yet. Perhaps there was no need to hurry. Jordan was evidently having extraordinary success in his attempts to undermine Napoleon, and he might not even need the Jedalar to accomplish his purpose. Her work was going well. Alex was happy here.

She was happy here.

She did not want to leave Gregor and Dorothy. She had grown accustomed to this place. Jordan might not have any sentiment for Cambaron, but to her it was now as much home as the cottage where she had been born.

Besides, the stained-glass dome was an accomplishment she wanted to share. She wanted to see Jordan's face when he saw what she had given to Cambaron. After the ball, after Jordan came, she would think about leaving.

After Jordan came.

Come upstairs with me, Gregor." Jordan tossed his hat and riding gloves to a footman and strode toward the steps. "I must dress. If I'm late for this ball, Dorothy will throw me out in the snow."

"Yes, she will." Gregor followed him. "And I will help her. The guests are already arriving. You could have come earlier. It's not kind to—"

"Nebrov is in Poland meeting in secret with Napoleon."

Gregor stopped on the stairs. "You're sure?"

"Janus sent me a message in Stockholm."

"Does he know the content of the meetings?"

"We can guess, can't we? He wants Napoleon to throw him Montavia and Kazan when he marches on Russia. The question being what prize has he got with which to bargain?"

Gregor started up the stairs again. "You think he's found another way to get the Jedalar?"

"I don't know," he said wearily. "I was told that the only one who knew the Jedalar was the craftsman who created it. I don't even know how Nebrov found out about its existence. Maybe he knows something else we don't."

"Or maybe he's merely trying to convince Napoleon what a trusted ally he'd be."

"I told Janus to watch Nebrov and send me word if he learned anything else. I don't want you to let Alex out of your sight for the next few months."

Gregor shook his head. "We've kept close watch. No stranger has come near Cambaron in the past three years without us knowing about it. Nebrov could not know they are here."

"I hope not." He shrugged. "There may be no danger. I just want to be sure we're not taken by surprise."

"We won't be." Gregor opened the door and strode into the bedchamber. "How was Sweden?"

"Cold." He took off his riding coat and threw it on the bed. "And successful. Napoleon will find he no longer has an ally in Sweden. Bernadotte will ally with Russia in case of invasion."

Gregor took his favorite seat in the corner facing the stained-glass window portraying Jordan's mother. "There's no doubt of the invasion, it's only a matter of when, isn't it?"

"Yes." He rang for his valet as he pulled at the folds of his cravat. "And it will be soon." He met Gregor's gaze in the mirror. "We've run out of time. I don't know how long it will take her to create the Jedalar. I can't wait any longer."

Gregor stiffened. "The Alliance could defeat Napoleon without the Jedalar. You said everything was going well."

"Napoleon has the greatest army of his career ready to march on Russia. If Russia falls, then there's a good chance Kazan will also fall. I won't take that chance." He jerked open his shirt. "I'll use any means at my disposal to prevent that from happening. I'll give her one more chance, but I can't afford to be patient any longer."

Gregor was silent and then said quietly, "Do you expect me to argue with you? Kazan must not fall." He stood up and moved toward the door. "But do not hurt her tonight. She has worked for three long years making that dome of flowers, and I've persuaded Dorothy to let her come to the ball to see it. Let her be happy."

The door closed silently behind him, but his words echoed in Jordan's mind.

Do not hurt her tonight.

A picture of Marianna came back to him as he had last seen her four months ago: childlike, innocent, eager.

His fist crashed down on the dressing table.

Goddammit!

Sit still," Dorothy said sternly. "I have to tie this ribbon in your hair."

"Why bother? No one is going to look at me when they can look at my dome." Marianna laughed excitedly. She felt so light and full of joy that she could have floated to the ceiling. "No one is going to look at anyone else. They're just going to dance and stare up at my beautiful windows."

"Then they'll have the most horrendous cricks in their necks. There!" Dorothy took a step back and appraised the white ribbon binding up the silky golden fall of Marianna's hair. "That looks properly Grecian. Now for the gown." She went to the armoire. "White, as is proper for a pure young lady of fashion."

"White, again?" Marianna made a face. "I've worn nothing but white for the past three years."

"This is a different white." She pulled out a simple high-waisted gown with a low, round décolletage. The material was of shimmering beaded silk that appeared more silver than white in the glow of the candles.

"It's beautiful," Marianna breathed. She reached out and tentatively touched the fabric and found it smooth and cool as window glass in winter. "But I've never seen it before."

"Because Madam Bradshaw just finished it yesterday."

Marianna turned to look at Dorothy. "You expected me to attend the ball?"

"Of course," Dorothy said gruffly. "Gregor and I decided it would not be just to keep you from seeing your triumph. Besides, you could not remain fifteen forever. I've already heard a few suspicious comments. It was time you made a few discreet appearances as a young lady." She unbuttoned Marianna's loose gown and let it drop to the floor. "Though I fear we'll have to whisk you away to London or Dorchester after tonight."

"No!" The instinctive rejection revealed just how irresolute had been Marianna's decision to leave Cambaron.

"We'll talk of it tomorrow." Dorothy dropped the beaded gown over Marianna's head. "If you'd consent to use Mary's services, I wouldn't need to play the abigail." She buttoned the back of the gown. "It's most damaging to my consequence."

"I can do it myself. I need no—" She stopped as she caught sight of herself in the cheval mirror. Her eyes widened. "I look . . ."

"Yes, you do." Dorothy sighed. "And I will definitely have to take you to Dorchester tomorrow. No one in their senses would believe Jordan would live in the same house as that woman and not seduce her."

That woman.

She was so accustomed to seeing the image of childhood projected by the loose gowns and braids that when she looked in the mirror, she was surprised to notice how her body had changed, rounded over the years. Her breasts, brimming over the fashionably low neckline, appeared almost voluptuous.

She shied away from the word. Titian's ladies were voluptuous, she was merely a trifle . . . full. "Is the neckline too low?"

"It's quite modest." Dorothy frowned. "I thought." She handed her a pair of long gloves. "Perhaps these will help."

Marianna made a face as she drew on the gloves. "I feel smothered."

Dorothy's gaze was still on the low décolletage. "You don't look smothered." She turned away. "And gloves are entirely de rigueur. You will no longer be permitted out of Cambaron's walls without them."

"Then I shall never leave the castle. I'm much happier in my workroom anyway." She whirled away from the mirror and hugged Dorothy. "Thank you," she whispered. "You and Gregor are so kind. It's such a lovely surprise."

"But you still prefer workrooms to balls."

"Not this ball. This is . . . different."

Dorothy kissed her on the forehead and cleared her throat before proceeding to give her instructions. "You will not dance that shocking new waltz. Even at a country ball that would not be permitted without sanction. You must be all that's shy and retiring. I'll stay by your side all evening, but the way you look tonight even a formidable bear leader like myself may not be sufficient to lend you countenance."

"Bear leader?"

"A spinster without a prayer," Dorothy said ruefully. "Or so I've heard myself described."

A surge of anger tore through Marianna. "If you're a spinster, it's because you choose to be. You're fine and beautiful, and you have a mind that half those men in the ballroom tonight would envy. They should not—"

"Hush." Dorothy's hand covered Marianna's lips. "I'm not embittered. I accept that men do not find me attractive. It's partially my own fault. I could have made a fine marriage. I have a respectable competence, and it would be considered a great coup for any man to be connected with the duke of Cambaron. I chose the path of strength, and gentlemen prefer women to be weak and accommodating. I could not bear it." She took a vial of perfume and dabbed a few drops on the pulse in Marianna's throat. "Roses. Isn't the scent fitting for your flower dome?"

"Very fitting."

"Now, smile, or I shall not let you go down and see their faces as they view your work."

Marianna's spirits rose as she thought of that wonderful prospect. She whirled toward the door. "I'll meet you on the landing. I have to show Alex how fine I look." She smiled over her shoulder. "He won't believe it's me!"

Men and women in elegant apparel crowded the hall, and Marianna could hear the strains of music from the ballroom.

"Slowly," Dorothy said as they started down the steps. "Let them see you."

"I don't want them to see me. I want them to see the windows."

"And I want them to see you. You're my handiwork and should be properly appreciated."

Marianna caught sight of Jordan just inside the

open doors of the study across the hall. He was smiling down at Lady Carlisle. Now, she was as voluptuous as even Titian could have desired, Marianna thought with a familiar flicker of annoyance. The well-endowed Catherine Carlisle was only the latest in a seemingly endless parade of women in Jordan's life. Marianna could not remember how many had succeeded the beautiful countess of Ralbon in Jordan's bed.

Yes, she could. She could remember every one. There was that enchanting red-haired Carolyn Dumark and then Helen Jakbar and then Elizabeth Van—

Jordan closed the doors of the study.

"Stop frowning," Dorothy admonished.

"Is that also forbidden by the *ton*?" But Dorothy was right. What did she care if Jordan chose to indulge his carnal appetites with that woman? This was a night for joy, and she would not allow anything or anyone to spoil it. "I don't see Gregor."

"He was going to supervise the lighting of the torches."

"I should be doing that."

"Not in that gown. Climbing around rooftops is definitely not acceptable behavior."

Marianna frowned uneasily. "They're looking at me."

"They certainly are. Perhaps a bit too much." Dorothy paused at the bottom of the steps before taking Marianna's elbow and nudging her toward the ballroom. "Come along. You're better off lost in the crush." She searched the throng and finally made a selection. "There's Sir Timothy Sheridan. You might find him companionable. He dabbles in poetry like your father, and he's certainly a safe partner for the dance. He'll only want to write a poem about your eyes and hair."

"What?" Marianna scarcely heard the words; her enraptured gaze was on the domed-glass ceiling in the center of the room. The circle of torches Gregor had lit outside around the dome made the flowers and vines blaze with color. Purple lilacs and ivory gardenias vied with the blazing orange-red of hibiscus. Dark green vines intertwined, separating and displaying the flowers. In each of the four corners peacocks with splendid turquoise and cobalt plumage pranced majestically among the blossoms.

"I did it," she whispered. "I did well, didn't I?"

"You did very well. It's beautiful," Dorothy said gently. "Now come and let me introduce you to Sir Timothy."

Dazed, Marianna let her lead her across the room to a fair-haired young man in the corner. The flowers above them cast exotic shadows on the gleaming floor as the dancers moved gracefully in the steps of the cotillion. The sight was everything Marianna had hoped it would be.

She cast a glance over her shoulder at the closed door of the study. Not quite everything. It would do no harm for him to leave that woman and come and tell her that her dome was every bit as good as she knew it to be.

Come, Jordan!" Dorothy threw open the door and marched into the study. She stared intimidatingly at Catherine Carlisle, who hurriedly moved away from the duke. "You will excuse him, I know. He has many demands on his time tonight."

It was clear to Jordan that Catherine was not pleased but chose not to engage Dorothy. Instead, she concentrated her efforts on him. "Of course." She smiled sweetly at Jordan. "You will return soon, Your Grace?"

Dorothy whisked Jordan away before he could answer.

"And what have I done now?" Jordan asked as he straightened his cravat. "As usual, it's clear you're displeased with me."

"Besides behaving in your usual shocking fashion and staying half the evening alone in that study with that bovine creature, you've done nothing at all," she hissed, a smile pasted on her face. "You may go back and continue your disgusting pursuit of that demimondaine . . . after you tell Marianna you like what she's done."

He didn't look at her. "I don't have to tell her. Everyone is singing paeans of praise."

"Then tell her. She has a right to hear it from you. Why have you been avoiding her?"

"Don't pick at me, Dorothy," he said quietly. "It's not safe tonight."

"Fustian. I will not have tonight less than perfect for Marianna."

"So I'm to add my praises to those of the mob. Very well, where is she?"

She nodded across the room. "With young Sheridan. He's quite taken with her."

He glanced at the corner she had indicated, but there were too many people blocking his vision. "He has a passion for infants?"

"Infant?" She looked at him in surprise. "That's right, you've not seen her tonight, have you?"

He had been careful not to seek out Marianna. He didn't want to look at her or talk to her. He had wanted to lose himself and forget her existence, but Dorothy had foiled that plan.

Don't hurt her tonight.

He felt something twist inside him. Well, so much for Gregor's injunction. He had made the attempt, but Fate appeared to be against him. He might as well get on with the business. He started across the room. "You want me to pay my respects?" he said roughly. "Then let's get it over with. Though I don't see why you think I—" His stride faltered as he caught sight of Marianna.

A promise fulfilled, beautifully, sensually fulfilled.

"Infant?" Dorothy murmured.

Christ, it was as if these last three years had never happened. He was back in the tower room, watching her, wanting her. Relief streamed through him as he felt himself harden, ready. Yes, this was the response he needed. Lust was savage, mindless, without pity. If he let it take control, then he could do anything he had to. Any tenderness and softness would be submerged.

As it *must* be submerged.

"Jordan," Dorothy said warningly.

"Be quiet, Dorothy." He smiled recklessly. "I'm only doing what you wanted me to do."

"I didn't think— You haven't been—"

"You mean I've been as tame as Alex's pony so long you thought I was ready to be turned out to pasture. Perhaps I'm weary of doing tricks." His gaze went to young Sheridan. "But judging by the way that presumptuous puppy is staring at Marianna, he might be willing to perform for her." His mouth tightened. "I don't believe I care for his manner toward my ward. Make an excuse and take him away."

"I will do nothing of the sort."

"You will." He shot her a glittering glance. "Or I may decide to call him out."

"You don't mean it," Dorothy said, horrified. "He would have no chance with you."

"Then take him away." The bastard was staring at her breasts as if he would like to free them, lift them in his palms, and then bring his mouth—Jordan could almost taste the softness, feel the peaking of nipples beneath his tongue. He could no longer identify Sheridan's desire from his own. "Quickly," he said, between his teeth.

"I won't leave you alone with her. Do you want to ruin everything I've worked for?"

"We're not alone. I believe you said there would be at least two hundred guests here tonight."

Marianna had seen him. She stopped in mid-sentence and smiled tentatively at him.

My God, she was exquisite.

"Jordan, you brought me here to protect her," Dorothy said desperately.

"And you've done very well, but it's over now."

"What's happened?"

"Don't meddle with something you don't understand. Just accept that the situation has altered."

"I would understand, if you explained. I have a true affection for the child and—"

"It appears she's no longer a child."

"Jordan, you've been very kind to her. I even thought— Blast you, why have you changed?"

He didn't answer as he crossed the few yards. Then he took Marianna's gloved hand and brought it to his lips. "A triumph, Marianna."

The color flew to her cheeks. "You like it?"

"A triumph," he repeated with perfect sincerity. "My ballroom will be the envy of every hostess in England. I couldn't be more pleased or more impressed by your skill." He nodded carelessly to Sheridan. "How do you do, Sheridan? I believe my cousin has a favor to ask of you. Something to do with arranging transport home for a few of the guests . . ." He trailed off and turned to Dorothy. "I'm sure Sir Timothy will be all that's accommodating."

Sheridan looked uncertainly at Dorothy. "Of course, I'm at your service, ma'am."

Dorothy's lips thinned. "*You're* a true gentleman, sir." She turned on her heel and stalked through the crowd with Sheridan scurrying after her.

Marianna said, "She's angry with you. Why?"

"I'm not fulfilling expectations. Or perhaps I am. It's all how one perceives the situation." He held out his hand. "May I have the honor of this dance?"

She took an eager step forward and then shook her head. "It's a waltz. Dorothy says I mustn't dance the waltz."

"It's forbidden? Don't you tire of doing what Dorothy and Gregor tell you to do?"

"No. Yes." She stared at him, puzzled. "You've always wanted me to do what they tell me to do. You're confusing me."

"I'm merely asking you to dance." He held out his

hand again. "Don't you want to waltz beneath your splendid dome?"

"Yes." Her eyes were bright, and her smile was suddenly as reckless as his own. "Oh, yes." She put her hand in his. His hand cradled her waist, and he swung her out onto the floor.

She felt as if she were flying, swooping, held tight to the earth only by Jordan's hand at her waist. Yes, this was right, this was what she had wanted. To let Jordan take her on this magical journey, to fly, to spin, to share. It made the evening perfect, complete. She tilted her head back and stared up at the glass above her.

Flaming torches.

Light against darkness.

Shimmering color and beauty swimming in dizzying circles.

"Stop it," Jordan said.

"What?"

"I said, stop it. Look at me."

She did so, and she experienced a tiny shock that jarred her from the euphoric spell. His green eyes were glittering, narrowed on her face. Recklessness. Sensuality. Mockery.

She had been so happy when she had seen him coming toward her that she had barely noticed his change in demeanor.

He smiled. "Looking at me may not be as satisfying, but I can't tolerate being ignored for glass and paint. Have I mentioned that besides being atrociously spoiled, I also have a tendency to be intensely jealous?"

She shook her head. "That's not so."

His brows lifted. "No?"

"You're not jealous at all. I've watched you with—" She stopped. She didn't really want him to be aware of how closely she'd monitored his liaisons with those women. Then she realized she didn't have to admit it. He had never made mention of it, but he had known.

"I've watched you too," he said quietly.

She experienced a queer sense of nakedness, as if all the fragile barriers between them were tumbling down. She hurriedly looked back at the ceiling. "You don't care enough about anything or anyone to be jealous."

"Then why did I tell Dorothy to take young Sheridan away or I would put a hole in his handsome head?"

Her eyes swung back to him in shock. "You're joking."

"Dorothy didn't think it was amusing. It came as a surprise to me too." He swung her in a wide, swooping circle. "But what is between us has never been guided by ordinary rules, has it? Just when we become accustomed to one set, the game changes."

She couldn't seem to look away. "And has it changed?"

"Yes." His gaze moved to the nakedness of her upper breasts. "Thank God. I was beginning to feel like a eunuch."

She felt a sudden tingling and swelling as if his hands were stroking her. She swallowed. "Dorothy would say that remark was most indelicate." She suddenly burst out, "And to my knowledge a eunuch does not require a harem such as yours."

For an instant the mockery in his expression changed, and she thought he was going to smile. Then the hint of softness vanished. "I told you I'd seek consolation. If you'd been ready to take me three years ago, a harem wouldn't have been necessary." He smiled. "Come to me tonight, and I promise I'll rid myself of any entanglements."

She inhaled sharply as she felt the muscles of her stomach clench. "I *hate* this. Why are you being so— It's this stupid gown, isn't it? I wish I'd never worn it."

"And I wish you'd worn it sooner. It clarifies the situation. But we both know the gown isn't the cause. We would have come to this anyway."

"I don't know any such thing. I was happy here. I thought—" She was not certain what she had thought, but it certainly wasn't that she would be thrown into this sudden turmoil of feeling. "I felt safe."

An indefinable emotion flickered in his expression. "I never promised you safety. Not unless you gave me what I needed."

She stiffened as she realized his last words held no sensuality, only a harsh determination that transported her back to that night by the campfire in Montavia.

Mother of God, what a fool she was. She had been so contented, she had blissfully ignored the faint stirrings of apprehension she had experienced this afternoon. She whispered, "The Jedalar. That's what this is about, isn't it? You think I can give you the Jedalar now."

He glanced at the dome above them. "You've become an exceptional craftsman."

Hurt twisted within her. "I told you I wouldn't give it to you. Not ever."

"I have to have it, Marianna. I've delayed as long as I can. I knew you had the skill to create the Jedalar over a year ago. I hoped I wouldn't have to ask it of you."

Tears stung her eyes, and she fought them back. "Did you think because you've cared for Alex and me all this time that I'd soften and give it to you? I owe you nothing. I've taken this dark place and given it back to you full of light and color."

"Yes, you have." He looked into her eyes and said roughly, "And I don't want you soft. I want you strong. I want you to fight me and make me fight you. You *have* to fight me."

"I will." Her voice was unsteady. "Please, let me go. I don't want to be here anymore."

"When the music ends. We have to talk."

"Now!" She could bear no more. She broke away from him and hurried across the room. She heard the rustle of whispers among the dancers. She had probably ruined herself in their eyes. What did she care about them? All that mattered was that, to her profound relief, he wasn't pursuing her.

She almost collided with Gregor as she ran through the doorway.

"Marianna."

He looked so troubled, she tried to smile. "The torches were beautiful. Everything was beautiful, Gregor."

"Give him the Jedalar," he said in a low voice. "He does not want to hurt you, but he will. He will break you any way he can, and I cannot help you now. Give it to him."

Her smile vanished as a wave of overwhelming desolation swept through her. She was alone. Gregor, whom she had thought her friend, had abandoned her.

She pushed past him and ran up the stairs.

Gregor turned and stood waiting as Jordan strode across the ballroom toward him.

"She's gone upstairs?" Jordan asked as soon as he reached him.

Gregor nodded. "There's no use following her. I am sure she won't answer the door. You frightened her."

He had frightened her, Jordan thought, but he had also hurt her, and that was much worse. "I want you to take Alex and leave the castle tonight, at once. Go to Southwick to the *Seastorm* and take it down the coast."

"To what destination?"

"No destination. Just show the lad a fine time."

"For how long?"

He shrugged. "A few days. Then bring him back to Cambaron."

His gaze searched Jordan's face, and then he stated, "But Marianna will not be here when we return."

"No, I'm taking her to Dalwynd."

Gregor smiled sadly. "No doubt to find a way to convince her to give you the Jedalar?"

Jordan looked at the stairs. "What do you want me to say? That I'm going to keep up this ridiculous farce? It's gone on too long. Your dove is no longer a child, she's a woman. Yes, I want the Jedalar. Yes, I want her in my bed. If I can find a way to get both at

Dalwynd, I'll do it. But I assure you, I most certainly will have her before you see her again." He smiled fiercely. "And there's nothing in heaven or hell you can do to stop me this time."

"I know. At last, you have found an excuse to take what you want. It is very sad. There will be much pain for both of you."

"Then so be it. Send word to me at Dalwynd if you hear anything from Janus."

Gregor nodded gloomily and started up the stairs. "I will go and get the boy."

Marianna closed the door of her room and tore off the long gloves with shaking hands. She removed the beaded gown and thrust it far back in the armoire. She never wanted to see that beautiful garment again. She quickly slipped on the loose gown she had discarded earlier in the evening, snatched up a shawl, and ran from the room. She tore up the long, winding staircase to the tower room.

She skidded to a stop just inside the door.

Jordan sat at her worktable, his legs stretched out before him. "We didn't finish our conversation." The candle on the table cast flickering shadows on the long planes of his face. "I thought you'd come here. I frightened you, and it's the only place you feel safe, isn't it?"

She turned and took a step toward the door.

"I'm taking you away tomorrow."

She whirled back to face him. "No!"

"Not far. We're going to my hunting lodge, Dalwynd, just ten miles to the south."

"Why?"

"Because you've inspired a good deal of affection among my people here. I prefer to have you in a place where you're likely to be more amenable to persuasion." He glanced around the tower room. "And where you don't feel safe."

"I won't go with you. I've already decided to take Alex and go to Dorchester with Dorothy."

He shook his head. "Alex has already started on a journey of his own."

She stared at him in disbelief. "Alex is in his bed asleep."

"He was until Gregor woke him and told him of the great adventure he was taking him on."

Alex! Panic tore through her. She jerked open the door and flew down to Alex's room.

Gone!

She stared down at the rumpled covers of the bed, her stomach churning.

"He will be quite safe as long as you do as I wish," Jordan said from behind her.

She crossed her arms over her chest to keep them from trembling. "Gregor would never hurt Alex. He's only a child."

"But he knows many of Kazan's children will die unless we find a way of protecting them. When it comes to choosing who is to receive his protection, he will choose Kazan."

Gregor's words came back to her. *I cannot help you. Give him the Jedalar.*

"He won't hurt Alex," she said stubbornly.

"Perhaps not, but he won't give your brother back to you either." He met her gaze. "I promise you won't see Alex again until I have the Jedalar. You'll never know if he's safe or not."

She stared at him. His expression was absolutely relentless. "You're a terrible man," she whispered.

He smiled crookedly. "It's entirely possible." He turned to leave. "Be ready to leave at first light. I know you won't want to distress Dorothy any more than necessary by needless farewells."

It was all a nightmare. It seemed impossible that she had been so happy earlier in the evening when her life was now in such chaos.

"It doesn't have to be this way." She turned to see him standing in the doorway watching her. "I must be a little mad, but I'm driven to give you one more chance to change your mind. Promise to give the Jedalar to me, Marianna, and you'll have Alex back by tomorrow evening. Everything will return to the way it was."

Nothing could ever be the way it was. Everything had changed. Was her promise to Mama worth this risk to Alex? What did she care if a dozen nations were destroyed, if Alex was safe? But was there a risk to Alex? She couldn't believe that either Gregor or Jordan would hurt him, so the risk was really to Marianna. Alex was the only person on earth who really belonged to her, and Jordan would keep his promise to deprive her of Alex. After years of being more mother than sister to him, the threat was enough to terrify her.

She couldn't break her word to Mama without a battle. After all, it was only a matter of finding out where Gregor was keeping Alex and getting him back.

She said coldly, "I regret to disappoint you, but I won't give you any such promise."

"Oh, you're not disappointing me. On the con-

trary, after years of restraint, it will be a relief to indulge the sinful nature Gregor swears I've overcome."
He smiled. "It was a last opportunity for me as well. I
can't tell you how glad I am that you saved me from
it."

CHAPTER 9

Dalwynd came into view just after noon of the next day. The large thatch-roofed stone hunting lodge was located beside a small lake that was covered by ice and surrounded by pine trees.

Jordan slipped from his horse as soon as they reached the stable yard and then lifted Marianna from her mare. He released her at once and strode toward the door. "Mind the ice on the step."

His manner was careless, almost impersonal, as it had been since they had left Cambaron at dawn that morning. She slowly followed him into the lodge, entering a huge square room with several doors opening off it. A gleaming oak staircase with elaborately carved banisters and side pickets led to the upper story and a long hall that overlooked the lower parlor.

"I think you'll be comfortable." Jordan took off his hat and gloves and tossed them on an inlaid marquetry table just inside the door. "It's a bit chilly in here. I'll start a fire."

He was treating her with the politeness he would

have shown an honored guest, she realized with annoyance.

He crossed the room and knelt before the huge stone fireplace. "We'll have no servants while we're here. You'll have to rely on my humble self to care for your needs. I live very simply while I'm at Dalwynd, but that should be no problem for you. You've always complained Cambaron was too big."

She glanced around her at the "simple" parlor. A long table that would have seated twenty occupied the center of the room. Silver pitchers and crystal decanters gleamed on the intricately engraved sideboard resting against the far wall. Over the fireplace a tapestry in shades of greens and ivory depicted a spear-wielding Diana hunting a boar.

Jordan's gaze followed Marianna's to the tapestry. "My father purchased that atrocious object. He was always attracted to women who had an element of ferocity. I thought it strange because he was completely unable to match them in spirit and eventually grew to detest them." He struck flint, and the kindling flared. "You should know I've arranged to have two men quartered at the stable to care for the horses and lay fires and such." He paused. "With instructions that you not be permitted to leave the premises."

"I'm surprised you didn't just throw me into the dungeon at Cambaron," Marianna said bitterly.

"I'd never be so insensitive. You appeared to have a certain apprehension about it when we first discussed it. Besides, dungeons are no longer fashionable. Hunting boxes are all the thing these days." He rose and moved toward her. "It will be warm soon. Take off your cloak."

She didn't move.

"Take off your cloak," he repeated softly as his fingers undid the button at her throat. She shivered as his thumb brushed the sensitive cord of her neck. "It's not a barrier that can't be overcome." He slid the cloak off her shoulders and threw it on the wing chair by the fire. His gaze moved over the riding habit that was as loose and childlike as the rest of the clothes in her wardrobe. "And neither is that detestable garment. It's merely annoying."

"I intend to be as annoying as possible until you give Alex back to me." She added in exasperation, "This is all nonsense. I don't know what you hope to gain by bringing me here."

"I hope to persuade you to be sensible."

"What you deem sensible. You haven't been able to accomplish that in the last three years."

"Because Gregor took pity on the dove, and I found his pity a dreadfully contagious disease." He stepped forward and untied the ribbon that bound one of her braids. "But I'm over it now. Patience and the milk of human kindness are obviously of no avail. I can't do any worse than I— Stand still. I've always hated these braids." He untied the other braid. "That's better." His fingers combed through her hair. "Much better. I don't want to see it braided again while we're here."

The act was blatantly intimate, and her loosened hair felt heavy and sensuous as it lay against her back. He was not touching her with anything but his hands in her hair, but she could feel the heat of his body and smell the familiar scent of leather and clean linen that always clung to him. With every breath she drew she had the odd sensation he was entering her, pervading her. She hurriedly took a step back and asked, "Where am I to sleep?"

He smiled. "Wherever you wish to sleep." A burgundy-rich sensuality colored his voice.

"Then I wish to sleep in Dorothy's house in Dorchester."

He shook his head. "Not possible." He indicated the staircase. "There are four bedchambers. Choose which one you like. I usually occupy the one at the end of the hall."

She stared at him uncertainly.

"Did you think I was going to force you? I'm sorry to rob you of your first battle, but I have no taste for rape. I'm only furnishing a setting where we'll be close, very close. I'll let Fate and Nature do the rest." He nodded to a door leading off the parlor. "Your workroom. I've furnished it with tools and glass and paint."

"So that I can make you a Window to Heaven?" She smiled scornfully. "What are you going to do? Stand over me with a whip?"

"Whips aren't the thing either. I wanted you to have something to amuse you. I knew you were accustomed to working, and I thought it would please you."

She crossed the parlor and threw open the door to reveal a low-ceilinged room with exposed oak beams. She assumed the dark green velvet drapes covered a window. The room was not at all like her workroom in the tower.

But a long table occupied the center of the room and on that table were glass and tools and paints.

Relief soared through her, alleviating a little of the

tension that had plagued her since they had left Cambaron.

Salvation. She could work.

"And you, in turn, will amuse me." He gestured to the large, thronelike high-backed chair in the far corner. "I know you were reluctant three years ago to let me watch you at your craft, but circumstances have changed."

"Nothing has changed." She strode over to the window and jerked back the curtains to let light pour into the room, then went to the table and examined the tools. "I'll ignore you now, as I would have then."

"You wouldn't have ignored me," he said softly. "If I hadn't been a soft fool, you would have been in my bed before a week had passed. Perhaps that very night."

She whirled on him. "No!"

"Yes."

"You would have forced me?"

"No force would have been necessary."

Heat flooded her cheeks. "I'm not Lady Carlisle or that— I'm not like them."

"No, you're not like them. You're far more alive, and that's where both temptation and pleasure lie. From the beginning you've known what's between us as well as I have." He looked into her eyes. "You want me as much as I want you."

His tone was without a hint of doubt, and his certainty sent a jab of sharp uneasiness through her. "It's not true," she whispered.

"It *is* true." His tone roughened. "Every time I was with another woman, I wanted it to be you. Sometimes I pretended it was you. Wasn't it the same with you? Didn't you ever wonder what it would be like to—"

"No!"

"I think you did. Perhaps you didn't admit it to yourself, but weren't there moments when you woke in the middle of the night, and you would catch yourself—"

"I told you, no." She moistened her lips. "And I suppose you think if you seduce me, I'll be as weak as those other women and give you the Jedalar."

"It would simplify matters enormously. Perhaps I even told myself seduction might be a tool of persuasion. Gregor would say I have a tendency to lie to myself to justify taking what I want." He smiled crookedly. "But you would have come to my bed whether or not there was a chance of convincing you to give me the Jedalar. I couldn't have waited any longer. It was like kindling a fire and deliberately keeping it too low to warm you. I've grown damned cold in the last three years."

He turned on his heel and strode out of the room.

It was a lie. She didn't want him in the way those other women did. It was true he had always exerted a fascination for her, but that didn't mean she was—

She would not think about it.

She crossed to the window and stared out at the stable yard. Jordan was undoing the saddlebags on the packhorse, and as she watched, he turned and spoke to one of the men standing in the deep shadow of the stable. The man hurried forward to help, but Jordan waved him away. His dark hair shone in the cold winter sunlight, and his face was lit by the faint smile that was so familiar. She knew his body as well as his face, the lean, loose-limbed grace, the deceptively lazy way he moved.

But she did not know it the way Catherine Carlisle did.

She did not want to know it in that way, she thought desperately. Yet why had there been those times when she had awakened in the middle of the night with those shockingly sensual visions? How terrible that he had guessed that sinful weakness. It made her feel as if she had no place to hide.

Well, she must be stronger than she'd been in the past and distance herself from him. If she did not show him weakness, then he would see that bringing her here would gain him nothing.

You've been in that bedchamber all afternoon," Jordan called through the bedroom door. "Come out and have your supper."

"I'm not hungry. I'm going to go to bed."

"You will eat," he said pleasantly. "If you prefer, I'd be delighted to bring in your meal and serve it to you in bed."

She opened the door.

She had seldom seen him garbed so informally. He was without a coat or cravat, dressed only in Hessian boots, a loose white shirt, and black buckskin breeches that clung to his hips, thighs, and calves.

"What a disappointment. I thought I was to receive an unexpected gift." He gestured for her to proceed him. "Instead, I suppose we'll have supper before the fire while we talk."

"We've already talked. I see no reason for further discussion."

"No, that was merely a breaking of the proverbial ice." He followed her down the steps. "I find seduction is impossible without speech. Now, I realize what a handsome rascal I am, but it's my eloquence that always carries the day." He seated her at the table and sat down across from her. "I cooked this delicious repast myself. I know you'll want to sample the results of my labors. Eat."

She picked up the spoon, dipped it into the venison stew and tasted it. It was very good.

He was looking at her expectantly.

"It has too much salt."

"Zounds!" He clutched his chest with both hands as if he had received a mortal blow. "An arrow in the heart." He shrugged. "Or perhaps only in my self-love."

Incredibly, a smile tugged at her lips before she could stifle it. She had seen that playful mockery in a hundred different situations over the years and had responded without thinking. It was clear habit was going to be an insidious enemy.

"Ah, you see." He smiled at her. "Your situation is not so frightening. I'm still the same man. You're merely seeing another side of me."

"I'm not frightened."

He ignored her protest. "You were frightened when you came to Cambaron, but now I think you have a fondness for it. To conquer fear, it's only necessary to become familiar with the beast."

"What an apt description," she said coolly.

He chuckled with genuine amusement. "It is, isn't it? Gregor claims my soul is part beast, part angel, and has been trying to shift the balance for years." His smile faded. "He's wrong about the angel, but I guarantee you'll find the beast quite interesting. You have only to stroke him, and he'll come and lay his head on your lap."

Her gaze instinctively went to his thick dark hair, which was tied back in a queue. She had seen his hair loose about his shoulders but had never touched it. She quickly looked down at her stew. "That reminds me of a tale my father once told me about a maiden and a unicorn. When that beast put his head in the maiden's lap"—she took a spoonful of stew—"he got his horn chopped off."

He stared at her in astonishment and then threw back his head and laughed uproariously. "Lord, what a delight you are. It's clear I shall have to be exceptionally careful of my 'horn.' "

She flushed. "I didn't mean—"

"Don't spoil it by remembering all of Dorothy's rules and strictures. For a moment you were the girl I knew on the *Seastorm*."

"Dorothy's rules were meant to keep me safe from the beasts that roam the world."

"Touché. Hoist by my own petard." He picked up his spoon. "I believe I'd best have nourishment before the next engagement."

She was relieved that he had fallen silent. She was finding that the distance she had sworn to keep between them persisted in shrinking, the past blurring with the present. She had always found matching wits with him exhilarating, and there had been something darker, more exciting, in the exchange tonight.

The silence lasted until she broke it herself. She put down her spoon and said formally, "I've finished my meal. May I go to my room now?"

"No." He smiled as he saw her jaw set mutinously.

"You may work all day, but the hours between dark and time to retire are mine. You can talk or be silent as you wish, but you won't leave me." He gestured to a green and ivory patterned Chippendale wing chair beside the hearth. "However, you'll find that chair is far more comfortable."

It also had the advantage of being across the room from him. She jumped up from the table and quickly moved to the hearth. Then she sat down in the chair he had indicated, her spine straight, her hands clasped on her lap.

The amusement in his smile annoyed her. "This is foolishness. I can't just sit here and look at you," she said in exasperation.

"I realize it's a terrible burden. But I find it infinitely pleasant looking at you." He grimaced. "Even in that hideous garment." He stood up and moved toward her.

She stiffened warily, but he dropped down on the hearth a few feet away and linked his hands over his knees. The movement pulled the buckskin even closer over his thighs, delineating every muscle.

She quickly shifted her attention to the fire. "I want you to tell me where you've taken Alex."

"Somewhere safe."

"You have no right to do this to—"

"I don't wish to talk about Alex." His voice was lazy as he leaned his chin on his knees. "I want to tell you what you can expect of me."

"I can expect arrogance and a complete lack of humanity."

"Oh, I'm very human. I'm not used to virgins, but I'll try to be gentle the first time. It won't be easy. I've wanted you too long."

Heat flooded her cheeks as her gaze flew back to his face. His expression was impassive and his tone almost casual, as if the act were a forgone fact.

"After you become accustomed to me, there are things I can teach you, ways that will increase both our pleasure." He smiled. "I was steeped in decadence from the time I was a lad, and you might as well benefit. For instance, do you know how sensitive a woman's breasts can be? How cold and heat can bring pleasure or restraint? How a strange and different position can bring a pleasure so intense, it will cause you to cry out?"

She swallowed. "You know I don't. I don't wish to know such things."

"Because you've never experienced them," he said softly. "What if I told you that what you feel when you're working is nothing in comparison, that it can be every color, every texture that you can imagine."

"I wouldn't believe you."

"Then I'll have to convince you, won't I?" He leaned back against the stone fireplace, his lids half-closed, his lips curved with sensuality. "I'd like to show you, but you're not ready for that yet. Instead, I'll tell you what to expect." His tone suddenly sharpened. "No, sit back down. If have to touch you, I won't be able to control myself."

He was tensed, an animal about to spring. She was suddenly aware that his outward laziness was masking a tension that held an element of violence.

She slowly sat back down in the chair.

The tension gradually ebbed out of him. He leaned back again. "I've imagined how we'd come together a thousand times, in a thousand different ways. I even dreamed about them. The one that nearly drove me mad involved the chair."

She stared at him, unable to look away.

"Do you remember the cushioned chair I was going to have brought to the tower room?" He nodded toward the door across the room. "It was going to be exactly like that one in the workroom here. Big, high-backed, strongly built, with wide arms. I could see myself sitting in it, watching you as you worked, watching the way your hands moved, caressed the glass. Your hair is hanging down your back as it is now, and I want to jerk you to your knees and bury my hands in it." His voice became hoarser. "I'm hurting, I'm in a fever to touch you. I want your hands around me, to caress me as they do the glass." He closed his eyes. "But I can't move. I have to sit in the chair and wait for you to come to me."

Her breasts were lifting and falling with every breath. Dear God, she could see that scene as if it were before her.

"The wind is cold blowing in the windows, but I don't feel it. I'm *willing* you to look at me. Finally, you do. You turn and you see the expression on my face and you know.

"You're afraid, at first, but then you turn away from the table. You walk slowly across the room and stand before me. You reach and touch my mouth with your fingers." He opened his eyes, but she knew he wasn't seeing her, he was seeing the woman in the tower. "I can't wait for you to take off your gown. My hands are in your hair, pulling you down on me. I'm inside you and your legs are over the arms of the chair and I hear you gasp." His hands clenched into fists. "You're small, but you take all of me, and your hands are on my shoulders and your nails are—"

"Stop it." Her voice was strangled. "I won't hear any more."

He drew a deep, shuddering breath. It was a moment before he spoke again. He said in low voice, "I'll be sitting in that chair tomorrow, watching you work."

A wave of heat scorched through her. She felt as if even the tips of her fingers were burning. "I'll pay no attention to you. I won't even realize you're there."

"Then it will be exactly like my dream, won't it?" He smiled. "And perhaps you'll look up and see me and know I'm waiting for you."

She shook her head and jumped to her feet. "I won't stay here any longer. I'm going to my room."

He nodded. "That would probably be best. I find I have even less restraint than I thought. Perhaps we'll have a longer time together tomorrow evening."

She moved quickly toward the stairs.

"Do you remember the legend of Scheherazade?" he called after her. "She told the caliph a tale each night for a thousand and one nights. Shall we see how many of my dreams I can recall for you?"

She didn't answer. She felt as if she were on fire. She had to get away from him.

"Tomorrow night I believe I'll tell you about the stallion and the mare. We're in the south pasture watching them, and you turn to me. . . ." He chuckled. "But that's another story."

"I don't want to hear it."

"Not even a little bit? Admit you're curious."

She was curious, she realized with a sense of panic. His words held a raw power and fascination, the picture he had painted had stirred, mesmerized her and made her feel— Sweet heaven, perhaps he was right. Perhaps she was as lost to lust as he was.

She looked down at him from the landing. Catlike, sensual, he hadn't moved from his relaxed position on the hearth. Firelight lit the planes of his lean, irregular, face, revealing strength and a beauty where there should have been no beauty.

"Pleasant dreams, Marianna," he said softly.

T he chair!

She woke gasping, her heart pounding.

Her breasts were swollen, the tips sensitive as they brushed the coverlet.

She was shaking uncontrollably, and there was a strange ache between her thighs.

Jordan sitting watching her, his hands on the wide arms of the chair.

Hunger. Heat. Emptiness.

She hadn't really gone to him. It hadn't happened. It had only been a dream, an erotic reflection of the story Jordan had told her.

The chair . . .

Y our hands are shaking," Jordan observed. He shifted in the chair and slung one leg over the arm. "Be careful you don't cut yourself."

"I won't cut myself." She glanced away from him as she carefully cut a petal-shaped piece of glass. "If you'll stop talking and disturbing me."

"You have circles beneath your eyes. Did you have trouble sleeping?"

"No."

"I did. I didn't sleep at all. I thought about you lying in your bed down the hall just a few yards away. It was most disturbing." From the corner of her eye she saw him begin to swing his foot. "To entertain myself, I started thinking about stained glass and the interesting things you could do with it."

"I've been fully aware of those things for a number of years."

"But you haven't explored all the possibilities. I'll tell you what I have planned, if you like."

"I do not like."

"Well, it could be a little advanced for you. Later, perhaps. The stallion and the mare will be interesting enough discussion for this evening. Are you looking forward to it?"

"No."

"I think you are. After all, satisfying your curiosity isn't dangerous. I'm even permitting you a sense of outraged virtue by forcing you to listen to my scandalous confessions. Every woman enjoys knowing what hell she puts men through."

"I don't enjoy it."

His mockery faded. "My apologies then. You're not like other women in that respect. You have no malice." He continued on a lighter note, "But you do have curiosity, and I shall seek earnestly to appease it."

She didn't answer, and he fell silent.

The air seemed too heavy to breathe.

He was watching her.

He was thinking about her.

He was waiting for her.

The chair.

Did you dream about the stallion last night?"

"No," she lied.

"Did he mount you from behind?"

She didn't answer.

"Was the stallion me?" he asked softly.

She turned her back on him and pretended to hold the panel up to the window to hide the color flaring in her cheeks.

"What a pretty backside you have. Small and pert and tight. It's no wonder I have such wicked thoughts."

"You should not have told me such terrible things," she said desperately. "You would not say such things to Dorothy."

"I would not say such things to anyone but you. Dorothy is a fine woman, but she's bound by the very rules she thinks she flouts. She will never take the final step and tell those people she detests that they mean nothing to her." He paused. "But you have an honesty and boldness she lacks, an honesty I've never found in another woman."

She might be honest, but she did not feel bold. She was beginning to tremble with the strange weakness that invaded her whenever she was in the same room with him. Last night she had sat, with hands folded in that chair by the hearth, staring at him in helpless thrall as he wove that picture of lust and depravity.

And when he had let her go to her room, the dreams had come.

Her hands were shaking again. She quickly put the panel on the table before she dropped it.

"Your cheeks are flushed. Strange. I didn't think it

was particularly warm for this time of year. It even snowed last night. Do you suppose you're coming down with a fever?"

"No."

"One can't be too sure." His gaze went to the window where long, thick icicles hung from the eaves. "This evening I think I must tell you at least one interesting cure we could try when the fever comes again."

You're proving remarkably resistant." Jordan's legs were stretched out in front of him and crossed at the ankle. "It's been almost a week, and neither of us has been sleeping properly." His forefinger idly traced the design of the deep floral carving on the arm of the chair. "If we continue for another week like this, it may be quite detrimental to our health. Put an end to it, Marianna."

His hands were beautiful, tanned, well shaped, with long, graceful fingers. Lately, she had found herself obsessed with watching his hands as they gestured or merely lay quiet on the arm of the chair.

The chair.

She wished she could forget the images it brought to mind, but they were always with her. Even if she could forget it, she thought bitterly, she now had a store of such erotic pictures. He had seen that she lived in a world where sight of the simplest object would bring memories of Jordan sitting by the fire weaving his tales of seduction.

"Why are you hesitating?" he asked softly. "You once told me that you believed as your father did that a spirit should be free. Why are you letting yourself be bound? You know what you want."

Her breasts were swollen, her body aching. He had only to be in the same room, and the response came unbidden. God help her, she was like that mare he had described, mindless, in heat, wanting only to be mounted.

But she was not an animal.

"Why else did you come here with me?"

She whirled on him. "You know why. Alex. You forced me to come here."

"I gave you a reason to come here."

"No!"

"You knew Alex was not in danger." He shook his head. "Be honest with yourself. You wanted what I wanted. The fire had been burning too long and too low for you too." His voice thickened. "It will never end until you take what you want, Marianna."

"It's you who wish to take what you want."

"Have I taken? I haven't even touched you. I've merely opened the doors and let you look in and see what's waiting for you inside."

The doors of a room lit with all the dark, exotic colors of desire.

"Come in," he urged softly. "You'll like what you find."

She shook her head.

He sighed. "I suppose it was too much to hope that even you could be that honest. Shall I give you an excuse? Come to me tonight, and in two days' time I'll take you to see Alex."

She turned and looked at him. "You'll give him back to me?"

"No, but I'll let you assure yourself of his well-being." He stood up and moved toward the door. "You see? You'll be sacrificing yourself for your poor brother held by the evil duke of Cambaron. Even Dorothy could understand such a splendid act of virtue."

He was leaving, she realized. It was the first time he had left her alone in the workroom since the second day they had come to the lodge. "Where are you going?"

He glanced over his shoulder. "I'm going for a ride. I'm feeling a great need to expend energy, and you're failing to cooperate. I'll be back by dark." He paused. "Unless you wish me to stay."

She didn't answer.

The next moment he was gone.

She was relieved to be without his disturbing presence, she told herself. Now she could concentrate on what was important to her. She reached out and picked up her cutting knife and then stopped.

It was too quiet.

Yet it was as if he were still in the room with her. She slowly turned and looked at the chair.

I suppose it was too much to expect that even you would be that honest.

It will never be over until you reach out and take what you want.

I only gave you a reason for coming here.

Was it true?

She had a terrible sinking feeling she had yielded far too easily when he had told her she was to come here.

The fever of need he had built had come too quickly not to have been smoldering, waiting for a spark to ignite it.

The fascination he had exerted had held her captive for three long years, and even when she had been most annoyed with him, she had never been able to dismiss him from her mind. It was as if he had possessed her from that first moment in the church in Talenka.

She walked heavily over to the chair. She reached out and touched the smooth wood of the back.

A shudder went through her as she felt the lingering warmth from his body.

She had lied to herself.

Sweet Mary, it was true.

He did not return before dark. It was almost midnight before she heard the sound of his horse in the stable yard.

She ignored it and kept on working. From that moment of realization she had thrown herself into a maelstrom of work, trying to block it away from her, trying not to think.

"Go to bed, Marianna."

She knew he was standing in the doorway, but she didn't turn around. She had to close herself away from him. "Go away. I don't want to see you."

"It's late. Go to bed."

So that she could lie awake another night? "Go away."

"And let you get so tired that you'll be careless and have more scars on your hands tomorrow?" he asked roughly.

"It's none of your concern."

"No, it's not my concern." He was standing behind her. "It's my obsession." He reached around her and took the cutting knife from her hand. "Go to bed."

The heat of his body surrounded her, and she smelled the scent of leather and horse and cold wind. She stood there, strained, unyielding.

She *wanted* him.

Something snapped, uncoiling within her.

She closed her eyes, and her breath released in a long sigh. She leaned back against him.

He stiffened, and she could feel the hardness of muscle and tendon. "Marianna?"

It was over. She couldn't fight any longer.

"I don't like this," she whispered. "It . . . hurts."

His other arm joined the first in encircling her, cradling her back against him with a strange tenderness. "Only the wanting hurts," he said thickly in her ear. "That's why it has to stop—the rest is beyond anything."

"Do you promise?"

He laughed huskily. "Oh yes, I promise." He held her for a moment more and then took a step back and began unbuttoning her gown. "I'll promise you the world, if you want it."

"I don't want the world," she said. Poor Jordan, she thought dully, he always believed that in the end he had to pay for what he wanted. How terrible to live with a cynicism that deeply ingrained.

It seemed odd to be standing here like a weary child while Jordan undressed her. She *was* weary, and her body had grown so accustomed to aching with need that she accepted it without question. The gown fell to the floor, and she stepped out of it. "I don't want anything from you."

"Turn around."

She didn't want to turn around. She wore only a thin chemise, and she felt suddenly shy and uncertain.

"Turn around. I want to see you."

She slowly turned to face him.

She saw his expression.

She was no longer weary.

"You do want something from me." His hands went to her hair, hovered, and then brushed the tresses back with a gossamer-light touch. "Come here." He reached out and pushed the chemise down to her waist and then brought her to lean against him.

She began to tremble. Her breasts were swelling, the nipples pebble-hard as they touched the crispness of his shirt.

His hands were on her bare back, his fingers drawing sensual circles on the smooth flesh. "Lord, you're soft."

His hands slid down and cupped her bottom and then pulled her into the hollow of his hips.

Arousal. Stark. Rigid.

Her trembling became a long shudder of need.

"Shh. It's all right. This is what you want." He moved her carefully against him, letting her feel the strength of him.

He thought she was afraid. If she could have spoken through the hot mist of need, she would have told him she was beyond fear. She was aware only of what she had to have from him. Her hands clutched his shoulders, and she pressed against him. Hard.

He froze. "Gently. We have to go gently."

After a week of tantalizing arousal she could not think of gentleness. "Do it." Her words were muffled in his shirt. "Now."

"I couldn't be more in agreement." His hand reached up between them and cupped her breast in his palm, his thumbnail flicking the taut nipple.

She arched upward with a low cry.

He slid the chemise down from her hips. "Spread your legs, Marianna."

She obeyed without question. He had described every intimate part of her body and what pleasure he would bring to it. This was part of it . . . his hands on her. She held on to him, or she would have fallen as his fingers plucked gently at the hair surrounding her womanhood. She held her breath as he went lower, searching until he found the small nub.

His thumb flicked and then pressed hard.

Her eyes widened in shock. Fire and pleasure. Need.

Her breath was coming in little pants as his thumb pressed, rotated. The muscles of her stomach tensed with every motion. She moved closer, offering him more.

"You like that?" He pressed harder, his other hand holding her at the small of the back. "It's only the start." His fingers fell away from her. "I think we'd best hurry. Come, we'll go upstairs to bed."

"Here." Her gaze was drawn to the chair.

He understood at once. "No," he said firmly. He started to pull her toward the door.

She refused to move. "Here."

"You're not ready— I'd hurt you."

"Here."

"Dammit!" He whirled on her, his nostrils flaring. "Why are you making this so difficult? Do you think I'm used to being with virgins? It's *killing* me. I'm trying to—" He broke off as he saw her expression.

"You obstinate woman. You don't know what's good for you."

"Here."

"Oh, what the devil!" He pulled her down on the floor. "I told you I'd be gentle with you. I don't like to be made a liar."

"The chair . . ." she whispered.

"Later." He pushed aside her legs and came between them. He made an adjustment in his clothing. "This will be painful enough for you. I wanted a soft bed and clean sheets and the things a woman should have when she—" He was pressing against her. He stopped and looked down at her, his chest rising and falling with every breath. "I didn't want it to be like this."

"I don't care. It doesn't matter." She bit down on her lower lip. Why did he not move and stop the emptiness? She instinctively arched up against him.

"Don't!" He moved carefully into her. "Don't move."

Stretched. Throbbing. Empty.

She arched against him again. More. She had more, but it still wasn't enough.

His features were contorted above her as if he were in pain. "No," he said between his teeth.

She was suddenly furious with him. "You've said yes for over a week. Now isn't the time to say no to me. It's not fair."

He looked down at her with glazed eyes. "Heaven forbid I be accused of such a crime." His hips moved back, and for a panic-filled moment she thought he was going to withdraw.

He plunged forward to the hilt.

Pain!

She cried out, her head arching back on the rug.

He stopped, his weight on her, filling her completely.

He closed his eyes. "Shall I stop?"

The pain was fading, and she was becoming accustomed to the bold clublike hardness within her. She should feel full, but spasms of sensation were shooting through her. She knew what came next. He had described it to her every night of their stay here, and she would not be robbed of it. "No."

"Good." His laugh had a note of desperation as his lids flicked open. "I don't know if I could have stopped anyway." He drew out and then plunged deep. Again. And again. And again.

Rhythm. Hunger. Fast. Slow.

His hands beneath her buttocks, lifting her to every thrust. He was making low sounds deep in his throat, primal, animal sounds that made her own excitement more intense. Her head thrashed back and forth on the floor as the need became wilder, the tension tighter.

It was growing, coming nearer. "Jordan," she gasped. "Jordan . . ."

He began rotating within her, his fingers seeking out the nub he had found before.

"Up," he said hoarsely. "Come up to me."

She was sobbing, her hips moving upward in rhythm to the motion of his thumb, helplessly obeying every command.

"More!"

Her spine arched off the floor. She cried out as he reached her womb.

He held her there, suspended, pulsating. The sensation was indescribable. Her mouth opened to scream.

He put her legs on his shoulders and kept her there. "Come to me," he said through his teeth. "Now."

She moaned, unable to move, the spasms growing. "Let it come."

She mustn't scream. Only animals screamed when they mated.

She could not stand it. The tension climaxed, and she convulsed.

She screamed as her her nails dug into his shoulders!

Beyond anything.

He had said it was beyond anything, and he spoke the truth.

She was only vaguely aware of him changing position, easing her, moving, still stroking deep. Was there more? She wondered hazily.

Then he went still and an instant later gave a low cry. He fell forward, his arms around her, holding her. He felt weak, in need, in her embrace. Jordan was never weak, never in need, and yet, in this moment, he needed her.

Her arms tightened fiercely about him.

Beyond anything.

May we go upstairs now?" Jordan asked as soon as his breathing steadied. He lifted his head. "You probably have bruises. This floor is damnably hard."

She stared up at him dazedly. He was still within her; she felt as if he had been there forever, a part of her. "I . . . don't think so." Perhaps she was bruised, but it didn't matter. It was a small price to pay for what had gone before. "It felt . . ." She did not go on. There were no words.

"I'm glad your first time was not a disappointment." His lips gently brushed her forehead before he moved off her and adjusted his breeches. "But now it's time to go to bed." He stood up and pulled her to her feet. "Ready?"

Her knees felt weak, and she swayed. He caught her and lifted her in his arms.

Her glance fell on the chair, and, incredibly, she felt a faint stirring.

"Oh no." He instantly shook his head. "I'm beginning to regret telling you about that particular vision. We have to go slowly." He left the workroom and climbed the stairs two at a time. "Everything in its time."

She became suddenly aware of her nakedness against his fully clothed form. It gave her an uneasy feeling of vulnerability that caused a little of the dreamlike sensuality to disperse. "Where are you taking me?"

He shifted her in his arms and opened a door. "Your chamber, my lady. I thought you'd prefer it to mine." He laid her on the bed and turned away. Only embers remained in the fireplace, and Jordan was moving about the room in darkness. "It's easier to accept new experiences if you're surrounded by the familiar."

Clever, she thought drowsily, Jordan was always very clever. "I believe you're a trifle late. I've already accepted the new experience."

"Not entirely." He was suddenly on the bed beside her, drawing her into his arms.

Solid, warm flesh. Naked flesh.

She instantly flinched away from him.

"Gently." His hand gently stroked her hair. "You'll grow used to me in your bed. It's only the next step."

"You have your own chamber," she said stiltedly. "You need not be here with me. Dorothy says, even in marriage, gentlemen usually only pay their wives visits in order to indulge their lust or beget children."

"I admit it's not my custom either, but I find I want this. Indulge me."

"I don't wish to indulge you. It makes me feel . . . uncomfortable."

"Did your father only pay visits to your mother's bed?"

"No, but then our cottage was very small."

"Would he have occupied a separate room if he'd had a residence as large as Cambaron?"

"No." She was silent a moment. "But that was different. There was not only lust between them, there was true feeling."

He kissed her temple. "And is there no feeling between us?"

"Not love," she whispered. "You do not love me, and I do not love you. There is something . . . but it's not what they had."

"Perhaps it's something far more interesting. I've noticed that given time, what people call love usually degenerates to mawkish sentiment." His arms tightened possessively around her. "At any rate I intend to stay here with you. Become accustomed to the idea."

He would not be dissuaded, and she was too weary to argue with him at the moment. He had said it was not his custom; perhaps it was only a whim, and he would grow bored after tonight. She tried to relax her stiff muscles.

The room was silent, the darkness comforting. She was beginning to grow drowsy again when he asked in a low voice, "Was I brutal to you?"

"What?"

"I . . . wanted to be gentle," he said haltingly. "I was afraid I'd remind you of what happened to your mother."

He meant that horrible night and the beasts who had raped and tortured Mama. Strange, she had not even connected the two acts. Her need had been so great, if there had been violence, it was she who had provoked it. "You weren't like them."

"Did you see it?"

"No, when the soldiers came, she made me take Alex out the back door and run to the forest. She said it was my duty to take care of him, and I mustn't come back until after the soldiers left." She swallowed to ease the tightness in her throat. Why was she telling him this? She didn't want to remember that night. Yet the words kept coming, tumbling out into the darkness. "I didn't see them, but I heard them. I stayed close because I wanted to find a way, any way, to help her. I couldn't leave Alex. She made me promise. I had to listen . . . I couldn't leave Alex."

"Christ."

He drew her closer, and her tears rained down on the warm flesh of his shoulder. "I kept my promise and didn't come back until they left. They had hurt her . . . terribly. They thought she was dead, but she wasn't. She didn't die until the next morning." She closed her eyes. "I couldn't stay. I had promised her— I went to the priest and left a note on his doorstep to tell him what they'd done to Mama. I don't even know where she's buried. I asked them to bury her next to Papa. Do you suppose they did?"

"I'm sure they did."

"I don't guess it matters. She wasn't there anyway. I stayed there and held her hand, but she wasn't there anymore. She had gone somewhere else."

"She was very brave."

"Yes." She was silent a moment. "I've never spoken about that night. It . . . hurts to even think of it. I don't know why I—"

"Perhaps because it was time to make peace with it."

"Peace?"

"Guilt. You had to choose between Alex and your mother and the promise you had given her. You loved her, you wanted to help her, and you stood by and let her die." He said roughly, "It was a choice no one should have been forced to make, dammit. No one should carry a burden like that."

She had never allowed herself to consider that it was guilt that kept that painful memory from healing. Yet now she could not see how she had ever been able to ignore it. "There should have been something I could do."

"Against a troop of soldiers? You would have died, Alex would have died, and your mother would still have died. You did the only thing possible."

"She shouldn't have died. There should have been something I could do."

"Hush." His hand pressed her face into the hollow of his shoulder. "It's done, and you have no blame. Believe me."

She drew a shaky breath. "Why should I believe you? Are you a priest to grant me absolution?"

"A priest? Good God, you should know better than that after the last week." He suddenly chuckled. "But after years of having Gregor try to pound the iniquities out of me and a conscience into me, I've become something of an expert on guilt." His lips brushed her nose. "And you don't have a particle."

She didn't quite believe him but was aware of a slight easing of the pain from the wound that had never closed. Perhaps there was some truth in what Jordan said. She had already acknowledged his cleverness, and no one could deny his experience in the infinite facets of wickedness.

"Now please have the goodness to go to sleep, and I shall do the same." He kissed her temple. "You've completely exhausted me both physically and mentally. I never imagined I'd be called upon to do anything tonight but service you as a good stallion should. You never cease to surprise me, Marianna."

And he never ceased to surprise her, she thought as she closed her eyes. Seducer, scoundrel, a man who had relentlessly undermined her will and taken her body, and yet, when she least expected it, he gave her gifts. . . .

She was sleeping deeply, like an exhausted child.

What the devil was he doing in her bed? Jordan wondered. His decision to stay in her bed had been an impulse, and he was not given to impulses. Except in the act itself he preferred to maintain a certain distance. Yet he had cared enough to argue with her to remain here.

Jordan shifted away from her, staring into the darkness.

After three years the battle was over, and he had won. Not that there had been any doubt of the outcome. He had deliberately set out on a course of seduction, and he was too skilled not to succeed with an innocent like Marianna. She had been fighting herself as well as him, and it had only been a matter of time before she capitulated.

He had won. Why did he feel so little satisfaction?

Lust? He had wanted her again almost immediately after he had left her, but it was was not only lust.

He moved to the edge of the bed, sat up, and swung his legs to the floor. He would ignore this reluctance to leave her and go to his own room. By tomorrow he would have regained his objectivity and realize this unrest was only a temporary madness. Now that his body had been sated, his mind would be clear and he could concentrate on trying to persuade her to give him the Jedalar.

He was crossing the room toward the door when he noticed the dying embers in the fireplace. It would do no harm to lay wood on the fire so that she would not wake to a cold room. He knelt, built up the fire, and stoked the blaze until it flared brightly.

Always before, after he had succeeded with a woman, he had felt a sense of triumph and then almost immediately the stirrings of boredom and discontent. None of those emotions were present now, and he was uneasy about identifying what he was feeling.

He glanced over his shoulder at the woman in the bed.

No, not just a woman. Marianna.

He slowly stood up and moved to look down at her. Her golden hair was a silky cloud on the pillow, and her mouth was soft and vulnerable. God, he did not want this. All he had wanted was release from passion. He wanted to regard her as a woman to take or discard. He had never thought he would be caught in the trap he feared most.

Possession.

CHAPTER 10

She woke to see him standing naked at the window, staring out at the dawn sky.

Shock rippled through her, jarring her to wakefulness. She had studied the paintings of great artists, but she had never seen a nude man before. She found him far more pleasing than even the men created by Michelangelo. To her eyes they had seemed pale and overly brawny, while Jordan was tanned, sinewy, full of power and elegance. Tight buttocks flowed into lean, strong legs, and his shoulders were corded, not bulging, with sleek muscle.

She must have made some sound, because he turned and looked at her. "Good morning."

He was perfectly at ease in his nakedness. She wished she could be as composed. "Good morning," she whispered.

He stared at her without expression, and she had the uneasy feeling he was angry with her. That impression lasted only an instant before he smiled, once more drawing charm about him like a glittering cloak. "You're looking at me as if I were about to devour you. Do I appear so formidable?"

"No." She found herself telling him the truth. "Actually I was thinking you were quite splendid. Much more comely than that statue of David by Michelangelo."

"I thank you." He bowed, somehow making the gesture graceful even in his nudity. "I don't believe anyone has ever likened me to a biblical statue before. I seem to provoke more earthy comparisons." He started toward the bed. "How do you feel? Are you sore?"

"No." She was aware of a little soreness between her thighs, but she would not confess it to him. He had already discovered too many of her weaknesses. She had not thought surrender would bring this overwhelming intimacy. Why did she not admit it—she had not thought at all. She had flowed to him as helplessly as a leaf caught in a current, caring only for the ease he could give her. She sat up in bed, drawing the covers to her throat. "I'm quite well."

"Good." He sat down on the bed beside her. "Then we can proceed."

Alarm shot through her. "I didn't say that I wanted to— I'm not sure— This is not a good thing."

"It's a very good thing. I thought you'd be having second thoughts this morning. Dorothy has done her work too well."

He slowly pulled the cover down to her waist, his gaze fixed on her naked breasts. "It's always a good idea to get right back on a horse after the first lesson. Otherwise you have a tendency to lose the rhythm of the pace."

That brought to mind the erotic tale he had spun

of the stallion and the mare, and she could feel the muscles of her stomach clench with excitement.

He noticed the response, and he looked up at her face. He said thickly, "I need you. I've been standing at that window for hours waiting for you to wake. Will you take me, Marianna?"

The same hot, helpless tide she had experienced last night swept over her. Why did it go on? She had hoped that once she had given in to lust, it would be over. Yet she wanted him as much in this moment as she had last night.

He bent down, his mouth hovering over her breast. "I promise I'll reward you, if you do."

She gasped as his warm tongue stroked her nipple. "I told you I don't want rewards."

He widened her legs and entered slowly, his very deliberateness tantalizing. "You want this one. First, we'll make sure you weren't lying to me about your soreness." He began to stroke, thrust, gently and then a little harder. "And later we'll go on to the second lesson . . . and the reward."

She closed around him, tightening, as the spasms of need began. She began to pant, her fingers clutching the counterpane of the bed. "What are—" She broke off and arched upward as his fingers found her. She forgot what she had started to ask.

But Jordan had not forgotten. His hands reached under, gently pinching, kneading her buttocks. He bent closer until his lips were in her hair and began to whisper in her ear.

You've worked long enough. I'm beginning to feel grievously neglected." Jordan leaned back in the chair. "I'm sure you need some fresh air. Let's go for a walk."

He just wanted to get her away from the workroom, she thought in exasperation. "I've worked only a few hours in the past four days. I'm going to finish this panel."

"What a stubborn woman you are." He shifted restlessly. "It's not as if you're going to use the blasted panel. Gregor says you have a pile of discarded ones in the storeroom in the stable."

She looked down at the tulip she was cutting. "One never knows. Beauty is never a waste of time."

"That's true." He chuckled. "But I prefer active beauty to passive." He paused. "And I particularly prefer you active." His tone deepened, became honey-sweet. "Come here."

"No." She ignored the familiar heat that moved through her. "I want to finish this panel before we go to see Alex tomorrow."

He went still. "Alex?"

She turned to look at him. "You promised me."

"For God's sake," he said harshly. "You know he's come to no harm, and you can't pretend that's why you're in my bed."

"No, that's not why I let you—" She broke off and said wearily, "I cannot help myself. It's like a sickness."

His anger flared again. "By God, if it's a sickness, it's one you revel in."

She couldn't deny it. In the last four days she had existed in a haze of sensual hunger. They had come together more times in more diverse ways than she could count, and it was never enough. He had only to look at her in a certain way or touch her casually in passing and her body readied.

And he was always touching her. She had gradually come to realize he used touch not only to arouse but to establish possession. He would lift her hand to his lips in the middle of a conversation and then go on talking as if the caress had never happened; he would knead the nape of her neck as she sat at his feet before the fire; he would brush her hair for her before they retired, talking idly, his fingers playing with the strands.

Each touch, each word, each mundane act, was drawing her closer into the web of intimacy.

He smiled, and his face lit with charm. "Pleasure isn't a sickness, pleasure is joy," he coaxed. "You love everything I do to you. Say it, Marianna."

She didn't have to make the admission. He knew very well she was completely under his spell. At first she had floated along, accepting everything, but gradually she had become aware Jordan was not equally swept away. Not that he did not want her; no question existed on that score. But there were times when she caught a glance, a watchful expression, that gave her pause. It was as if he were trying to shape her to his needs, an idea that brought both anger and fear. She knew how strong was Jordan's will, but she would not be the mindless voluptuary he was trying to mold. "It doesn't matter how I feel. It is what I am." She hesitated and then said in a rush, "I want you to let me go. I've decided this cannot go on."

His smile vanished. "It *will* go on."

She turned to look at him. "How long? Until you grow tired of me?"

"I cannot imagine that circumstance."

"I could name at least six ladies who are very familiar with that circumstance since I came to Cambaron."

He frowned. "It's not the same."

"It is the same. Why do you need me? You are not a constant man. Next month you will bring another woman here and—"

"Will you be silent! For God's sake I told you it was not the same."

"No." She ran her fingers through her hair. "I know it's . . . different somehow. But it's a difference I cannot bear."

"You're not being rational. You cannot bear pleasure?"

"Not if it means . . . I feel smothered."

"Nonsense."

"You want something from me," she went on haltingly, feeling her way. "Perhaps you have already grown bored with me. Perhaps you're merely pretending so that I will come to trust you enough to give you the Jedalar. Is that it?"

"You know I'm not bored with you. Will you stop ranting at me?"

"How do I know? You're a very clever man. Maybe Lady Carlisle never knew when you grew bored with her." She drew a deep breath and then said evenly, "And I'm not ranting. I'm saying what I'm thinking. Though you've seen that I've had little capability for reasoning of late."

The anger suddenly left his expression, and he leaned his head against the high back of the chair. "Quite true. I didn't want you to think, only to feel. Thinking would have gotten in the way." He added quietly, "Do you wish to wring a confession from me? Very well. I'm weary of deceiving you anyway. It sticks in my throat. The Jedalar has nothing to do with this." He paused. "I intend for you to belong to me."

She gazed at him incredulously. "Belong? I'm not a slave to belong to anyone."

"I wish you were. I'd like nothing better than to build you a lovely cage where I held the only key. The ordinary ways a man owns a woman are not to my liking. The bonds aren't strong enough."

She shook her head dazedly. "This is outrageous. I don't understand you."

"Neither do I. I learned a long time ago that it's foolish to try to hold on to anyone. Everyone walks away eventually. It's better to walk away first and not look back. That's what I intended to do with you, but something happened. You touched me . . . and held me." He smiled crookedly. "I assure you, I've been fighting it with all my strength."

"Then let me go."

"I can't." His tone was abruptly laden with frustration. "I can't, dammit." He drew a deep breath and then said mockingly, "So I decided I had to find a way to make you stay. It would be pleasant if you would succumb to bribery like an ordinary female, but I know you wouldn't. However, I do have another weapon. You have a remarkably sensual nature. I suppose you've noticed I've endeavored to entice you to yield to me every time and every way I wanted you. Such submission becomes a habit that forges the strongest of chains."

Chains. She shivered as she realized that she had nearly let it happen. How close she had been to letting him rule her life as he had her body. Would trust have come with the dependence he had begun to instill in her? At some point would she have given him the Jedalar just to please him? The thought was frightening. "Why are you telling me this?" she whispered.

He shrugged. "My feelings for you have always been confused. Perhaps I want you to fight me before I destroy all I value in you. I found you cannot enslave without being enslaved." His smile was sardonic, but his voice had thickened. "I have the sickness too. I cannot look at you without wanting you."

Desire, raw, powerful, and uncompromised by any other emotion. Well, what had she expected? What else was there between them? Yet the knowledge brought unbearable pain that terrified her with its depth. She had to bring an end to this emotional chaos before it became intolerable. She must find a way not only to leave Jordan but Cambaron. "I want to see Alex."

He shrugged. "Then you shall see him. We don't have to go to him. I'll send word for Gregor to bring him to Dalwynd tomorrow."

"He's that close?"

"Close enough." He paused. "Put your cutting knife down."

She shook her head. "I told you I didn't want to go for a walk."

"Neither do I. Come here."

She turned to look at him.

He was no longer lounging in the chair but sitting upright. He smiled at her. "If you're determined to leave me, it can do no harm to let me have a few last hours of pleasure. There are still many things for you to learn."

She stared at him in disbelief. "You've just told me you wish to put me in a cage, and you expect me to—"

"Why not?" His long, graceful fingers moved slowly, tracing the grooves of the carving on the arms of the chair.

The chair.

"Come here, Marianna. Remember? I can't come to you."

He was talking about the dream, his dream, the dream that woke her in the middle of the night.

His green eyes were narrowed on her face, and his lips were heavy, sensual. Color darkened the bronze of his cheeks, and there was the faintest flare to his nostrils. "Do you want to run back to Dorothy and be like her for the rest of your life? Don't you want to taste and feel everything there is to feel?" His hands tightened on the arms of the chair. "I *want* this, Marianna."

She could feel his need. The air between them vibrated with it. She had become accustomed to satisfying his every desire because in doing so she satisfied her own. Her body was readying now, she realized helplessly. It made no difference that she knew what he was doing. Her heart was pounding, and she felt the familiar aching emptiness between her thighs.

"You want it," he said. "Another memory, another pleasure. There have been so many, what's one more time?"

He was everything that was beautiful and elegant and seductive. Satan could not have been more alluring or more persuasive when he had tempted Eve.

"Are you afraid? Why? Do you doubt your resolve?"

"I'm not afraid."

"Then come to me."

She slowly started toward him.

He held her gaze. "That's right," he whispered. "Let me have you. Let me bring you pleasure."

She stopped before him. She could see the pulse leaping in his temple. She wanted desperately to reach out and touch him.

What was one more time?

It did not have to be a surrender. She would be leaving him soon; she must find Alex and escape from this trap that had proved so alluring. Yet surely now that she knew what she was fighting, she could be strong enough to take what she wanted and walk away from him.

"You cannot have me," she said clearly. "I will not belong to you."

He went still, his eyes holding hers.

"But I will take you now. Not because you want it, but because I do."

He smiled. "A challenge? You don't have the experience to best me in this arena. But, by all means, do try."

The dream required she touch his lips with her fingers.

She did not. She reached out, untied the ribbon that bound his queue, and pulled it from his hair. "And if I don't like every aspect of your dream, it will be as different as I wish it to be."

Watchful, he said nothing.

Her fingers combed through his hair, enjoying the thick silkiness. She was trembling, and she knew he could see it. She didn't know how long she could maintain this pose of dominance when her knees were shaking so badly she could barely stand. She knew he wanted her. Why did he just sit there? "Well?" she said impatiently.

His brows lifted. "You expect something of me? But you said I couldn't have you. I wouldn't think of offending you by disobedience." His head turned, and he pressed his lips to the soft skin on the inside of her forearm. "Until you give me permission."

Heat tingled up her arm. She swallowed. "Jordan, I—"

"That's permission enough." He jerked her down on his lap. His lips roamed over her throat while fingers tore at the buttons on the back of her gown. His head lifted, to reveal eyes blazing with feeling. "Stand up." He didn't wait for her to comply but stood her on her feet. "Is this different enough for you?" He tore the gown and shift off her, and they fell in strips at her feet. He pulled her back on his lap, facing him, adjusting her legs over the wide wooden arms of the chair.

He reached beneath her, and two fingers plunged deep while he freed himself with the other hand. He stroked, rotated, stroked again.

She gasped, her fingers closing on his hair.

He bent her back, his mouth closing on her right breast, and he sucked long and hard, tonguing her nipple in rhythm to the probing of his fingers.

She bit her lower lip to keep from screaming. The sensation was indescribable. Her thighs stretched wide over the hard, smooth wood and Jordan's fingers. . . .

He lifted his head. "Do you belong to me?"

She was barely aware of the content of his words. She looked up at him dazedly.

His fingers left her, and he made an adjustment. He plunged deep, filling her to the quick. "Do you belong to me?" he repeated.

Her hands plucked at his shoulders. "Jordan, I can't—"

"Do you want me to move?"

"Yes," she whispered.

His hands pressed down on her hips, sealing her to him. He was still, his chest moving in and out with his labored breathing. "Then tell me you belong to me."

Chains. A sudden burst of anger tore through her. "I will *not*."

He did not move, and she felt the waves of lust and frustration emitting from him as a tangible force. "Damn and blast you." He started to move, his hips rotating upward in a wild, thrusting, driving motion.

She could only hold on to his shoulders and ride the storm until the final explosion. It seemed to go on a long time. She could hear herself making little animallike cries as she took him and took him. . . .

He buried his head on her breast, still flexing within her. She couldn't move as shudder after shudder of release rippled through her.

"Tell me you belong to me," he said in a low voice.

"Let me go."

"You'll tell me someday."

She felt a frantic need to escape. "I'm not comfortable. Let me stand up."

He lifted his head, and a reckless smile lit his face. "But we're not finished."

She stared at him in bewilderment. He could not want her after that wild climax of feeling.

She was being moved, shifted to his lap, with her legs over one arm of the chair. He was still within her, and he bent her back over his arm, his lips caressing her nipple. "Isn't this pleasant?"

"What are you doing?"

"Waiting. I'd be a fool not to take advantage of such a vulnerable position when you're being so cruel as to want to leave me. Who knows when I'll be granted such a privilege again?"

She felt him hardening within her.

"Close your legs and let me feel your tightness." His lips brushed her ear. "I told you only a little of my dream. There's still much more to come."

This had been a mistake, she thought in despair. She had believed she was strong enough to take what she wanted without yielding more of herself. She should have known better. He had seized control, and at this moment she felt more owned than ever in her life.

"Hold me," he whispered as his fingers searched and found.

As the pleasure started, she instinctively tightened around him, giving him what he demanded.

A terrible mistake.

Is it safe to slide on?" Alex ran to the edge of the lake and looked out over the glittering ice. He stuck out a booted toe and probed at the icy surface. "This is a fine place. May I stay with you, Marianna?"

"No, the ice is still too thin, she said, answering the former question. She pulled him back from the danger. "And I would love for you to stay with me. Why don't you ask Jordan?"

"Jordan, may I?"

Jordan broke off his conversation with Gregor and shook his head. "We need you to help Gregor protect Cambaron while we're gone."

Alex frowned. "Then I want Marianna to come back with me."

"But Marianna needs to rest. That's why she's here," Jordan said gently. "She became very tired working on that lovely flower dome. You don't want her to become ill, do you?"

Alex said quickly, "Marianna's never ill." His worried gaze went to Marianna's face. "But she does look . . . pale."

"I feel perfectly fine," Marianna said firmly, with a barbed glance at Jordan. She would not have him making Alex anxious. "And I'll be back with you at Cambaron before you know it."

Alex asked Jordan, "Why can't she rest at Cambaron?"

Jordan smiled. "Does she ever rest at Cambaron? We'd have to seal off the tower room."

Alex chuckled. "And the stable storeroom and the ballroom and—"

"What if I promised not to work?" Marianna said to Jordan, challenging him. "Then there would be no reason for me not to go back to Cambaron today."

Jordan gave Alex another glance. "Could we trust her?"

Alex shook his head.

Jordan smiled blandly at Marianna. "How well he knows you. I suppose we'll just have to keep you here until you're more rested." He turned back to Alex. "But there's no reason for you not to visit more often. Gregor can bring you back in a few days. We'll get you a pair of skates, and if the ice is hard enough, we'll have a few lessons."

"I can learn to skate?" Alex's eyes lit with excitement. "Marianna too?"

"I'm sure she would be a fine skater," he said silkily. "But we'd have to watch her carefully. She's always had an affinity for thin ice."

She wanted to reach out and strike him. She whirled away. "Let's go for a walk along the shore, Alex." She added pointedly to Jordan, "You don't have to come with us. I'm sure you and Gregor have many things to discuss."

To her surprise he nodded. "We'll watch you from here. Don't slip and fall. The snow is hard-packed, but there's thin ice beneath it." He smiled at Alex. "There will be a cup of hot chocolate waiting for you after your walk, and then maybe we'll have a game of chess. Would you like that?"

"Oh yes."

Marianna took Alex's hand and set out. The snow crunched beneath her boots, and the sun shimmered brilliantly on the white surface. Gradually the vigorous activity caused her anger and frustration to ebb. She would not let her anger with Jordan spoil this time with Alex. "I've missed you. Have you been well?"

He nodded. "Gregor took me on a splendid trip on the *Seastorm*. I saw Captain Braithwaite again. He's got lots more gray in his hair now."

"But you're back at Cambaron now?"

He nodded again. "But I haven't been able to ride much. The ground has been too icy." He was silent a moment and then whispered, "You're not really ill, are you? Not like Mama? You're not going to—"

"No!" She stopped and fell to her knees before him. She gathered him in her arms and rocked him tenderly. He had not mentioned Mama for a long time and never mentioned the night she died. She had not realized how vivid the memory still was to him. "I'm just a little tired. I'll be back with you just as soon as I can."

"Not if it's going to make you more ill," he said quickly.

Blast Jordan. "It won't make me ill." She framed his cheeks in her gloved hands. "And perhaps when I come back, we'll go on our own journey, just the two of us. Would you like that?"

His eyes lit eagerly. "Where would we go?"

"We'll have to decide that later." She kissed him on the forehead. "But for now let it be a secret between us."

"Could I take my horse?"

She stood up. "We'll discuss that when the time comes." She took his hand and continued to walk. "How is Dorothy?"

"Fine," he said absently. He looked out to the lake. "Perhaps we could wait until after I come here again to go on our trip." He added hastily, "Not that I'm sure we wouldn't have a splendid time, but we wouldn't want to hurt Jordan's feelings when he's planned everything so nicely."

"No, we wouldn't want to hurt Jordan's feelings." She tried to keep the irony from her voice. Jordan, the seducer, the magician who could spin a web so glittering, you wanted to stay caught in it forever. Even Alex was helpless before him.

"Marianna!"

They turned to see Gregor waving his arm at them.

"Chocolate!" Alex turned and ran back toward the lodge.

"Be careful," she shouted after him.

He laughed and kept on running, sliding over the snow.

She smiled and shook her head at her own foolishness. When was a seven-year-old boy ever cautious? Particularly Alex, who lived every minute as if there would never be another?

Alex had already disappeared into the lodge when she arrived at the stable yard, but Gregor stood waiting on the step.

"I am sorry," he said quietly. "I could not stop him."

She felt the heat touch her cheeks and deliberately pretended to misunderstand him. "No one can stop Alex when there's a cup of chocolate waiting."

"I thought Jordan would bring you back within a few days." His gaze raked her face. "Has he hurt you?"

Had he hurt her? Not physically, but she was beginning to feel that the pain would never stop unless she could find a way to leave him. "You must know he's not a violent man."

"He does not need to strike a blow to bring pain." He shook his head. "If you would give him the Jedalar, I would have reason to try to interfere."

"Try?" She smiled bitterly. "I thought you told me you always won your battles with Jordan."

"That was a long time ago. With every loss Jordan learned. It would be difficult to take away something he wanted now."

And he would not even make the attempt as long as there was a possibility that Jordan could wrest the Jedalar from her. She was alone.

Well, she had been alone before. She did not need his help. She turned and opened the door. "I need a cup of hot chocolate myself. It's growing chilly out here."

Alex and Gregor stayed until late afternoon, and the tears stung Marianna's eyes as she watched them ride away.

"They'll be back in a few days," Jordan said quietly.

"Alex *needs* me," she said fiercely.

"I need you."

He turned and went back into the lodge.

She followed him. "You didn't tell me Alex was at Cambaron. I thought you'd sent him away."

"We brought him back. He's happiest at Cambaron. There was no use upsetting him unduly." He turned to look at her. "And I didn't tell you he was at Cambaron because I knew that you'd immediately decide to make the attempt to go to him. We're too close to Cambaron here at Dalwynd." He smiled faintly. "For the woman who walked seventy miles to Talenka, the distance would be nothing."

"But you knew he'd tell me."

"I promised you could see him. I don't break my word. It only means I have to be more vigilant."

"This can't go on." She turned and walked to the window and stared blindly out at the frozen lake. She asked suddenly, "What would you do if I gave you the Jedalar?"

She could sense his sudden tension across the room.

"What?"

"That's what you want. What if I gave it to you? Would you let me and Alex go?"

"Yes," he said slowly, "I would let you go. I'd let you ride out of Cambaron with enough money to make you and Alex comfortable for the rest of your lives. I'd stay at Cambaron and promise not to look for you for a full month. I'd give you your chance to be rid of me." She heard him move, and then he was behind her, not touching her. "And then I'd come after you and find you and bring you back." His arms slid around her waist. "But we both know you're not going to give up that easily. You might try to trick me by dangling the Jedalar in front of me, but I'm not in any danger of having to bargain with you yet." His lips gently feathered her ear. "Poor Marianna, you're sad and tired, and life isn't fair, is it? Come sit by the fire. I'll fix your supper."

A thundering crash at the front door!

Marianna woke to hear Jordan's low curse as he leaped from the bed.

Another crash!

"What is—" She was talking to air; Jordan was no longer in the room. She jumped from the bed, slipped on her robe, and ran out of the room and down the stairs.

Jordan was crouched on the doorstep, bending over a giant bearlike form.

"What is it? What's happened?" Her fingers were trembling so badly, she barely managed to light the candle on the table by the door. "Who . . . ?"

"Gregor." Jordan's voice was hoarse. "Gregor, goddammit."

Fear tore through her. She took a step closer, holding the candle higher.

Blood on the snow. Blood on Gregor's quilted tunic. She fell to her knees beside him. Was he dead? Dear God, so much blood . . . and his face was chalk pale. "Is he . . . ?"

"He's not dead. He won't die." Jordan's voice was fierce. "Get linens for bandages." He straightened and with an effort lifted Gregor's enormous bulk in his arms. "I won't be able to manage the stairs. I'll lay him before the fire."

She ran to do his bidding. Gregor was hurt. Gregor could die. Sweet, wise Gregor . . .

Alex!

Gregor had been with Alex. Whatever fate had befallen Gregor must also have struck down Alex.

Alex might be lying somewhere on the snow, hurt, unable to defend himself.

With shaking hands she took out an armful of linens and flew back to the parlor. Gregor was lying on the rug in front of the hearth. Jordan had already unbuttoned his tunic and grabbed one of the linens from her.

"Jordan." She tried to steady her voice. "Alex."

"I know." He was trying to staunch the bleeding in Gregor's upper chest.

"Alex is alone out there. We have to go after him."

"We will." He sat back on his heels. "The wound's not too deep, but he's lost a good deal of blood."

"Will he live?"

"I've seen him survive much worse."

"Was it a wild animal?" She was shaking so badly, she could barely stand. "What did this to him? A wolf?"

He shook his head. "Knife wound."

"Knife? He was attacked? Robbers?"

"We'll have to ask him."

"But he's in a faint. You stay here with him, and I'll go after Alex."

"No," Jordan said sharply. "We don't know where he was attacked. Gregor will have to tell us."

"I can't wait. What if—"

"I'm . . . sorry." Gregor's eyes were open, looking up at Jordan. "I was . . . stupid. I've grown too soft with the life here. Should go home . . ."

Marianna felt a rush of relief. If he could speak, he couldn't be too badly hurt.

"Well, your stupidity is not going to prove fatal. It's a good thing you're as big as you are. Anyone with less blood would be a corpse now." Jordan's voice was light, but his hand was infinitely gentle as he brushed the wild mane of hair back from Gregor's face. "Where did it happen?"

"They were waiting for us. . . ." Gregor trailed off and then roused himself. "Seven men. They knew we were coming."

"Do you know who they were?"

"I recognized only one—Costain."

Jordan cursed beneath his breath. "Where?"

"Down the road . . . other side of bridge . . . about . . . six miles . . ."

"Gregor," Marianna whispered. "Alex?"

"They took him." His eyes closed. "That's why . . . they wanted him. Southwick. They took the road toward Southwick. . . ."

He was in a faint again.

"Why would they take Alex?" she whispered.

"I'll have to leave at once." Jordan stood up and moved toward the staircase. "Stay here and take care of Gregor. I'll get dressed and ride to Southwick."

She felt a chill as she looked down at Gregor's still body. Seven men, he had said. If Gregor's tremendous strength had not prevailed, the danger to Jordan would be as great. "Alone?"

"There's no time to go to Cambaron to get help."

"You could take the two men you have on guard here."

"No, I want them here to take care of you."

"Sweet Mary, why? Do you think I'm going to run away when Alex is in danger?"

"No." He looked down at her from the landing. "But you'll stay here and not leave the house, and the guards will stay also. Do you understand?"

"The only thing I understand is that I want Alex back." She recalled something else Gregor had said. "Who is this Costain?"

"We'll talk later." He threw open the door and strode into his room. "I have to get to Southwick at once."

Gregor woke again four hours later. "Jordan?" he whispered.

"He went to Southwick." She pressed the cool cloth to his temple. "He's been gone some time now."

"Alex." He shook his head. "He won't find him. It was too far . . . it took me too long. I . . . failed." He closed his eyes. "Ship . . ."

A chill went through her. "Ship?"

"Why else . . . Southwick? Ship . . ."

"Don't talk." She pressed a cup of water to his lips. "Drink."

He swallowed the water. "I am sorry, Marianna. Failed . . ."

"You couldn't know this would happen. You could have been killed. It was one man against seven."

"We were so careful. Should have been safe. Betrayed. I suspected nothing." He closed his eyes. "But they were waiting. . . ." He drifted off again.

Southwick.

A ship.

Who was waiting?

She was beginning to fear she knew the answer.

Gregor woke twice more during the night and appeared to be gaining more strength with each passing hour. Marianna sat by the fire tending him, waiting.

Jordan did not return until well after daybreak.

"How is he?" he asked as he strode into the lodge.

"Better." She braced herself. "Where is Alex?"

"On a ship that sailed two hours before I arrived at Southwick." He paused. "A ship bound for Montavia."

"Nebrov," she said numbly.

"Not Nebrov. One of his lieutenants, Marcus Costain. Nebrov is in Poland meeting with Napoleon. Passage was booked for a Marcus Costain and his nephew, James Lakalb."

"Are you sure it was Alex?"

"I made inquiries on the dock. Costain booked a separate cabin for the boy and told the agent his nephew was ill and would have to remain in his cabin for the entire journey."

Alex was a prisoner. Alex, who spent most of his waking hours outside, careening joyously around Cambaron, was going to be confined in that small space for the long journey to Montavia. It was too painful to consider. She suddenly recalled something else Jordan had said. "How do you know Nebrov is with Napoleon?"

He hesitated. "I received a message while I was in Sweden."

She stared at him in disbelief. "You suspected he might be planning to make some move to do with the Jedalar. That's why you brought me here; that's how all this started."

"It wasn't a suspicion, only a vague possibility," he said harshly. "We've been watching carefully since the moment you arrived at Cambaron. There was not one sign that Nebrov had discovered where you were."

"You didn't tell me," she said dully. "I could have taken Alex and run away."

"We didn't *know*."

"I wouldn't have taken the chance. Not with Alex's safety." She stared directly into his eyes. "But you chose to do it."

"I tried to—" He met her gaze and then said wearily, "Yes, I made the choice."

She stood up and moved toward the staircase. "I'm going to pack my clothes, and then we're going to go to Southwick. We're going to board the *Seastorm* and follow Alex to Montavia."

"We can't do that," he said. "Not yet."

"Not yet!" She turned on him with blazing eyes.

"Alex is alone and afraid. When he reaches Montavia, that monster may kill him as he did my mother."

"No, he won't. You're not thinking clearly. Nebrov doesn't want Alex; he wants you. He only took Alex to lure you to him." He added, "I once told you that was the danger."

"And you still let him be taken."

"We'll get him back."

"Now!"

"We're going back to Cambaron first." He lifted his hand as she started to protest. "You don't take a hostage without leaving terms. No terms will be given to me because Nebrov would be afraid I'd ignore any threat to the boy if it meant losing the Jedalar. He'll make sure his terms are delivered to you personally. And then we'll take the messenger."

"What good will that do?"

"I want him," he said coldly. "Costain's men were lying in wait for Gregor and Alex. Someone at Cambaron had to have told them when they left the castle. I don't like traitors."

"We don't have time for you to indulge your taste for vengeance."

"It's not only vengeance. He may know something. Nebrov has the advantage, but anything we learn may help." He added, "I assure you that within a few hours we'll know everything he does."

Torture.

His tone was so savage, she should have been sickened, but she was not. She didn't care what Jordan did to any of those beasts, if it would get Alex back. "And then we'll go after Alex?"

"I promise you, the moment we have as much information as we can gather, we'll set sail for Montavia."

One part of her realized that Jordan's way was the most reasonable, but she didn't want to wait. She knew too well the brutality of which Nebrov was capable. She kept remembering her mother's pain-racked body and hearing—

"Very well," she said. "I'll wait two days and no more. After that, I'll find my own way to get to Montavia."

She quickly climbed the steps and closed the door to her room.

Alex. She leaned back against the door as fear and sorrow overwhelmed her. It seemed impossible that only yesterday afternoon she had laughed as she watched him running along the bank.

She would not cry. Tears would do no good. They would not get Alex back. She crossed the room to her armoire and started drawing out her gowns. She had to keep herself busy and not let herself think of what might happen to him.

She must hold on tight.

CHAPTER 11

Y ou could go without me," Gregor said. He shifted restlessly in the back of the wagon. "I am delaying you. I can follow tomorrow when I have more strength."

"You go with us," Jordan told him. "It will take only an hour or so more to reach Cambaron."

Gregor looked at Marianna, who was waiting on the seat of the wagon. "I think an hour means a great deal to her at this time. Though she is taking this better than I thought she would."

"Because she hasn't exploded and torn us to pieces? I wish she would. She's wound too taut. She may break." His gaze went to Marianna's pale, strained face and then quickly shifted back to Gregor. He smiled mirthlessly. "At least you're safe from her wrath. You've already been punished for your sins."

"Not enough. It was a very great sin."

"My sin. My responsibility. If he dies, it will be—" He broke off and then said, "But he's not going to die." He drew the blanket higher around Gregor. "Try not to move or you'll start the bleeding again.

Besides the inconvenience of having to take your corpse back to Kazan, I'm going to need you."

He went around to the front of the wagon and climbed onto the seat beside Marianna.

Dorothy was waiting in the courtyard as the wagon rolled through the gates.

She stepped forward. "I'm sorry about the lad," she said to Marianna. "I'm sure Jordan will get him back."

"You know?"

"I sent a rider with a message before we left Dalwynd to tell Dorothy the boy had been taken." Jordan jumped down from the wagon. "I thought it would save you distress." He lifted her down from the wagon. "God knows, there isn't much else I can do right now."

"You've probably already done quite enough," Dorothy said grimly. "I don't understand any of this. But if it has anything to do with that Corsican, you had no right to involve the child."

"Do you suppose you could refrain from heaping guilt on my head and see to Gregor? The trip wasn't easy for him." He smiled bitterly. "And, yes, I know, that's my fault too."

"I'm glad you admit it." She immediately took charge, directing servants, sending for the physician in the village. Then, taking Marianna's arm, she whisked her toward the front door.

"I'll be waiting in the study, Marianna," Jordan said quietly.

She nodded but didn't look at him as she let Dorothy lead her into the castle and up the stairs to her chamber.

"You're as cold as a block of ice," Dorothy said as she knelt at the hearth and stoked the flames. "Come and get warm."

Marianna wanted to tell her that no fire could rid her of this chill, but Dorothy was being kind. She crossed the room and held her hands out to the fire.

"Why would they take the boy? Do they think Jordan will ransom him?" Dorothy asked.

"Perhaps." She had never told Dorothy the details of her life before she came to Cambaron, and there was no use confiding in her now. She would not have understood a world so violent and alien to her own. "If you please, I don't want to talk about it now."

"Of course." Dorothy moved brusquely toward the door. "Will you come down to supper?"

"No." Jordan had said she must stay in her room in order that Nebrov's messenger would have to come to her. He had set a watch in a room down the hall and would know who came and went.

"Then I'll see that something's brought up to you." Dorothy paused at the door, hesitating. "And I wish you to know that I do not condemn you for going with Jordan to Dalwynd. Your loss of virtue was not your fault, and I shall still look on you exactly as I did before."

"What?" Marianna raised her head and stared at her in bewilderment. Virtue? What difference did a loss of virtue make when Alex was gone? Mother of God, what did it signify if she became the whore of Babylon? All that mattered was making sure Alex was saved. Then, as she stared at Dorothy, she realized it did matter to her. She evidently considered it of great importance, or she would never have mentioned it at this time. She might loudly embrace the rights of women, but the strictures of the *ton* had been more deeply ingrained in her than she knew. Even though she protested and denied it, Marianna was less in her eyes than she had been before.

She had broken the rules.

"That's all I wished to say. Now we'll forget this unfortunate incident and go on as before."

As the door closed behind her, Marianna stared into the flames. Dorothy was wrong; they could not go on as before. She would continue to love Dorothy for her kindness, but there would always be a barrier between them from now on.

Dorothy is bound by the very rules she thinks she flouts.

Jordan had said those words. Jordan had known what she had never guessed. Clever Jordan.

But not clever enough to keep Nebrov from taking Alex.

She sat down in the wing chair before the fire and closed her eyes.

Let the messenger come soon, she prayed. She could not bear this waiting much longer.

An envelope was slipped under her door a few hours later.

She heard a faint rustle and turned her head to see a white envelope cross over the threshold like a poisonous snake.

She leaped from her chair and was at the door in seconds but made no attempt to throw it open and look for the messenger. Jordan had promised he would be intercepted. Instead, Marianna ripped open the envelope and scanned the note inside before running down the stairs and into the study.

She threw the note on the desk in front of Jordan. "Here it is. It was slipped under my door. Now, let's *do* something about it."

He picked up the missive and read it. "It's what we expected."

Exactly what they expected, Marianna thought sickly. A death threat to Alex unless she surrendered herself to Nebrov at his estate at Pekbar before the month's end. "We have to leave at once."

"I've already sent word to ready the *Seastorm*," Jordan said. "We'll set out in the morning for Southwick." He rose to his feet. "Wait in your room. I'll need to talk to you as soon as I'm done."

"Where are you going?"

He glanced over his shoulder, and she inhaled sharply as she saw his expression. "The messenger."

It was after midnight when Jordan came to her room. He glanced at the cases beside the bed and said, "I see you're ready to depart."

She had paid little attention to gathering belongings, concentrating only on keeping herself from going mad while she waited for him. "I packed for Alex as well. He'll need something to wear when Nebrov releases him." *When* he releases him, not *if*. She had to keep believing they would save him. She asked, "Who was the messenger?"

"William Stoneham."

At first she did not recognize the name. He had always been just William, the name on Alex's lips a dozen times a day. When realization dawned, shock rippled through her. Cheerful, dapper William who had taught Alex to ride. William, whom Alex trusted only a little less than Gregor. "It couldn't be him. He loved Alex."

"Not as much as he loved the pounds Costain paid him to betray your brother. He told Costain where Gregor and Alex were going yesterday and that they would be unescorted."

She shook her head to clear it. These people she had thought she knew so well, she had not really known at all. The safe cocoon of Cambaron was unraveling, leaving her feeling dazed and naked.

"He was to notify Costain's man in Southwick when he delivered the message." He smiled grimly. "Unfortunately, he won't deliver the news in person. I left William's hand intact so that he could write the note we'll dictate, but his other extremities are sadly damaged."

"Dictate? What do you want him to say?"

"We may have need of dividing our forces. He'll send word that I was summoned to London and plan to come to Montavia at a later date and that only Gregor will be escorting you to Montavia."

"Did William know anything else?"

"No." He paused. "Marianna, we can't let Nebrov control the terms."

She stiffened. "What are you saying? I won't have Nebrov angered and chance having him hurt Alex."

"Sit down, Marianna."

"I don't care what games you're playing with Napoleon. Alex is not going to be part of them."

"I said, sit down." He gently pushed her down onto the chair. "And listen to me. Do you think

Nebrov is going to release Alex even if you give yourself in exchange?"

She had to believe it, she thought desperately.

"Shall I tell you what's going to happen? He'll capture you, renege on his promise to release Alex, and use him to make you give him the Jedalar. Do you want to see Alex tortured before your eyes?"

"No!" Her hands clenched the arms of the chair. "It won't happen. I'll give him the Jedalar."

"I can't let you do that."

"You can't let—" She stared at him in horror. "You'd let him die?"

"He won't die," he said harshly. "Do you think I'd allow Alex to be sacrificed? I'd let you give Nebrov the Jedalar and then find a way to take it from him later, if I thought that would save Alex." He knelt before her chair. "It wouldn't. After Nebrov has the Jedalar, the first thing he'd do would be to destroy anyone else who has knowledge of it. He'd kill both you and Alex. Think, Marianna, you know what he is."

She did know and had a terrible fear that Jordan was speaking the truth. Mama had told her often enough that power usually bred dishonor. It was only desperation that had led her to ignore that knowledge.

He didn't speak for a moment, letting his words sink in. "Our only chance is to find a way to catch him off guard and take Alex away from him. To do that, I'm going to need your help." He paused. "You're going to have to give me the Jedalar."

"I knew it would come to that," she said bitterly. "It's what you always wanted, wasn't it? What a wonderful opportunity."

He flinched. "Yes, it's what I wanted, what I have to have. But I won't let you be hurt by it. Trust me, Marianna."

"I don't trust you. Why should I?" She met his gaze. "You would have kept me in a cage. You let that monster take Alex."

"Then don't trust me. Just do what's best for Alex."

"That's my intention." She wearily leaned back in the chair. She had no choice. He was right, the Jedalar could be the key to freeing Alex. She had to run the risk.

Forgive me, Mama.

But her mother would never have wanted her to endanger Alex. She would have done what she had to do to save her family and tried to salvage what she could later.

"Very well." She sat upright in the chair. "We'll find a way to trick Nebrov by offering him what he wants. But it may not be as simple as you imagine. What do you know of the Jedalar?"

A little of the tension left him. "I know that a good many years ago Czar Paul of Russia decided that Moscow should have a means to repel invaders who laid siege to the city. He was rumored to be none too sane and loved to dress up in military uniforms and play soldier, and this was to be his finest act of military genius. He ordered a tunnel built from some point in the heart of Moscow to a point several miles beyond the perimeter so that his forces could circle around behind any besieging enemy and surprise them. The tunnel was built in great secrecy; the workers were blindfolded when they entered and left the tunnel. After the tunnel was finished, the czar became obsessed with keeping his secret safe. He realized that not only could his army attack a besieging force, but an invading army could enter Moscow and take it without a battle. He was terrified someone would discover the plans that showed the location and map of the tunnel, so he devised a means to disguise the map in a place no one would think to look. He commissioned the fashioning of a magnificent stained-glass window for one of his palaces. He had heard of a great craftsman Anton Pogani who was working on a church in Montavia and sent for him to do the work."

"The Window to Heaven," Marianna said.

Jordan nodded. "Pogani and his wife agreed to come to Moscow to do the czar's bidding. When they arrived, they found that not only was the window to be a work of art, but the glass was to be laid in such a way that it would furnish a secret map of the tunnel. An intricate task, but Pogani accomplished it."

"Grandmama accomplished it," she corrected.

"But no one knew it wasn't her husband who did the work. The czar was greatly pleased. He burned the plans and map of the tunnels and made arrangements for the immediate installation of the window in his palace." He paused. "And ordered the execution of Anton Pogani and his wife since they knew the secret and could not be permitted to live. They must have been warned, because they fled Moscow that night and took the Window to Heaven with them."

"They weren't warned," Marianna said. "They knew after they'd been in Moscow only a short time that the czar would never let them leave Russia alive."

"How?"

"The workers who built the tunnel," she whispered. Even now the horror of the act made her ill. "When they were no longer needed, the czar had them murdered. Seven hundred and sixty-seven human beings."

"I didn't know that."

"Grandmama couldn't let him reap the benefit of those murders," she said fiercely. "So she took his precious tunnel away from him. She knew as long as she had the Jedalar that he would feel threatened, that he would never be able to draw a safe breath."

Jordan nodded. "But they didn't return directly to Montavia. Anton was wounded in the escape, and they had to find a haven until he could recover. Kazan borders Russia, and they went there instead. They threw themselves on the mercy of the ravin and asked sanctuary. Kazan would not become involved in a dispute with Russia, but the ravin agreed to hide them until Anton could travel."

"And tried to steal the Window to Heaven while they were about it," she said sardonically.

"What did you expect?" Jordan shrugged. "Kazan sits on the doorstep of a giant. It's only practical to try to discover how to fell him if necessary." He continued, "But your grandparents fled again, this time to Talenka, and sold the Window to Heaven to the church. To steal the Window from the church would have caused a great deal of trouble with the papacy. Since Kazan wanted the Jedalar only as a safeguard anyway, the ravin decided not to make a move as long as there was no danger of it being used against her country." He paused. "And when the czar had the great kindness to be murdered, it lessened the threat enormously. I suppose your grandmother was very grateful to be safe at last."

"She knew we'd never be safe, that we'd need a weapon. That's why she made Mama memorize the exact design of the Jedalar. And why my mother made me do the same thing."

"It wasn't a weapon," he said harshly. "It was a trap. She had no right to make you guardians of a secret that dangerous. She should have smashed the blasted window herself."

"But then you and Napoleon and Nebrov would have nothing to claw and fight over." She smiled bitterly. "And when the Window was smashed, they still came after us. Mama would have been killed, even if she had known nothing. They kept asking her over and over where she had hidden the design on which the window was based." She tapped her temple. "The design is here and only here. Yes, it was a trap, but without it we would have had nothing with which to fight. Besides, she had good reason for running the risk."

"The treasure room in the tunnel?"

She was prepared for the question. Her mother had said they would undoubtedly know about it. "What treasure room?"

"There were rumors the czar created a room in the tunnel to store his treasures. Did your grandmother hope to go back and compensate herself for the Window to Heaven?"

"Why should I tell you? You don't need to know. I shall tell you nothing that's not necessary."

"Not even to save Alex?"

"We *will* save Alex, but I'll give you only what I must."

His gaze narrowed on her face. "You accused me of risking Alex. Don't do the same thing, Marianna."

"How dare you?" Her eyes blazed. "I would never put him at risk. I had to stand by while Mama died protecting Alex and me. Do you think I'll let her die for nothing? I love Alex. I don't know why I'm even talking to you. I doubt if you even know what love means."

"Perhaps not." He smiled with effort. "I admit I've not had extensive experience with that particular emotion." He rose to his feet. "If it's not revealing too much to such a callous barbarian, will you tell me how long it will take you to make another Window to Heaven? Nebrov can't expect you to produce a work of the same quality as the one in Talenka overnight but—"

"It's already done."

He went still. "I beg your pardon?"

"As soon as I felt I had the necessary skill and precision to complete it, I made the Jedalar. Did you think all I was doing for the past three years was taking dancing lessons and waiting for time to pass?"

"There was also the small matter of creating the dome for the ballroom." To her surprise there was a hint of pride in his smile. "I suppose I should have guessed you would never give up. You're far too determined."

"So are you, and so is Nebrov. I had to make sure I had something with which to bargain if Alex or I were ever in danger."

"And, of course, you couldn't trust me."

"I could trust no one. Particularly you."

"Just how did you manage to create a window of

that scope and size without any of us knowing about it?"

"Grandmama made sure that everyone assumed the Jedalar was spread out throughout the window's twenty-three panels, but that wasn't true. The map occupied only one panel that was three feet long and two feet wide. A panel that size can be easily enough hidden."

"Where?"

She hesitated. Silence on the subject of the Jedalar had been ingrained in her since childhood, and it was a habit she found difficult to break. "It's in the stable storeroom among the panels I discarded."

He gave a low whistle. "Very clever. According to Gregor, you discarded such a large quantity that it became commonplace for you to banish your work to the storeroom. How many panels are out there?"

"Over thirty." She added, "And we're going to take them all to Montavia."

"May I ask why?"

"Because then neither you nor Nebrov will know which is the Jedalar," she said, "until I choose to tell you."

"I'd be deeply grateful if you would not link us together verbally. Even though you clearly do it in your mind."

She did link them together. She had no choice. Jordan was the enemy. Even if he helped her save Alex, he would still try to take the Jedalar from her. She did not know if it could be done, but she must try to save both the Jedalar and Alex.

At the moment it seemed an impossible task. All the anger that had kept her functioning was draining out of her at an alarming rate, and she was so exhausted she could barely sit upright.

"Go to bed," he said roughly. "You can't go on like this."

She shook her head. "I couldn't sleep."

He moved behind her, and his hands cupped the back of her neck.

She stiffened.

"Relax." He started to massage the tense muscles of her nape. "It's not as if I haven't ever done this for you after you've worked all day."

She had a sudden vision of herself sitting at his feet before the fire, his hands moving on her with possession and strength until she had been dazed with contentment. Dazed and dazzled with everything he had done to her during those days at Dalwynd.

His thumbs probed gently. "It loosens the—"

"Don't touch me."

He kept kneading her nape. "It's easing you, blast it."

"Don't touch me!"

His hands fell away, and he stepped back. "Do you think I'm trying to seduce you?" he asked quietly as he moved around the chair to stand in front of her. "I'm not a fool, Marianna. You were in need, and I was only trying to help."

"I don't want your help."

"But you may need to accept it before this is over. Doing battle with me over trivialities will sap both our strength and may get in the way of saving Alex." He stared directly into her eyes. "No matter how much you dislike me at the moment, I believe you know I keep my word. Until Alex is returned to you, I will make no attempt to take anything from you but your cooperation." He smiled crookedly. "However, after my guilt is expiated, I promise nothing. You know my morals are sadly unstable." He turned and moved toward the door. "We'll be leaving before dawn for Southwick. I'd appreciate it if you'd try to get some rest. It would be a great bother having to pick you up off the road if you fainted from exhaustion."

It was still dark when Marianna reached the courtyard the next morning. Torches burned bright in their sconces before the front door. Servants bustled to and fro preparing for the departure, and Dorothy was overseeing their efforts.

"This is most undignified." Gregor shrugged off the help of a solicitous footman and climbed awkwardly into a wagon drawn before the door. He grimaced as he settled himself on the pallet. "I told Jordan I was strong enough to ride, but he insisted I be coddled like an infant."

Marianna could see why he had made the decision. Gregor's face was drawn and bloodless in the merciless light. "Are you sure you're well enough to make the sea journey?"

"What is there to do on a ship but rest? By the time we reach Kazan, I shall be strong as a bull."

"Kazan? We're going to Montavia."

"Jordan has decided we should sail directly to Kazan and negotiate with Nebrov from a position of strength."

She could see little advantage in such a move. "How kind of him to inform me. Where is Jordan?"

Gregor nodded toward another wagon by the stable. "He is seeing to the crating of your panels." He chuckled. "What a clever little dove you are proving to be. I never guessed what you were doing."

"It's not clever to do what you have to do." She saw Jordan coming out of the stable and strode across the courtyard toward him. She asked him, "You've packed all of them?"

"I'd hardly leave one behind when it might be the Jedalar."

"But I'd wager you examined every panel very carefully before you had it crated."

He smiled. "Of course. I even measured them. Every one of them is three feet by two feet. Some of them looked a bit more intricate than others, but I could tell nothing. Any one of them could be the Jedalar. I had the crates marked with a description of the contents to save time when you decide to retrieve it."

"That will be helpful." She changed the subject. "Why are we going to Kazan? Gregor says you wish to negotiate from a position of strength, but I don't want Nebrov to think we're offering him resistance."

"Nebrov won't destroy his weapon just because he perceives it to be threatened. Besides, we may need help after we get the boy away. According to Janus, Nebrov's power has been growing in Montavia. It would be safer to take Alex to Kazan."

After they got him away.

Jordan sounded so matter-of-fact that she felt a surge of hope. She could tell herself that all would go well and Alex would be safe, but it was difficult to make herself believe it.

Jordan's brows lifted. "Satisfied?"

"No, I won't be satisfied until Alex is free. But we will go to Kazan."

"I'm glad you agree." He inclined his head mockingly. "We should have the last of the crates loaded within a few minutes. Be ready to start."

"I'm almost ready. I've only to say my farewells to Dorothy."

"I've already bid her good-bye," Jordan added dryly. "And was nearly frozen by her disapproval. She seems to think I've arranged Alex's abduction just to lure you farther into my wicked web and—" He stopped, his gaze narrowing on her face. "What is it? What's wrong?"

"Nothing."

He shook his head, studying her expression. He said slowly, "It's Dorothy. What did she say to you?"

"It doesn't matter."

"What did she say?"

She shrugged. "That she forgives me my lack of virtue."

"Christ."

She smiled with effort. "I'm sure she considers herself very generous to a woman who is ruined in the eyes of all respectable people."

He gave a low curse. "She hurt you."

"She couldn't help it. She didn't even realize the hurt was there. She thought she was being kind." She turned away from him. "I'll be ready to leave in a few minutes." She suddenly thought of something and asked over her shoulder, "What favor did you do for her?"

"Favor?"

"When I first met Dorothy, she told me you had once done her a great service."

"It was nothing of particular note." When she stood waiting, he shrugged and said, "No one would publish her books. I bribed McArthy and Son to do it."

"I see." She felt his gaze on her back as she crossed the courtyard to the steps where Dorothy now stood. Poor Dorothy, her finest triumph had been provided by one of the oppressive males she condemned.

"I will go with you, if you wish," Dorothy said gruffly. "It's not seemly for you to travel with Jordan in this fashion."

Even now, when Dorothy considered her ruined, she was still striving to put things right. Marianna felt a flicker of warmth mix with the sadness. She could not condemn Dorothy for not being all that she wanted her to be; she must accept her for what she was. "Montavia is not like England. You would not understand it. You will be happier here." She gave her a quick hug. "Good-bye, Dorothy, thank you for all your kindness to me."

"You will find the boy," Dorothy said brusquely. "And you'll be back at Cambaron by summer."

Marianna merely smiled, then turned and went down the steps to the wagon where Jordan was now waiting.

Without looking at Dorothy, he lifted Marianna onto the seat and then climbed up himself.

"Wave farewell to her," Marianna said in a low voice.

"The devil I will."

"She has a great fondness for you. She will be hurt if you're cold to her."

He shot her a look. "And what about your hurt?"

"I don't need you to fight my battles." Then she demanded, "Wave farewell to her."

"Obstinate woman." The faintest smile curved his lips. He lifted his hand in Dorothy's general direction and then snapped the reins to put the horses in motion.

As the two wagons rolled out of the gates of Cambaron, Marianna glanced over her shoulder at the castle. Lord, how frightened she had been the first time she had caught sight of those four towers. Three years of her life had been spent within those stone walls. It was strange to think that she would never see them again. No matter what the outcome of this journey, she and Alex would not return to Cambaron. She felt an instant of poignant regret and then firmly dismissed it. Cambaron had never really been her home, and she must remember what Grandmama had always told her.

"What are you thinking?"

She looked around to see Jordan observing her.

She was not about to tell him she never intended to return to the castle. Yet Jordan was a part of Cambaron, and she had a sudden desire to share this leavetaking with him. She said haltingly, "Grandmama often had to travel from place to place in order to do her work, and at first she was very unhappy. She would just start to love a place and feel comfortable, and she would have to give it up and leave again. Then she suddenly realized that she wasn't really giving up anything, because with every window, every panel she had created, she had left a part of herself behind. She said 'Leave your mark, Marianna, and no one can ever take anything away from you.' "

"She sounds like a very wise woman."

"Very wise."

She again looked back over her shoulder at the castle that had sheltered six hundred years of power and privilege. Generations of nobility had come and gone; even royalty had cast their tall shadows in those halls. Yet she would defy any of them to claim they had brought more to this place than she had.

She whispered, "By God, I've left my mark on you, Cambaron."

CHAPTER 12

"Smell it, Marianna." Gregor lifted his head and sniffed enthusiastically. "There are no scents on earth like the ones here in Kazan."

Marianna obligingly sniffed, but she could tell little difference from the scents here and those at Domajo and Southwick. "Very nice."

"You needn't be polite. We all know Gregor suffers from an incurable malady," Jordan said as he joined them at the rail of the ship. "He believes that even the air in Kazan is sweeter, the horses bigger and faster, and the people stronger and more intelligent."

"I believe it because it is true," Gregor protested. "You will see, Marianna." He took her arm and pulled her toward the gangplank. "Come, Jordan, why are you tarrying?"

"The horses have to be saddled and unloaded." He followed them down the gangplank. "The palace is over four miles from the dock. It would be pleasant to have some form of transportation, don't you think? Even though Cambaron horses are only adequate compared to Kazan's vastly superior horseflesh."

"Palace?" Marianna asked.

"If we're to receive help, we must petition the ravin," Jordan explained. Then, as he saw her worried frown, he added, "It's only a formality. Kazan has no desire to let Nebrov keep a weapon that could be aimed at them."

"This has gone on too long," Marianna said. "We don't need another delay." The journey from England had seemed to last an eternity, stretching her nerves to their limits. The idea of having to linger in a foreign palace was unbearable.

"There's a possibility that there may also be some information waiting for us," Jordan said. "Janus is watching Nebrov, and he has orders to send identical messages to the ravin at the same time he sent them to me."

"There they are." Gregor strode toward the horses being led down the gangplank. He soothingly stroked the nose of his big stallion. "Here we are on hard, firm ground again," he crooned. "You will be much happier now." He swung onto the saddle. "Come, let us go." He didn't wait for them but spurred ahead down the cobblestone street.

Marianna shook her head in wonderment. She had never seen Gregor so full of joy. His scarred face had been luminous. "He's so happy."

"He's home," Jordan said simply.

"He must care a great deal for you to stay in England."

He lifted her onto her saddle. "I know that fills you with amazement, but, yes, he does care about me." He swung onto his horse and nudged him forward. "And, of course, there is always the matter of duty. Gregor always does his duty."

In spite of the mocking words she became aware of an odd tension suddenly charging him. It dawned on her that he could be mitigating the difficulty of getting the ravin's help. "What's wrong?"

"Nothing is wrong. Everything is perfect. Ask Gregor."

"You don't like Kazan?" Her forehead knitted in perplexity. "But isn't protecting Kazan the reason you're determined to get the Jedalar?"

"I never said I didn't like Kazan. It's far more home to me than Cambaron."

The words were restrained, almost noncommittal, but there was something beneath them, something in his expression. Then she realized what it was. Why, he truly loved this country. In spite of his mocking words regarding Gregor's passion for his homeland, his feeling was just as deep. But, being Jordan, he would not lift his mask to reveal it. "It's not at all like Cambaron."

Nothing could be less like that rocklike bastion of power than this city. Exotic onion-shaped towers and tall, graceful needle-thin spires abounded here. Instead of the sod or stone houses she was accustomed to seeing in the English countryside, the principal building material here appeared to be wood. Nearly all the houses and shops were flat-roofed and similar in design, but each had its own stamp of individuality, such as a lacy carving on a window box or colorful tiles on a doorstep. As they picked their way through the marketplace, she noticed each booth or stand had its own copper or porcelain samovar over a small fire.

She pointed at a tall flumelike structure at one side of the market where crowds of people had gathered. "What is that?"

"An ice slide. Every town and village in Kazan has at least one."

She watched a little boy careen madly down the ice-coated funnel and land in a thick bank of snow. He picked himself up, whooping joyously as he ran around to get in line at the ladder again.

"Alex will love it." she said eagerly, without thinking. "Can we—"

But Alex was not here. Alex might never—

"Yes, he will," Jordan said firmly. "We'll probably never get him off it."

Hope. She must not despair; they still had hope and determination. Looking away from the children on the slide, she quickly changed the subject. "Gregor says the reason you hate Napoleon is because you love Kazan. Is that true?"

"Gregor has a habit of simplifying things."

"Is it true?"

He shrugged. "I suppose it's true."

"Why? It's not your country."

"Because I wasn't born here? Cambaron was given to me. I chose Kazan."

"It's so . . . different."

"More than you know." He smiled crookedly. "The first months I was here, I hated it. The people of Kazan didn't realize what an honor it was to have me in their midst. They cared not a whit for my title or my money. I was not a savant, nor had I proved myself in battle. Therefore I was nothing. It was a very chastening experience for the spoiled hellion I was at the time."

"Why did you stay?"

"There were reasons." He grimaced. "One of which was anger. I would *not* be considered of unimportance. So when Tartar raiders descended on Kazan, I went with Gregor and his men to the steppes."

"War?"

He nodded. "Kazan is nearly always at war with someone. Our land is rich only in minerals, but we have a valuable sea link to the Mediterranean."

"*Our* land?"

"It became mine on the steppes. I bought it with blood."

She shivered at the simple words that revealed so much. Those wars had changed him, hardened him, burned away the softness, and left him one with these strange, brutish people.

He was looking at the fluted towers of the distant palace, and she again became aware of some indefinable emotion seething just below the surface.

"Are you apprehensive about meeting with the ravin?"

"Not apprehensive." His tore his gaze away. "Let us say, a trifle disturbed." He spurred forward. "Come. At the speed Gregor is traveling, he'll be sitting in the audience chamber before we even reach the palace gates."

Gregor was not sitting in the audience chamber; he was pacing impatiently as Marianna and Jordan walked into the room. "I've sent a message that we are here. It should not be long."

"Not unless it's deemed wiser to keep us waiting," Jordan said. "One never knows."

"You are being unfair," Gregor told him. "She will come."

Marianna felt a ripple of shock. She?

"Jordan seldom feels it necessary to be fair to me. You should know that by now, Gregor."

Marianna turned toward the doorway and the woman who had spoken.

Another shock, this one of stunning proportions. She *knew* this woman. She had spent hours studying that strong, beautiful face. It was older now, with tiny crow's-feet at the corners of the slanted green eyes, but it was still beautiful and even stronger.

"I'm always fair to you. I'm merely cautious. You know how I hate to be disappointed." Jordan came forward and lifted the woman's hand to his lips. "You look lovely as always and perhaps even a little younger."

Jordan's mother. Marianna continued to stare in astonishment. Jordan's mother had died when he was only a baby, and yet, looking at the two standing side by side, Marianna had no doubt they were mother and son.

"Of course I look younger," the woman said. "I've decided I shall never grow old. Next year I intend to order all the clocks in Kazan stopped."

"And all the calendars burned," Gregor added. He lumbered toward her. "I shall see to it personally."

A brilliant smile lit her face as she turned to him. "Gregor. Have you been well?"

He nodded. "Well enough."

"With the tiny exception of a knife wound in his chest," Jordan remarked.

The smile faded from her face. "Who?"

"Nebrov's man, Costain."

Her expression hardened. "Did you kill him, Jordan?"

"Not yet."

"Why not? Do it yourself, or I will see that it's done."

"I believe the matter concerns me, Ana," Gregor said mildly.

"Be quiet, Gregor. I'm not too pleased with you either. You must be getting feebleminded to let yourself be wounded by that vermin."

She was the one who was being unfair, Marianna thought with irritation. "He was *not* feebleminded. There were seven men," Marianna interjected. "And he walked six miles in the snow after they wounded him."

The woman turned her head. "Ah, you have a champion. You must be Marianna Sanders." Her keen glance raked Marianna from head to toe. "Gregor wrote me a good deal about you. I would like to see the window you did of me." She grimaced. "Though that's the only part of Cambaron I shall ever want to see again."

"I thought you were dead."

"I would have been dead, if I'd stayed there." She turned and stared challengingly at Jordan. "It was strangling me."

Jordan ignored the provocation. "Marianna, I'm honored to present Her Majesty, Ana Dvorak, Ravin of Kazan." He smiled. "And you'll be delighted to know you don't have to curtsy. It's not the custom in Kazan. A mere inclination of the head to show respect is all that's required."

"Providing that one feels such respect," Ana Dvorak said with irony. "I suppose that Gregor's wound is connected to the message I received from Janus three days ago?"

"You've had word?"

She nodded. "Come with me and we'll talk." She turned to Gregor. "Find her suitable quarters. Sandor is somewhere about. I will see you at supper." She impulsively reached out and touched his arm. "I'm not entirely unpleased to see you, *mado*."

"You are very pleased to see me," Gregor corrected.

She chuckled. "Perhaps."

Marianna turned to Gregor as soon as they departed. "Why does everyone at Cambaron think she's dead?"

"Because she wished them to think it. We planned it very carefully so that everyone would believe she drowned in a boating accident. That way there would not have to be a body."

"We?"

"She needed me. I helped her."

The sentences were spoken with utter simplicity as if his helping Ana Dvorak could be the only course of action whenever her need for him arose.

Gregor led her from the chamber. "Ah, Sandor." He hailed a bearded young man hurrying down the corridor. "The ravin wishes quarters for the *belka*. Near the garden, I think."

"Certainly." Sandor inclined his head respectfully to Gregor. "If you will follow me?"

"What is a *belka*?"

"It is an outsider, anyone who does not belong to us."

The term was certainly fitting. She had never felt more the outsider than in this strange land. She returned to the subject Sandor had interrupted. "Why did she wish them to think her dead?" she asked

Gregor as they followed the young man down a labyrinth of corridors.

"She told you. She could not bear it." He shook his head. "She should never have gone to Cambaron, but she was young and willful and would not listen. Her blood was hot, and when she met Jordan's father, she thought only of—" He stopped and nodded his head at Sandor a few yards ahead. "I should not say more now. The ravin should be spoken of with respect before her subjects."

The ravin, Jordan's mother, the woman who had come back to life. Marianna's mind was whirling as she murmured, "Jordan said his mother departed this life when he was two."

He chuckled. "Did he indeed? Jordan never likes to lie."

"She left him. She left her child." She shook her head. "How could she do that? If she wasn't happy, why didn't she take him when she left Cambaron?"

His smile faded. "He was the future Duke of Cambaron. She would never have been permitted to take him with her. She was not even allowed to take him for a walk without a maid in attendance. She would not have been permitted to leave herself, so the deceit was necessary. She knew Jordan would be well cared for and never want for anything."

Except a mother.

Everyone walks away eventually.

When Jordan had said those cynical words, she had never dreamed he had also included his mother.

"Do not condemn her." Gregor's gaze was on her face. "It was not a good thing she did, and it brought her much pain. But, for Ana, it was the only thing to do."

She remembered the impression of challenge and tension she had received when Jordan and his mother had confronted each other. "I don't think Jordan understands that either."

"The emotions between them are not easy to define. They are much alike."

"When did he learn she was alive?"

"When he was a lad of nineteen. We had been watching and receiving reports on him through the years, and Ana decided we could wait no longer." He grimaced. "He was rapidly acquiring all the vices of his father and putting them to use with all the vigor of his mother. She sent me to England to school him."

"Will this be suitable?" Sandor threw open a door and stepped aside. "If not, there is another down the corridor that overlooks the fountain."

She barely glanced at the luxurious chamber, receiving only a vague impression of pale gold draperies, light, and space. "No, this will be fine."

Gregor smiled. "Very good, Sandor. Thank you."

Sandor inclined his head and quickly strode away.

"I will see that your bags are brought to you." Gregor added gently, "I know that all of this is a little bewildering for you, but this is a fine place. You will like it here. I look forward to showing you my homeland."

"We won't be here long. We'll have to leave for Montavia almost immediately."

"It does not take long to love Kazan." He turned. "Rest now. We usually eat at twilight. I will come and escort you to the dining hall. Do not worry about any other surprises, Ana will see that we dine alone tonight."

When she was alone in the room, she moved over to the bed.

Rest? Besides her worry and tension regarding Alex, her mind was whirling with implications of the scene that had just taken place. Resentment, challenge, unquestioning affection, and loyalty had all been present in that audience chamber today, none of which should have had this impact on her. She was here to save Alex, not become involved in the tangled lives of others.

Everyone walks away eventually.

She would not feel sorry for that child who had been abandoned. Understanding did not bring justification. Jordan had no right to try to cage her to assure himself that she would not leave him. He had not even displayed regret and as much as said he would make the same attempt after he had freed Alex for her.

Everyone walks away. . . .

Jordan and his mother were standing talking by a huge recessed window when Gregor and Marianna walked into the dining hall. The last purple-gold rays of twilight surrounded them, and Marianna was again aware of how much alike they were. The same tall, strong body, the dark shining hair, the boldness, the wariness.

Jordan looked up and saw her. He politely inclined his head to the ravin before he crossed the room toward them.

"You're comfortably settled?" he asked.

She nodded. "What message from this Janus?"

"Costain delivered a captive to his estate at Pekbar three days ago."

"Alex?"

"It was night, and Janus wasn't able to get a good look at him."

"It *has* to be Alex."

"What do we do now?"

"Now we eat a fine dinner." He took Marianna's arm. "And tonight we sleep well so that we'll be rested for our journey to Montavia tomorrow."

"We must make plans," Marianna said impatiently.

"I have a few ideas I'll need to mull over. We'll discuss them in the morning. The ravin is furnishing us with a large troop of men to accompany us."

He had addressed her not as Mother but as the ravin. He was deliberately distancing himself from her, Marianna thought as she glanced at the woman standing by the window. Ana Dvorak's shoulders were thrown back, and she was staring indifferently at them. Yet Marianna had the impression she was not truly indifferent. Lonely? No, that was too absurd. In her white satin gown and glittering emerald coronet the woman was everything that was bold and regal.

"Seat Marianna, Jordan." Even as he spoke, Gregor was moving across the room toward the ravin. "I will sit by Ana. We have many things to discuss."

Marianna watched as Gregor bowed and said something to Jordan's mother. She threw back her head and laughed, her expression coming vibrantly alive. He took her arm, escorted her to the head of the table, and seated her with elaborate courtesy. Every word, every gesture, reflected a familiarity of long standing.

"They know each other well," Marianna murmured.

"From the cradle," Jordan said. "They grew up together. They're distant cousins, and Gregor's father was the captain of the guard in the Dvorak household."

She looked at Gregor's scarred face. "Was Gregor in the army too?"

"For a number of years, but when Ana Dvorak became ravin she made him chief adviser."

"I don't understand how your mother could become the ravin. Gregor said she was only a noblewoman when she married your father."

"In Kazan the throne doesn't automatically pass from father to son." Jordan seated Marianna far down the table from Gregor and his mother and then took the place across from her. Distance again, she thought absently.

Jordan continued, "Kazan is surrounded by potential enemies and can't afford the indulgence of a weak or foolish ruler. The Council of Nobles choose one from their ranks who they judge will be the strongest ruler. When the former ravin died, there was no ruler for two years until they finally chose Ana Dvorak."

"A woman?"

"Dorothy would be scandalized by your surprise," he said. "I'm sure she would be delighted that Kazan offers women an opportunity to prove their worth."

"I'm equally delighted." She added pointedly, "It's just not common practice for men to be fair. Even in Montavia this could not be."

"The council decided she had proven herself. After her father died, she had ruled her own lands for ten years and made them flourish. She rode at the head of her vassals and repelled bandits and raiders from across the border. She built bridges and aqueducts. She took care of her sick and even opened a hospital here in Rengar. Yes, she was without a flaw." He smiled sardonically. "Of course, there was that small mistake of a marriage in England, but that was of no account. The ceremony was not performed in the traditional Kazan manner, so it clearly was not binding."

"But she didn't marry again?"

"No." His smile became mocking. "After being wed to my father, I'm sure she had quite enough of marriage. It would only have gotten in her way."

"You resent her."

"Do I? It's a possibility. I also admire her. She's a brilliant woman. She rather reminds me of you."

"Me?" She shook her head. "I'm nothing like her."

"You have the same vitality and intensity." He paused. "And the same appetite for pleasure."

The sensual words came out of nowhere, catching her off guard and bringing the physical response that he had so carefully cultivated during those days at the hunting lodge, the tingling between her thighs, the swelling of her breasts. The mask was suddenly off, and this was not the man who had carefully tamped down any hint of sexuality on the journey from Cambaron but the totally erotic being he had been at Dalwynd.

He smiled as he read her expression. "Don't be alarmed. I intend to keep my promise. I just thought I'd remind you it's still there, waiting. For both of us." He glanced at the servant who had appeared at her side bearing a silver tray on which were arranged an assortment of baked meats. "Try the chicken. The ravin's cook has created a lemon sauce that's quite superb."

He wants her still." Ana bit into a chicken wing with delicacy and gusto, her moody gaze on Jordan and Marianna. "This is not usual for Jordan."

"Marianna is not usual," Gregor said. "And neither was what he felt for her."

"I see nothing so unusual about her." She frowned as she studied Marianna. "Why is she fighting him?"

"Do you suppose it could be because she regards him as the enemy? She loves her brother, and she holds Jordan responsible."

"He will get the boy back."

"And there's the small matter of the Jedalar we are trying to steal from her."

Ana dismissed the argument with a wave of her hand. "We are in the right."

"Right is usually in the eye of the beholder."

She nodded thoughtfully. "There are problems, but most women are taught to be guided by their bodies, not their minds."

"Marianna is not 'most' women."

"You said she let herself be taken by him. She is clearly a young woman with a young woman's passions."

The conversation was making him uneasy. At first he had thought he had seen signs of envy, but now he realized Ana's feelings were far more complicated. "The battle is between them, Ana. You cannot make a gift of her to him just because he wants her. You sent me to England to make sure he was not spoiled by getting everything he wanted."

"This is different."

It was different only because Ana wanted it to be different. "How would you have felt if your husband had possessed a mother who wanted him to have you, regardless of your inclination?"

"There was no question of that," she said bitterly. "They all hated me in England."

"For good reason. You were rude and wild and wanted your own way. You cannot trample over people and expect them to love you."

She glared at him. "I don't trample over people." Scowling, she then amended her own statement. "Well, not as a common practice."

His laughter boomed. "I admit you've grown gentler over the years. Now, you are more like a pouncing tiger than an attacking lion." He looked at Marianna again. "She did a splendid panel of a tiger that reminded me of you."

Her attention returned immediately to the previous subject. "Jordan is generous and can be very charming. There is no reason he should not have her. She could not find a better lover or protector."

His laughter faded as he saw where she was drifting. There would be trouble if she decided on this course. He said slowly, "You cannot buy him, Ana."

"Don't be ridiculous. I'm not trying to buy him." She lifted her chin. "I have no need to buy anyone."

"That is true. Now believe it yourself." He lifted his glass of wine to his lips. "He will come to you in time."

"Will he?" Her lips curled bitterly. "When I am old and gray and pitiful? I've waited too long already.

What does he want of me? I cannot be anything but what I am."

"Be patient. You've hardly been a sweet and sacrificing mother," Gregor said mildly. "Any more than he's been an understanding, forgiving son."

"I don't want his forgiveness."

"Then what do you want from him?"

She was silent a moment and then said haltingly, "He need not be so cold. It would not be too much to expect friendship, would it? After all, we do have a common goal."

He could sense the hurt she would never show Jordan. He wanted to reach out and touch her in comfort, but he knew she would not accept it. This wound went too deep. "It will come in time."

"You said that before," she said impatiently.

"Ah yes, you fear gray hair and creaking bones. But how can that happen when I'm going to burn all the calendars?"

She smiled reluctantly. "Would you really do that for me, Gregor?"

"Of course. Do you wish for a fountain of youth? I will venture forth immediately and find it for you."

"I'm not sure I would like to be young again. I was very stupid when I was young."

"We are all stupid before we gain experience."

"You were never stupid," she said softly. "You were always exactly as you are now." A shadow crossed her face. "Were you truly almost killed?"

"No, I've had far greater wounds. All the blood frightened Marianna."

"I won't have you die," she said with sudden fierceness. "Do you hear me? I won't have it. What would I do without you?" She grimaced as she realized what she had said. "You see how selfish I am. I'm not sure you're right regarding my improvement in character."

"It is all you. The bad and the good combine to make the whole. It is the entire Ana Dvorak that matters."

She looked down into the wine in her goblet. "The entire Ana Dvorak has certain needs that you do not fulfill. Are you going to come to me tonight?"

"No."

Her hand tightened on her goblet. "I will not wait forever for you."

"This is very good wine. Your own vineyards?"

"Yes. You injure my pride by your refusal. Other men desire me."

"I desire you." He smiled at her. "How could I not desire you? You are everything that a man could want in a woman."

"Then why do you— I will not humble myself again like this."

"Yes, you will."

"Why should I?"

"Because you know that no one loves you as I do. You are curious to know how it would feel to bed a man whose love is as great as mine."

She smiled beguilingly. "If you truly love me, you will come to my bed."

"It is because I love you that I do not. Sadly it is as bad for your character to indulge your every wish as it was for Jordan."

"I am not Jordan."

She did not realize how much she resembled Jordan in this moment. Green eyes glittering with annoyance, the beautiful mouth tight with willfulness, the explosive energy lying just beneath the surface. The only difference was that Jordan masked his emotions beneath that air of cynicism, and Ana hid hers behind a wall of pride.

"No, Ana," he said gently.

A mixture of disappointment and anger flared in her expression. "I'm not a nun. Do you want to know how many men I have had in my bed since last I saw you?"

"No, I do not want to know."

"When I go back to my rooms tonight, I will send for a man who does not find me—"

"No, you will not." His gaze met her own. "Not while I am here."

"You cannot expect me to—" She broke off and then nodded jerkily, her voice uneven, "Not while you are here. Never while you are here." She glanced quickly away from him. "You are a very difficult man, *mado.*"

"I am a very simple man."

"Who must always have his way." She squared her shoulders and smiled recklessly. "Well, I will not be defeated on all fronts. I think I must see that Jordan is made happy, if I am not."

He should have known she would return to do battle. "You took away his mother, and now you wish to provide him a mistress to soothe the hurt? It is not a trade you can make, Ana."

"You will not allow it?"

He nodded at Marianna. "She will not allow it."

Ana's gaze raked the delicacy of Marianna's features, the fragility of her small body. "I doubt if she's a match for me. I think I must accompany you on this journey to Montavia. Nebrov will hesitate to attack if I am along."

"I am not so confident."

She smiled brilliantly. "And besides, I must be there to protect you in case your wits fail you again. Yes, I will definitely go to Montavia."

He opened his lips to argue with her and then closed them. Perhaps Ana should go with them. Marianna's will was strong enough to resist Ana's coercion, and, for all he knew, Ana's effort might bring about the prize she wanted most in the world. A common goal, she had said, meaning the defeat of Napoleon, but now Marianna offered the possibility of another common goal.

Poor dove, he was about to offer her up to the tigers.

"Why are you not arguing with me?" she asked warily.

"But I want you to go to Montavia." He smiled at her and added with complete truthfulness, "I always want you with me, Ana."

The morning was frigid, and the breaths of the horses milling about the courtyard were like plumes of smoke. Marianna was mounted and waiting impatiently when Jordan came out of the palace.

He was dressed all in black even to the seal fur on the collar of his cloak, and he appeared lean, tough, and faintly sinister in the early light.

"Good morning." He mounted his horse and gathered the reins. "I regret to keep you waiting, but I was having a discussion with the ravin. It seems she's going with us."

She frowned. "Why?"

He shrugged. "Who knows? What she says isn't always what she means." He took stock of the waiting horsemen. "But she apparently meant it when she said she'd furnish us with quite a large troop. This is almost an army."

"How long are we going to have to wait for her?" she asked.

"Not long." His gaze returned to the palace. "There she is now."

Ana Dvorak looked very much like the warrior in her stained-glass window, Marianna thought, as she watched the woman mount her black stallion and then ride toward them. The ravin was not wearing armor, but her back was straight, her seat on the horse magnificent, and her manner bold and autocratic.

"I don't suppose you'll reconsider? This is not necessary, you know," Jordan said as she reached them. "There's no use putting you in danger as well."

"I'm touched by your concern. But I do think it necessary, and I rule here, not you, Jordan." She gestured for him to ride ahead. "Now run along with Gregor. I wish to speak to the *belka*."

"Why?" Jordan asked.

"I'm merely being cordial to a guest. You gave me no opportunity to become acquainted with her last night."

Jordan hesitated and then glanced inquiringly at Marianna.

Sweet heavens, Marianna thought, he was behaving as if the woman were going to cut her throat. She was not sure she was looking forward to becoming acquainted with the ravin, but there was nothing to fear.

"Go on," she said curtly.

He shrugged and nudged his horse into a gallop.

"He is very protective," the ravin said as she guided her horse along side Marianna's. "It is a fine quality in a man."

"If one wishes protection."

"Don't be absurd. A woman always needs protection."

"Do you?"

"I'm the ravin. I have an army to protect me."

"And before you were the ravin?"

Ana Dvorak burst into laughter. "Very well, I admit it. I would have hung a man up by his toenails if he'd offered me protection."

"Even Gregor?"

Her face softened miraculously. "Gregor will not listen. He never offers, he just gives of himself." She frowned. "But I am not here to talk of Gregor, and I'm not here to answer your questions."

"You said you were here to become acquainted, Your Majesty," Marianna said.

"No, I'm here to tell you that you should take Jordan back to your bed."

Marianna's eyes widened in shock. "I beg your pardon?"

She shrugged. "I'm not like Jordan; I have little subtlety. Men are prone to dance around a problem, when confronting it would bring an instant solution."

"And I am a problem?" Marianna asked carefully.

"You're angry with Jordan, but it's nothing that can't be resolved. It's foolish to ruin your future over a present dispute. Of course, Jordan cannot offer you marriage, but you'll find him a very generous protector."

"Oh, will I?"

"And if you don't trust him, I'm prepared to en-sure that you're well cared for when he leaves you. I will give you a comfortable income and a lovely house here in Kazan. Gregor says you're very fond of your brother. I will see that he gets a fine schooling and an opportunity to succeed in any career he chooses." She looked intently at Marianna. "Is there anything else you could ask?"

"Yes, I wish to ask one more thing." Marianna's voice was shaking with anger. "Did he tell you to speak to me?"

"Jordan does not tell me anything. I make my own decisions." She studied Marianna's expression. "You're very angry. I don't think you're prepared to be reasonable."

"Reasonable? You consider it reasonable for me to become a whore at your bidding?"

"I did not— Well, perhaps I did, but it was for your own good."

"And what if I had offered you the same sugges-tion?"

"In your circumstances I would have considered it a fine—" She stopped and then said bluntly, "I'm not in your circumstances. I *want* this for Jordan."

"You're just like him," Marianna said in disbelief. "Nothing matters but what you want." She drew a deep, shaky breath. "No, thank you, Your Majesty. I don't want your fine house or your son. All I want is your help in getting Alex back and then to say good-bye to both of you."

Ana took in Marianna's face and blazing eyes, then gathered her reins. "No doubt worry over your brother has made you a trifle overwrought. Think about it. I will talk to you later." Her gaze slid away from Marianna before she added, "It would be best if you did not tell Jordan of our discussion."

"Why? I'd think you'd want him to know how helpful you're being to him," Marianna spat.

"I did not succeed yet. One does not boast of failures." She kicked her horse into a gallop and rode toward the head of the column.

Marianna was shaking so badly, she could barely sit her horse. Anger. Yes, it was anger that was almost making her ill. What did she care if the ravin considered her worthy only of a temporary place in Jordan's life? She wanted no place at all. None of the other words had cut or disturbed her.

"Take deep breaths." Gregor was beside her. "And think of cool, clear water. It sometimes helps."

Marianna took a long, deep breath. It did not help.

"What did she say to you?"

"She offered me a fine price to become her son's whore."

He sighed. "I thought as much. Ana has always been overly blunt."

"Blunt? I wonder why they ever chose her to be ravin. She could start a war just by being in the same room with a foreign envoy."

"True." He smiled. "But she is usually not this bad. Her emotions are getting in the way of her thinking. She is becoming desperate."

"Desperate" was the last description she would use for the arrogant woman who had just left her.

"You do not believe me, but she is desperate." Gregor cast his eyes on Jordan at the head of the column. "She loves him. She has always loved him."

"You don't desert a son you love."

"You are as hard as he is," Gregor said. "He has never forgiven her. When he came to Kazan the first time, she thought he might relent, but there has always been a barrier."

"And she wishes to bridge it with me?" she asked incredulously.

"She is desperate," he repeated. "And determined. Be wary of her."

"Tell her to be wary of me," Marianna said grimly. "I'm not a bone for her to throw to her son."

"You are angry with her, and that is right," Gregor said. "But also try to understand her. Sometimes she is like an impatient child. Ana has led a hard life and made many mistakes, but she will give everything when called upon. She has always been my friend, and I've never had a better one."

"I don't want to understand her. I don't want her for my friend," Marianna said. "And I don't want to be another of her mistakes."

"I am not doing well here." Gregor grimaced. "I will go and talk to Ana and see if I can do better."

Marianna watched him ride toward Ana Dvorak.

She had known all along that Jordan would never offer her marriage. Everyone knew a duke had to make a great marriage, and besides she wanted no permanent liaison with a man who would try to dominate and cage her. The ravin's words meant nothing to her. She was only angry that the woman had insulted her by assuming she was not worthy of being anything but a toy to be enjoyed and then thrown away.

She was not a toy. She had worth.

It was not hurt or shock that she was feeling. It was only anger.

• • •

What have I done now?" Jordan asked. He dropped down beside Marianna on her sheepskin pallet beside the campfire. "It must be something particularly horrendous. You've been glowering at me all day."

"I've not been glowering. I've scarcely seen you today. As far as I'm aware, you've done nothing other than be yourself."

He flinched. "Ah, what a wicked condemnation."

"Besides, what you do is of complete indifference to me as long as it doesn't affect Alex."

He gave a mock shiver. "The winds are cold tonight." He looked at his mother sitting across the fire with Gregor, and his expression became grim. "If I haven't committed any major sins, it must be the ravin. What did she say to you today?"

Marianna's gaze followed his to Ana Dvorak. The ravin was staring at Marianna with proud defiance. Marianna knew she could not hear what they were saying, but she had the impression there was fear beneath that pride. A fierce rush of power coursed through her. She knew Jordan would be angry at his mother's interference. With a few words she could drive the wedge between them deeper. She could soothe her own stung pride and receive a small portion of vengeance.

"It must have been something fairly poisonous," Jordan said. "Was she telling you of my iniquitous past?"

She would tell him. Why should she protect the woman? She was no martyr to take punishment and turn the other cheek. What did she care if there was something childlike and vulnerable about the ravin in this moment?

"Well?" Jordan asked.

Mother of God, she could not do it, she realized with frustration. "Why should she have to tell me about your past? Everyone knows how badly you behaved. Still behave," she corrected herself. "Does it please your vanity to believe the only subject of conversation is yourself?"

"Are you saying it was not?"

She glanced again at the ravin and then at the fire. "She's an arrogant, unpleasant woman, very much like yourself. She irritated me with her lack of respect for my craft. She doesn't understand that to create a work of art is just as important as ruling a country."

His expression lightened. "A grievous sin. I agree the ravin is more prone to value a well-disciplined army than a fine painting. You must educate her regarding her duty as patron of the arts."

"I won't be here to educate her. Do it yourself. She is your mother."

"Is she?"

"Yes, you cannot deny she is your mother by not addressing her as such. Or is that only another way to sting her?"

He stiffened. "You just said she was arrogant and unpleasant. Why are you defending her?"

"I'm not defending her. I'm merely remarking on your foolishness. I don't care about the conflict between you. You obviously resent her for leaving you. Perhaps you're right. I had a mother who loved and cherished me. I'm not familiar with cold, self-serving women like the ravin."

"She may have many deplorable qualities, but she

isn't cold, and as for self-serving, she's served Kazan
well at some sacrifice to herself."

"Stop waffling and make up your mind. Are you
going to forgive her for her sins or not? Is she worth
your affection or isn't she?"

"I do *not* waffle." A frown creased his forehead.
"Stay out of this, Marianna. This is none of your
concern."

"I'm not trying to interfere. It is nothing to me."
Yet, to her frustration and amazement, she realized
she had been trying to interfere. After swearing to
avoid involvement, she had jumped headlong between them. She quickly changed the subject. "How
many days will it take us to get to Montavia?"

"Another two days to reach the northern border,"
he said absently, still frowning. "Nebrov's lands are
located in northeast Montavia. His principal residence
is Pekbar, which is two days' ride from the border."

"Then we'll be able to start negotiating with
Nebrov within two days," she said, relieved.

"No."

She stiffened. "What do you mean?"

"The negotiations won't start until you and Gregor
reach the steppes a day later. He doesn't know you've
created a new Jedalar yet. You'll set up, and Gregor
will send a message to Pekbar for Nebrov to come to
you. He'll tell him that you'll trade the Jedalar for
Alex instead of yourself."

"What if he doesn't agree?"

"I don't believe there's any doubt he will agree.
Time is growing short, and it will be much more
convenient having an already completed Jedalar than
just a craftsman who has to be coerced into doing the
panel. Pekbar is surrounded by mountainous terrain.

When he accepts the trade, you'll tell him the window is too large and fragile to take overland, and he must come to you at your camp on the steppes. You'll specify he has to bring Alex for the trade."

"You know he won't bring Alex."

"No, but he'll come himself. He won't risk having the Jedalar smashed again, and since he knows Gregor would be a fool not to have a substantial force with him, he'll have to withdraw a sizable number of his own army from Pekbar to crush any resistance."

"You think he's going to steal the Jedalar and still keep Alex?"

"I think he's going to try to steal the Jedalar and take you as well." He paused. "He wants not only the Jedalar, but also the woman who knows everything about it."

She had been working her way to that same conclusion. "Then I'm to be the bait while you raid Pekbar and free Alex."

He nodded. "Gregor will take half our forces for your protection. I'll take the other half, and go to Pekbar and get the boy."

"How?"

"With a force this size there are many options."

"You're going to attack the castle?" She shook her head. "That sounds too dangerous for Alex."

"Not as dangerous for Alex as it is for you. We'll need at least a day to get Alex away and safe over the border to Kazan. Perhaps more. If you and Gregor can keep Nebrov from suspecting we're going to make the attempt, we'll have a better chance of succeeding."

She nodded. "Very well."

"You're accepting this too calmly." His tone was

edged with uneasiness. "It may not be that simple. We still don't know how Nebrov found out about the Jedalar or how much he knows. He may even know which panel contains the map." He paused. "And I don't have to tell you how vicious he can be when he's frustrated in getting what he wants."

No, he didn't have to tell her, and she was not at all calm. She shivered as she realized she would soon see Nebrov. She would be as close to him as she was to Jordan right now. She smiled with effort. "I'm not worried. I'll have Gregor and all those fine soldiers of the ravin. That's more than I had when I last encountered him." She looked away from him. "It all seems very hazardous. What if something goes wrong?"

"I can't promise you that it won't," Jordan said quietly. "But it's the best plan that I could devise. If you can think of a better one, let me hear it. You call me vain, but I wouldn't let Alex die for my self-love."

He was not closing her out; he was letting her have a part in saving Alex, she realized with a surge of warmth that banished a little of the dread. She said haltingly, "I was angry. It could be that you aren't vain."

His lips turned up at the corners. "I appreciate the measure of doubt." The faint smile disappeared. "You agree to the plan?"

"If you can think of nothing safer for Alex."

"I can think of nothing safer for either of you." He added harshly, "Do you think I want you in danger? If I thought you'd agree, I'd have had Gregor meet with Nebrov and send you back to Rengar."

"You said Nebrov wants the Jedalar *and* me. The bait would not be as tempting." She shuddered. "No, it has to be me."

"Then we'll meet here on the Bordlin steppes in four days' time."

"Four days . . ." For bad or good, in four days it would all be over.

Her gaze went to the purple mountains to the south that marked the border between Kazan and Montavia. Alex was beyond those mountains.

Alex and Nebrov.

CHAPTER 13

Jordan's hands clenched the reins as he watched the column of soldiers wind its way down the mountain trail toward the distant steppes. Marianna's hair shimmered in the sunlight as she turned to speak to Gregor. They were too far away for Jordan to hear her words, but he could see there was no hint of a smile on her face. He could not remember her smiling since Alex was taken. What the devil did she have to smile about? he thought bitterly. She was frightened her brother might be killed at any moment, and he had compounded the horror by sending her as bait to the man she feared most in the world. Christ, he had not wanted to let her go. He had exaggerated the danger she would face so she would not demand to come with him to Pekbar, but Nebrov was always a threat.

"You are afraid for her," Ana said. "You should not worry. Gregor will take care of her."

"I know." Jordan turned to her. "Gregor takes care of all of us, doesn't he? I've often wondered why he bothers. We're not really worth his efforts."

"You mean I'm not worth his effort."

"I didn't say that."

"But you meant it." She shrugged. "You're probably right. I'm not a virtuous woman. But I'm a strong woman, and I take care of my own now." She smiled. "Why do you think I insisted on coming with you? I realize it's a little late, but I must prove that I no longer run away from responsibility."

"You need to prove nothing to me."

"I didn't say I wanted to prove anything to you. I know your mind is closed to me. I need to prove it to myself." She turned her horse. "Enough of this chatter. Let us go to Pekbar and get the boy."

Two days later Gregor and Marianna set up their tents on the steppes, and Gregor immediately sent a rider to Pekbar with the message. Nebrov's reply came the next morning.

"He's coming?" Marianna asked as Gregor scanned the note.

"He's coming," Gregor answered, glancing at the foothills a few miles away. "He should be here by tonight."

"Why isn't he coming at once? It could be a trick. If the messenger could travel this quickly, Nebrov could be right behind him."

He shook his head. "I surmise he wishes to arrive after darkness falls. It is easier to hide deception at night."

"He will attack?"

"Of course, if he thinks it possible to succeed." He smiled gently at her. "Do not frown. It is my duty to make sure he does not think that possible." He turned to Niko, who stood a few feet from them and said, "It is time, my friend. The foothills."

Niko nodded and hurried away.

"The foothills?" Marianna asked.

"Nebrov will not bring his entire force when he comes to camp. It is too open here, and he has respect for Kazan's army. I believe it probable he will leave a sizable force in the hills and have them sweep down to surprise us."

"How can you be sure?"

"Nothing is sure, but he has few options on this terrain. If I am right, Niko will hide his men in the hills and rid us of that threat."

"You seem very certain of victory."

"Kazan's borders have always been challenged by one army or another, and we know these mountains. We have learned to hide and hit. Run and hit again. Most forces are too rigid and sluggish to respond to such attacks."

"Nebrov also lives in these mountains."

"But his army showed no great power to adapt when he tried to conquer Montavia. He relied on sheer numbers and arms to overwhelm the enemy. It is my belief he lacks imagination."

She shivered. "I hope you're right."

"You are frightened." Gregor shook his head. "Have you so little trust in me? I will guard you."

"I know you will. It's just that—" She fell silent, trying to find words to explain the fear that paralyzed her whenever she thought about the coming encounter. "I know you must think me a coward. It's because of *him*. He makes me feel helpless."

"You are not a coward, and you are not helpless unless you let yourself be." He changed the subject.

"It is good he has delayed his arrival until tonight. He will linger in the foothills to deploy his troops, and that will give Jordan more time to free Alex." His face clouded. "God knows he will need it. Finding a way to enter that stronghold alone will not be easy."

"Alone!" Her gaze flew to his face. "He's going to go into the castle alone? He told me there would be an attack." He had not really said that, she realized. He had merely not denied it when she had made the assumption.

"There is no time to lay siege."

"Alone," she whispered.

"Sometimes one man is safer than a battalion. They will not be expecting it. He will meet with Janus and learn where they're keeping Alex. Then he'll scale the wall and try to free the boy before they know he is there."

"He didn't tell me. Mother of God, and he said my meeting with Nebrov was more dangerous." She clenched her hands into fists at her sides to keep them from shaking. "Is he mad? He's not a bird that can fly in and out of a castle without being noticed."

"It is the only way."

"How can you say that? What if this Janus is wrong about his information?"

"Alex will still be safe. Jordan will make very sure that he's not exposed to any danger. Nebrov's men would not dare hurt his hostage."

"And what about Jordan?" she asked fiercely. "Will they hesitate to kill him? You know they won't. If they catch him, they'll murder him without a thought."

"He's not so easy to catch. His time here in Kazan

was not all spent in palaces. He has proven himself in many battles against our enemies."

"Hitting and running, you said. Where is he going to run to at Pekbar? They'll capture him and—" She stopped, her throat dry with terror. "You should never have let him do this."

"He had to do it," Gregor said simply. "I could not have stopped him. He held himself at fault for the boy's capture."

And she had reinforced that guilt. She had spit bitterness and spite at him and had not even bid him good-bye when they had parted. "Go after him. Help him."

Gregor shook his head. "This is the way he wants it. We must continue with the plan. Besides, it's too late. I would not get there in time."

He meant that by the time he reached Pekbar, either Alex would be free or Jordan dead.

The terror gripped her, making her chest tight until she could scarcely breathe. "This was a mistake. Aren't you supposed to take care of him? You should have told him to find another way."

"If it is a mistake, then there is nothing to be done about it. If you wish to help Jordan, try to make sure Nebrov does not suspect he has reason to hurry back to Pekbar. His horses will be tired from the journey here, and he will not push them on the return without reason."

And he would run those horses until they dropped dead in their tracks if he knew what was transpiring at Pekbar. "It still may not be enough time."

Gregor's eyes narrowed. "You are as pale as the moon. Why are you so upset? If Jordan dies, you will be free of him. Isn't that what you want? Of course, we will have to find another way to rescue Alex. That will not be simple, but you know we will do it."

She turned on her heel and went into her tent. She didn't want to face even Gregor's kindly inquisition when she felt this naked and vulnerable. Her limbs were shaking, and her stomach was churning with panic.

Jordan could die.

She had not let herself consider the threat to anyone but Alex. She had been so filled with guilt and anger that she had been unable to—

Guilt?

She closed her eyes as the realization struck. She had blamed Jordan because she had not been able to shoulder her own guilt. She had already admitted to herself that she had not been forced to go to Dalwynd. She had gone because she had been helpless to resist the power that had pulled her toward Jordan from their first meeting. She could have fought him, made an attempt to find where Gregor had taken Alex. She had done neither. If she had not given in to temptation, she would have been with Alex to protect him from harm.

If Jordan was guilty, then she shared his guilt as she had shared his lust.

No, for her it had been more than lust. Desire alone would never have led her to take such a step; it had only been the mask to keep her from looking deeper. What she had felt was far more than lust.

And she had not even told him good-bye. She had let him go without a word.

Please, God, don't let him die.

•   •   •

Steady," Gregor murmured in her ear. "He cannot hurt you. I will be with you every minute."

Marianna drew a deep breath as she watched the column of torchbearing riders approach. Soldiers had also carried torches that night Nebrov had come to the cottage. The light had illuminated Nebrov's face, and her mother had recognized him and sent Marianna running to the forest with Alex.

Now he was coming again.

"You need say nothing," Gregor told her. "I will speak for you."

Nebrov was close enough now for her to see his face. He did not look like a monster. His features were delicate, his dark eyes large and almost soulful. His silky brown pointed beard made his triangular face appear longer and his thin lips fuller.

"Good evening, Damek." He reined in his horse before them and slipped gracefully from the saddle. He was a small man, only a few inches taller than she, and meticulously dressed, from his shining black boots to the fur trim on his elegant gray cloak. His gaze went to Marianna. "This is the girl?"

"I'm sure you've had descriptions of her." Gregor gestured to the tent. "Shall we go inside? It is a cold evening, and I would not want you to become chilled. Unless you have doubts about your safety?"

Nebrov took off his doeskin gloves and tucked them in his belt. "Why should I have doubts when I've given instructions that the boy dies if any harm comes to me?" He strode into the tent ahead of them, then turned to stare again at Marianna. "Actually she's far more comely than I had heard. Draken must have enjoyed her. It's always pleasant when one's objectives provide alternate satisfactions." He paused.

"The mother was quite handsome, too, but I was too angry to fully enjoy her. This one appears far more meek and pliable."

A welcome anger poured through Marianna, melting the ice of fear that had held her silent. "We will not talk about my mother."

Nebrov raised his brows. "Perhaps she has more spirit than I thought. Tell me, what tricks did His Grace teach you? Would I enjoy them?"

"You are here for the Jedalar," Gregor reminded him. "Where is the boy?"

"Did you think I'd bring him here? I left him in a safe place in the foothills with instructions not to be brought to your camp until our negotiations have borne fruit." He smiled at Marianna, revealing tiny crooked teeth. "I was delighted to learn that Draken had persuaded you to create a new Jedalar. It will save me time. Where is it?"

"Where is Alex?"

"I told you that—" He broke off, then went to the entrance of the tent. "Costain," he called out, "go get the boy."

Shocked, Marianna quickly looked at Gregor. Had they been wrong? Had Nebrov brought Alex to trade?

Gregor gave an almost imperceptible shake of his head.

A trick. He meant Nebrov had been prepared for the demand and was attempting to deceive them.

"Costain?" Gregor repeated. His expression hardened, and his scarred face was truly terrifying in the lamplight. "You should have invited him to join us. I have been eager to meet with him again."

"Marcus told me of your wound," Nebrov said.

"You must have great stamina. He thought he'd killed you."

"He tried diligently."

Nebrov dismissed the subject as of no importance. "Well? I've sent for the boy. Are you going to continue to whine, or will you show me the Jedalar?"

"I'll get it." Marianna went to the table on the other side of the tent and drew from beneath it a glass panel depicting scarlet roses climbing a gray stone wall.

"Give it to me!" Nebrov had followed her and snatched it from her hands. He held it up to the lamp, his eager gaze raking the flowers, square stones, and labyrinth of thorny vines and leaves. "It could be . . ."

He had not been surprised at the smallness of the Jedalar, she realized with a sudden chill. He had expected it. Everyone else assumed the Jedalar was the entire Window to Heaven, but Nebrov had been aware the map required only one panel. It was clear he knew more than Jordan had known. But how much more?

"Or it could be of no importance at all." Nebrov fixed his attention on her. "You could be trying to hoax me. Would you be that unkind?"

With effort she kept her voice steady. "And risk my brother's life?"

"The reports I've received say that you're a devoted sister, but Draken could be using you. Costain told me he had seduced you, and women have been known to choose a lover over family duty." He pursed his lips, thinking about it. "Draken would not willingly give up the Jedalar. He is a trifle soft on occasion, but he is not a fool."

"We are here," Gregor said impassively. "He feels an obligation toward the boy. However, we do not promise not to take the Jedalar back from you after Alex is freed."

"That would be a very complicated affair," he said. "No, my guess is that Draken thinks that I will accept the Jedalar, give you the boy, and go my way. That will make the girl grateful, and she will be willing to cooperate and put Jedalar and Zavkov together."

"Zavkov?" Gregor asked.

Nebrov raised his brows. "Draken didn't tell you?" His glance shifted to Marianna. "But I'm sure you told Draken everything, didn't you? He's reputed to be adept at getting what he wants from women. Yes, he must have known. What's a key without a lock?" His eyes narrowed on her pale face. "Ah, that frightens you. You did think to fool me."

"How did you know about the Zavkov?"

"It was a long, involved procedure. I have informants in Kazan, but I heard only rumors there about the Jedalar and a room in the tunnel filled with gold and jeweled objects, so I journeyed to Moscow. I found one of Czar Paul's advisers who had dealt with the supervisors who built the tunnel." He grimaced. "It was not an easy task. Like your grandparents, he had been targeted to die because he knew too much. He paid off his executioner and fled to the country to hide. Even after all this time he was most reluctant to speak, but I persuaded him before his unfortunate demise." He paused. "He told me the Jedalar was designed to be only half the answer."

Gregor glanced thoughtfully at Marianna. "Indeed."

"So you can see that, even if this panel is the right

one, it is not enough. I must have someone who can put the puzzle together." He smiled at Marianna. "And it is only reasonable that the person who created the Jedalar would know how to accomplish that feat."

She moistened her lips. "And what if I can't do that?"

"It would be unfortunate . . . for you."

"It's not wise to issue threats in an enemy's camp," Gregor observed.

"Not unless one feels safe to do so. I feel infinitely safe." He looked at Marianna. "So if this is not the correct panel, you'd best give it to me at once."

"Why do you feel safe?" Gregor asked. "Is it because Costain's mission was not to get the boy but to give word to your men in the hills to attack?"

Wariness appeared in Nebrov's expression. "Do you accuse me of breaking a truce?"

Gregor laughed. "But of course. We expected nothing else. That was why we took precautions."

"Your precautions will do you little good," Nebrov said contemptuously. "My forces outnumber you. It's true I hoped for a surprise, but it is of little account. If you surrender now, I may permit you to live."

"How kind," Gregor said. "But let us see what report Costain brings back from the hills before we take advantage of such benevolence." He strode to the table and reached for a bottle of wine. "All this talk has given me a tremendous thirst. Marianna?"

She shook her head.

"You'll forgive me if I don't offer you wine, Your Grace. It's not our custom to pamper an enemy within our gates." He beamed. "We prefer to slaughter them."

"You will not have time for your glass of wine. It is only a few miles to the hills, and they should be here soon. They were only waiting for word."

Gregor poured wine into a wooden goblet. "Then I will take it outside and wait for my tragic end." He gestured to Marianna. "Would you care to join me? I've always dreaded the thought of dying alone."

"You are mocking me," Nebrov snarled. "You will see that—"

An outcry rose from outside the tent.

Gregor tensed, the smile faded from his face.

Nebrov nodded. "You see?" he asked softly. "It has started."

"Then I must confront it. Perhaps you should stay in the tent, Marianna. I have decided a solitary death is more meaningful."

She was already at his side. "You invited me to join you. I won't stay here with this mongrel."

"Very well." He cast a glance over his shoulder at Nebrov's livid face. "Perhaps you'd better accompany us to protect her. She has value for you, and you wouldn't want her to be killed by accident. You've already made too many blunders." He made a clucking sound with his tongue. "Smashing windows, allowing your victims to die before revealing their secrets. It would be amusing, if it was not so sad."

Nebrov's face flushed as he strode toward the entrance. "I shall take great pleasure in making sure it takes you a long time to die. You have great strength. I might even manage to stretch out your agony for an entire month." Triumphantly, he stared at the edge of the camp where several soldiers blocked the view.

"You will learn the price of—" He broke off in mid-sentence and then muttered a low curse.

Marianna stiffened in shock as her gaze followed Nebrov's. The crowd had parted to permit a single rider to pass through, a rider leading a horse behind him. She heard the sigh of relief that issued from Gregor beside her.

"Niko." He stepped forward as the horseman came near. "I trust everything went well?"

Niko nodded. "Four escaped. Eight prisoners. We have not counted the dead."

"Excellent. You have done—" His glance fell on the saddle of the horse Niko was leading. He stiffened. "What is this?"

For the first time Marianna realized the horse was carrying a macabre burden. A soldier in Nebrov's livery was slung across the saddle.

Niko grinned. "A present."

Gregor strode forward, thrust his hand into the bloodstained hair, and lifted the dead man's head. He swore beneath his breath. "Costain."

Niko's grin widened. "He squealed like a pig when I stuck him."

Marianna swallowed to ease the sudden queasiness in her stomach.

"You cheated me, Niko," Gregor said grimly. "I did not ask for this present."

"I did not say it was a present for you," Niko said. "It is a gift for the ravin. She offered a pouch of gold to the man in the troop who brought her Costain dead." He frowned. "But I do not think he will be a sweet-smelling gift by the time we rendezvous with the ravin. We had better leave him here. Will you bear witness the kill was made?"

"Oh yes," Gregor said grimly. "I promise I will discuss this kill in great detail with the ravin."

Nebrov was staring in disbelief at Costain's body. "The fool," he said harshly. "By God, they're all inept fools."

"I suggest you leave," Gregor said. "I am in extreme bad temper at the moment. I might forget that you still hold the boy and give the ravin another gift."

Nebrov looked down at the panel he was still holding. "This is not the Jedalar, is it?"

"No," Marianna said. "It's not the Jedalar."

"I'm surprised you admit it."

"Because I want you to know that you leave here with nothing of value. You will still have to negotiate with us for Alex."

"You took a great chance."

"There was a possibility you might bring Alex. I had to make the attempt."

"You were willing to risk the child for Draken." His lips curled. "He has you so besotted, you will do anything for him. I believe you actually love the bastard."

She didn't answer.

"Is it true?"

"Why should you want to know how I feel? It is nothing to do with this."

His eyes narrowed in suspicion. "It is everything to do with this. Why are you so reluctant to make the admission?"

He was searching for the motive that had driven her to take such a chance. If she did not furnish him with one he would believe, he would begin to explore other directions. He must not do that; he must be convinced. Jordan must have as much time as possible.

She met his stare directly and said the words she had not wanted to say, the words that were still too new and barbed with hurt. "I love him."

He studied her for a moment. "Fool. I hope your passion for him is worth the boy's life."

Gregor shook his head. "Kill the goose that could bring you the Jedalar? As long as the boy lives, you have a chance of forcing Marianna to do what you wish."

"There are other ways to force compliance." He sneered. "If my man hadn't been careless, her mother would have talked."

"She would never have told you anything," Marianna said. "Nor would I. Kill Alex, and you will never have the Jedalar."

Uncertainty flickered briefly in his face. "We will see. I will consider your words. I may decide to bargain again with you." He smiled unpleasantly as he mounted his horse. "Or I may send you the boy's head. You will have to wait and see. It's exceptionally easy to crush a young child." He dropped the climbing rose panel on the ground in front of her. It did not shatter, but a large crack appeared at the upper-left corner. He nudged his horse forward until the animal's front hooves crushed the fragile glass. "Like that. It is something for you to remember while I make my decision."

He whirled his horse and galloped out of the camp.

"Don't look like that," Gregor said gently. "He would not kill the boy. He only wanted to make you suffer."

She looked down at the broken glass at her feet. The scarlet roses were like glittering drops of blood on the earth. "He has made me suffer." She stared at Costain's body sprawled across the horse a few yards away. She wished it were Nebrov's body. Ever since that terrible night she had been afraid of Nebrov. His gigantic shadow had darkened every moment. Now fear was being ousted by anger. He had killed her mother. He might still kill Jordan and Alex. Someone must put an end to this evil.

"We must break camp at once," Gregor said. "We want to be out of Montavia and halfway to the Bordlin steppes by the time Nebrov reaches Pekbar. He will be in a rage when he finds Alex gone and is bound to ride after us with every man in his command."

"If Alex is gone," she said dully. If Jordan was not dead.

The thought sent another bolt of terror through her. She had spent a sleepless night trying to bring fear under control, but it was here again, staring her in the face. Jordan could be dead, and she wouldn't even know it. He could have slipped into that castle and been captured—

She was suddenly impatient with herself. She was giving Nebrov every particle of the misery and heartache he had wished to incite. Jordan was more clever than any man she had ever met. He alone could free Alex despite the odds. She refused to let Nebrov win any more victories from her. She nodded brusquely. "You're right, Gregor. We'll start at once for Kazan."

"Jordan will still be alive when we reach there, Marianna. You must have faith."

She glanced at him and saw both understanding

and pity. He had been there when she had told Nebrov she loved Jordan. She wanted to tell him she had lied, that she had only been trying to delay Nebrov. It was impossible. She had been able to convince Nebrov because her words had rung with truth. Gregor, who knew her well, would not believe a denial.

"You will not tell him?" she asked haltingly.

He shook his head. "We have already robbed you of too much." He paused. "I am sorry, Marianna."

He was sorry because he knew that there could be no happiness or permanency in such a love. He was sorry because Jordan was the Duke of Cambaron and she was a craftsman. He was sorry because he knew Jordan's passion would eventually fade, and she would be left with ashes. She smiled bitterly. "Don't be sorry. Nebrov is right. I'm a fool. You should never be sorry for fools. It only encourages them never to seek wisdom."

She turned and went into her tent.

I don't like it," the ravin said. "You did not tell me you were going to practice this madness, or I would have had you confined in Rengar." She glanced down the hill at the castle. "I will go with you."

"You will stay here," Jordan said emphatically. "I have no desire to lose my life because you believe any plan you didn't make yourself is no plan at all."

"One man alone? Of course that's no plan at all." She turned to Janus. "How strong are Nebrov's forces here? How long will it take us if we lay siege?"

Janus shrugged. "Two weeks."

"Which is two weeks too long," Jordan said. "And

we don't know if Nebrov gave orders for the boy's execution in case of an attack." He glanced at Janus. "Alex is being kept in the tower nearest the south wall?"

Janus nodded. "The door will be unlocked and unguarded at midnight for a period of fifteen minutes, no more."

"What if the guards took your money and plan on taking Jordan's head as well?" the ravin demanded. "Bribery is always unreliable."

"True," Janus said. "And they fear Nebrov."

"You see?" the ravin demanded of Jordan.

"Then you'll have the opportunity to swoop down and rescue me." Jordan turned and started down the steep hill. "So we'll all be happy."

"I won't be—"

He was not listening to her, Ana realized. Her hands clenched into fists as she watched him move like a shadow. Why would he not listen to her? She was tempted to call her captain of the guard and tell him to stop the fool before he killed himself.

If she did, he would never forgive her.

If she didn't, he might be dead before morning.

Gregor would tell her to leave him alone. He had trained Jordan well, and if anyone could pluck the boy from that tower, it would be her son. Gregor would tell her that she must regard Jordan as she would any of her own soldiers.

But he wasn't one of her soldiers; he was her son.

She looked up at the night sky. Clouds were covering the moon, but that advantage might not last. Another thing over which she had no control.

Sweet Jesus, she hated being helpless.

•   •   •

The iron door creaked as Jordan carefully opened it. In the silence it sounded like a crack of thunder to him. He cast a quick glance over his shoulder. The guards on the rampart gave no indication they had heard; they were still talking idly.

He stepped into the cell.

An overpowering odor of filth assaulted him.

Where the devil was Alex? He dared not call out. He took another step forward, peering into the darkness.

The corner. A small figure huddled in the far corner.

He moved across the cell, his boots sinking into straw and fecal matter. He felt a surge of anger. For God's sake, he would not have kept a cockroach in this place, much less a child.

Now he was close enough to see the glitter of Alex's eyes. Poor lad, he must be terrified. He wanted to call out to reassure him, but it was too dangerous. Just another few steps, and he could risk a whisper.

Pain tore through his kneecap.

He grunted and tottered on one leg.

Alex viciously struck at the other knee with vicious accuracy.

Jordan fell to the floor and reached out blindly as he saw Alex bolt past him toward the door. His hand closed on the boy's ankle, and he jerked him off balance and down to the floor.

Alex struggled wildly, wriggling in his grasp.

"Alex!" Jordan hissed. "Stop! It's Jordan."

Alex froze. "Jordan?"

"Or what's left of him. What did you hit me with?"

"I took the leg off the stool. I thought you were one of them."

Jordan released Alex's ankle. How much time had elapsed during the struggle? "We have to get out of here. The guards will be back soon."

Alex was already moving toward the door.

"Wait." He stood up and limped ahead of him. "Stay behind me."

"How are we getting away from here?"

"We're going over the south wall."

They had reached the courtyard and from their vantage point the forty-foot wall appeared an insurmountable barrier. Jordan expected an argument, but without a word Alex followed him until they reached the rope that Jordan had used to scale the wall.

"I'm climbing to the top," he whispered. "When I get there, I want you to tie the end of the rope around your waist very securely. When you're finished, tug on the rope and I'll pull you up. Can you do that?"

Alex nodded.

Jordan began climbing, his feet bracing against the wall. How long did he have? The fifteen minutes must be almost up. He pulled himself up on the ledge and glanced down.

Alex was already knotting the rope about his waist. A sharp tug on the rope immediately followed.

Jordan began to pull Alex up. The boy was a dead weight, and by the time Alex was on the ledge, Jordan was breathing so heavily, he was sure the guards on the rampart would hear.

"Now comes the hard part," he whispered as he untied the rope from Alex's waist. "We have to move very fast. I'm going down ahead of you, but when I reach the quarter-way point, you've got to follow me. Brace your feet on the wall and hold tight to the rope."

Alex's eyes widened. "But I don't know—" He drew a deep breath. "You'll be right below me?"

Jordan grinned. "So close that you'll crush me if you let go of that rope." He started down the other side of the wall.

Four feet.

Six feet.

Twelve feet.

He stopped and waved at Alex.

Alex hesitated, gazing down at the ground.

Who could blame him, dammit? The lad was only seven years old. Jordan had decided to climb back up to Alex when the boy started down the rope.

Jordan breathed a sigh of relief. He waited until Alex had almost reached him before beginning to move downward again.

Twenty-five feet.

Thirty feet.

A shout from the direction of the ramparts!

"Hurry!" he called to Alex, no need for whispering now that they had been seen. He reached the ground. "Jump! I'll catch you!"

Alex released the rope and fell to his arms.

"Jordan, they're going to shoot!" Alex cried out, his gaze on the ramparts.

Jordan set him down and grasped his wrist. "Run for the hill!"

He glanced back as they started up the steep incline. Soldiers were streaming out of the gate.

A bullet whistled by his ear.

At least they'd had no time to launch a mounted attack. In another minute he and Alex should be out of range. Once they reached the horses at the top of the hill, they should be safe. It was nearly impossible for anyone to overtake horses from the ravin's stable. He must just make sure to block the boy from those bullets spitting from—

The ravin!

"Dammit, no! Go back!" Jordan shouted.

She paid no attention. She galloped down the hill with two horses in tow and reined in her stallion before them. "They saw you! I told you it was a stupid—"

"Be quiet," he said through clenched teeth. He tossed Alex onto the smaller horse and slapped the animal on the buttocks to send it at a run toward the ravin's forces on the hill. "And get out of here!"

The ravin's eyes blazed at him. "You get out of here!"

Another bullet whistled by him as he pulled himself onto the saddle. "That's my intention. If you would—"

He did not hear the bullet, but he saw the ravin's eyes widen in horror.

"Jordan!"

CHAPTER 14

The red tents billowing on the barren Bordlin plain looked like a cluster of radiant butterflies that had mistaken a desert for a garden.

Marianna could see a number of people milling about, but they were still too far away to recognize. Any one of them could be Jordan.

Or none of them.

"What if they aren't here?" she whispered.

"They will be here." Gregor started down the hill. "Come. We will go and find your Alex."

She nudged her horse into a trot. Her heart was pounding, her palms cold and clammy. She must not be nervous. God would not let Alex or Jordan die and that monster live.

But God had let Mama die.

As she and Gregor drew closer, she quickly eyed the crowd who were gathering to greet them. No Jordan. No Alex. No Ravin.

The tents. They had to be in the tents. Just because she didn't immediately see them was no sign they were not here. The ravin's forces would not have abandoned them at Pekbar—

"Marianna."

Alex!

He stood several yards away, garbed in ragged trousers and shirt, a broad smile on his face and a wooden basin in his hands.

She slipped from her horse and was running through the crowd toward the small figure. He looked like a Gypsy boy, she thought tearfully, all tousled black curls and big dark eyes.

"Alex!" She dropped to her knees and pulled him into her arms. "Alex, you're—"

"Let go. I can't breathe," Alex said gruffly. In spite of his words, his arms were holding her just as tightly. "Stop crying, Marianna. I'm quite all right."

She pressed her cheek to his. She had forgotten how endearingly fragile his child's body felt in her arms.

"You're getting me wet," he said impatiently. He had evidently tolerated enough affection for the moment.

She drew back but kept her hands on his shoulders. She wanted to keep on touching him, assuring herself that he was here. "I'm sorry."

A smile illuminated his face, and his fingers went up to touch her tear-streaked cheek. "You're wet too. You're going to drown us, Marianna."

"Are you well? Did they hurt you?"

A shadow crossed his face, and his gaze slid away from hers. "A little." He quickly called beyond her shoulder to Gregor. "Hello, Gregor. You're a day late. We got here yesterday afternoon, right on time."

He chuckled. "I regret my tardiness. We took a

longer route to avoid running into your former hosts.
It is good to see you, lad."

"It's good to see you, Gregor." Alex knelt to pick
up the basin that had gone flying from his hands
when Marianna had grabbed him. "I have to take this
to Jordan. The wound—"

"Wound!" Marianna inhaled sharply. "What
wound? Are you hurt?"

"No, I told you, Jordan—"

"Jordan's hurt?" She jumped to her feet. "How
bad? What—"

"Hush, Marianna," Alex said. "If you would listen, you'd know by now."

She stared at him in astonishment. The maturity
and authority that echoed in his words were foreign
to the Alex she knew. And the change was not only
in his voice, she realized. His face was thinner, the
baby fat gone, and dark circles were imprinted beneath eyes that met hers with a fearless clarity.

"Jordan isn't hurt either." He turned and started
across the camp, motioning for her to follow him.
"It's Ana who was shot."

"Ana!" Gregor was off his horse in a heartbeat.
"Where is she?"

Alex pointed to the large tent at the edge of the
camp. "It was a bullet that—"

Gregor muttered something beneath his breath and
ran toward the tent.

"He doesn't listen either," Alex said in disgust.
"She's not badly hurt. Jordan says the wound in her
shoulder is clean. It's only a question of keeping it
so."

She tried to keep her tone casual as she asked,
"Jordan is well then?"

He nodded, and suddenly his expression was filled with enthusiasm. "It was splendid. We climbed a rope up the wall and— Well, Jordan climbed it and then pulled me up to the rampart. Next time I'll do it myself."

"There will be no next time," she said firmly.

The shadow returned, wiping the childish enthusiasm from his face. "I hope not."

But he was not sure. All the security he had known at Cambaron had vanished, and he was again the little boy who had thought a warm blanket a treasure in a cold world. It was not fair. Anger soared through her. "I promise that you'll be safe now. Have I ever lied to you?"

"No, but sometimes bad things happen that no one can stop. I forgot that." He straightened his thin shoulders. "But if you try hard, sometimes you can make it better."

What terrible things had happened to him in these weeks that he had tried to make better? "Alex, are you—"

"Jordan was worried," he interrupted. "He said you were in no danger, but last night after supper he rode up to the hills. I think he was watching for you."

"Was he? I don't see why. He was telling you the truth. I was quite safe, and Gregor and I didn't have any grand adventures like you did."

"You wouldn't tell me if you did," he said shrewdly. "You'd be afraid I'd be worried."

Another flash of maturity. "Well, I'm anxious to hear all about yours."

"When I have time." He frowned. "Ana needs me now."

She looked at him in astonishment. "The ravin?"

"Ana," he corrected. "She helped save my life, you know. Now I have to help her."

"I'm sure she has many people here to help her."

His jaw set. "*I* have to do it." He looked toward the tent. "There's Jordan. Here's the basin, Jordan," he called out. "Shall I fill it with hot water?"

Jordan.

He was standing in the entrance of the tent looking at her.

"Jordan?" Alex demanded impatiently.

"Oh." He tore his gaze away from Marianna. "Yes, please."

"Come on, Marianna." Alex ran toward a steaming kettle hung over a small fire outside the tent. He stopped and faced his sister. "Why are you just standing there?"

Marianna didn't realize that's what she was doing. At the moment she wouldn't have been aware of fire pouring from the heavens. *He* was alive and well and staring at her as if . . .

What? She didn't know. She didn't care.

He was alive.

"All went well?" Her voice sounded breathless even to herself.

"No, but we got the boy. That's what's important."

"Yes." She must stop staring at him. Everything she felt had to be written on her face. "Thank you."

"You don't need to thank me for retrieving what I lost." He paused. "How are you?"

"Didn't Gregor tell you? Everything went just as you planned."

"I didn't ask how the plan went," he said roughly. "How are *you*, dammit?"

Leaf-green eyes that could quickly change expression from cynicism to humor. She had lived for years with the toughness, sensuality, and dry wit that was Jordan Draken, and yet now everything about him seemed new to her.

He stiffened, his eyes narrowing. "Gregor wasn't telling the truth. Something happened."

Something of extreme importance to her but not to him. She shook her head. "It wasn't pleasant seeing Nebrov again, but it wasn't terrible either."

"Marianna, help me." Alex's demand broke into her awareness. "Hold the basin."

She hurried over to the fire and did as he asked. She kept her gaze averted from Jordan as Alex carefully ladled hot water from the kettle into the basin.

Jordan was behind her but not touching her. She had not heard him move but felt his presence with unerring instinct.

"Your hands aren't steady," he said in a low voice. "You'll burn yourself." Both of his arms reached around her, and his hands covered hers. "I'll help you."

His touch was warm and strong; the familiar scent of him filled her nostrils. She hadn't been trembling before, but she was now. He had held her like this during that first moment of surrender at Dalwynd, and memories were flooding back. "I don't need this."

"I know." His words were nearly inaudible. "But I do."

Alex threw the ladle back in the kettle and took the basin from her. "Is that enough, Jordan?"

"No." Then he glanced at the bowl. "Yes." His

arms fell to his sides and he took a step back. "Take it into the tent."

"I'll go with you," Marianna said. She couldn't stay here with him. She was too shaken and vulnerable, too aware of all the things of which she would have been robbed if he had died at Pekbar. "How did she become wounded?"

"The alarm was given as we were climbing down the wall. I told her to stay on the hill but, as usual, she paid no attention. She galloped down to bring us our horses."

"She saved your life?"

"She is quite sure she did. In truth we had time to reach the hill, and I would have much preferred not to have been forced to worry about her as well as Alex." He smiled. "But it was quite a splendid effort, and I think you may have to do another window of her. She appeared more Valkyrie than Galahad."

"Who shot her?"

"One of the guards. I cannot put a name to him. We were in something of a hurry when we departed Pekbar." His lips thinned. "But I made sure that whatever his name is, it would be immediately engraved on his tombstone."

"But the ravin will recover?"

"Ana," Alex corrected her as he moved toward the tent.

Jordan's brows raised. "For some reason he resents the use of that title."

"Why?"

"I have no idea." She started to follow Alex, and Jordan fell into step with her. He was so close, his thigh brushed against hers as they walked. "You'll have to ask him."

"He may not answer me," she said, troubled. "He's changed."

"Yes."

"What happened to him?"

"I have no idea. He won't talk about it." He glanced at her. "And I wouldn't ask him, if I were you. He'll tell you when he's ready to do so."

"But perhaps it's only . . . it may only be temporary."

Jordan was silent.

"You don't think so?"

"No."

"You don't appear concerned. They *hurt* him."

"I'm concerned that they hurt him but not about the change. I know you regret it, but he's stronger now and better able to defend himself." He suddenly chuckled. "And to attack in turn."

"Attack?"

"You'll see." He stepped aside and gestured for her to precede him into the tent. "Probably in the immediate future."

She frowned in puzzlement as she entered the tent.

Gregor was kneeling beside a sheepskin pallet on which lay the ravin. Alex was moving brusquely about the tent, putting down the basin, gathering clean cloths from the table.

Gregor looked up and smiled at Marianna. "She is not badly hurt."

"I'm very badly hurt," the ravin corrected sourly. "I'm in great pain, and I'm having to put up with the most supreme indignities."

"She is always bad-tempered when she is ill." Gregor's big hand gently brushed back a lock of hair from her forehead. "With a tongue as foul as a swamp bog."

"How disgusting. And untrue." She glowered at Marianna. "Why are you staring at me? Does it please you to see me weak and helpless?"

She did appear a trifle drawn, but her innate forcefulness and fire still burned brightly. "I will tell you when you display either of those qualities," Marianna said. "At the moment I recognize only bad temper." She glanced at Gregor. "And a tongue as foul as a swamp—"

"Enough. I'm surrounded by enemies." She glared at Alex as the little boy dropped to his knees beside her. "No! Go away."

He paid no attention as he dipped a cloth into the hot water.

"Jordan, why did I bother to save your life if I am only to be tormented by this fiend?"

"Bad judgment?" Jordan suggested.

Alex untied the bandage on the ravin's shoulder to reveal a puckered, swollen wound.

"You will not touch me," she said forcefully.

Alex carefully dabbed at the edge of the wound.

Ana went pale, her teeth biting into her lower lip.

"Gently," Gregor said quickly.

"He does not know the meaning of the word," Ana said. "Every four hours he descends on me and puts me through this torture."

Alex's jaw set. "Jordan says it has to be kept clean."

"I've had enough of it." She glared at him. "Get out of my tent!"

He continued to dab at the wound.

"Gregor, pick him up and carry him out of here."

Marianna took a protective step forward.

"No." Jordan placed his hand on her arm, stopping her.

"He appears to be doing no damage," Gregor said. "Someone must do it, and I do not believe you would strike a child."

"He is not a child. He's a demon." She gasped as the hot water touched the torn flesh. "And he will not *stop*."

Alex paused a moment in his ministrations and then turned to Jordan. "I think you all should leave. She's trying not to weep and will be ashamed if you see her weakness."

Marianna stared at him in astonishment.

"You're the one who is going to leave," Ana said.

Alex turned back to her, glaring fiercely into her eyes. "I stay. They go. It has to be clean."

The ravin's eyes widened in shock.

"Ana?" Gregor asked.

"Oh, very well," she said grudgingly. "You might as well leave. He obviously will show me no mercy." She glanced at Gregor. "You stay. I must have someone to protect me."

"I am not sure I am in a mood to protect you. Before Alex told me you had been shot, I was ready to do you violence myself. I did not like you going behind my back and putting a price on Costain's head."

"They killed him?" she asked eagerly. "Who?"

"Niko."

She smiled with satisfaction. "Good."

"Not good. You will not interfere again in my concerns."

"It was my concern also. You are my subject, and therefore it was my duty to protect you."

"Ana."

"Oh very well. What does it matter? He is dead now anyway." Her glance shifted warily to Alex. "You should take heed, boy. If you hurt me, I may put a price on your head too."

"No, you won't," Alex said as he dipped the cloth back into the hot water.

Jordan nudged Marianna toward the tent entrance. She cast a disbelieving glance over her shoulder at the little boy and the ravin. How odd they looked together, and yet there was an almost visible bond between them.

"I'm not sure we should have left them," she said as soon as they were outside the tent.

"She won't hurt him. This battle has been going on since we arrived here yesterday. Alex insisted on being the one to care for her. He even stayed awake all last night so that he could wash the wound."

"He did?" The image that came to her was ludicrous: a little cub protecting an injured lioness. "You shouldn't have let him. He needs his rest."

"I couldn't have stopped him," he said dryly. "Besides, it kept him busy. I didn't want him worrying about you. I was doing quite enough of that for both of us."

The words were sweet and meant too much. She tried not to dwell on them. "I suppose it will be all right for him to stay with her for now. I'll go get him later."

"He might not come." When he saw her stricken expression, he added harshly, "For God's sake, don't look like that. It won't be because he loves you any less. You haven't lost him."

"He might blame me for what happened to him."

"How could he? It wasn't your fault."

"Perhaps it was. You said that I wanted to come to Dalwynd."

"It wasn't true. Don't you know that a man who is seducing a woman will say anything to get his way?"

Not Jordan. Jordan would not lie.

He stopped, and his hands closed on her shoulders. "Listen to me. He doesn't blame you. If there's fault, it lies at my door."

She shook her head. "He's changed."

"Life changed him, not you." He shook her gently. "And for the better. Can't you see it? It's not every child who could face down the ravin. Before he was a good lad, but now—" He stopped.

"Now what?"

"He reminds me of you the first time I met you."

"When I was dirty and hungry and fierce as an animal."

"None of that mattered." His hands opened and closed on her shoulders in a curiously yearning manner. "Even in the darkness you served the sunlight."

She wanted to break away, but she couldn't move. He had looked at her like this in the tower room when the sunlight had made her dizzy with joy and she had first thought she had seen behind the mask he wore.

"I was cast out also," Gregor said from behind them. They turned to see him striding toward them. "It seems Alex thought I was a distraction. Ana will have to protect herself."

Marianna welcomed the interruption that shattered the spell. She glanced away and said quickly, "I need to go to my tent and wash away this dust before I go back to Alex."

"And rest a little," Jordan said. "There's no hurry. You've been riding all day."

"I don't need to rest. Tell Alex I'll be with him shortly."

Not that he needed her, she thought wistfully as she walked away. Jordan said she had not lost him, but what she was feeling at the moment was very much like loss. It was foolish to feel sorry for herself. Alex was safe and Jordan was safe. An hour ago she would have asked nothing more from life. It seemed that as soon as danger faded into the background, greed took hold, and she wanted everything she could not have.

Well, she could have Alex. Jordan might be out of reach, but Alex loved and needed her. He just had to be reminded of the ties between them.

As soon as she arrived at her tent, she took off the jacket of her riding habit and splashed cool water on her face and throat. She had always loved the sensation of water on her body. One of the panels that she had brought with her in the wagon was of a waterfall cascading over moss-covered rocks. She had tried to remember this sensual feeling as she had crafted the pale blue of the water.

The panels.

She wished she had not remembered them. Nebrov had knowledge of the Zavkov, and that meant it was no longer enough for Marianna just to keep her silence. Not if she was to keep her promise to her mother and fulfill the duty she had known she must perform since childhood.

There were no ifs about it, she thought impatiently. The promise must be kept. There was no excuse not to do so now that Alex was safe. The act would drive the final wedge between her and Jordan, but perhaps that was for the best. Now that she had realized how much she loved him, she was like a hungry child trying to grab every moment, every experience. That first moment she had seen Jordan outside the ravin's tent had been torture, staring at him, wanting to touch him to make sure he was really safe. She had wanted to step forward and take him, claim him, but therein lay the danger. There was only one way for them to be joined, and that way would eventually destroy her. No, she must be done with him so that she would not be tempted to return to that mindless creature she had been at Dalwynd.

She deliberately blocked the pain the thought brought. Evidently she was not ready to come to grips with leaving him yet, she thought wearily. She would be better able to face these problems after she had rested.

A moment later she was curling up on her pallet and closing her eyes. Darkness was welcome, darkness was safe, darkness brought forgetfulness. She had always loved the light, but she did not want it now.

She would rest for just an hour and then go fetch Alex from the ravin's tent.

Only an hour . . .

She thinks Alex is rejecting her, dammit." Jordan's hands clenched into fists at his sides.

"She cannot turn back the clock," Gregor said quietly. "She must realize the boy will never be the same."

"I know. And she will blame me for that too."

"She is not unfair. The change is still new to her,

but her hurt will heal. Who should know better how life can scar?"

Jordan flinched. He had added his measure of cuts to form those scars. "I share this particular blame." His lips tightened grimly. "I want Nebrov."

"As do I. He has claimed too much from us." He paused. "And he is not going to give up. He is not foolish enough to pursue us into Kazan, but he will still try to find a way to find the tunnel."

"Without the Jedalar?"

"He mentioned something else. Zavkov."

Jordan frowned. "What the devil is that?"

"I do not know, but Marianna did. He called it the lock for the key. Evidently the Jedalar is only part of the answer."

It made sense. Though the complete map was contained in the panel, there would have to be someone to interpret it, and the czar had trusted no one. "You say Marianna knows?"

"And was dismayed that Nebrov did. It frightened her."

"Enough to make her give us the Jedalar?"

Gregor shrugged. "It is possible. I thought I would let you discuss it with her."

"I will." He glanced in the direction in which Marianna had vanished. "But not now. We still have time."

"Not very much."

"I know that," he said harshly. "What do you expect me to do? She's tired and frightened and hurting."

"When this started, you would not have cared about her, if it meant keeping Kazan safe."

"Not now!" He turned and stalked away. Gregor

was right, but that did not make the choices easier. He did not want to coerce and use her, and God knows he did not want to hurt her again. Why couldn't she see that it was better that he find the tunnel rather than Nebrov? Kazan would use it only for its own defense, but it would be a disaster if that map was given to Napoleon.

She would not see because she trusted no one but herself. She had revealed only the details she had been forced to give him to save Alex, and he doubted if she would be willing to confide any more now.

What the devil was Zavkov?

Marianna did not wake until almost midnight and came back sluggishly to awareness.

Alex . . . She should not be sleeping. Alex needed her.

Alex was not here! Nebrov had him and—

Panic brought her fully awake, but relief immediately followed as she realized that horror was over. Alex must still be with the ravin, and she had only to fetch him.

She splashed water into her face and made a scanty attempt at tidying her hair before leaving the tent.

The camp was silent, and except for the guards on the perimeter, everyone appeared to be sleeping. Jordan was in one of those tents. A memory came back to her of his lean body sprawled naked next to her on the bed, his arm curved possessively about her.

She veered away from that image. She did not want to think of Jordan and definitely not of those days at Dalwynd. Her body's response was too ingrained not to—

A lantern still burned in the ravin's tent.

Had she taken a turn for the worse? Marianna ran the last several yards to the tent and threw up the flap.

She stopped just inside the threshold. Alex was curled up on the pallet beside the ravin, his curly head nestled on her naked shoulder.

A sharp pang pierced her at the sight of them. Even in conflict the bond had been apparent, but now they could be mother and son.

She must have made some noise because the ravin opened her eyes, and her gaze flew to where Marianna stood.

Marianna took another step into the tent. "He must be making you uncomfortable. I'll take him now."

"No!" The ravin's arm tightened around Alex. "It's my good shoulder. He just fell asleep. Leave him alone."

"If you are not uncomfortable, then he must be. He needs to go to bed."

"Does he look uncomfortable?" the ravin challenged. "It is you who are uncomfortable with him being here." She nodded toward the low stool beside the pallet. "Sit down. We must talk."

"I don't wish to talk. We'll wake Alex."

"Nothing could wake him but the horn of Gabriel. He was up all of last night tending my wound. Jordan could not get him to rest. He would not be asleep now if he had not dozed off from exhaustion." She looked at Alex, and her hand gently stroked his curls. "He does not look like you. He is dark, and you are fair."

Marianna reluctantly moved to the stool and sat down. "He favors my mother."

"He's a handsome boy. She must have been beautiful."

"Yes."

Her attention shifted to Marianna. "You are jealous. You do not like him being here with me."

"I'm *not* jealous. I know you're ill, but he is only a child. He has no business tending—" She broke off and nodded wearily. "He is all I have. I don't want to lose him."

"You won't lose him. You have given him love and performed your duty through all his life. It will bind him to you." She smiled without mirth. "Believe me. It is a truth I know well."

"But you chose to cut that tie with Jordan."

"Because I was young and selfish. I had married a weak man who thought he could steal my strength. When he found I was not going to let him do it, he made my life a misery. I was a stranger and alone in that cold land. I had to escape."

"And leave your child."

"Do you think I wished to do it? I loved him. He was my salvation, but I could not bear it there." She shrugged. "If I had stayed, he would have lost me anyway."

"I cannot see that."

"No?" Her eyes glinted. "My husband had started to beat me. I have a terrible temper, and I would not have tolerated that for very long. I would have killed him." She smiled sardonically. "I preferred fleeing England to being hanged for murder. You, no doubt, would have stayed and meekly borne any abuse for duty's sake."

"No, I am not meek, and I probably would have

left Cambaron as you did." She paused. "But I would have found a way to take my child with me."

"As I should have done," the ravin whispered. "I'm not denying my guilt. Do you think I have not regretted it? It seemed impossible at the time, but I should have found a way." She looked down at Alex. "But I have been punished enough for it. At first I was only happy to be back in Kazan, but then I began to think of Jordan. Every time I saw a child, I realized what I had given up." Her finger tenderly traced the line of Alex's brow. "I am not a monster. Even if I could, I would not steal moments like this from you."

Marianna felt tears stinging her eyes. She did not want to feel sorry for this autocratic woman. She did not want to be drawn any deeper into Jordan's and Ana's lives.

The ravin continued in a low voice. "But perhaps you would permit me to borrow a few? I never had them with Jordan, and now he will not even give me understanding."

The humbleness of the request touched her, and she deliberately hardened her heart. "Sleeping children are endearing. It's when they're awake that the challenge comes."

"I could meet the challenge. If you permit me."

Marianna stared at her, torn with indecision. The woman was asking for what she did not want to give. She needed Alex more now than at any time in her life.

But maybe Alex did not need her, she thought suddenly. It could be that during this period of healing, he needed to help heal another's wound. Perhaps she was being selfish to him as well as the ravin. It was difficult to know what to do. No, she realized sadly, it was only difficult to admit what she should do. "I won't have you shouting at him."

A flicker of relief crossed the ravin's face as she recognized her victory. "You think he minds? He is tougher than you know. We understand each other."

Marianna experienced another wistful pang. She wished she understood this new Alex as well as the ravin did.

"You must become reacquainted," the ravin said, as if reading her mind. She grimaced. "But I don't suggest you be shot in order to accomplish it. It is very painful."

Marianna smiled faintly but firmly insisted, "I won't have you shouting at him."

The ravin made a face. "Oh, very well. I will try to curb my tongue. Though it is not my nature."

"I agree." Marianna rose to her feet. "I will let you sleep now. Do you wish for any help with your wound?"

The ravin shook her head. "You're not going to wake the boy?"

"No. He appears comfortable enough for the night." She moved toward the entrance. "Tell him I will see him in the morning."

"Wait."

Marianna looked back over her shoulder.

"I thank you," the ravin said haltingly. "I know you are not happy about this."

"No. I'm angry and hurt and, yes, jealous." She smiled without mirth. "And, like you, I want my own way."

"Then why are you doing it?"

"Alex. You may be better for him right now than I am." She paused. "And when you have the responsibility of a child, you must always do what's best for him, not yourself."

The ravin flinched. "That was a cruel jab."

"Yes, I wanted to hurt you." She shrugged. "I thought it would make me feel better."

"Did it?"

"No."

She went outside and stopped to draw a deep breath of cold air. She wanted to go back and snatch Alex up in her arms and run away with him. In many ways this was worse than the night Costain had taken her brother. Affection could be a dangerous enemy, and the ravin had stored up years of love to lavish on a child. And there was the added bond of shared danger between them.

She would not go back. She had made the choice. At least she would not have to worry about Alex while she fulfilled her promise to Mama.

And the sooner she fulfilled it, the better. Now that there was nothing to keep her here, it was time to make plans to leave.

The horses were being sheltered a quarter-mile away from camp, where the grass was abundant enough for grazing. Gregor had assigned only two men to guard them. With so many horses to watch, it should not be difficult for her to avoid detection and slip her own mare away from the others.

She glanced across the camp at the shadowy shape of the wagon containing the panels. It was located near one of the large tents, possibly Gregor's or Jordan's. No guards were in sight, but Jordan was too clever to leave the Jedalar unwatched. He knew her very well and would be prepared for her to make an attempt.

It would not be easy, she thought wearily.

But difficult or not, it must be done.

Jordan strode into her tent the next morning. "Where is it?" he demanded.

She whirled to face him, then flinched as she saw his expression. "Where is what?"

"For God's sake don't pretend ignorance. I know it has to be somewhere in your tent. You were seen last night."

"You mean you had me watched?" She moistened her lips. "Then your spy must have told you I went to the ravin's tent to see Alex."

"And immediately afterward you went to the wagon and took something from it."

"Did I?"

"You know you did. Where's the Jedalar, Marianna?"

She glared at him defiantly. "I don't know what you mean."

He grabbed her shoulders. "Tell me."

"Why should I? So that you can steal it from me as your mother stole Alex?"

"I'm not responsible for what the ravin does or says. No one has stolen Alex from you. What the hell happened in that tent last night? Is that what this is all about?"

Her jaw set, and she did not answer him.

He drew a deep breath and tried to control himself. "Dammit, why didn't you wait? I was going to talk to you about the Jedalar. Why did you have to do this now?"

"We've talked about it before. We don't agree."

"Thousands of people could die if Napoleon gets that map." When her expression didn't change, he went on. "I've seen you talking to Niko. Do you like him?"

"Of course I like him."

"Did you know his family lives near the Russian border? They would be the first to be slaughtered. You've seen what Nebrov's army did to the towns in Montavia. Do you want to see that happen here?"

"Napoleon won't find the tunnel. None of you will find the tunnel."

"Gregor says that Nebrov knows about something called the Zavkov. If you don't help us, he may find the tunnel."

"He can't find it without the panel."

"And, by God, he's not going to lay his hands on it." Jordan's expression hardened. "Because you're going to give it to me."

"I am *not*. The panel is mine, and I won't— Put me down!"

He was carrying her out of the tent. "I didn't want to do this." Still retaining an iron hold on her arms, he set her down before Gregor. "Search the tent."

Gregor shook his head sadly and disappeared inside.

"No!" She started to struggle, her gaze fixed desperately on the entrance of the tent. "Let me go."

"Stop fighting me. Do you think I like doing this? Goddammit, you forced me."

"I didn't force you. I only took what was mine." She butted her head against his chest. "I won't let you do it."

He pinned her arms to her sides and held her immobile. "Marianna, don't . . ." His voice was thick with pain as he looked down at her. "Don't you see? I've got to take it."

She suddenly stopped fighting. "Please . . ." She looked up at him with glistening eyes. She had to make him understand. "My promise. I have to keep my promise."

"I found it," Gregor said from behind her. "She cut a slit in her sheepskin pallet and slipped the panel inside."

They had found the panel. It was over.

Through a veil of tears she watched Jordan examine the panel. It was a complicated work depicting a bed of yellow flowers at the apex of the panel where three winding streams joined paths. "Daffodils," he said. "I should have known. . . ."

He remembered the story she had told him of the first panel she had made. So many memories, so many ties, and now all to be forgotten, broken.

"I'm sorry, Marianna," Then he burst out violently, "No, by God, I'm not sorry. I'm glad this damn battle is over. Now, forget about it. Let me worry about the tunnel and Nebrov."

"I can't forget about it," she said. "I'll never be able to forget about it. I promised my mother, and you're making me break my word." She blinked and quickly lowered her eyes to the ground. "You've got what you wanted. May I go back into my tent?" Her voice shook. "I don't want to look or talk to either of you for a very long time."

He nodded curtly. "Go on."

She walked heavily into the tent and closed the flap.

It was over.

• • •

You'll have to ask her about this Zavkov," Gregor said.

"I'll talk to her after supper. She's had enough defeats for one day."

"Yes, she took it very badly." Gregor looked down at the panel. "Do you think these three streams are branches of the tunnel?"

"I don't know." And at the moment he didn't care. All he could see was Marianna's drained face in that moment before she had gone into the tent. He thrust the panel at Gregor. "Study it and see if you can make any sense of it. I don't have the stomach to look at it right now."

"This is only half the answer to the puzzle. What if she won't tell us about the Zavkov?"

"I hope she doesn't. Then I'll have an excuse for going after Nebrov now instead of later." He smiled savagely. "Extracting information from that bastard will bring me infinite delight."

The sun was setting when Jordan strode into the ravin's tent. He glanced at Alex, who was sitting by his mother's pallet. "Run along to your sister. She needs you."

"Marianna?" Alex frowned. "Why?"

"Just go to her."

Alex looked uncertainly at the ravin. "Will you be able to do without me?"

Ana nodded, her gaze on Jordan's face. "I will be fine." She added with irony, "I have my son here to care for me."

Alex ran out of the tent.

"You're angry with me," the ravin said. "I admit I'm puzzled. It's difficult to commit any heinous acts while lying flat on one's back."

"I'm not angry." He paused. "Marianna needs to have the boy with her. I know you're ill, but from now on I want you to do without him."

"Marianna asked you to intercede?" the ravin asked slowly. "Why didn't she come to me herself?"

"She didn't ask me. She just said . . ." Jordan stopped. "Last night after she left you, she took the Jedalar from the wagon and hid it in her tent. This morning I took it away from her."

"And now you're filled with guilt and want to give her everything in your power to take away the pain." She smiled faintly. "We are very much alike. I had a similar reaction quite recently."

"We're not alike," he said. "I don't run away and leave the people who belong to me."

She stiffened. "Ah, at last it's out in the open. No, you run away before they belong to you. That way you never have to risk them leaving you." She shook her head. "But it doesn't help, does it? There are always those who slip under your guard. I think this *belka* did."

"Keep the boy away. You don't need him."

"Keep him away yourself. Do you think I'm chaining him?"

"Yes, it's what you do to all of us."

Her eyes widened. "What?"

"You keep us all chained to you. Ask Gregor. He's been at your beck and call since you were children."

"We're not talking about Gregor. You said us. You?"

He was silent a moment and then said slowly, "From the time I was a child, they told me I was like you. I thought about you a good deal when I was growing up. I had precious little in common with my dear father." He smiled crookedly. "Did you know that for a while I actually hated him because I blamed him for driving you to your death?"

"No, I didn't know that."

"It was quite a shock when I found that I had blamed him unjustly. I felt cheated and foolish, and I thought I hated you as much as I did my father. I fought Gregor about coming here, but he made me come anyway."

"I told him to make you come."

"Then I met you, and you were exactly what I imagined you to be. All the force and fire and strength. I'm sure you'll feel very triumphant to know it was you who drew me back here until I came to love Kazan."

She started to raise a hand as if to reach out to him, but then let it drop when she saw the hardness of his expression. "You didn't want to tell me this. Why did you?"

"Because I know that you've always wanted it from me. Now I've given it to you. You don't need another captive at your chariot wheels. Release the boy and give him back to Marianna."

"Christ, you do think I'm—" She closed her eyes for a moment and then opened them. Her voice was trembling when she spoke. "Marianna knows that she could take the boy, if she wanted to. She chose not to do so."

"I don't believe you. She said you had stolen him."

"Then she had her own reasons for telling an untruth. I wish you would go away and discover them. I believe I'm very tired."

She was pale and drawn, and for the first time since he had met her he became aware that she was no longer a young woman. He had been filled with frustration that he had been forced to come and bargain with her, and he had deliberately tried to hurt her. She had such strength, he had not thought he would succeed to this extent. "If I've been mistaken, I apologize," he said. "Marianna was upset. Perhaps she said things that—"

"I cannot find Marianna," Alex said from the entrance to the tent. "Did she go for a ride?"

Jordan stiffened. "She's not in the camp?"

Alex shook his head.

Jordan turned and moved quickly toward him. "Go find Gregor and tell him to meet me at Marianna's tent."

"Her own reasons," the ravin repeated from behind him. "Gregor said she was not the usual sort of woman. Poor Jordan, and that painful confession for nothing. You put her in a cage, and she refuses to stay there. I'd wager your *belka* has flown our auspices."

"And left Alex? There's only one thing that would have made her do that."

"Ah, the tunnel. But you said you had the Jedalar."

"That's what she wanted me to think. Christ, she played me for a fool."

He strode out of the tent.

Gregor was waiting for him when he reached Marianna's tent. "She is not here. There is a slit in the back where she must have slipped out."

"Is her horse gone?"

"I have not had time to question the guard. I would assume it is." He paused. "I did go to the wagon and counted the panels. Three are missing."

"The one Nebrov destroyed, one to practice her little trick on us, and the real Jedalar. She must have taken two panels from the wagon last night and hidden one outside the tent."

"And is now on her way with the real Jedalar to get this Zavkov." Gregor gave a low whistle. "You have to admire the dove. It was well done."

"I don't have to admire her," Jordan said through his teeth. "I want to throttle her." He turned away from the tent. "Get Niko and at least twenty men. One of them has to be a good tracker."

"None is better than Niko. Don't worry, we will capture her before morning."

"I don't want to catch her. I want to follow her."

"And gather everything up in one scoop." Gregor nodded. "There are moments when you are not entirely stupid, Jordan. Of course, that could be due to my superior training." When Jordan did not smile, he added quietly, "Do not be too angry with her. She used what weapons she had."

"She used my pity and softness to make a fool of me. She deceived me. You're damn right I'm angry." He turned and strode toward the horses. "We'll leave within the hour."

I've come to bid you good-bye," Gregor said as he entered Ana's tent. "I've given instructions that you're to be taken back to Rengar."

"Toted in a wagon like a sack of flour," Ana said, making a face. "What indignity for a ravin. Where is Alex?"

"Running about the camp, fetching and carrying for Niko and the others. He is worried about Marianna, and Jordan wished to keep him occupied. It will be your duty to comfort him after we leave."

"I hear and obey." She smiled bitterly. "It should be no task at all. According to Jordan, I need only beckon, and everyone falls beneath my spell."

"There is some truth to that." He fell to his knees beside her. "But it surprises me that he expressed it."

"He was upset about the *belka*." She paused. "He cares for her. It is not only lust."

"Yes, but he may never admit it. He is very angry with her now."

"Because she deceived and left him. It must seem that all the women in his life betray him. She should hate me. Poor girl, neither Jordan nor I make life easy for those we love." She reached out and touched his hand. "He thinks I'm some sort of evil Circe. I'm not, am I?"

He chuckled. "If you were, I'd be your first victim. Do I look like a swine?"

"You look beautiful." She reached up and traced the ugly scar on his face. "You always look beautiful to me."

He captured her hand and brought it to his lips. "I know."

"How vain you are."

"You see beauty because you see love."

A shadow crossed her face. "Jordan said you were chained to my chariot wheels."

"Do you have a chariot? I thought they were out-dated."

"I'm serious. Have I been selfish?"

"Yes." He smiled. "But it's a selfishness I would never do without." He leaned down and pressed a kiss on her forehead. "I must go. I want to see you well by the time I return to Rengar. Do you understand?"

"I will be." She clutched his hand more tightly. "Why?"

He raised his brows inquiringly.

"Why do you give me so much but not all?"

"You do not know?" A loving smile lit his face. "I'm surprised you have not guessed."

"Tell me."

"Because I am selfish too."

"You are not selfish. You give to everyone."

"Because it pleases me. Is that not a form of selfishness? I have loved you all my life, but I don't want bits and pieces of you. When I was younger, I used to think it might be enough, but gradually I came to the realization that I am not a man who could bear a half-filled cup."

"I am not a half-filled cup," she said tartly.

"It could be the description is inadequate. Perhaps the problem is that you have always brimmed over the edge. At first you would not look at me because I was not comely and charming as you found Jordan's father. I had always been there like an old sheepdog trailing at your heels."

She tried to laugh. "Better a sheepdog than a swine, I suppose." She swallowed. "Jordan is right. I'm not a good person. I did hurt you."

"Not with intention." He lifted her hand to his

lips again. "And then you did finally look at me, but you were still preoccupied with fighting the demons you had created for yourself. You had to prove you had worth, you had to see Kazan safe and prosperous, you had to lure your son back to you."

"You helped me try to do all those things."

"Yes, I helped you, but I won't cheat myself by accepting a minor place in your life."

"You were never minor. How can I convince you? Dear God, what do you *want* of me?"

"I want it all. Nothing else will satisfy me," Gregor said simply. "And someday, when you give up your guilt and come to terms with yourself, you will be able to give it." He rose to his feet. "It is time I left. I will send Alex to you."

"Take care," she whispered.

"Of course. What talisman do you think has kept me alive all these years? Selfishness made me the most cautious of men." He smiled teasingly as he repeated softly, "I want it all."

Niko came riding back to the troop. "She is heading north, over the mountains."

Jordan's gaze went to the mountains. Russia.

"Moscow?" Gregor murmured.

"Not necessarily. The Zavkov might be hidden somewhere close to the border."

"What if her destination is Moscow? It's a long, hard trip for a woman alone."

"She's not a fool. I'm sure she took food."

Gregor raised his brows skeptically. "Enough to last her through a trek like that?"

"She can care for herself. When she was little more

than a child, she traveled by foot halfway across Montavia."

"This is different. There are few towns and villages between here and Moscow. She cannot hunt. How will she—"

"She may not be going to Moscow." He nudged his horse into a gallop, leaving Gregor and his apprehensions behind.

She had used pity to disarm and blind him. He would not permit her to do it again.

CHAPTER 15

I t is going to be Moscow." Gregor's breath puffed in the frigid air as he added, "I do not understand it. How does she know the way? Niko said she is traveling as if she were following a map."

"That's not surprising," Jordan said. "Her mother made her memorize the Jedalar. I'm sure she would have given her exact directions as to how to reach the other half of the puzzle."

"It is very cold." He cast Jordan a sly glance. "But we have seen no sign of wolves. That is good. They get very hungry during the winter."

"Be quiet, Gregor."

"I am only trying to protect the Jedalar."

"I know exactly what you're doing."

"Wolves have sharp teeth and strong jaws that can destroy flesh and bone with one crunch. Just think what they could do with our precious glass panel. Perhaps you should send Niko ahead to keep her in sight."

"I don't want her to know we're following her."

"It is worth the risk. She is probably concentrating

too much on an empty belly and keeping alive to look behind her."

Jordan muttered a curse.

Wolves have sharp teeth. . . .

They had seen no wolves, dammit.

. . . *and strong jaws that can destroy—*

"Niko, go ahead," he snapped. "Keep her in view, but don't let yourself be seen."

She has run out of food," Niko said. "There was enough grass for the horse to graze today, but she made nothing to eat for herself when she camped last night."

"She will probably come to a village soon." Gregor bit into the tender piece of roasted rabbit. "And she has plenty of flesh on her bones. A few days without eating will not hurt her." He pulled off a piece of meat from the spit and extended it to Jordan. "Have some more. There is plenty. The hunting was good today, and we still have six fine rabbits for tomorrow. There's nothing like a full belly to make you sleep well."

The bastard expected him to refuse. He took the piece of meat and ate it. Then he took another piece and ate that too.

"She is hungry." Niko's tone was laden with reproach.

"What do you expect me to do?" Jordan asked in frustration. "Go and deliver her supper to her so that she'll know she's being followed? We're too close, dammit. She should be in Moscow in another week."

"Yes, let her eat then. It is good for a woman to

suffer," Gregor said. "It humbles them and makes them aware of the sins they commit against us poor men. Is that not right, Jordan?"

Jordan gazed directly at Gregor and said with precision, "Quite right." He got to his feet and stalked away from the campfire. He was sick of both of them and sick unto death of this long journey. He wanted it over.

If he wanted it over, what must she feel like? She believed herself alone in this wilderness. He knew loneliness. It was worse than hunger or fear.

Hunger.

With a low curse he turned, stalked back toward the fire, picked up one of the rabbits, and headed for the trees where the horses were tethered.

"Niko says she is camped by the river about four miles from here," Gregor called after him.

Jordan reined in his horse in the woods a good distance from Marianna's campfire. What the devil was he doing here? he wondered in exasperation as he slipped from his saddle and tied his horse to a tree. He grabbed the rabbit he had slung over his saddle and started through the forest. He had no idea how he was going to get this blasted animal to her without revealing his presence. Dead rabbits didn't fall from the sky and into a cooking pot. He should have let her—

She was gone.

He stopped at the edge of the trees several yards from the brightly burning campfire. Her sheepskin pallet was spread before the blazing logs, but Marianna was nowhere in sight.

Alarm jolted through him. Where the devil was she?

Then he saw her.

She was standing barefoot in the shallows of the river, a spear carved from a gnarled tree branch in her right hand. Her gown was hiked and tucked into her waistband, and she reminded him vaguely of the Diana in the tapestry in the hunting lodge. She raised the spear, peering down at the moonlight-burnished water.

A glimmer appeared on the surface.

She struck!

And missed.

She waited patiently as minutes passed.

A shimmering movement to her right and she whirled, bringing the spear down with the same quickness as the trout she was stalking.

She missed again.

She waited again.

On the third attempt she was victorious.

He heard her cry of triumph as she held the fish high and waded back to the shore.

He faded into the shadows as she neared the campfire. In the flare of light she no longer looked the triumphant huntress. Her face was thinner than in their first meeting in Talenka and pinched with cold. She was shivering, her bare legs tinged blue from standing in the icy water. Lord, how long had she been in that river before he had arrived?

He took an impulsive step forward. He wanted to wrap her in warmth and safety, take away the cold and the hunger.

He stopped when she began tending to her own needs. She wrapped herself with a sheepskin blanket and sat down, rocking back and forth before the fire.

She continued in that manner for a long time before she was warm enough to turn and pick up the trout. It was a good-sized fish. She would eat tonight and perhaps tomorrow.

Jordan strode back to his horse. She had not needed him. She had adapted to the situation and provided for herself. She was as strong in her own way as his mother was in hers.

He mounted his horse and headed back to his own camp. It had been a long, cold journey for nothing. He should be annoyed and frustrated.

He should not be filled with this damned pride in her.

Jordan . . .

Marianna drowsily opened her eyes in the middle of the night with a strange sense of peace and contentment. Why had she been concerned? Everything would be fine. He would forgive her for what she had to do. This conflict between them was not of any real importance.

A sharp gust of wind ruffled the surface of the river and caused the fire to flare higher. She shivered as she came fully awake. She drew her blanket tighter around herself as a desolation swept through her that was colder than the wind.

A dream. She must have been dreaming.

Jordan would never forgive her, and she would never ask it. Their paths had parted and would never again be intertwined. She must become accustomed to that truth and arm herself against these agonizing moments.

But how did you arm yourself against a dream?

The fish is gone," Niko said to Jordan. "And she has had to leave the river and go farther inland."

He looked hopefully at Jordan.

Jordan said nothing.

"I have been thinking," Niko said. "Mikel brought down several fat pheasants yesterday. I could go ahead of her and leave one of them on the trail for her to find."

Jordan shook his head.

Niko frowned. "It would do no harm. She would still not know we are following her."

"It would do harm."

Niko uttered a low exclamation as he whirled his horse and sent it flying down the trail.

"Why would it do harm?" Gregor was studying Jordan's face.

"Perhaps I want her to suffer."

Gregor shook his head. "It is not vengeance. You would have helped her three nights ago."

Jordan was silent a moment and then said, "She must do it on her own."

"Why?"

"For God's sake, we're going to take away the fruits of her victory," Jordan burst out. "I'll be damned if I steal away the victory itself. Not one woman in a thousand could make this journey without help. She deserves to know she did it all herself."

Gregor nodded understandingly. "Interesting. You are no longer angry with her?"

"Oh yes, I'm angry. I want to throttle her. That has nothing to do with this."

"Interesting," Gregor said again.

She has snared a rabbit." Niko's voice had as much pride as if Marianna had magically produced the animal from thin air. "It took her all day, but she did it."

"That is good." Gregor beamed.

Murmurs of approval came from the troop, and several gave smiles of relief. One young man made a face and exchanged money with another.

Gregor turned to Jordan and said, "I hope you are capable of subduing our dove yourself. I am not certain you will receive help from Niko or any of the others."

Jordan knew what he meant. Over these weeks on the trail the troop had watched and gradually become caught up in Marianna's struggle for survival. With every small victory she had won more of their respect.

The *belka* was no longer an outsider.

"And what about you?" Jordan asked Gregor.

"Kazan must be safe. I will do what must be done," Gregor said. "Will you?"

"Yes."

"You are sure? We are only two days' journey from Moscow. The time to act is coming."

And by God he would welcome it. His nerves were stretched to the breaking point with standing by and watching Marianna struggle against odds she was not prepared to meet. The conflict between them would resume, but at least this blasted journey would be over. "Don't worry. When we reach Moscow, I'll be ready to do what's necessary."

• • •

She did not go to Moscow. The next day she turned south and then rode west.

Niko came riding back to the troop just after noon. "She has stopped."

"She's made camp?"

Niko shook his head. "I think she has reached her destination."

Jordan's hands tightened on the reins. "Where?"

"Three miles from here. There is a village and, on the hill, a grand palace. She tied her horse outside the palace and went inside."

"Did anyone come out to greet her?"

Niko shook his head. "The palace is deserted. It looks as if no one has been there for years."

"Then I believe we can assume she has reached her destination." Gregor glanced at Jordan. "Do we go after her at once?"

Jordan nudged his horse forward. "You're damned right we do."

She was here!

Relief poured through Marianna as she set down the cloth-wrapped Jedalar and leaned it against a wall of the foyer. Heaven knows, there had been times when she had thought she would not make it.

The palace was everything her grandmother had told her it would be.

She looked up at the curving green-and-white marble grand staircase to the long windows of the landing. A huge crystal chandelier wept glittering tears above her.

Emptiness.

Coldness.

It was as if the inhabitants of the palace had just walked out. The door had been unlocked, and no protective cloths covered the rich tables and chairs. Dust was everywhere.

She stiffened. An unlocked door?

Nebrov?

Fear rushed through her until she remembered that the doors at Cambaron had never been locked. No one dared to steal from the rich and powerful. If Nebrov had beaten her here, she would be facing him now.

She closed the door, and the sound echoed hollowly off the high ceilings. Nebrov was not here now, but who could say how much time she had? If she did not set to work at once, she would have to wait until tomorrow. The insertion must be done while the sun was still high.

Her brow wrinkled as she strove to recall the detailed instructions Mama had given her. The hall to the left should lead to the chapel. She picked up the Jedalar and moved quickly down the hall.

Jordan reined in his horse at the bottom of the hill. The bold rays of the midafternoon sun lit the palace, which shone with a rainbow of colors. It was truly an ice castle; snow and ice covered half of the gray marble structure that appeared more Greek than Russian with its classic pillars and graceful, low-roofed wings. Long icicles hung from eaves. Ice formed a mirrorlike surface on the stones of the courtyard and on the four steps leading to the front entrance. Even the bank of stained-glass windows that stretched across the front of the palace were frosted, each one glowing like an individual flame captured in crystal.

Marianna's horse was tied to an ornamental post in the courtyard.

"The quarry is in sight," Gregor said. "Do we storm the palace?"

"No, find quarters for the men in the village. I'll go in alone."

"Ah, what bravery, what self-sacrifice."

Jordan ignored the flippancy. "And question the villagers about any newcomers who have arrived here. We don't want Nebrov surprising us."

"I will do better than that," Gregor said. "I'll send Niko to double back and watch for our demon friend."

Niko groaned in mock despair.

Gregor ignored him, his gaze going from the palace to the fluted towers of Moscow. "This palace is very close to the city. It could be one of the exits for the tunnel."

"I'll place a sizable wager it is," Jordan said.

Gregor turned to Niko. "Well, come along, my friend, let us get these men under a roof for the night. I am certain Jordan will summon us if we are needed."

Niko grimaced. "You care nothing about getting me under a roof for the night."

"I promise tomorrow night you will have both a warm fire and a dry roof." He lifted his hand to Jordan. "I will come to you tomorrow morning to see if you have triumphed or merely survived."

Jordan watched them ride down the hill toward the village and then again looked up at the palace.

She was there within those walls.

In a moment he would see her, talk to her.

He started up the road toward the palace.

She struck him on the back of the neck as he entered the front door!

Marianna was standing behind the door and would have hit his head if he had not seen the shadow of the club on the floor and whirled to face her. Even the glancing blow made him grunt with pain.

When she again tried to bring down the club, he grabbed it and tore it from her grasp. Her weapon turned out to be a tree branch. "Dammit, are you trying to kill me?"

She whirled and tried to run away.

He caught her by the hair, jerking her to a halt.

She did not cry out from the pain as another woman would have done. Instead, she turned her head and sank her teeth into his arm.

His grasp on her hair loosened, and she broke free. She dashed across the foyer toward the staircase.

He caught her on the sixth step and tumbled her to her knees. The next moment she was on her back, and he was astraddle her, pinning her arms above her head.

"Let me go!"

"The devil I will."

"Fool," she muttered. "I was a fool. I led you here. I should have realized . . ." She started to struggle again. "But you can't have it!"

"Stop fighting. You'll hurt yourself."

She glared up at him. "Or you!"

"Not me," he said thickly. "In case you haven't noticed, I've begun to enjoy this."

She froze as she realized the truth of his words. In her position she could scarcely miss the hard arousal pressed against her body. "You won't rape me," she whispered. "You wouldn't do that."

At the moment he wasn't as certain as she seemed to be. The sudden physical struggle had released all the anger and frustration that had built over the months. He was having trouble thinking, and the mindless hunger was readying him. His hips moved in the most sensual of caresses, rubbing against her. "How can you be sure?"

A shiver ran through her. Her teeth sank into her lower lip. "I know you."

"I thought I knew you." His lips brushed her throat. She smelled of wind and pine and an acrid scent that was vaguely familiar. It didn't matter. She also smelled of woman, and that scent was more arousing than any perfume. He licked delicately at the pulse in the hollow of her throat. "But that didn't stop you from deceiving me and then trying to kill me."

"I wouldn't have done that. I was only trying to knock you unconscious. I had to stop you."

His hips moved again. "From doing this? Why? You like it. Right now, you want nothing more than to wrap your legs around me. Isn't that right?"

She drew in a deep, shaky breath. "Yes, that's what I want, but I'm not going to do it. I'm not going to let you use me to rid yourself of anger. You won't rape me, and I won't be seduced."

"We fought this battle at Dalwynd."

"I'm stronger now."

He studied her face. "Yes, you are." He smiled. "But did it ever occur to you that will only make the battle more interesting for both of us?"

"Let me up. I feel as if I'm stretched on a rack."

"Don't you like it? I do. I can feel every muscle and soft place in your body. I think if I entered you from this position, you would find it very exciting. Do you remember what pleasure you received stretched over the arms of the chair? I can see the way—"

"Let me up." She suddenly burst out, "If you're going to rape me, do it!"

He would not have to rape her. She was already trembling and in need.

Her eyes blazed up at him. "Do it! Otherwise, let me be free of you."

He did not want to let her free. He would never free her, he realized. Not in this lifetime or the next. The knowledge sent a wave of shock through him.

She stiffened. "What's wrong?"

He couldn't let her go, and if he tried to hold her, she would never stay. "There's a good deal wrong," he said grimly. "And I wish I hadn't become aware of it in this particular instant." He released her arms, then swung off her and moved to one side. "Get up."

She lay still, surprised at the sudden victory.

"I said get up," he repeated harshly. "And, for God's sake, stop looking at me like that. It makes me want to—" He broke off and moved farther away on the wide step.

She slowly sat up and brushed her hair out of her eyes. "Why did you—"

"It's cold as Hades in here." He stood up and started down the steps. "I'll get wood for a fire.

You've had a few hours to explore. Is there a small room that will be easy to heat?"

She indicated a door to the left of the foyer. "There's a fireplace in that anteroom."

He nodded, then said, "Don't try to run away. Gregor and the men are in the village. We'll track you down, if you do."

"You needn't worry. I can't run away," she said quietly. "Not until I do what I've come to do."

The ax came down, biting into the wood.

Jordan struck again, hitting the log as if it were a mortal enemy.

Marianna shivered as she watched him from the window. She had been aware of his anger, and to see its release in violence was a chastening sight.

Chastening and vaguely erotic.

Vulcan.

He was as primitive as Vulcan wielding his hammer. She could see the bulge of muscle on his thighs as he braced himself before each blow, the pull of tendons in his shoulders beneath the black shirt. A wave of heat went through her as she remembered that moment when she had lain stretched beneath him on the stairs.

The hammer striking the anvil.

No, she would have been no passive anvil. She would have matched him blow for blow. She had felt her will melting with every touch, every moment that passed.

And he had known it. He always knew her every intimate response. He had known he could have her, and he had let her go.

Jordan stacked the logs in the fireplace, set the kindling, and struck flint. "What is this place?"

"The palace belonged to Czar Paul."

"It looks as if no one has been here for a long time."

"No one has. The czar was assassinated in 1801, and the royal family had no knowledge of this place. He had it built by the same workmen who built the tunnel."

The kindling caught fire and flared. "And were later killed?"

"Yes."

He sat back on his heels, looking into the fire. "The lock for the key."

She didn't answer.

He didn't take his gaze from the fire as he asked quietly, "Where's the Jedalar, Marianna?"

She might as well tell him. If he searched, he would find it anyway. "It's in the chapel down the hall. Do you want to see it?"

"Not now." He stood up and stoked the fire. "I hope you'll give it to me later. I don't want to be forced to take it." He turned and strode toward the door. "Watch the fire. You must be hungry. I have food in my saddlebag."

If he had only come an hour later. . . . She wondered if she had time to run to the chapel and complete her work. No, she decided. What she had to do would take too long. And she must not be discovered until it was done.

No, that wasn't the true reason. She wanted this time with him. When he found out what she had done, he would never want to see her again. It wasn't too much that she take this little for herself.

The fire was burning brightly when he returned to the anteroom, and the chill had almost dispersed. He threw his saddlebags on the hearth and shrugged off his cloak. "I unsaddled your horse and put him in the stable. You shouldn't have left him standing outside so long."

She said defensively, "I was coming back to care for him when I saw you and Gregor down the hill."

"And decided to remove my head from my body."

"I told you I didn't mean to harm you."

He rubbed the back of his neck. "Then you didn't succeed."

"Did I really hurt you?"

"You most certainly did." He studied her expression. "I believe you're displaying concern. How peculiar. You must be plotting something."

"No." She moved over to the saddlebags. "Not at the moment. I'm too hungry. If you'll make a spit, I'll skin the rabbit."

"That's why I brought in the branch you used to club me with. Sit down and rest. I don't need help." He looked at the dust-covered chairs and added, "You'll stay cleaner if you spread your cloak on the floor and sit on that instead of those chairs."

"I haven't worried about cleanliness for weeks." Still, she did as he suggested, then sat in front of the fire. She watched him as he began to whittle one end of the club. "Where did you send Gregor?"

"To the village. He'll be back in the morning to see if I've survived." His lips curved ruefully. "I'll tell him it was not an easy task." He looked from her face to the large round window gracing the wall across the room. The stained glass depicted a scarlet sun shooting out golden rays of light as it sank down behind purple hills. The sun pouring through the brilliant panes cast a long beam of multihued light that struck and formed a radiant circle on the oak floor in the center of the room. "That's very beautiful. Your grandmother's work?"

She nodded, her face lighting eagerly. "Grandmama did all the stained glass in this palace. Wasn't she wonderful?"

"Yes." He glanced at the window again. "But I think the work you did at Cambaron is better."

Her eyes widened in astonishment. "You do?" Then she immediately shook her head. "No, that couldn't be true. She was a magnificent craftsman. No one did better work than Grandmama."

"Until Marianna."

"Truly?" she whispered.

"Truly."

Happiness surged through her. He meant it, and though it might not be true, it was wonderful to hear praise from his lips. "You should see her windows in the chapel. That's where her best work is displayed."

"And where you took the Jedalar."

Her smile faded. Everything always came back to the Jedalar, casting a cloud over every joyful happening between them. "Yes."

"Why?"

She looked away from him. "Do you wish me to skin that rabbit or not? I've gotten quite skilled at the art in the past weeks."

For a moment she thought he was not going to allow the evasion, but then a smile lit his face. "I know." He knelt on the hearth and drawled, "By all means. Such crudities are totally beyond me."

Her spirits lightened as she recognized the lazy, mocking tone she had heard a thousand times at Cambaron. The coming conflict between them was inevitable, but it was not to be yet.

Eat." He frowned. "You've had only a few mouthfuls."

"I've had enough." It was true she had eaten only a little of the rabbit roasting on the spit in the fireplace, but she was satisfied. Her appetite must have lessened due to the scant fare on the journey here. "You eat the rest."

"You've got to be hungry. You've not had a bite since last night."

"How do you know?" Then she shook her head as she guessed. "You were that close to me?"

He shook his head. "Niko."

"I feel very stupid. I never realized anyone was following me."

"You weren't stupid. Niko is an expert tracker, and we stayed several miles behind. You did better than most men would have done." He looked away from her into the fire, and the next words came awkwardly. "I was proud of you."

Her eyes widened. "You were?"

"Yes."

"Why?"

"I suppose it's due to a few unimportant qualities I've noticed in you. You never give up. You have a fine mind, and you're brave as a lion. Oh, and one more reason." He still was not looking at her. "Because you belong to me."

She tensed. "I don't belong to you."

"Not yet. I have to make it so." He looked up and held her gaze. "Will you wed me, Marianna?"

She stared at him, stunned. "Wed?"

"I've decided it's the only way you'll stay with me. You would never break your vows."

Her astonishment caused her to blurt out the first thing that came into her head. "Your mother broke hers."

"She had reason. My father was the worst kind of bastard. I'm not stupid enough to follow his example."

"You don't mean this."

"Why not?"

"You're the Duke of Cambaron. You know such a marriage is unacceptable."

"You've been listening to that balderdash Dorothy has fed you," he said roughly. "I accept such a marriage, and I'm the only one who counts. The rest of the world can go to perdition."

She shook her head.

"Do you think you're unworthy of me?"

She lifted her chin. "Why should I think that? I'm probably too good for you."

He chuckled. "Then we agree."

"But it's not what I think. They will—"

"I'm tired of listening to what 'they' think." His expression turned grim. "I want you as my wife and, by God, I'm going to have you."

"Because I wouldn't be your mistress."

"I wouldn't be satisfied if you consented to that now. I want more."

"Why?"

He was silent, as if searching for words. "I love you," he finally said haltingly.

She felt an incredible burst of joy. It was a miracle, an unbelievable gift. She wanted to—

It *was* unbelievable.

A deep thrust of pain tore through her as she realized how gullible she was to have had that initial response. She swallowed to ease the tightness in her throat. "How very convenient."

He muttered a curse beneath his breath. "Convenient? I've never said 'I love you' to any woman before, and you say it's convenient? It's not convenient. Do you think I want this? It hurts like the devil."

It did hurt, and the pain was growing with every moment. "You said I wasn't stupid, and yet you expect me to believe you," she burst out. "I won't be duped again, Jordan." She tightened her lips to keep them from trembling. "I always thought you honest. I didn't think you'd lie to get me to give you the Jedalar."

His eyes glittered with anger. "Christ, I can *take* the damned Jedalar. It's here in this palace."

"But you don't know how to put the puzzle together. You need me for that."

"I need you." He added, "But not for that. If I have to do it, I'll figure it out for myself. It's not—" He stopped as he saw her expression. "I'm wasting my time. You don't trust me."

"Can you blame me?"

He smiled crookedly. "No, I suppose it's too much to ask. It's clear I'll have to prove myself."

She shook her head wearily. "There's no time."

"Nonsense, we have all the time in the world." He

took a few moments to subdue his exasperation and annoyance. "After we finish with this business, I shall set out to court you."

After they finished with this business, he would not even wish to look at her. The thought sent a surge of panic through her. She wanted to reach out and touch him, fill herself with warmth to ward off that chill future. "No!"

His lips tightened grimly. "Resign yourself to it. I'm going to find a way to have you. I'm even willing to be as civilized and correct as even Dorothy could wish. What the devil else do you want from me?"

She said unsteadily, "I want what we had at Dalwynd." She paused, then added, "Now."

He went still. "Even though you have no trust in me?"

She nodded. "I don't have to trust you to know that you will bring me pleasure."

"Oh, I'm to be a toy for your pleasure?"

"Isn't that what you wanted of me at Dalwynd?"

"Not entirely. As a matter of fact, during that period my motives were often muddled even to myself." He shrugged. "But I have no objection to the role. You can be assured I'll endeavor to please. Take off your clothes."

She stared at him in bewilderment.

"Well, since you're so eager, you surely didn't expect me to waste time seducing you?" He started to unbutton his shirt. "You evidently have no need of sweet words."

"I don't remember you ever giving me sweet words." The words of seduction he had spoken to her had all been raw and shimmering darkly with sensuality.

"But you listened to them with all the attention of an acolyte to Venus." She became aware of the faint bite beneath his usual mockery. He stripped off his shirt. "I've never seen a woman so eager to be convinced."

"You're trying to hurt me."

"Why should I try to— Yes." His lips twisted. "But why should that make a difference?" He sat down and began to remove his boots. "A bit of conflict can be exciting as a prelude to bed play."

It did make a difference. She did not want bitterness and pain to mar this last encounter.

"But perhaps I'm wrong. Perhaps you want more from me."

She had hurt him. No, she must not believe she had that power. She must not believe any of the things she desperately wanted to be true. In this place, at this time, he was the enemy. She took off her cloak and dropped it on the floor. "No, that's all I want."

"The devil you do!" His eyes were blazing. He took a deep breath, and she could almost see him put on the mask of mockery and sensuality. He leaned back in the chair. "Then you'll have to shed more than that cloak. I'm beginning to get bored. Shall I help you?"

"No." Her hands were trembling as she went to the fastening of her gown. "I'll do it myself."

"Ah, what an independent spirit you have. Have I ever told you how much I admire that quality?"

"Even while trying to crush it?"

"I never wanted to destroy your spirit. I just wanted to channel it so that no one could enjoy it but my humble self." He stood up, shed the rest of his garments, and then resumed his seat, completely at ease in his nudity. "I visited a sultan in Morocco once who had a splendid palace in which to store his charming treasures. I did not envy him at the time." His voice hoarsened as his gaze went over her now-naked body. "I do now. Would you walk to the center of the room?

"Why?"

"To please me. I promise I will please you in turn."

She started slowly across the room. She was acutely aware of his gaze on the hollow of her spine, the curve of her buttocks. She abruptly stopped and turned to face him. "This is ridiculous. I feel like a slave on an auction block."

"What a terrible experience for a woman of independence. I had no such intention. Just another few steps."

She hesitated, and then she suddenly realized what he wanted. She took four more steps, and she was in the radiant circle of color formed by the sunlight streaming through the stained-glass window. She felt the warmth of the sun's rays on her naked body.

"Splendid," he said softly. "You look like a Nereid from beneath the sea."

She glanced down at herself and felt a strange thrill. It was like looking at a stranger. Her body was criss-crossed by scarlet and gold lines and, where there were no brilliant streaks of color, soft muted pinks vied with lavenders. She wondered what color her hair was in this light. She reached up to touch it and then turned her head back and forth; her hair felt heavier and more sensual as it swung about her shoulders. Her entire body felt different, as if it belonged to someone else. "Nereids should be cool and blue."

"Perhaps in the panels you fashion." She heard him rise from his chair. "My Nereids bask in sunlight, and there is nothing cool about them."

He stepped into the circle of color and became one with it.

Nude. Magnificent. Aroused. His cheeks were hollowed, and his light eyes shimmered as they looked down at her. "Isn't this amusing? Tell me, do you suppose we look like figures in a stained-glass window?"

"No." She swallowed. "Stained-glass windows must be on display."

"And I'm a trifle shocking for public display." His gaze went to her breasts. "And so are you, my love."

She knew what he meant. She felt her entire body ripening and readying and a tingling ache beginning between her thighs as she looked at him. Lean, muscular, and streaked with fire, he was the most beautifully sensual creature she had ever beheld.

"You like this, don't you?" he whispered. "And why shouldn't you? When you were making your beautiful windows, you must have sometimes felt that you were part of them." He paused. "Or wanted to be part of them." He took a step closer. "And now you can."

She was trembling. He was towering over her, and she felt small and helpless and completely woman.

He took her hand and brought it to his body. "I've always been jealous of your work. Did you know that?" He closed her hand around him. A shudder went through him as he held it in place. "You would never share it with me, and I wanted all of you." His other hand went out to cup her breast. "You're so tiny, your hand barely goes around me." He urged softly, "Think how we look now. Imagine us as the figures in one of your panels."

She was imagining it. She could see him. . . .

Dear heaven, she could see both of them. Her breast was lifting and falling beneath his hand as his thumb teasingly flicked her nipple.

"Am I part of it?" he whispered.

"Yes. . . ."

He smiled. "That's not enough." He suddenly lifted her, wrapped her legs about his hips, and plunged deep! "I want to be all of it."

She cried out, her hands clutching his shoulders.

"Take me!" His voice was a guttural growl. His hips worked frantically back and forth as he held her sealed to him. "All of me!"

She was moaning, grunting, savagely trying to press closer, as if she were a different woman from the one who had stepped within that circle of light. She was vaguely aware of him falling to his knees and then pushing her down on the floor. The wood was cold on her back, but the sun was warm on her body, and Jordan was hot. . . . His face was only a dark shadow above her, but his body was outlined in a fiery radiance.

Vulcan, she thought feverishly. Vulcan striking . . .

His dark hair had come loose from its queue and brushed her breasts with every thrust. "Think—of—me." He punctuated every word with a deep plunge. "I need to be—"

"Be still!" she gasped. "I can't think at all. I don't even know what you—"

She arched upward as explosive release tore

through her. She was aware of Jordan's hoarse cry above her.

They lay there, joined, in the pool of light, while shudder after shudder ripped through them.

"And you think you can give this up?" he asked in a low voice.

He was the one who would give her up, she thought sadly. "I don't want to talk about it."

She thought he was going to protest, but after a moment he said, "Very well. I suppose I'm satisfied with my progress to date. I hope my services proved satisfactory?"

She moistened her lips. "Let me up. I want to go back to the fire."

"In a moment." He swung off her and then lifted her to a kneeling position in the brilliant circle of light. "I have another window I want you to remember." He knelt facing her, took her hands, and looked into her eyes. "It is true, you know. I do love you. I love your body and your mind and your soul." He lifted her hand to his lips. "I want all of them. I'm sorry I don't have much to give in return. I'm selfish and arrogant, and Gregor will tell you that my soul is constantly in jeopardy."

He had a great deal to give. He had wit and courage, intelligence and honesty. She wished desperately to reach out and gather everything he was to her, but she could not do it. The risk was too great.

She said nothing.

He shrugged. "I see that you agree with him." He drew her into his arms. "It will do you no good. Fate is definitely on my side." His hand stroked the back of head, and he slowly rocked her back and forth. "Why else would we have been brought together, if not to belong forever? None of it would make any sense at all."

She should not let him hold her like this. She had not expected tenderness. It was much harder to bear than passion, and would only make the parting harder.

She did not move. She could not give him up. Not yet.

Her arms tightened around him, and they knelt there until the last rays of the sun faded and the radiant circle slowly vanished from around them.

CHAPTER 16

"Why do they call you the Duke of Diamonds?" Jordan's tongue gently traced the aureole around her nipple. "What brought that to mind?"

"I remembered something Dorothy said a long time ago."

"And you're just wondering now?"

"She said it had something to do with pouches of diamonds and women. . . . I think I didn't want to know."

"Then why are you questioning me?"

Because now she had a hunger to know everything about him, the bad and the good. She wanted to savor every aspect, every quality. She would have only memories later, and those memories must be of the complete man. "Tell me."

"It was a long time ago," he said impatiently. "I don't practice such idiocies any longer." He rubbed his cheek back and forth against her breast. "And it's not for my wife's ears."

"But I'm not your wife."

"You will be."

She did not argue with him. She had no wish to spoil the moment. "I want to know."

He raised his head. "You won't like it."

She looked at him from beneath her lashes and murmured teasingly, "It cannot be any worse than what I know of you already."

He flinched. "What a comforting thought. However, I beg to disagree." He lifted her hand and pressed his lips to the palm. "There are details of my unsavory past that you don't know and should not know." He asked absently, "What on earth is that smell?"

She stiffened and tried to tug her hand away. "What smell?"

He sniffed her palm. "I noticed it before. It's familiar, but I can't quite place it. . . ."

"Horse," she said quickly. "I told you that I had little chance to bathe on this journey." She forced a smile. "And you should not be so ungentlemanly as to remark on it." She had to distract him. "Or are you merely trying to avoid my question? I want to know about the Duke of Diamonds."

He frowned. "By God, do you never give up?"

He had dropped her hand, but she must be quite sure the memory of that scent was blotted from his mind. Her jaw set, and she said, "Evidently everyone in the *ton* is familiar with the reason they call you that. I think it completely unfair you should know everything about me, and I—" She stopped as he made a gesture of surrender.

"It was only an absurd conceit. At the end of an evening of pleasure I'd leave a leather pouch of diamonds for the lady. The pouch would contain one diamond for every time she had pleased me." He looked away from her. "It aroused a certain competitiveness that intrigued me."

He was not telling her everything. "Dorothy said there was something else . . . that they laughed when they spoke of it."

"Dorothy should not have even discussed this with you." He shrugged and then said curtly, "It was the places I left the pouch in that they found amusing."

"The places—" Then she understood, and heat flooded her cheeks.

"I told you that you wouldn't like it."

"I don't like it!" She sat up and reached for her cloak. "I find it wicked and depraved." She jumped to her feet, flung the cloak about her, and strode toward the door. "As I find you."

"For God's sake, where are you going?"

"Away from you. There must be somewhere in this huge place where I can avoid seeing—"

"It was years ago. I was scarcely more than a boy." He was on his feet, following her into the foyer. "Come back to the fire. You can't go wandering around in this cold."

"You were never a boy. You were born a wicked, lustful scoundrel who—"

"Why are you so angry?" He grabbed her by the shoulders. "I only told you what you asked of me."

"I didn't think—" She hadn't thought it would hurt so much. She hadn't thought the picture of that wild boy and his debaucheries would fill her with this anger and pain. She had been wrong. She did not want to know the complete Jordan Draken, if it meant she had to think of those women in his past. "It should not surprise you that I'm shocked at such an act."

His eyes narrowed on her face. "It wasn't shock." He added softly, "Jealousy?"

She quickly shook her head.

"Why not? If you'd told me you'd had your own Duke of Diamonds, I'd have wanted to kill him . . . and you." He took a step closer. "But then I have reason. I've already told you I love you."

"You don't—"

His lips covered hers, smothering the words, his tongue entering to joust and play. She was breathless when he finally lifted his head. "And I think you must feel a similar affection for me. Or something very near it."

"No," she whispered.

He smiled recklessly. "Then you must be feeling cheated. I can think of no other reason for this display. I shall have to rectify the omission immediately."

"What do you— Jordan!"

He had picked her up and was carrying her toward the staircase.

"I want you under me," he said hoarsely as he climbed the stairs. "As you were this afternoon, but with nothing between us." He paused at the sixth step. "I believe this is right."

"I don't want this."

He laid her on the steps and then straddled her. He impatiently pushed aside her cloak. She gasped as she felt flesh on flesh, hardness against softness.

"Then convince me, and you won't have it." His thumb and forefinger pulled gently on the tight curls surrounding her womanhood. "Convince me."

A hot shudder went through her, and her breasts swelled.

The moonlight streaming through the long windows on the landing touched the crystal chandelier beyond his shoulder with icy radiance. Cold and heat. Darkness and fire. Dominance and submission. She tried to retrieve the anger that had faded into the shadows of sensuality. "I'm not one of those women to whom you gave those pouches. I won't have you treating me—"

"Shh." His fingers touched her lips, silencing her. "It will never be like that with you." His eyes were suddenly glinting with mischief. "Though I may give you diamonds someday." He felt her stiffen and bent forward to whisper in her ear. "There are two huge diamonds that my barrister keeps for me in London. They're very beautiful with a clear, bold fire. Like you, Marianna."

"I don't want diamonds."

"But you'll want these." He slipped two fingers deep within her. "Because we'll put them here."

She gasped and arched upward.

His fingers thrust slowly back and forth. "I like the idea of you wearing my diamonds, love." A third finger joined the others, and the rhythm quickened. She bit her lower lip to keep from crying out. "I believe you'll like it too. I hope you'll wear them as you work, dine, ride, and walk. Every time you move, you'll find they rub together and bring you a burst of pleasure."

The erotic words were as inflaming as his fingers within her, stroking her to fever pitch. She was barely aware of him moving, adjusting her position. He smiled wickedly as he whispered, "And it will be my great privilege to remove them when we do this."

He plunged deep, ramming her to the quick.

She cried out and reached out blindly for him. He lifted her legs about his hips and rode her with a passion that was almost brutal in intensity.

She was whimpering, her fingers clutching helplessly at his shoulders. The sensations were unbelievable. She thought she could bear no more, and then he gave her more and it was not enough. He was everything that was savagely male, and she was female accepting with equal primitive wildness.

When the explosion came, she convulsed, her scream echoing off the high arched ceiling.

His breath came in short, labored gasps as he lifted his head to look down at her. "I was too rough. Did I hurt you? Are you well?"

She was, except for a weakness that pervaded every limb and a feeling that the world had ended and been reborn. "You didn't hurt me."

"I had to make you see." His hand gently stroked her cheek. "The Duke of Diamonds was a long time ago, another man. The only time I'll resurrect him is for you, when it brings you pleasure." His gaze held hers, willing her to believe. "It's only for you now. Forever. Do you understand?"

"Yes."

"But you still don't trust me." It was a statement, but she knew he wanted her to deny it.

In this moment she could almost trust him, almost believe he loved her.

Almost.

"I'm cold," she whispered.

Hope faded from his expression, and he forced a smile. "And no wonder." He moved off her and stood up. He pulled her to her feet and draped the cloak about her. "Come back to the fire." He took her hand and led her down the stairs. "I believe I said that before. I must admit I'm delighted you didn't comply."

She had the cloak, but he was totally nude. "You must be cold too."

He shook his head. "I feel as if I'll never be cold again." He closed the door of the anteroom and led her to the rug before the fire. "Lie down. I'll hold you until you go to sleep."

As he had held her at Dalwynd. She had been so full of fear and resentment during those weeks that she had not appreciated those precious moments of intimacy. Well, she had tonight and would savor it to the full.

She cuddled close to him before the fire. She would not think of tomorrow. He was holding her with exquisite tenderness, and tonight she could pretend everything he said was true. She could pretend he loved her more than he wanted the Jedalar, that his passion was only for her.

And that there was a love that could last forever.

Ah, this is very good."

Marianna drowsily opened her eyes to see Gregor standing in the doorway.

"For God's sake, Gregor." Jordan snatched the cloak from the floor next to them and covered Marianna. "Didn't it occur to you to knock?"

"I was in a great hurry." He beamed. "And there is no shame in this room. You are very beautiful together." His smile faded. "And it is better I find you here than Nebrov."

"Nebrov." A cold chill went through Marianna as

she sat up and brushed her hair back from her face. "He's here?"

"Not yet. Niko says he will be here within two hours."

"How many?" Jordan asked.

"A hundred men, perhaps more. Riding hard."

"Against twenty." Jordan muttered an obscenity. "Did they know Niko saw them?"

Gregor shook his head.

"Then we can still surprise them." Jordan began to hurriedly dress. "They'll have to come through the hills as we did. There has to be a place where we can—"

"No," Marianna said. "Bring him here."

Jordan gave her an impatient glance. "What?"

"Bring him to me."

"The devil I will."

"You don't have enough men to fight him."

"That may not be so," Gregor said. "One of our men is worth three of Nebrov's."

"That still leaves you outnumbered," Marianna said. "Hide your men here in the palace and then go meet Nebrov and tell him you'll bargain with him. Tell him if he'll spare you and your men that you'll surrender me and the Jedalar." She held up her hand as Jordan started to protest. "Then bring him to me here. He can't take his entire force into the palace. You'll have a chance to defeat them."

"Let us be very clear. I'm supposed to bring him to you?" Jordan asked carefully. "Do you have any idea how enraged he must be with you?"

"Of course I do. I also know he won't kill me until he's sure he knows where the tunnel is located," she said matter-of-factly. "And that will give us a chance to rid ourselves of him once and for all."

"Goddammit, I won't make you bait again!"

"You've never made me anything I didn't choose to be. I choose to do this now." She turned to Gregor. "Tell him. If we cut off the head, the snake will die. His men won't attack if we kill Nebrov."

"That is true," Gregor said. "But severing that head may be difficult."

"But we have a better chance here than you do attacking his full force in the hills."

"She is right," Gregor said to Jordan. "And if we are defeated, he will still come here for her."

"Not if she comes with us."

"I won't come with you." She met his gaze. "You'll have to tie me on my horse. Bring him here."

"Why the devil are you being so obstinate?"

"Because I'm right." She added wearily, "And because it has to end. You told me once that he would never give up. Nothing has changed." Her expression hardened. "Except that he's hurt Alex. I can't let him keep harming the people I love. He deserves to die."

"He will die. But not here. Not with you—"

"Bring him here or I'll ride out and meet him and bring him myself."

"Blast you," he said softly, his tone laden with frustration. He stared at her another moment before whirling on his heels. "Come on, Gregor. We've had our orders. Let's go get the bastard for her."

"I'll be waiting in the chapel," Marianna said.

Jordan glanced at her over his shoulder.

She shook her head. "I won't be praying for deliverance. I told you the Jedalar was there. Nebrov won't be fooled again. I'll have to show him what he wants to see."

"You swore you'd never do that."

"Circumstances have changed. I have no choice."

"You know that I'm going to be there. Whatever you show Nebrov, you show me." He paused. "Even after we rid ourselves of Nebrov, you'll still lose."

"I know I'll lose." Not in the way he meant, but in a manner that would be more devastating than he could dream. "I'll have to face that when it happens."

"Marianna . . ." He took a half-step toward her, then stopped. "Dammit, there's no time." He turned and strode out of the room.

Gregor hesitated. "You must not blame him. He does not want this."

"I don't blame anyone." She was beginning to believe Jordan's words about the inevitability of fate. Nothing else could explain the tangled threads that had interwoven all their lives. "No, that's not true. I blame Nebrov."

He searched her expression. "You are no longer afraid of him."

"I wish I could say that was true," she said wearily. "But I can't let the fear stop me. For years my fear made me think I was helpless. I'm not helpless. He killed my mother, and he hurt Alex. I'm not going to let him hurt anyone ever again."

"Gregor!"

It was Jordan calling from the hall. Gregor hesitated and then walked out.

She waited until she heard the sound of their horses' hooves on the stones of the courtyard before quickly throwing on her clothes. She left the ante-room and headed toward the chapel.

She had two hours, perhaps less. With the preparations she had made after she had first arrived, it should be enough time.

She threw open the door of the chapel and paused for a moment, staring up at the glorious stained-glass window over the pulpit.

She had told Jordan she was not going to pray for deliverance, but she muttered a prayer beneath her breath anyway.

Sometimes Fate had to have a little help.

They were coming.

Marianna tensed as she heard the clatter of boots on the marble floor of the hall. Fear tore through her as she realized Nebrov would be walking through the door in a matter of seconds.

She looked up at the stained-glass window. "Help me, Grandmama," she whispered.

She must not be afraid. Everything was ready.

But suppose something went wrong? It might mean—

"If you think you'll avoid punishment by having our meeting in a chapel, you're destined to be disappointed," Nebrov said. "I promised Draken his life and safe passage, but the bargain did not include your own."

She braced herself, stood up from the pew on which she had been sitting, and turned to face him.

Nebrov's large eyes were glittering with excitement and triumph as he moved down the aisle toward her, closely followed by Jordan and four soldiers dressed in the green-and-gold uniform of Nebrov's army. "Good afternoon, Your Grace," she greeted him.

"The Jedalar," he said impatiently. "I do not have to tell you how annoyed I will be if you try to trick me again. So annoyed, I will be forced to cut your throat from ear to ear."

"There's no need for threats," Jordan said. "She's promised to show you what you want."

"I will give you the Jedalar." Marianna looked at the soldiers. "But do you really want them to see it? Czar Paul found witnesses both a danger and an inconvenience."

He hesitated and then waved his hand in dismissal. "Wait outside in the hall."

Marianna waited until the door closed behind the guards before moving toward the altar.

"Where are you going?" Nebrov asked sharply.

"The Jedalar is behind the altar." She retrieved the glass panel. "I'll have to climb on the sacrament table to replace the left lower panel in the window with the Jedalar. I'll need someone to hand me the panel."

"I'll do it." Jordan strode down the aisle to stand beside the altar. He took the Jedalar and looked down at it. "A rainbow . . ."

"Grandmama always said that life was always full of rainbows and that we must follow them," she said in a low voice. "She said great treasures always follow."

"What treasures?" Nebrov was beside them, peering down at the panel. "Was the tale true? Is there really a treasure room in the tunnel?"

"She said the czar had plans for such a room. I suppose you'll have to see for yourself." Marianna lifted her skirts and climbed up on the high marble table. She worked gently at the panel she had previously loosened and withdrew it from the window. She handed it down to Jordan in exchange for the rainbow Jedalar. It took her only a few moments to secure the Jedalar in place.

She glanced over her shoulder and nodded with satisfaction. "It's positioned correctly. The sun is behind a cloud now, but I think we should see something in a few minutes."

"See what?" Nebrov asked.

"I imagine we're about to see what we came for." Jordan lifted Marianna down from the table. "The map?"

"Yes." She moved out from behind the altar. "The complete map of the tunnel. The sunlight pours through the panel and—"

A brilliant stream of sunlight flooded the chapel, and no further explanation was necessary. Magnificent colors and dark shadows were cast over the chapel.

Nebrov made an exclamation and moved toward the left side of the chapel where the rainbow panel's shadow fell on one of the large white-veined marble blocks that composed the floor of the chapel.

Jordan followed him, but Marianna stayed where she was beside the altar. She knew what they were seeing. The arcs of the rainbow intersected with the veins in the marble in a pattern that was both complicated and detailed. "Zavkov marble. All of the marble for this palace was taken from a small mine in Zavkov, Siberia. My grandmother spent weeks there searching for just the right veining in that marble block so that it would form the precise blend with the Jedalar."

"The lock and the key," Jordan murmured. He

lifted his head to look at her across the chapel. "Brilliant."

"There's a small square here that might indicate a treasure room." Nebrov bent over the block. "It appears to be at this end, near the beginning of the tunnel." Nebrov whirled to face her and snarled, "But it does not show the entrance. What good is the map without the entrance?"

"The czar knew where the entrance was," Marianna said. "The passages were intricate and required a map, but he knew exactly how to get into the tunnel."

"And so do you." Nebrov's gaze narrowed on her face. "Where is it?"

"I'll tell you." She paused. "When you promise me safe passage as you did Jordan and Gregor."

"I don't have to promise you anything. I could force the information out of you."

"Yes, but that would take time, and I can see you're eager to find the tunnel. Isn't that worth the satisfaction you might have from any revenge against me?"

"Perhaps." He shrugged. "Very well. You have my word."

Which meant nothing, as she well knew, but it had been necessary to pretend reluctance to avoid suspicion. She indicated the floor behind the altar. "The third stone. It's hinged from below and lifts easily. There are stairs leading down into the tunnel."

Nebrov strode eagerly forward.

"Wait." She went to the table and lit one of the two oil lamps she had put there in readiness. "You'll need this."

Nebrov had already lifted the stone and was peering down into the darkness. He took the oil lamp from her and started down the steps. He stopped on the third step and cautiously tried the stone door to make sure it lifted easily from below before looking up at them and smiling grimly. "Oh no, I have no intention of going down there alone and have you seal me away in the tunnel."

"Shall I call your men?" Jordan asked.

"Not until I see what's in the treasure room. You both shall accompany me." Nebrov added to Jordan, "I wouldn't think of denying you the pleasure of seeing what you've striven to find all these years, Draken." He climbed back to the floor, pulled his pistol, and gestured toward the waiting darkness. "After you?"

Jordan started down the steps.

Nebrov turned to Marianna. "And now you."

She tried to keep her expression impassive. "If we're all to go, then we'll need another lamp."

When he nodded curtly, she lit the second lamp on the sacrament table, turned, and started down the steps.

Jordan was waiting for her at the foot of the stairs. "What a strange scent there is down here," he murmured.

He knew!

Or perhaps not, for he took a step back, training his eyes on Nebrov.

Nebrov gestured with the pistol. "Go on. Straight down the main tunnel, no branching off." His glance was eagerly flicking back and forth as he followed them down the dark corridor. "The treasure room was on the left," he muttered. "Where the devil is it?"

"We haven't gone very far," Marianna said. Jordan was hesitating in front of her. No, he mustn't stop now!

She deliberately stepped on the back of his boot to nudge him forward a few more steps. "Perhaps it doesn't—"

"There it is!" Nebrov's gaze was on a dark square opening now on his immediate left. "You fools, you would have gone right past it!"

"It's too dark down here," Marianna said plaintively. "I can't see anything."

Nebrov was already in the middle of the room, lifting his lamp high. "Chests," he said excitedly, looking all over the large room. "Chests and . . . kegs! His eyes widened in fear as he realized where he was standing. He started to back from the room.

"Run!" Marianna shouted at Jordan as she hurled the oil lamp to the ground. "Back to the chapel!"

The gunpowder she had spread across the threshold exploded into a wall of flame imprisoning Nebrov within the room!

Jordan grabbed her elbow, and they tore down the corridor toward the steps leading to the chapel. "Christ, there was no treasure room, it was a powder magazine."

"Hurry!" she gasped out. "Those kegs will explode soon. I spread gunpowder for a little distance down every branch of the tunnel. The timbers supporting the tunnel will catch fire. . . ."

A shrill scream that chilled her blood caused her to glance over her shoulder.

Nebrov had plunged out of the room, but he was engulfed in flames as he tottered after them like a horrible creature from a nightmare.

"Don't look at him!" Jordan pushed her toward the stairs now just ahead of them. "Get up those steps."

A whoosh like a breath of wind went through the tunnel, and she knew the burning Nebrov had ignited the trail of gunpowder in the main tunnel. Another hideous scream and Nebrov was lost to view in a sea of flames.

"God!" Jordan was trying to beat out the flames that leaped from the tunnel floor and reached the skirt of her gown.

"Stop it! You'll burn your hands."

Jordan continued to beat at the flames with one hand while he pushed her the final few steps to the surface. "Did you have to seed the entire tunnel? Wasn't the ammunition room enough?"

She pulled herself onto the floor of the chapel. "I had to be certain."

Jordan slammed down the stone door. "And nearly got yourself burned to death."

Her breath was coming in harsh gasps. "Had to be—"

"Certain," Jordan finished. "How close is the powder room to this palace? Are we all going to be blown to bits?"

She shook her head. "It's halfway down the hill. Your hands . . . let me see your hands."

He ignored her. "It seemed closer."

"I don't think—"

An explosion rocked the palace!

Jordan grabbed her and rolled with her until they hit a wall. She lay there watching as a long, jagged crack snaked across the marble floor and explosion after explosion followed one another.

She heard crashes and screams of panic from the hall, but no one ventured into the chapel.

At last the explosions stopped, but the chapel was filling with thick black smoke, curling up from below through the cracks in the floor.

"We have to get out of here," she whispered. "All the tunnels below the palace will be on fire by now."

"Is there another way out of here?"

She shook her head. "We'll have to go out through the palace."

He stood up and pulled her to her feet. "I doubt if anyone will try to stop us. From those screams I'd say Nebrov's men are concerned only with saving themselves." He propelled her down the aisle toward the door. As she stepped over the gaping crack in the marble, she could see the glimmer of flames below like a glimpse into the bowels of hell. Nebrov was down in that inferno, and she had condemned him to a horrible death.

She was in a holy place and should not feel this deep sense of satisfaction.

"It's done, Mama," she whispered.

"Come on." Jordan threw open the door. The corridor was empty as he had predicted and filled with clouds of black smoke. Her eyes were stinging by the time they reached the foyer, and she could barely discern the crystal chandelier that lay shattered on the floor.

Then they were outside, and clean, cold air was in

her lungs. There was smoke here also, and half the hill seemed to be in flames. The courtyard was in chaos, with panicked horses and soldiers running about shouting shrilly.

"There you are," Gregor said, relieved, as he appeared suddenly beside them. "I was about to dash in and rescue you. It is kind of you to save me the trouble. Nebrov?"

"Dead." Jordan's arm tightened around Marianna's waist as they dashed across the courtyard. "Let's get out of here. The fire is going to break through the floor of the palace any minute. Are all the men safe?"

Gregor nodded. "Why shouldn't they be? There was no battle. The moment the explosions started, everyone was in a hurry to get out of the palace. They thought the end of the world had come. I sent our men down the hill with the horses away from the flames." He grimaced in disgust as he nodded at the screaming men in the courtyard. "These are not soldiers."

By the time they were halfway down the hill, the palace was engulfed in flames. Marianna looked back over her shoulder, and sadness overwhelmed her.

"He deserved to die," Jordan said quietly. "If you hadn't done it, I would have."

She stared at him in surprise. "I wasn't thinking of Nebrov."

"No?"

"Grandmama's work. All her beautiful windows . . ."

Gregor chuckled as he and Jordan exchanged glances. "Of course, you would think of the windows instead of that vermin. It is entirely natural, eh, Jordan?"

But Jordan was no longer looking back at the burning palace but down the hill at the gaping cavity caused by the explosion. He would not let her blame herself for Nebrov's death, but she knew he would hold her at fault for the destruction of the tunnels he had wanted for Kazan. "I had to do it."

"No, you chose to do it," he said grimly. "There's a difference. You must have spread the gunpowder in those other branches of the tunnel before Niko even caught sight of Nebrov and his men."

"Don't you see?" she asked, desperate to make him understand. "Grandmama created the Jedalar. She was part of that horror in the tunnel, and she had to make it right. She made Mama and me promise that the tunnel would never be used to kill anyone again. She even planned exactly how it could be done. She was the one who spread the rumor about the treasure room. She knew the czar planned to use that room for arms and gunpowder and—" She stopped as she saw Jordan's face was completely expressionless. She had not thought he would forgive her. She said wearily, "Yes, I chose to do it. Even if I had made no vow, I would still have destroyed the tunnel."

"Why?" Gregor asked.

"Because my grandmother was right. War is evil, and the tunnel was a weapon of war. Go fight your wars with the weapons you have." She gazed steadily at Jordan. "I'm glad I did it."

"Well, I'm not glad. I'm furious with you." He took her elbow and pushed her down the hill toward the waiting troop. "But I can wait to express my displeasure until we get you to the inn and see if you have any burns."

Great heavens, she had momentarily forgotten

those flames that had nearly devoured them. "I'm not burned. It was you who—" Her glance had dropped to the hand holding her elbow, and she inhaled sharply. Angry red weals crisscrossed the back of his hand; his palms must be even worse. "You're hurt!"

"Hurt is an accurate description." His lips thinned. "And pain doesn't tend to make my temper any better."

"I'm so sorry," she whispered. "I never meant for you to suffer."

His expression did not soften. "Then you shouldn't have blown up that tunnel. You may have hurt a great many people with one stroke."

She shook her head. It was useless to argue with him on a subject on which there could be no agreement.

"I have a medicinal cream in my saddlebag that will help," Gregor said.

She again glanced back over her shoulder at the burning palace. She wished there was a medicine that would ease the pain from the wedge she had just driven between them.

Why was she mewing like a mournful cat? she thought impatiently. She had known what she was doing and what the result would be. Now, she had to accept it.

Dear God, she wished the pain would go away.

When they arrived at the inn in the village, Gregor took charge. His booming voice sent the innkeeper and servants scurrying to arrange for rooms, baths, and food for all of them and clean bandages for Jordan's burns.

Within an hour Marianna found herself immersed in a tub of hot water in a simple but pleasantly furnished bedchamber. She washed her hair three times, but it still retained a faint hint of smoke.

She leaned back in the hip bath and wearily closed her eyes. It might take a long time to rid her body of the smell of that disaster in the tunnel, but she would never recover from the tragedy itself. She had given up too much with that one act.

"We'll have to be miles away from this place by tomorrow morning."

Her eyes opened to see Jordan standing in the doorway. He was dressed in black buckskin trousers and a loose white linen shirt. He had worn black and white that first night at Dalwynd, she remembered. No, she must not think of Dalwynd.

Her gaze flew to his hands, which were now neatly bandaged. "How bad are they?"

"Only minor blisters." He came into the room and shut the door. "Did you hear me? We have to leave for Kazan tomorrow." He strode over to the tub and reached for the large toweling cloth the servant had set beside it. "I know you need time to rest, but there are fires breaking out from that burning tunnel all the way to Moscow. Czar Alexander is bound to send someone to find out the reason." He held out the towel. "Stand up."

She got to her feet, and he enveloped her in the towel and lifted her out of the tub.

"Your hands!"

"Be quiet." He patted her awkwardly with the towel. "The czar is nervous now anyway, with Napoleon on the horizon. His response won't be pleasant when he discovers he was this vulnerable to attack."

"Then he should thank me. Napoleon can no longer attack him through the tunnel."

"That's going to be little comfort when he finds out he had a weapon that might have defeated Napoleon and you destroyed it. I want you on your way to the border when that happens."

"I thought you were angry with me."

"I am." His tone was clipped, his expression set and hard, and the waves of frustration and displeasure he was emitting were nearly tangible.

"Then why are you trying to protect me?"

"One has nothing to do with the other."

He was still patting her with those poor bandaged hands, she realized with exasperation. "Will you stop?" She took the towel away from him and wrapped it around herself. "You'll hurt yourself. And why does one have nothing to do with the other?"

"I have no intention of cheating myself out of what I want because you've done something for which I'd happily wring your neck." He glared at her. "No one is going to take you away from me. Not the Czar, not Napoleon, not Wellington, and not you either."

Hope flared within her, but she was afraid to acknowledge it. "You still wish me to be your mistress?"

"Haven't you heard anything I've said? We will wed as soon as we reach Kazan." He added grimly, "If I can keep the ravin from executing you for your idiocy."

Wed. She felt the breath leave her body. She had not permitted herself to believe him before and after what she had done. "Why?"

"Now isn't the time to ask that question, if you expect a tender declaration of sentiment."

"I'm not going to ask you to forgive me. I did what I had to do."

"I know." For an instant his expression lost a little of its hardness. "I'm not so unfair that I would fault you for something I'd do myself. I'd have taken the Jedalar away from you if I'd found a way. You did something that I find unacceptable, but that doesn't mean you're unacceptable. None of that has any bearing on what's between us."

"No?" she whispered.

"Except that it makes me angry enough to want to rip that towel off you and throw you into a snowdrift," he said harshly. "For God's sake, don't you know there's no question of forgiveness between us? I cannot think of anything you could do that would make me not want you." He walked to the door and opened it. "Go to bed. Be ready to leave at dawn tomorrow."

The door slammed behind him.

There had been nothing sentimental or tender in his manner or words. He had given her only anger and understanding, harshness and a promise of eternal endurance.

She stared at the door, feeling bewilderment . . . and the beginning of joy.

Darkness had fallen when she turned the knob of Jordan's door.

Jordan was lying on the bed, still fully dressed, staring out the window at the flaring fires marching across the landscape.

He turned his head toward her. "I told you to go to bed."

She couldn't see his expression, but his tone was not encouraging. "I had to see you. I won't be able to sleep otherwise." She closed the door and came toward him. "Are you in pain?"

"Yes, and I don't take it well at all. So you'd better go back to your room and leave me alone."

"I can't do that."

"You'll regret it. When I'm hurt, I have a tendency to strike out blindly."

"Then I'll find your conduct unacceptable." She lay down beside him. The words she had come to say were difficult for her, and she did not want to see his face. She turned her back toward him and fitted herself spoon fashion against his body. "But I won't find you unacceptable. Not ever."

She felt him stiffen against her. "Those words sound vaguely familiar."

"They're beautiful words. You've never been so eloquent."

"By God, you're easy to please."

"No, I'm very difficult to please. I require everything." She paused. "But I'll give everything in return."

He made no motion to put his arms around her. "For instance?" he said, his words were muffled in her hair.

"I will fight any battle for you. You want this Napoleon defeated? I will help you."

"You should have thought of that this afternoon."

"I will give you children. I think I would be a good mother." She said haltingly, "And I will give you my work. It is the most important part of me, and it will be difficult to share, but I will try." She hesitated and then said in a low voice, "And I will love you as long as I live."

There was a silence, and then he asked politely, "Is that all?"

She started to turn to him in indignation, but his arms were suddenly around her, holding her still.

"Let me go," she said, struggling. "I know you're in pain, but you're being most unkind, and I—"

"Hush," he said thickly. "I was joking."

"I don't think this is a moment for amusement."

"I wasn't amused. I didn't know what to say, so I—" He stopped and drew her closer. "I didn't know what to say."

And when Jordan was touched or moved, he hid behind that mask she knew so well. The anger flowed out of her, and she lay still. "You say, 'Thank you, Marianna. I realize I'm not worthy of you, that I'm an insensitive, blundering cad, but I will strive to mend my ways.'"

She expected him to laugh, but he did not. "It won't be easy. I'm not insensitive, but I like my own way, and there will be times when I'll blunder and hurt you." His voice deepened and became unsteady. "But there will never be a moment I do not love you."

Tears stung her eyes. "And there will never be a moment I don't love you." She added, "Though there will be times I'll close myself in my workroom and forget I have a husband."

"The devil you will."

She kissed his wrist above the bandage. "The devil I will."

Papa would have thought this a strange declaration, she thought dreamily, and this setting just as bizarre. His romantic poet's heart would have been grievously offended, and yet she would have had nothing different. A love that had already survived hardship and challenges did not need flowering gardens and pretty words to validate it.

They were silent, staring out at the fires.

"What are you thinking?" she asked after a long while.

His lips brushed her ear as he whispered mischievously, "I was wondering if you'd call me an insensitive cad again if I made love to you."

"You're not going to make love to me. I won't have you hurting those hands."

"No?" She thought he was going to argue, but he pulled her closer. "Very well, this is pleasant too. But I must have been a very inadequate lover, if you think I need hands." He looked back out the window. "It's a good thing the snows have limited those fires to the line of the tunnel. If they'd spread to the fields, it would be a hungry spring for—" He stopped, and she heard him draw a sudden breath.

She turned her head to look at him. "Jordan?"

"Nothing." He kissed her absently. "I just had a thought. I'll have to consider the possibilities. Of course, it will depend on when Napoleon actually arrives in this area of Russia. . . ."

He had trailed off, his gaze remaining on the trail of fires leading to the gates of Moscow.

He was already making plans, plotting, trying to nullify the damage caused by the loss of the tunnel. She lay quiet, letting him think. It did not matter that he was barely aware of her presence. He would come back to her, she thought contentedly. What a wondrous and magical realization.

From this day forward he would always come back to her.

CHAPTER 17

They started for Kazan the next morning, setting a hard, fast pace on the long journey to the border.

They were up before dawn and didn't stop until the last light faded from the sky. By the end of the day Marianna was too exhausted to do anything but fall into a deep sleep in Jordan's arms.

She was almost numb with weariness when they finally saw the towers of the ravin's palace at Rengar.

"This won't be pleasant for you," Jordan said quietly. "It's the ravin's duty to protect Kazan, and she was counting on that tunnel. I'll try to protect you, but she will be—"

"Don't protect me," Marianna said. The last thing she wanted was to be a bone of contention in the battle between them. "I did it, and I'll take the consequences. Stay out of it, Jordan."

Jordan shook his head. "I find that an exceedingly uncomfortable position. The last time I gave in and let you have your way, you tried to burn down the Russian countryside." He held up his hand as she started to protest. "But I promise I'll see what transpires before I rush to your defense."

The ravin met them in the courtyard. She looked entirely well and as robust and forceful as ever. Her gaze searched Jordan's face. "Success?"

He shook his head.

The ravin uttered a low exclamation. "I should have gone myself."

Gregor laughed. "Your presence does not necessarily guarantee success."

She motioned impatiently. "Does Nebrov have possession of the tunnel?"

"You might say that," Jordan said. "He's in the tunnel even as we speak."

Jordan was deliberately baiting the ravin. He had not been in her presence more than a few moments, and already the air was vibrating with tension. "He's dead." Marianna nudged her horse forward to confront Ana. "And I burned the tunnel. No one will ever have possession."

"You burned—" The ravin's brow furrowed with anger. "By God, you had no right to do such a thing. Do you know what damage you've caused?"

"I had the right." She glared back at her. "And I took it. No damage has been done to anyone but Nebrov. I've rid you of the threat he posed."

"And what of Napoleon?"

"He will not have the tunnel either."

"Do you know the size of the army he's planning on bringing into Russia? What if he decides Kazan is another plum for him to pick?"

"Then do what you would have done before you decided to use the tunnel." She slipped from her horse. "I don't care what you do. Where is Alex?"

"I have not dismissed you."

She put her hands on her hips and demanded, "Where is my brother?"

They exchanged glare for glare. Finally, the ravin said grudgingly, "I sent him to the south garden when I had word Jordan had entered the city. You were not mentioned, and I did not want him unduly distressed."

"Where is this south garden?"

The ravin gestured to a servant and said curtly, "Take her."

Marianna cast a glance over her shoulder at Jordan, but he was staring at the ravin, clearly girding himself for battle. Marianna had lost her temper and not handled the interview with the ravin well, and he would probably compound the damage. Well, let them sting each other. She would worry about it later. Now she only wanted to see Alex.

She followed the servant into the palace.

My God, what an arrogant piece of work," the ravin said as she turned back to Jordan and Gregor. "I should have thrown her into prison. I may still do it."

"That would have been monstrously inconvenient," Jordan said as he got down from his horse. "As I intend to wed her tomorrow."

"Wed?" The ravin's eyes widened. "What nonsense is this?"

"And wed her again by English law when we return to Cambaron."

"Two ceremonies?"

"I have two countries. I want to make sure she belongs to me in both." He smiled crookedly. "As you remarked, I hold on tightly to what is mine, and Kazan did not recognize your marriage to my dear father."

"You cannot wed her. Not only is it most unsuitable, but she destroyed our plans!"

"Then we must make new ones. As soon as we check our defenses, I'll set out for Moscow again."

"Why?"

"To see the czar and discuss an idea that occurred to me when I was watching the tunnels burn." He turned to Gregor. "Will you be my *vadsar* tomorrow."

Gregor nodded. "It would be my honor."

"He will *not*," the ravin said. "This marriage will not take place."

Jordan stared right into her eyes. "Why not? Do you dislike her?"

"That has nothing to do with it."

"I think you respect her. Liking will follow."

"Why are you doing this?"

"I love her," he said simply. He paused for a moment and then said haltingly, "I hope you will attend the wedding."

He walked into the palace.

The ravin stared after him in bewilderment.

"A victory," Gregor said quietly. "And she gave it to you."

"Victory? She may have destroyed Kazan."

"We are not so weak that we cannot rally from this blow." He shrugged. "And she is right—she had more claim on the tunnel than any of us."

"You approve of this marriage?"

He nodded. "And so will you, once you recover

from the first anger. If you can make her your friend, you may get what you've always wished."

"I do not choose my friends for what they can bring me." She hesitated. "And it would do no good to try anyway. She resents me."

"And, of course, you've given her no cause. You've treated her as a whore for the bartering; she thinks you've stolen the affections of the child she loves, and now you want to throw her into prison."

"I didn't tell her I was going to throw her into prison."

Gregor chuckled. "But you would have if she hadn't outfaced you."

"She did nothing of the sort."

"She did." A smile lingered on his lips. "Why do you think Jordan loves her? She shares many of the qualities he admires in you. If he weds her, he will be reminded of you every day even when he is at Cambaron." He added softly, "And he will grow accustomed to admitting to himself he loves those qualities in her. That is why you must sanction this marriage."

"Must? You do not say must to me, Gregor."

"Must," he repeated. "Let him go, Ana."

"Let him go?" Her tone was suddenly laden with pain. "I've never had him. You're speaking as if I were the Circe Jordan believes me to be."

"He does not believe that to be true, but from the moment he came to Kazan that first time, you did everything you could to claim him." He grimaced. "And you're a very powerful woman, Ana."

"It did no good."

"Because he's as powerful as you. He has to come willingly to you. You cannot force it. He has taken the first step in asking you to attend the ceremony. Sanction the wedding."

"I will not do it. You cannot ask me—" She broke off. "She will take him away. You said she likes Cambaron. They will live at that cold castle and give me grandchildren I will never see." She tossed her head and turned away. "I will not let her do it. I will think of something."

"Throw her into prison?"

"Perhaps that wasn't a good idea," she conceded.

"Make her welcome in Kazan." He paused. "Or I will return with them to Cambaron."

Her eyes widened. "You would desert me?"

"You sent me to him in the beginning, and he has dominated your life since the moment you left that weakling husband and came back to Kazan. I'm growing weary of this conflict between you. I told you how to make peace." He said with abrupt forcefulness, "You want a son? I will give you one. He will not be Jordan and will probably be as big and ugly as a gorilla, but he will be yours." He added softly, "As I am yours."

"You would not leave me," she said unsteadily.

"Free him and free yourself, or I will claim my own freedom."

He turned on his heel and walked away from her.

"Blast you, Gregor, you cannot leave me!"

He did not look back.

Marianna paused in the arched doorway leading to the garden, her gaze hungrily going to the little boy playing by the reflecting pool.

She scarcely recognized Alex as the thin Gypsy she

had left many weeks ago. He had gained weight, and his curly hair was neatly trimmed. He was garbed in a quilted tunic and boots similar to the ones she had seen other Kazan children wear on the streets of Rengar. The ravin's influence, no doubt, she thought grimly. She wondered what other influences the woman had brought to bear in her absence. The ravin, too, was a woman who wanted to leave her mark.

Well, she would soon see. She drew a deep breath and then called, "Alex!"

He turned and saw her. He did not speak for a moment and then uttered a joyous whoop and ran toward her.

Her eyes closed as her arms enfolded him. So warm and dear.

However, he almost immediately tore away from her. "You shouldn't have gone away," he said fiercely. "I'm very angry with you."

"I had to go. I didn't want to leave you."

"That's what Ana said. She said you wouldn't have left me if it hadn't been very important."

"She did?" Marianna asked in astonishment.

Alex nodded. "But you should have taken me with you."

"There was a possibility I might have had to meet the people who were bad to you."

A shadow crossed his face. "Did you?"

She nodded. "But they will never trouble you again, Alex."

His expression didn't lighten. "You should have taken me with you," he repeated. "It wasn't fair. You're my sister. You didn't let me take care of you."

"You were taking care of the ravin."

"I would still have come with you."

"I thought you liked her very much."

"I do like her, but that's different. We don't belong to each other." He frowned. "You must promise not to go away again without telling me."

A surge of warmth and joy rippled through her. "I promise." She gave him a quick hug. "I have something else to tell you. Jordan and I will wed tomorrow."

A brilliant smile lit his face. "That means that you'll be with him forever, doesn't it?"

"That's exactly what it means," Jordan said from the doorway. He came forward to stand beside them. "As you're Marianna's eldest male relative, I'm here to ask you for her hand."

Alex nodded gravely. "But you must treat her very well."

"I shall endeavor to do so," Jordan said with equal solemnity. "You must remind me, if you see me faltering."

"I will." Alex turned to Marianna. "Do you have to ask Ana for his hand?"

"Good heavens, I hope not." She made a face. "I don't think the ravin likes me as much as she does you."

"Ana," Alex corrected.

"Why don't you like us to call her the ravin? It's her title, Alex. Just as the servants at Cambaron call Jordan His Grace."

"That's different." He frowned. "When people call her the ravin, it reminds me of the big black birds that used to swoop down and raid the cornfields near the castle. Ana's not like that."

"Her enemies would not agree," Jordan said dryly.

"But she has no enemies here, so she should not be called that." Alex turned to Marianna. "And I think she would like it if you asked permission to marry Jordan."

"I don't believe this is the time to ask her anything," Jordan said. "Though I did ask her to attend the wedding."

"You did?" Marianna asked. "Why?"

"Because she is his mother," Alex said in disgust. "Don't be stupid, Marianna."

The mother he would never acknowledge, and yet he had invited her to share the important day. "Why?" she asked again.

Jordan shrugged. "A whim."

No whim would have prompted such an action from him. "Did she say she would attend?"

"Of course she will come," Alex said.

Jordan smiled. "If she deigns to honor us with her presence at dinner tonight, perhaps you will be able to persuade her."

The ravin did not honor them with her presence at dinner that night, and neither did Gregor. After they had eaten and put Alex to bed, Jordan strolled with Marianna back to her quarters.

"How does one marry in Kazan?" Marianna asked.

"Much as it's done anywhere else. The ceremony will be held in the palace chapel. I've chosen Gregor as my *vadsar*."

"What is a *vadsar*?"

"The guardian for my bride. It's an ancient tradition from the time when a tribal leader would send an emissary to another chieftain to fetch his bride. They would often have to journey though hostile territory, and the bride was a great prize. Therefore the emissary had to be the bravest and the boldest."

"Gregor, the *vadsar*." Marianna smiled. "It suits him well."

"He will meet you at the door of the chapel and bring you to me. We kneel facing each other, and the priest says words. Then we exchange vows before witnesses. I've asked Gregor to find an appropriate gown for you to wear."

"What is appropriate?"

"Brides wear sky blue in Kazan. It's considered the color of felicity."

"And what do grooms wear?"

He looked at her innocently. "Why, white, of course. The color of virginity. All bridegrooms must be virgins in Kazan."

"Truly? It is—" She stopped as she saw he was chuckling. She made a face. "It's well you were only joking. They would never permit us to wed unless that requirement changes. What color do grooms really wear?"

"Black, for mourning." He took a step back as she turned on him. "A small jest, love. There's no color designated for men. We wear what we please."

"That doesn't seem fair."

"Even in Kazan life is sometimes unfair for women. Though the ravin is doing all possible to alter that state." He stopped before her door and inclined his head in a slight bow. "Good night, my love. Until tomorrow."

She looked at him uncertainly. They had not come together in passion on the hard journey here, but she had known he wanted her. She had thought his restraint was due to the lack of privacy on the trail and assumed they would be together tonight.

He smiled and shook his head as he saw her expression. "Haven't you noticed? I'm courting you. I decided one more night of abstinence won't be too much of a strain for me."

"I don't understand."

His smile faded. "We will spend a good deal of time here in Kazan. I wanted to show the members of the ravin's court that I hold you in honor. It's too late at Cambaron but not here."

Happiness surged through her. "It doesn't matter."

"It matters," he said quietly. A mischievous smile lit his face. "Instead, I shall spend tonight contemplating my sins and deciding on a new and interesting fashion in which to make your wedding night memorable. There must be some way I can combine the two."

Sin and sensuality and a bridegroom who was the master of both. She felt a ripple of heat as she looked at him. "If there is, I have confidence you'll find it."

"So do I."

He was leaving her, and she didn't want to let him go yet. Tomorrow seemed a long time away. "Do you think the ravin will come?"

"I doubt it." He shrugged. "It makes no difference."

"It does make a difference," she said impatiently. "Why do you pretend it doesn't? You care for her."

His expression hardened. "It's senseless to talk of this."

"It's senseless to ignore it. I know you care for her. I saw your face when I gave you the window with her image."

"It was a magnificent work."

"It was your *mother*. For heaven's sake admit it and forgive her."

"You're being very forgiving yourself. Did I mention she was thinking of throwing you into a dungeon?"

"It doesn't surprise me. She's a hard woman."

"Then let us drop the subject."

"We can't. Because neither of you can forget each other, and I won't have her standing in the shadows for the rest of our lives. I'd much rather face her in the sunlight."

His face softened. "You stand the sunlight much better than the ravin, my love."

"Because I'm young and strong, and I'm to marry a strong man, not a weakling as she did. If you cannot forgive her, understand her." She held up her hand as he started to speak. "That's all I have to say, but it had to be said."

"Why?"

"I told you." But she had not told him everything. She had not told him that even though the ravin had coveted Alex's affection, she had not let her brother think badly of Marianna. "I would rather have her for an ally than an enemy."

"But there's something more, isn't there?"

She should have known Jordan would sense and probe for the entire truth. "Yes." A smile lit her face. "She doesn't raid cornfields."

The gown Gregor sent to her quarters was of sky-blue silk and would have been called ridiculously outmoded by the *ton*. The simple round neck was encrusted with pearls, but instead of having a fashionable high waist, it flowed to the floor, shimmering with beauty. It rather reminded Marianna of the gowns worn by the first duchesses of Cambaron.

"You are very lovely," Gregor said when she reached the chapel. His big hand squeezed her own. "Come, I will take you to your husband."

Husband. He meant Jordan. It was Jordan who stood at the altar. She experienced a dazed feeling of incredulity.

Then, as Gregor led her down the aisle, the disbelief disappeared. Jordan was dressed in a heavy gold-and-white quilted tunic over black trousers tucked into knee boots. He was as beautiful as Gregor claimed she was, and by God, he was *hers*.

She was vaguely aware of a sea of strangers, of Alex smiling at her from the front pew.

And the ravin sitting beside him.

Marianna's pace faltered. She had not really expected Jordan's mother to be here.

Then Jordan was holding out his hand to her, and she saw nothing but him. She took it joyously. This was their moment, the time that belonged only to them.

She started to turn to the priest.

No, there was something wrong. This time did not belong only to them. There was always a past and future as well as the present.

And there was something she had to do.

She whispered to the priest, "One moment."

She felt Jordan's surprised gaze on her back as she whirled around, walked over to the ravin, and stared directly into her eyes.

She said clearly, "Alex said I should ask you for Jordan's hand in marriage."

The ravin blinked in surprise but quickly recovered. "Besides the irregularity of such an action, it is a little late for formalities."

"Alex doesn't think so, and neither do I. May I marry your son?"

"He cares nothing for my wishes."

"On the contrary I find myself craving approval from all and sundry." Jordan's tone was light as he joined Marianna and took her hand again. "Matrimony is a fearsome step, and one I doubted I'd ever take."

The ravin stared at him uncertainly. "You wish for my permission? You are joking?"

Marianna held her breath. She knew how tempted Jordan would be to hide beneath his usual mask of mockery.

Jordan's smile faded, and he was silent a moment before he said quietly, "I'm not joking, Ana."

Ana. Not Mother. Marianna smothered a sigh of exasperation. Well, at least it was not Your Majesty or ravin. What had she expected? They were both hard and stubborn, and wounds did not heal overnight. It was a start.

Ana smiled brilliantly and then said gruffly, "I suppose the match is not totally unacceptable to me." She turned to Marianna. "The windows in this palace are without character or color. Perhaps while Jordan is in Russia with the czar, you will stay and lend me your skill?"

A concession, but hardly a compromise. "It would be my pleasure. Jordan says we must stay here until we're sure Kazan is safe from Napoleon, and I'll go

mad without work to do. Perhaps later you will come
to Cambaron and see the work I did there. Jordan says
my dome is very impressive. You might see something
that would please you."

"Cambaron?" Ana's eyes widened in horror. "I
will never return to that place. It is—" She stopped as
her gaze encountered Gregor's. "It is a possibility."
She turned to Jordan and lifted her chin. "But you
must not expect me too soon. I am a busy woman,
and I cannot constantly be at your beck and call—and
it could be I have other plans for my life. Perhaps
when your first child is born, I will come." She
glanced challengingly at Gregor. "Well? Is it
enough?"

He shook his head. "I want deeds, not words."

She drew an exasperated breath as she gestured impatiently at Marianna. "Well, what are you waiting
for? It is rude to keep the priest waiting."

Marianna smiled, then turned to Jordan and held
out her hand. "Your mother is right. We must not
keep the priest waiting."

He led her to the altar. "I'm happy you finally
decided to get around to me," he murmured. "For a
moment I wasn't sure if you weren't wedding the
ravin."

"I am," she whispered, trying to make him understand. It was not going to be an easy task to make a
man as possessive as Jordan let others within the circle.
"Just as you're wedding Alex. We are not alone in
this, but that is a good thing. We've both been too
much alone. Now, I wish us to be joined in all ways."

"It sounds very crowded. I hope we don't have to
invite both of them into our marital bed?"

"Jordan, I mean—" She stopped as she saw the smile that lit his face.

"But in other circumstances it seems a good plan." He knelt on the cushions at the foot of the altar. "My dear love, I appreciate the gentle way in which you're trying to tell me I must share you, but it really isn't necessary. I'm sure that will be a constant battle between us, but not where Alex is concerned. I accept that he's part of you." His brows lifted. "Now, may we proceed with the wedding?"

Yes, there would always be battles and challenges in the life before them. They would both be changing and working, and because of their natures, they were bound to be constantly in conflict.

But there would also be love and loyalty and building together. They would leave their mark on life as she had left her mark on Cambaron.

She could hardly wait for it all to begin.

She smiled eagerly as she reached out and took his hands in her own. "Yes, I'm ready now."

EPILOGUE

September 15, 1812
Moscow, Russia

After a horrendous trek through Russia and battle losses mounting to the thousands, Napoleon reached the gates of Moscow. General Miloradovich, head of the Moscow garrison, asked for a cease-fire while he led his men out of the city. His request was granted. Napoleon moved into a city that appeared almost completely deserted, fully expecting Czar Alexander to sue for peace.

Later that evening Moscow was set ablaze.

Napoleon arrested four hundred incendiaries who declared they had set the fires on the orders of the director of police. Before the fires were put out, over two thirds of the city and most of the essential supplies stored there had been destroyed.

In the Kremlin Napoleon waited in vain for over a month; Czar Alexander did not sue for peace. The emperor finally departed Moscow to search out provisions at Kaluga, ninety miles to the north. That march started a nightmare retreat through a barren, frozen land.

It was the beginning of the end for Napoleon Bonaparte.

He's back in Paris!" The ravin strode into Jordan's study and waved in Jordan's face the letter she had just received. "But it is not the Paris he left. Napoleon's empire is crumbling, the French have lost faith in their great hero."

"It is about time," Gregor murmured.

Jordan scanned the letter, and a smile lit his face. "That means the allies will be gathering for the kill." He rose to his feet and moved toward the door. "Gregor, send a message to have them ready the *Seastorm*. I'll go to Marianna's workroom and tell her the good news." He grimaced. "And try to tear her away from that chapel window she's creating for Ana. I doubt if she'll regard journeying to help defeat the emperor of more importance."

"Notre Dame is in Paris," Gregor murmured.

Jordan understood at once. He threw back his head and laughed. "Excellent. Marianna would lead a charge against Napoleon herself, if it meant she would be permitted to see the Rose Window at Notre Dame."

"You are really leaving?" the ravin asked, startled.

"Of course." He glanced back over his shoulder. "And so should you, if you wish to protect Kazan. Once Napoleon surrenders, every country in Europe will be scrambling to grab territory for itself."

"No one will be permitted to snatch Kazan," she said fiercely.

"Then you'd better be there to prevent it, Mother," he said as he left the study.

He had spoken abstractedly, his thoughts on the coming victory. He did not even realize what he had called her.

"Mother," she whispered.

"You have made great strides during these last months," Gregor said behind her. "It was bound to bear fruit. Go with him now, and the final bonding will occur. Stay and it may take much longer."

"Are you going with him?"

"No."

She had known that would be his answer as she had known this moment would come. She had been prepared for it since the wedding those many months ago.

I want deeds, not words.

"Kazan needs my help."

"You have a son to protect Kazan. Do you doubt that he and Marianna won't be able to hold their own with the rulers of Europe?"

"No, but this is not a fair test."

"It is not a test. It is a choice."

She turned to look at him. Scarred and beautiful. Relentless and kind. Her lover who was not her lover.

But not for very much longer.

She walked toward him. "I love you, *mado*."

"I know." His gaze searched her face. "But do you choose me?"

"You ask a great deal, and you may not like what you get. You know how possessive both Jordan and I can be. If I choose you, it is forever. I would never let you go. I will treasure and smother you. I will give a bag of gold for the head of anyone who so much as bruises your fingertip."

He chuckled. "Then I must be very careful not to shake hands with anyone of even moderate strength."

"I'm not joking. I'm giving you warning."

"I believe I could survive." His smile faded. "Do you choose me, Ana?"

She did not want him to look this grave. She had caused him too much worry in the past, and now she wanted only smiles and joy for him. "Oh yes, I choose you. In all ways. In all things." A brilliant smile lit her face as she came into his arms and nestled there. She felt right and free and as wrapped in splendor as one of Marianna's stained-glass windows. "With all my heart."

Read on for a preview of

Iris Johansen's

novel

STALEMATE

#1 NEW YORK TIMES BESTSELLING AUTHOR

IRIS JOHANSEN

TAKES YOU TO THE EDGE OF SUSPENSE

STALEMATE

AN EVE DUNCAN FORENSICS THRILLER

STALEMATE

The phone was ringing.

Ignore it, Eve told herself, her fingers moving swiftly on the skull reconstruction she'd given the name Marty. She could call whoever it was back when she was through working. The phone was set for speaker and she could pick up if it was Joe or Jane. She was getting too close to that important last step in the sculpting.

On the sixth ring the answering machine picked up.

"I need to speak to you. Answer the phone, Ms. Duncan."

She froze, her fingers stopped in midstroke. Luis Montalvo. Though she had spoken to him only twice, that faint accent was unmistakable.

"I know you're there. You haven't left that cottage in the last week." His voice became faintly mocking. "Your dedication is admirable and I understand you're brilliant at your job. I look forward to having both focused soon on my behalf." He paused. "Do pick up the phone. I'm not accustomed to being ignored. It upsets me. You don't want to upset me."

And she didn't want to pick up the phone. He might jar her out of the zone of feverish intensity she needed when she was working this close to completion. Dammit, she had hoped he wouldn't call her again after she'd turned him down when he'd phoned her over a week ago.

"I won't give up, you know."

No, he probably wouldn't. Montalvo had been polite during the first call, and even after she'd refused his offer the second time he'd phoned, he'd displayed no anger. His voice had been smooth and soft, almost regretful, yet there had been a note beneath that velvet courtesy that had puzzled her. It had made her uneasy then, but tonight it filled her with impatience. She had no *time* for this now. Marty was waiting.

She strode across the room and picked up the phone. "Montalvo, I'm very busy. You've had your answer. Don't call me again."

"Ah, how delightful to hear your voice. I knew you wouldn't be so rude as to leave me hanging on that dreadful answering device. I hate impersonal machines. I'm a man of emotion and passion and they offend me."

"I really don't want to hear what you love or hate. I don't care. I want to get off this phone and forget you exist."

"I realize that sad fact. You're absorbed in your latest reconstruction, of that boy found buried in Macon. Have you named him yet? I understand you name all the skulls you work on."

She stiffened. "How do you know that?"

"I know everything about you. I know you live with a Detective Joe Quinn of the Atlanta Police Department. I know you have an adopted daughter, Jane MacGuire. I know you're possibly the best forensic sculptor in the world. Shall I go on?"

"That could all be public record. And how did you know about the boy murdered in Macon?"

"I have many, many contacts around the world. Do you want to know who killed him? I could find out for you."

"I don't believe you."

"Why not?"

"Because you're not even in this country. You're a scumbag of an arms peddler and you live in Colombia, where you can hide out and deal your poison to the highest bidder."

He chuckled. "I do like frankness. Very few women I know are willing to tell me the truth as they see it."

"Then I'm grateful to not be one of the women you know, you sexist bastard. If I were, I'd probably be tempted to cut your nuts off."

"Such violence, such passion. I believe we're very much alike, Ms. Duncan."

"No way." She drew a deep breath. "The answer is still no. I've no intention of coming down there and doing your reconstruction."

"You were very polite and businesslike, almost sympathetic, when I first made you the offer. The second time you were much more curt. I suppose you had Joe Quinn check me out?"

"Yes, of course. I don't deal with crooks and murderers."

"Everyone deals with whoever can make them the best bargain."

"I told you the last time that I wasn't interested in any of your fat fees."

"And I was duly impressed. I don't believe I've ever had anyone turn down a million dollars for a few days' work."

"Dirty money."

"Not true. All my cash is very well laundered."

"I thought you'd accepted that I wouldn't work for you."

"Because I didn't argue with you? I don't believe in spinning my wheels. I just go away and find another lure. It took almost a week for me to decide what that would be."

"And?"

"I'm convinced you'll be my guest in a very short time."

"Why?"

"That would spoil the surprise. I like to see a plan unfold like a beautiful night flower."

"You mentioned Joe and my adopted daughter. You touch them and I'll kill you."

"That violence again." His tone was amused. "I'd never be that stupid. That would be the trigger that would send you into the fray to take me down. I want your cooperation."

"I'm hanging up."

"Very well. I just wanted to offer you the opportunity to change your mind. It would make me happy if you would come to me for mercenary reasons. Much less stressful for all of us."

"Are you threatening me?"

"Heavens, no. You'd know it if I was doing that.

There would be no question. Won't you come and make me happy and become rich in the process?"

"No."

"Too bad." He sighed. "Good night." He hung up.

Eve slowly pressed the disconnect button. He had said he wasn't threatening her, but what else could she call it? It was subtle, but the threat was all the more chilling for the casual, understated way it was delivered. He'd been so calm when she'd turned down his offer that she'd honestly thought he'd accepted her refusal and was out of her life. It was clear she'd been wrong.

Should she call Joe and tell him Montalvo was still on the scene?

And have him think she was worried and rush home from the precinct?

She wasn't worried. She was uneasy. Montalvo had said her family was safe and she believed him. As he had perceived, any danger to them would make her angry and rebellious. He'd made no direct threat at all and he might just be trying to intimidate her into doing his job.

Maybe.

Yet he'd seemed to know entirely too much about her movements. Was she being watched?

Yes, she'd definitely tell Joe. But there was no use in alarming him right now. She'd tell him tonight when he came home for dinner. Okay, so she wanted to get back to Marty and she was afraid talking to Joe about Montalvo would keep her from doing it. She wasn't about to let Montalvo disturb her concentration on her work. That slimeball would probably enjoy the thought that he could control her to that extent. He might even call her again and try to reinforce that control. She'd be damned if she'd let him. She turned off the house phone and then her cell phone before moving back toward the reconstruction on the pedestal across the room.

Block Montalvo out of her thoughts. Think of Marty and the chance to bring him home. Think of the boy who'd been murdered and buried and left alone with no name or place.

That was better. Montalvo's words were blurring, fading away as she began to work.

Talk to me, Marty. Help me to bring you home. . . .

"Pity." Montalvo looked down at the phone. "I was hoping she'd give in to greed like a normal person. It's easy to be noble for an hour, a day, but then they start to think and perhaps dream a little. A week should have whetted her appetite and made her start making excuses why she should take the job."

"Not everyone thinks that money is the end-all of everything, Montalvo," Soldono said.

Montalvo smiled. "Almost everyone. It's unfortunate that Eve Duncan is in the minority." He rose from the carved chair at the head of the dining table. "Oh, well. One must make adjustments."

Soldono tensed. "Don't do it, Montalvo."

"She's giving me little choice. You're giving me little choice. You didn't talk to her, did you?" He shook his head. "I told you what you had to do, but you were looking for an out. I could see you scrambling frantically to avoid bringing her into the picture until time got away from you. Well, that time has come."

"Why her?" Soldono asked. "There's a fine forensic sculptor in Rio de Janeiro. Use him."

"Sanchez?" Montalvo shook his head. "Technically brilliant, but he's not what I want."

"Eve Duncan is an American citizen and she's known and respected by every police department on the planet. She turned down your money and you'll be stirring up a hornet's nest if you try to force her."

"And you wouldn't like that. The CIA tries to be very low-key these days."

"Let me try to get Sanchez for you."

"You don't understand."

"Then tell me."

He gazed musingly down at the depths of the wine in his glass. "It's a matter of passion."

"What?"

"I told Eve Duncan that I was a man of passion. It's true."

Soldono hadn't noticed any emotion in Montalvo, much less a passion. The man was brilliant and innovative, and he kept any feelings or thoughts hidden behind that faintly mocking smile. "Why Eve Duncan?" he repeated.

"She has passion, too. I've studied her file and nothing could be clearer. It's like a whirlwind spinning around her. She grew up on the streets with a drug addict for a mother and gave birth to an illegitimate child as a teenager. She turned her life around and went back to school and became a model mother. Then her daughter was kidnapped and presumably killed, but the body was never found.

Instead of being crushed, the lady became a forensic sculptor and tried to bring closure to other parents by identifying the remains of their missing children."

"I know all that," Soldono said impatiently.

"You know the facts, but you've never studied Eve Duncan the way I have. I believe I may know her better than she knows herself. I know what drives her. I know what makes her tick."

"Yeah, sure." He couldn't keep the sarcasm from his tone. "Passion?"

"Don't underestimate it. Da Vinci had it. Michelangelo had it. It's the difference between art and creation. Eve Duncan has it." His tone was smooth but hard. "And that's why I have to have her. Don't try to pawn anyone else off on me."

"Find another way. You promised me that you'd—"

"And I'd keep my promise if you'd kept yours." His tone was threaded with mockery as he continued, "But since the lady is not being accommodating, I must have cooperation from someone. You can see that, can't you?"

"No."

Montalvo's smile faded. "Then your vision had better improve quickly. I told you yesterday that if I didn't get the answer I wanted, I'd move. You obviously chose to think I wasn't serious. I'll give you another four hours to persuade her, Soldono. No more, no less." He looked at his watch. "Ten tonight."

"I can't strike a bargain like that."

"Of course you can. Don't bullshit me. You do it all the time. A life for a life." He turned away. "Finish your dinner. The tiramisu is magnificent. The chef will be upset if you don't try it."

Soldono was seething with frustration as he watched Montalvo walk away. Sleek, graceful, and as dangerous as a stick of dynamite too near the flames. Bastard.

Would he do it?

Why was he even questioning it? Montalvo didn't bluff and he would carry out any threat he made in exactly the method he'd outlined.

He had four hours.

He'd hoped to find a way to stop Montalvo without involving Eve Duncan, but time had run out. But was it to his advantage to make a trade for the woman? Why not let it go? He had to be sure it was worth it.

Four hours.

He reached for his phone and quickly dialed.

"Montalvo's given me four hours. Dammit, he'll do it. How the hell am I supposed to stop him?"

Venable was silent for a moment. "It's time you offered Eve Duncan a choice."

"Some choice. Okay, I'm on it. I'll call you back when I get through." He hung up and looked in his book for Eve Duncan's phone number.

Jane called me," Joe said as he came into the cottage two hours later. "She tried to reach you but she couldn't do it. She said she'd made reservations for us at the Doubletree in Phoenix and that I was to remind you that the show is this Saturday." He smiled. "I told her there was a fairly good chance that you'd remember."

"What?" Eve tried to shift her attention away from the skull. It was like fighting her way through a thick fog. "Of course I remembered." Eve managed to tear her gaze away from Marty. "It's a very important show for Jane. I wouldn't miss it. She should know that."

"Yeah." He went over to the phone and turned it back on. "She also knows that you've been working day and night to finish that reconstruction."

"Marty is difficult." She looked back at the reconstruction of the eight-year-old boy. At least, the forensic team's estimate was eight years. "I had to practically put his splintered facial bones back together before I could begin work."

"Do we have a clue who he is yet?"

She shrugged. "You know I never look at police files before I finish the reconstruction. The Macon police have photos of children who disappeared around the time that they estimate the boy was killed. We'll see if we have a resemblance."

"DNA?"

She grimaced. "Come on. The DNA labs are so backed up with current murders that they're not going to be in any hurry to process a five-year-old cold case." She pushed the hair back from her forehead. "But if I do a good enough job I have a chance to bring him home."

"You'll do a good job," Joe said. "But not if you get so tired you lose judgment." He headed for the kitchen. "Did you eat dinner?"

"I think so . . . I don't remember."

"Then we'll assume that you didn't. I'll warm up the beef stew in the refrigerator and put some garlic bread in the oven. That means you have fifteen minutes to clean up your studio and wash up."

"I can catch something later."

"Now." He opened the refrigerator. "Scoot."

She hesitated. Montalvo. She'd meant to tell him about the call from Montalvo as soon as he came in, but it didn't seem important now. As she'd worked on the skull, everything had faded but the reality of the work itself. Marty was important. The other lost children were important. She'd tell Joe about Montalvo later. "I should finish tonight. I want to do the computer 3-D image before we leave for Phoenix."

"The boy's been dead for five years. He can wait a little while longer." He glanced at her over his shoulder. "No arguments, Eve. I let you wear yourself into the ground because you give me no choice, but not this time. You'll have a fight on your hands. I'd bet you've lost five pounds this week."

"I don't think—" She wearily shook her head. Maybe he was right. She was exhausted and she probably had lost weight. This case had been particularly painful. She should be used to dealing with the cruelty of the monsters who killed innocent children after all these years of forensic sculpting. Yet the mindless brutality of the violence visited on this small boy had ripped aside the scar tissue. "I want to bring him home, Joe." Her lips tightened. "And I want to kill the son of a bitch who did that to him."

"I know," he said. "Give me a chance and I'll do the job for you. For that poor kid and for what his killer is doing to you." He slammed the refrigerator door. "I was hoping this damn obsession was lessening, but along comes a nasty case and you're right back where you were."

She stiffened. "This is what I do. This is what I am. Why are you so angry about it now?"

He didn't speak for a moment. "Because I'm tired. Because sometimes I can't stand to see you in pain. Because the years pass and I think the miracle will happen and it never does."

He was talking about Bonnie. She felt a ripple of shock. She couldn't remember the last time he'd spoken about her daughter. Yet Bonnie was always there, a silent presence. "I'll find her someday."

"A miracle," he repeated. "After all these years that's what it would take." He turned his back on her and moved to the stove. "Go get cleaned up. If I upset you anymore, you won't eat and I'll be defeating my purpose."

She studied him. Something was definitely wrong. His motions were jerky and that remark about Bonnie was an instant tip-off. She would have noticed earlier if she hadn't been distracted by both her work and the aftereffects of that call from Montalvo. "I'm not the only one who's upset. What the devil is wrong with you?" She crossed her arms over her chest to keep them from shaking. "And don't tell me that you're just fed up with living here with me. If you don't want to stay with me, no one is forcing you."

"Particularly not you."

"Shut up." She tried to steady her voice. "I don't have any right to ask you to stay. I'm an emotional cripple. As you said, I'm obsessed and I'll probably remain that way for the rest of my life. Sometimes I wonder why you haven't left me before this."

He didn't look at her. "You know why."

"Joe."

"I have my own obsession. Now, get your ass in

gear. We need to get some food into you." He shot her a glance. "It's okay. I'm over it. It just had to come out."

"Why now?"

"Why not?"

She hesitated, gazing at him. It wasn't over. She could sense the turbulence, the reckless energy whirling below the surface.

"You're down to ten minutes."

She tried to smile. "You used up five telling me what an obsessive wacko I am."

"Takes one to know one." He turned on the oven. "And you're my wacko."

She felt a sudden surge of warmth. He was the only man she'd ever known who could make her flit from emotion to emotion in the space of a heartbeat. She'd been angry, upset, defensive, and yet now she was feeling this powerful surge of affection. She turned away and headed down the hall. "Wackos of the world, unite."

"I only want to unite with one wacko and I fully intend to do it later tonight. After I feed you and stoke your energy level."

"Promises, promises."

She was still smiling as she stepped into the shower a few minutes later. She could feel a tingle of sexual anticipation and excitement start within her. Jesus, you'd think after all these years with Joe that sex wouldn't be this urgent. Wasn't it supposed to become merely comfortable after a while? Their coming together was just as wild and passionate as that first time. Her body was tensing, readying at the thought.

She took a deep breath and closed her eyes as the water flowed over her. She'd tell Joe about Montalvo's call over dinner, but right now she wanted to relax and forget about everything but Joe. . . .